ELYSE LARSON

The Hope Before Us

BETHANYHOUSE
PUBLISHERS
MINNEAPOLIS, MINNESOTA

The Hope Before Us

Cover design by Dan Thornberg

Published by Bethany House Publishers
A Ministry of Bethany Fellowship International
11400 Hampshire Avenue South
Bloomington, Minnesota 55438
www.bethanyhouse.com

Printed in the United States of America by
Bethany Press International, Bloomington, Minnesota 55438

Library of Congress Cataloging-in-Publication Data

Larson, Elyse.
The hope before us / by Elyse Larson.
p. cm. — (Women of valor ; 3)
ISBN 0-7642-2376-3
1. World War, 1939–1945—Medical care—Fiction. 2. World War, 1939–1945—France—Fiction. 3. World War, 1939–1945—Women—Fiction. 4. Americans—France—Fiction. 5. Women spies—Fiction. 6. Sisters—Fiction. 7. France—Fiction. 8. Nurses—Fiction. I. Title.
PS3562.A7522235 H67 2002
813′.6—dc21 2002002573

"We are going to win the war,
and we are going to win the peace....
The vast majority of the members
of the human race are on our side.
Many of them are fighting with us.
All of them are praying for us.
For, in representing our case,
we represent theirs as well—
our hope and their hope
for liberty under God."
—Franklin Delano Roosevelt
Radio Broadcast, December 9, 1941

Dedication

To our grandchildren—may our hopes become theirs.

Richard Larson

John Larson

Evan Larson

Justin Larson

Jennifer Larson

Jeffrey Larson

Patricia Larson

Karen Linden

Jeremy Linden

Timothy Linden

Daniel Linden

ELYSE LARSON is an author, photographer, and writing instructor. *The Hope Before Us* is her sixth published novel. Elyse and her husband live in Gresham, Oregon. They have three children and eleven grandchildren.

ACKNOWLEDGMENTS

I am deeply indebted to editor Sharon Asmus, painstaking about historical accuracy, talented in editorial skill, and endlessly encouraging to this writer. I want to thank artist Dan Thornberg, too, for the wonderful cover designs he has created for all of the WOMEN OF VALOR books.

Thanks to writer friends who have helped me with advice, encouragement, and prayers, especially Katy, Gail, Birdie, Marion, Woodeene, Marcia, Pat, Lauraine, Ruby, and Sandy.

Many thanks to my husband, Richard, who first made me aware of the cruelty of the U.S. internment of Japanese Americans and to Kenny Namba of Gresham, who served in the Nisei Combat Team and loaned me his copy of the military history of the 442nd Division. The facts about the actions of the Nisei Combat Team are as accurate as I could make them.

All persons in this novel are fictitious, except for a few known historical figures and the named heroes of the Nisei Combat Team. Lieutenant Masanao Otake, Staff Sergeant Yoshimi Fujiwara, Technical Sergeant Abraham Ohama, and Staff Sergeant Robert Kuroda were real decorated heroes, but only four out of hundreds from that division. The 442nd Division Nisei Combat Team became one of the most decorated divisions of WWII, earning more than thirty-nine hundred individual awards. This becomes more impressive when one learns that the combat team did not enter action until June 1944, less than a year before the war ended in Europe.

For the inspiration and factual detail of Em and Marge Emerson's story, I am indebted to the women who served in the Army Nurse Corps and as war correspondents who were willing to tell their stories. Their true experiences were more amazing than fiction dares to present.

Prologue

September 1944

Lieutenant Marge Emerson, U.S. Army Medical Corps, jumped from the landing craft into the waist-deep icy surf and floundered behind the GIs toward Normandy Beach. The weight of her musette bag on her back nearly dragged her under. Cliffs above the beach offered no gunfire now, but wrecked landing barges and blasted-out trucks still rose from the shallows and littered the sand. On the long floating docks to Marge's right, other landing craft disgorged army trucks, tanks, ammunition, barrels of gasoline, and all the supplies that the invading army needed to conduct war.

Marge had been ordered to France to join a field hospital team. Back in Wales, when she had pressed for investigation of an apparent suicide, she had unwittingly stumbled into a carefully laid plan to break up a Nazi spy ring in Britain. To protect her and their secret operation, the British Secret Service had spirited her away from Gilwern Military Hospital under cover of night. Sworn to secrecy, she hadn't said good-bye to friends, and she'd been ordered not to write to anyone. Letters to her would be detained so that no one could trace her whereabouts.

It was bad enough that her friends would worry about her, but what her sudden disappearance would do to her parents and to her sister, Em, really troubled Marge.

She sloshed onto the wet sand, looking for the person who would take her to Ste-Mère-Eglise evacuation hospital, where she was to link up with the team of nurses headed for Belgium.

The soldiers with whom she'd landed formed into lines and marched to waiting trucks. She stood at the water's edge uncertain which way to go.

"Lieutenant Emerson! Lieutenant Emerson!" a man's voice called.

She turned toward the dock. A tall soldier jogged toward her. He came at an easy run across the packed sand and halted a couple of paces from her. Saluting, he said, "Sergeant David Lewellyn, ma'am. I'm your driver."

She returned his salute and glanced at the insignia on his shoulder. "You're not Medical Corps."

"No, ma'am. Infantry. First Division. I'm a medic. I'm returning from a week's R and R in Paris. When the CO said there was a nurse who needed to be picked up, I volunteered. Rescuing is my specialty, and I figured you might need rescuing after coming across the Channel with all those Joes eager to make points with a nurse."

She laughed. "Sounds like you've been in the army for some time."

"Yes, ma'am. My jeep is over yonder." Without requesting permission, he lifted her wet bag from her shoulders.

Startled, because military women were supposed to carry their own bags, she said, "Well, thanks."

"You're welcome. A lot of army rules go against my grain. I was surprised they landed you in the water like the guys. It's a wonder you didn't have to swim for it, you being down there a foot shorter."

"They said the docks must be used for unloading supplies." Then she laughed. "I'm only a foot shorter than *you*. Most of the men don't reach your elevation. You must make a large target on the front lines."

"So they tell me. I figure I'm also a good cover for the boys."

She studied his face and saw no hint of bravado or bragging. "That doesn't seem to worry you."

"No, ma'am," he said quietly. The sun's reflection from the sand shined upward on his face, softening the shadow cast by his steel helmet. His craggy features seemed to glow. He reminded her of a guardian angel statue back home on the campus of the hospital where she'd trained. "How did you come to be a medic?" she asked.

"I'm a conscientious objector, ma'am. I don't hold with killing."

"Is this a matter of your faith?"

"Yes, ma'am."

They had reached the jeep. He tossed her bag behind the seat and moved to the driver's side while she climbed into the passenger seat. With a roar and minimal spinning of wheels, they headed for the road at the base of the cliff to join the line of supply trucks rolling inland.

Marge took care not to stare but found her eyes returning to his profile repeatedly. She had nothing but respect for conscientious objectors who risked their lives to save lives. She wished he'd say more about his convictions, but he drove silently as they ascended a ravine and moved into farmland divided by tall, battle-torn hedgerows. Something about Sergeant Lewellyn made her feel safe and settled after her distressing flight from Wales. She found herself wishing she could know him better.

Chapter One

Paris
October 1944

Em Emerson went to the window of her room in Hotel Scribe and looked down on the street. The sun broke through the clouds, igniting the scene. Paris! She was here at last. The beloved city, pride of France, had not suffered air raids or shelling. The buildings around her stood unmarred, turning the scene timeless.

Parisians, walking on the sidewalk below, looked healthy despite being thin. For the most part the women dressed attractively in bright colors. In the streets, however, the war and the Occupation had created a conspicuous absence of autos. In addition to military vehicles, the traffic consisted of bicycles and pedicabs, which were remodeled bicycles that looked like Chinese rickshaws.

After living in bombed-out London and driving through the war-savaged towns and landscape in Normandy, she found Paris incredibly beautiful. When she found time, she'd love to explore it for fun ... with Bob. At the thought of the older war correspondent who had championed her at every turn, her heart made a butterfly takeoff.

She had vowed not to fall into a wartime romance but had long since given up trying to talk herself out of her attraction to him. At first she'd thought her feelings simply sprang from gratitude for his kindness. As a female war correspondent, she was intruding into a male-dominated profession, and many of the men didn't welcome women journalists.

Em turned from the window and went to her desk, glancing at the last story she'd written. The men shouldn't be worried about competition. All the rules had been set up in their favor. Allied command banned women from the combat zones, so she couldn't report firsthand on battle action. Then whatever the women wrote, they had to wire to London for censorship. Consequently her stories were not always timely and sometimes made little sense, because she never could read the censored versions and add transitions for clarity. The men, on the other hand, wired their stories to the States immediately. Censors right here in Hotel Scribe went over them, letting the journalists read and polish the choppy versions before they sent them.

She needed to write up two more interviews with French civilians while the conversations were fresh in her mind. Sitting down, she zipped a clean sheet of paper into her portable typewriter and had just begun to type when the phone rang.

She snatched it up, trying to hold the thought of her next sentence.

"Hello," she said.

"Em Emerson?" The questioning male voice was not familiar.

"Yes. This is Em," she replied.

"I'm Brad Cummins, an acquaintance of Charles Jennings. He asked me to look you up while I'm here on business. I'm one of those civilians who tested physically unfit for military service, so I volunteered my business skills to come in after the fighting and help with the civilian recovery."

She stopped hearing him after the mention of Charles Jennings. Her heart leapfrogged to somewhere near her left collarbone. At the sound of Mr. Jennings' name, she tried to round up her stampeding thoughts. "How is Mr. Jennings? Is he still in Washington, D.C.?"

"No. As a matter of fact, I just left him yesterday in London. I have a message for you. May I come to your room to talk?"

Normally, she'd say no, but . . . "Where are you now?"

"Downstairs in the lobby."

No need to ask why he didn't want to meet her in a public place. Mr. Jennings was an official in the Office of Strategic Services, the OSS. Two years ago she'd volunteered for the secret service. After doing a background check, Jennings had politely rejected her, saying that she could serve her country better by continuing her career in journalism. A few days later she'd received her overseas assignment from her editor at *USA Living & Review*. His abrupt change of mind about needing a woman war correspondent had made her wonder whether Mr. Jennings had anything to do with her employer's decision, but she'd dismissed the thought as utterly unlikely. It still seemed totally improbable, and yet so did the fact that Mr. Jennings remembered her after all this time.

She'd been silent too long, and curiosity drove her to say, "Yes, Mr. Cummins. Do come up."

She hung up and went to the bathroom mirror to freshen her appearance. Her habit of running her fingers through her hair while she was thinking gave her an unkempt aura that would not likely inspire anyone's confidence in her. She didn't know why it felt important to appear self-assured, but she might as well try. Good thing pageboy style was in. Her naturally straight locks cooperated, turning under at the ends at her bidding.

When the tap on the door came, she dropped her brush, closed the bathroom door behind her, and marched to greet her surprising guest.

Short, slight, and almost hidden behind thick glasses, he looked like a typical 4-F who couldn't do military service. Her mom would say an Oklahoma breeze would sail him right to Texas. When Em invited him in, however, he moved like a canny outdoor ranch cat. Glasses or not, she suspected his quick glance registered everything in the room.

Closing the door, she said, "Please be seated." She gestured toward the chair beside her desk.

He took it.

She sat behind her desk at the typewriter, doing her best to look polite and not overly interested. "I'm surprised that Mr. Jennings should even remember my name."

"He certainly does. Why is a matter of anyone's guess. First, I must tell you, if anyone comes to your door while I am here, simply tell him we have a mutual friend, Carl Jensen, from whom I bring greetings. Officially, I'm an engineer on a consultation visit to a Renault auto plant." He leaned forward. "Now to get to the real point, Miss Emerson. I have a letter from Mr. Jennings, and I am to take him your response." He handed her a thin envelope.

She opened it and read quickly, then read it again thoughtfully.

Dear Miss Emerson:

This is to introduce you to my assistant, Brad Cummins.

You once applied for enlistment in our service. I wonder if you are still interested. We need you now. On the basis of our previous interviews and my current investigation of your qualifications, I can offer you a position as courier. You would continue working as a war correspondent and remain accredited to the Women's Auxiliary Army Corps, but you would have to go where WAACs are not allowed. I would arrange for you to take orders only from me and my staff.

You need only to say yes or no to Brad. If you decide yes, absolutely no one can know about our arrangement, especially your editor. Brad will give you the details.

Yours truly,
Charles A. Jennings
Office of Strategic Services

She had no memory to rely on for identifying his signature. The stationery contained no official seal, which made sense for secrecy but left her with little to go on. She frowned. "Mr. Cummins, may I see your identification?"

He reached in his pocket and handed her a small card. "We don't normally carry such, but Mr. Jennings told me to show you this."

At a glance the card looked official, but she realized now that she'd seen it, that anything could be forged, and she wouldn't know the difference. She returned the card to him. "Do you know the contents of the letter?"

"Only a little. I am to relay your answer. Then I will be told more."

She had been eager to work for the OSS two years ago. She'd wanted so badly to do something in the war that would really count. The more she learned about Hitler and the Third Reich and the concentration camps, the more she wanted an active part in the fight. She came from humble folks and instantly identified with every oppressed person. Her passion for justice had driven her to try to enlist in the OSS. When they rejected her, she never told anyone about applying or being rejected. Without conscious decision she had not told even her sister, Marge, who had enlisted in the U.S. Army Nurse Corps.

Now, as much as she loved journalism, she had to admit that reporting gave her little satisfaction toward making a difference in the war.

Mr. Cummins leaned back on his chair, waiting for her to say something.

Meeting his penetrating blue eyes, she thought again how deceptive his appearance was. At first glance he looked like the classic absentminded professor—except for his eyes. Now he was watching her like a cat waiting to catch a mouse. This was too important for her usual quick decision. She raised her eyebrows and said, "I need to think about this overnight."

He nodded. "Certainly. I'll call on you tomorrow afternoon. In the meantime I must take back the letter, and of course you must not discuss this with anyone else."

"Right." She handed the letter to him.

He rose from the chair, padded catlike to the door, and let himself out. She stared after him, already lost in speculation. What would such a decision mean for her? The good side might be that she could go to combat zones. General Eisenhower had been adamant that only men were allowed to go to the front lines. Therefore, women could not really report on the action that people at home longed to read about. Beyond that, what she did for the OSS obviously should help the war effort. Still she hesitated. For once she would look before leaping.

With Cummins gone, his unexpected visit almost seemed unreal. She didn't even have the letter to read again. Whatever had made Colonel Jennings think of her now, after two years? And what had inclined him to trust her enough to send Mr. Cummins? Was Mr. Cummins really from the OSS?

This was crazy. Yet why else had this man located her? The wording of the letter had somehow sounded like Mr. Jennings. She'd talked at length with him on half a dozen occasions. She ran her fingers through her hair and began to pace the floor. She always thought more clearly on her feet.

The negative side was what might happen to her personal life, what she had left of it. How would her duties with the OSS affect her relationship with Bob, for instance? And what would happen to her writing opportunities?

The phone ringing again interrupted her. Who could it be this time? A woman's familiar voice cried, "Em, is that you? Are you really here in Paris?"

"Vivienne! I was going to search the phone directory for your number." It was Vivienne Hugo. They'd met before the war when Vivienne had been in the United States with her young husband, a minor official at the French embassy. Em had interviewed her, and they'd struck up an immediate and firm friendship.

"Em, please to come and see me tonight. Bring your luggage and typewriter and stay here. So very quiet I will be for you to write, and I can guide you about the city. Oh, I want to show you Paris. Even after the Occupation, you may see something of why I love it. Do come. Please!"

Vivienne spoke, as Em's brother, Billy, would say, shotgun style. Her thoughts and words seemed to explode all directions, and some people found her difficult to follow. Not Em, however. Em thought the same way but had learned to control her tendency to talk too much and too fast in order to interview people. "This is wonderful! It's so good to hear your voice! I'm so glad you called! But how did you know I was here? I only just got in this morning."

"My dear Em, the Hotel Scribe I have called every day since General De Gaulle arrived in Paris. I was certain you would arrive soon. Now please do say you'll come for dinner, even if you are not allowed to stay overnight."

"I'd love to. Just tell me how to get there."

"The transportation I will provide. My brother, he will come for you in his old auto. What time shall I say for him? Can you be ready by six?"

"Yes. I'll meet him in the lobby—"

"*Non, non*. He will call for you at your room and escort you downstairs. Em, you must not be trusting of strange gentlemen in the lobby. French gentlemen especially."

Em chuckled at her teasing. "How will I know it is your brother at my door?"

"He is very safe. Joseph is Father Joseph now."

"A priest? I didn't know. I'll be ready. An evening with you will be such fun. I'm so glad you watched for me and called."

"My dear friend, I have waited for this day, and I have so much to tell. But first, I must not take you from your work. Tonight we shall talk. *Au revoir*."

"*Au revoir*, and *merci*!"

"Welcome." They both laughed at Em's two words of French. Certainly Vivienne's English had progressed much further than Em's Oklahoma-style French.

Em finished her last two articles and placed them in the courier bags to go to the censors in London. While she was downstairs, she asked about Bob and learned he'd been in a group accompanying General Bradley to the Front. She hadn't seen him since St-Lô. Now no one knew how soon he would return to Paris. With no hope of seeing him today, she decided to stay overnight with Vivienne.

As she put on a fresh dress uniform, she pondered again on what to do about joining the OSS. Part of her really wanted to, and yet she suspected such a move would make problems she couldn't even guess at, especially with Bob. Deciding overnight made her uneasy. Too many times in the past, her natural impulsiveness had gotten her into deep trouble, sometimes even hurting other people.

Marge had taught her to delay making important decisions for at least three days, and Em had found the technique helped on big decisions. She smiled, remembering how she'd once thought Marge missed a lot of fun by being too cautious. Then when Em ended up alienating her best friend without meaning to, she began to listen to her big sister's advice to slow down and think before acting.

Growing up on the ranch had made them both determined and resilient, but Em had always craved action. While Marge hadn't felt overly cramped by the small world of Tuttle, Oklahoma, Em did. That was why the OSS had attracted her when she first heard about it and also why she never told Marge about her effort to enlist. Did she still want to serve her country in the secret service? The answer hovered on the tip of her thoughts, but she purposely pulled herself away from making a decision. She must give herself more time.

The expected knock came on her door. She grabbed her topcoat, sat her cap on at an angle, and opened, expecting Vivienne's brother. She wasn't disappointed.

A tall blond man in the priesthood's white collar, black tunic, and pants stood before her. He smiled down at her. "How do you do? I'm Vivienne Hugo's brother."

"Father Joseph. I'm pleased to meet you."

"Indeed, the pleasure is all mine, Miss Emerson. So much Vivienne has told me about you. She's very fond of you."

"Thank you. And I'm fond of her. Please just call me Em."

"Certainly." He glanced at her typewriter case and overnight bag just inside the door. "May I take these for you?"

"Please, and thank you."

His smile gave him a boyish aura, despite the fact he had to be past forty from what Vivienne had told her. A closer look revealed some graying at the temples, scarcely noticeable because of his blond good looks. Father Joseph looked more like one of Hitler's ideal Aryans than like Em's idea of a Frenchman. His gray eyes held a soberness that startled her. His expression reminded her of soldiers she'd interviewed in the Gilwern hospital in Wales—especially those who had been in a lot of action.

She wondered what had led him to become a priest. Maybe if they talked long enough, she would find out.

On the way to Vivienne's she found conversation with him easy but also felt comfortable with his silence.

At Vivienne's apartment building, he parked in a sheltered area in the back. They entered a side door and climbed to the second floor.

Vivienne must have heard them coming, for she was standing in her open doorway with arms outstretched. "Em! At last you are here! Joseph, do take her coat and place her things to the yellow room. What a celebration we will have! Did I not tell you one day you would see Paris with me?"

Em returned her hug and then stood back to look at her friend. "It's been a long time—too long. I've worried about you so often, not knowing . . ."

Vivienne's face looked all eyes. She was so much thinner. Her blond hair was darker, and her cheeks had hollowed, giving her heart-shaped face a peaky look, yet she was as vibrant as ever.

"A long time, yes, when I think of the Occupation. But that is over. We shall rebuild, and we are so thankful to God that Paris was spared from destruction. Come in, come in! I hope you don't mind coming to the kitchen with me while I put finishing touches on our dinner. I do not have a maid, as when Piers was in the embassy."

"How . . . is Piers?"

Vivienne's smile faded, and her gray eyes darkened. "He is prisoner now in Germany. Germany holds two million of our men for slave labor. Piers hid when the conscription for workers was announced. He joined other men in the Resistance but had misfortune. One day the SS arrested him. Now I have no word from him for more than a year. I pray every day that he stays well and will soon come home."

Em swallowed. "I'm so sorry. I had hoped . . ."

Vivienne raised her eyebrows. "That he would have been spared? *Oui*, yes. We live on hope. I still do. But come along with me. Your arrival in Paris, it is a time to celebrate. Piers and I, we always celebrated each day's victory. He would want us to continue to do so." Vivienne slipped her arm around Em and led her to the kitchen. "I hope you will excuse—we eat in the kitchen. It is warm for sitting and talking. October brings much rain this year."

Em helped with small tasks, and by the time Father Joseph joined them, they were ready to sit and dine. He quietly gave thanks for the meal, and then helped Vivienne serve Em, making his sister stay seated while he fetched condiments and finally a custard dessert.

They lingered over cups of real coffee, albeit the powdered kind from Em's supply of army rations.

"St. Hilary parish, where Joseph serves, is near Epinal," Vivienne said, "but that area has become a battlefield, so he, when he can, stays in Paris with me."

Joseph smiled and nodded. "Presently I serve wherever I am needed."

"You mean the church moves you around like an itinerate preacher?"

He chuckled. "That is it. I am an itinerate preacher. My parish is France."

"That sounds very . . . nonspecific," she said.

The laughter left his voice. "It has been necessary to broaden my parish during the Occupation."

"Joseph, in his way, has helped in the Resistance. He even persuaded me to participate. After Dunkirk he smuggled trapped Englishmen out of France. When he ran out of Brits to help, he found he was set up for hiding and helping others. He began to assist Piers. So you see, his parish moved beyond his church boundaries."

"Wow! You must have many stories to tell," Em exclaimed. "My magazine has asked me to interview people here about how it was to live under the Occupation."

Vivienne set down her coffee cup, spilling as she did so. "You must not write about my brother or about me either. There are still those in France who disagreed with the Resistance, and some of them have the consciences of criminals." She mopped up while she talked.

"You mean publicity for either of you could be dangerous? As an outsider looking in, I thought the resistants were national heroes."

Vivienne stopped wiping the table, sent her brother a tentative look, and said, "France was near civil war before Hitler threatened us. We worked together for survival. Now that we are free again, those old factions already are regrouping. Joseph and I inadvertently made some enemies among the Socialist factions of the Resistance, as well as among some unscrupulous collaborators."

Em tried to digest this. "I didn't realize. Maybe I shouldn't be talking to any resistants."

"Joseph may be able to direct you to some who can safely tell their stories. But his own activities you must never mention."

Em turned to Father Joseph. "You have my word. I'll never write about you or Vivienne."

"I can give you names and addresses of a few heroes of France, but I won't be able to go with you to introduce you. Your task it will be to persuade them to talk with you. Also your transportation you must arrange. I will be leaving Paris in the morning."

"I'll work out something," she said. "I'd really appreciate knowing who to contact."

"Tell her about some of them," Vivienne said.

"Well, there's a group of nuns who hid thirty-five Jewish children until just days ago when the Germans were pushed out. Their parents, they went to concentration camps, but at least the children are safe and well cared for. It's been a daily miracle to keep them healthy as well as hidden.

"I know of a farmer south of Paris who single-handedly helped over eighty stranded Englishmen to escape. He did this while the Germans billeted their officers in his home, and his sister, who was living with him, didn't know about his covert activities. And then there is Marie-Anais, who hid a number of downed flyers and helped them escape from France into Spain, beginning in 1940, and she is now only seventeen herself. She is one you should interview."

"Stop! Wait! I have to write this down."

"I will make a list for you before I leave. Although, I must repeat, take great care to not mention my name to anyone."

"Agreed. I don't mind approaching strangers without an introduction."

He studied her for a moment and then nodded. "Good."

A series of firecracker explosions came from outside.

Father Joseph leaped to his feet and rushed to the window. In the same instant Vivienne switched off the light and joined him. Guided by the pale rectangle that marked the window's location, Em hurried to their sides. The kitchen looked down on the alley where Father Joseph had parked.

So this was how Vivienne had seen her and Father Joseph when they'd first arrived.

"Do you see anyone?" Vivienne cried in a stage whisper.

"No," Father Joseph replied.

"What was it? What happened?" Em asked.

"Gunshots. They didn't even bother with a silencer." Father Joseph's voice had turned cool and crisp. They both peered out.

Em joined them. "Can you see any movement?"

"No," Vivienne murmured. "Nothing."

Father Joseph whispered. "I'm going down there. Someone may need help."

Vivienne exclaimed, "No! Call the gendarmes. You don't know who might be down there."

"With Paris still unsettled, I don't trust the gendarmes. Collaborators may still be among them. Besides it would lead to involving you."

"Then stay right here and let someone else call the gendarmes."

"What if someone is wounded and needing help? I have to go. Say a prayer, and I'll be very careful."

Em, touching Vivienne's arm, felt her tremble.

Father Joseph hurried out, and after endless anxious minutes, Em saw him step cautiously into the parking court. Only two other old vehicles stood there. He ducked behind the first one. Em waited for him to reappear. Then she saw him, still crouching, hurry behind the other car. After another interminable wait he approached his own auto slowly. He bent down and disappeared inside the Renault.

This time he stayed out of sight for so long that Em said, "Should we go down too?"

"No!" Vivienne's tone brooked no argument.

Finally Em saw the dark shape of Father Joseph emerge from his car and, still bent over, dart back into the building. She let out a long-held breath.

Vivienne ran and opened the door for him. "What did you see?"

He came in and closed the door before speaking. "Laurence Pierre. I had asked him to meet me here later in this evening. I was going to drive him to a rendezvous. Vivienne, someone shot him through the head! He was just sitting there . . . as if he were waiting for me. And he was dead. The killer left a note."

Em's knees went weak. She wrapped her arm firmly around Vivienne's shoulders to steady them both.

Vivienne gasped and crammed her fist against her mouth. Then, muffled by her white knuckles, she cried, "He's only a boy! Fifteen!" Her voice broke.

"Many resistants are still boys," Father Joseph murmured.

Em held her tighter. "Come, let's sit down."

Vivienne limply obeyed. Then she looked up at her brother. "You mentioned a note."

"I found this." He handed her a crumpled piece of paper. "I hate to leave you after this shock, but his body must not be found near your apartment building. And I'll have to stay away from you until I can be certain I won't endanger you."

"Joseph, what about his mother? What can I tell his mother if she calls?"

"Pray she doesn't call until I can talk to her. Once she knows about his death, reassure her he is a hero, that he died for freedom." He moved toward the door. "Stay indoors until I telephone. Em, in some ways the war isn't over in France. You must keep this a secret. Do you understand?"

"I don't understand, but I won't say a word."

"And if anyone asks, you do not know me. For the time being, you have never met a Father Joseph."

Em nodded. "All right."

He left, and Vivienne read the paper in her hand. " 'Your robes will not save you.' Oh, dear God, they mean to kill Joseph!"

"Who? Who would want to kill him?"

"I . . . don't know." The microsecond of hesitation before Vivienne spoke, and the sudden carefulness in her voice, made Em feel that her friend did indeed know.

Chapter Two

Belgium
October 1944

Volleys of gunfire rumbled in the distance. A few shells shrieked overhead and hit the hillside west of the field hospital. Nurse Marge Emerson had not worked under gunfire before. She had joined a team of nurses at Ste-Mère-Eglise evacuation hospital only two weeks ago. They'd come directly to this field hospital, less than ten miles from the border of Germany, but the battle had remained a distant roar until now.

According to Marge's U.S. Army Medical Corps manual, field hospitals ideally set up two or three miles from the battle. She guessed the battle had crept closer.

Another shell screamed over. She braced for the explosion and then made herself focus on her patients in the post-op ward—checking temperatures, administering morphine shots as ordered, and giving reassuring smiles and comments to the soldiers who were conscious.

A few joked about the Germans to bolster her morale and probably theirs too. "You're purely safe if they're aiming at you. They can't tell directions very well."

"Yeah. Krauts never retreat. They just forget which way to go when they attack," remarked another.

The men's concern for her put Marge on the edge of tears. She throttled her sentiment and managed an amused smile. "Then I should only duck when I cannot see the whites of their eyes." The men chuckled and then grimaced because laughing hurt their wounds.

By the time Marge finished the morning rounds on her side of the ward, the ambulances began to arrive. The incoming wounded would create a rush in the admitting tent. Glancing down the line of patients she'd just tended, she decided she'd done all they needed for the moment, so she hurried out to join the nurses in the receiving area. After her, more nurses arrived, including Chief Nurse Louise De Mille. The women worked swiftly at triage, while stretcher-bearers and ward men brought in the wounded.

Each soldier wore a tag pinned to his breast pocket detailing the treatment he had received in the aid station at the Front. Most had received morphine. Medics and corpsmen had sprinkled sulfa into their wounds and had applied first-aid bandages. Those with serious bleeding had also received a unit of blood plasma.

The doctors moved among the stretchers checking each man. Those suffering from shock went immediately to the shock ward. Others they lined up for surgery. A few were ambulatory. Those went to the outpatient tent to have their wounds treated. They would soon return to duty.

Marge cut away soiled clothing from the first man to go to surgery. Then she and her tentmate Sally scrubbed and shaved the area around the wound. Marge wiped it with alcohol, painted it with iodine, and applied a sterile bandage. The man opened his eyes. She saw the fear that he would not voice.

"You're going to be fine, soldier. The doctors will fix you up like new."

He tried to smile.

Two orderlies came and lifted his stretcher.

Marge moved on to the next patient. She loosened a tourniquet, and then tightened it again, hoping the mangled leg could be saved. This man didn't open his eyes. He was ashen, and when she felt for his pulse, his hand was cold and clammy. "Sally, will you check his BP again?"

Sally fastened the blood-pressure cuff around his arm. In a few seconds, she called to a ward man. "Get this patient to the shock ward."

Marge worked on the next soldier, repeating the routine. She fell into an efficient system with Sally, prepping those marked for surgery, concentrating on one patient at a time. Twice she returned to check on the soldiers in her ward, then hurried back to admitting. She was dimly aware that the guns had quieted, and so had the rumble of ambulances. When they finally finished with the last wounded man in the receiving ward, early evening darkened the tent, and lamps had to be lighted.

Louise released Marge and Sally for supper. They slogged through the mud to their tent, the quarters for all the women, and grabbed their mess kits. In the mess tent the cooks ladled hot stew into their aluminum pans. They'd had coffee once during the rush, but no food for hours.

Marge sat on a bench at a table beside Sally, too tired and hungry to talk but knowing Sally must feel the same way. Army chow had never tasted better.

After a bit, Sally, a veteran nurse with this field hospital, paused between bites. "So how do you feel after your baptism under fire? You did well. I'll hand that to you."

"Well, thanks." This was the first time they had received so many casualties in just a few hours. "I'm beat, but sleep will take care of that. Do you know how many men went to surgery?"

"Over fifty, I'd say. We have six still in the shock ward. . . ." Her voice trailed off.

"What are their chances . . . the ones in shock?" Marge asked. She'd seen people die of shock in stateside hospitals despite having the best of equipment and nursing.

Sally straightened. "They usually make it. We've got a great staff of nurses in there, but these guys today are in really bad shape."

Marge sensed that Sally was not only tired, she was emotionally exhausted. Marge made a mental note to mention this to Chief Nurse Louise. Surely she and the other recent replacements could spell the nurses who most needed a break. Until their arrival, this field hospital had been understaffed because several nurses were ill. More than half the staff had been on duty since shortly after D day. Turning now to Sally, she said, "I don't know how you managed, as shorthanded as you were. The fatigue and lack of sleep is bound to get to you."

Sally stared into her coffee mug, then drank the last and straightened. "You do what you have to do. Fatigue is a small price to pay compared to what our men suffer. The payback comes when the guys wake up and you know they're going to make it. They don't complain, and they're so appreciative of everything we do for them."

Marge nodded. "That's the way most of them were at the station hospital in Wales too. Their attitudes made me want to work all the harder."

Already the station hospital and her friends in Wales seemed to belong to another life. She wondered what the nurses there thought about her disappearance. She'd made a habit of writing to her sister Em every week, and now that she couldn't, Em would be wondering, and soon she'd be worrying. And her folks back home in Oklahoma would be frightened.

She could only hope the British Secret Service would be quick about capturing the spies. Of course they'd given her no specific information, so she had no idea what might be involved. She hoped that her friends Jean and Nella would not be in danger. Surely they would be protected if they were.

Sally stood up, breaking into her silent worrying. "Shall we go see what our assignments will be for the night?"

"Okay."

After they washed and stowed their mess kits back in their tent, they learned they were to report back to the receiving area. Marge's adrenaline surged when she spied a new ambulance at the tent. Orderlies were unloading two more men. "Looks like it's not over yet."

"It's never over," Sally said.

They hurried into the admitting tent, where Chief Nurse Louise was directing Amelia and Dorothy to one of the wounded men. She looked up when Marge entered.

"Emerson, get this other man cleaned up for surgery. Peters," she said to Sally, "you go get some shut-eye and, barring any more rushes, report to me after breakfast."

"Yes, ma'am," Sally said. Then turning to Marge, she said, "See you later, partner," and left.

Marge prepared a basin of water, arranged cloths, towels, soap, alcohol, and iodine, and set to work. Amelia had already cut away the man's bloody jacket and shirt and had wrapped him warmly.

Marge loosened the sterile compress the medics had placed over the patient's wound. He was unconscious, and she was glad. Bullets had nearly severed his arm near the shoulder. It was a miracle he hadn't bled to death.

She worked gently, prepping the area, and finished just as Dr. Colville strode in and said, "We're ready for the next one."

"Here, sir," she said.

He read the man's tag. "Good. Get him in there."

A couple of orderlies lifted the stretcher and carried the man to surgery.

"Emerson, go relieve Mary Ellen in surgery," Louise said. "She's been on duty the longest."

"Yes, ma'am."

Outside the admitting tent a medic still waited beside the ambulance. Upon seeing her, he walked over and saluted. "Excuse me, ma'am. I wonder if you could tell me about my buddy."

She returned his salute. His voice sounded familiar. She looked closer at the face shaded and half concealed by the steel helmet. "Sergeant Lewellyn!" She could hardly believe that she was seeing the medic who had met her on Omaha Beach and had driven her to Ste-Mère-Eglise. They'd had a little time to get acquainted on the ten-mile drive, and that was all, but her first impression, that he was an unusual man, had been reinforced. Knowing there was little chance she'd ever see him again, she had said good-bye reluctantly.

Now here he was! She made no effort to conceal her happiness over seeing him. Meeting him here so unexpectedly was almost as good as receiving a letter from home.

Sergeant Lewellyn stared, and for a moment she thought he didn't remember her.

Then he exclaimed, "Lieutenant Emerson! In the dark, and with you dressed for the work out here, I didn't recognize you. Excuse me, ma'am, but can you tell me about my buddy? He had the shoulder wound."

She smiled. "I just prepped him for surgery. You said his shoulder. When I cleansed the area, it looked as if the injury didn't go beyond fracturing the humerus. Maybe his shoulder isn't involved."

"Oh, God, I hope so," he exclaimed. Then he straightened to attention. "No offense, ma'am. I wasn't using the Lord's name in vain. That was a prayer. A shattered shoulder would put that farmer out of business. He really is a farmer back in Ohio. A man needs a good shoulder to do the work on a farm."

"I hope his arm will be normal again."

"Yeah. I had a time stopping the bleeding."

"You did a good job. He was in stable condition and ready for immediate surgery."

"Thank you, ma'am. I'm glad it was you who tended him. If I get back here tomorrow, could you let me know how the surgery went?"

"I'll try," she said. "I'm on my way now to relieve a nurse in surgery. Good-bye, Sergeant. Good to see you again."

"Good-bye, ma'am. My pleasure."

On the way to the operating theater Marge found herself wishing they could dispense with the protocol of saluting and greeting by military title out here in the field hospitals. At the moment she could totally agree with Colonel Herschel back in Gilwern. Protocol was a bother.

Sergeant Lewellyn had remained vivid in her memory for several reasons. Perhaps the greatest was his strong faith in God. Marge herself had moved from being a devoted believer during her early years to becoming uncertain about her faith in nursing school. Seeing children die of cancer, especially one little girl she'd become particularly attached to, made all of her faith turn into one big question mark. Now the lunacy and suffering of the war had battered her childhood faith so thoroughly that she didn't know what to believe about God.

When Sergeant Lewellyn had appeared and was open about his faith, she'd questioned him first out of curiosity and then out of sincere interest.

He'd said that as a youth he had determined to try to live as one in whom Christ dwelled, just as the Bible indicated. Then when war came, he couldn't see Jesus shooting anyone, so he volunteered to be a medic.

Marge, seeking an answer for her own conscience, had said, "But then, should we let Hitler take over the world? Can't we defend ourselves and our way of life?"

His answer, that the only way to achieve peace would be to stop fighting, had not settled her own questions at all, but his ideals had made her wish she could agree with him.

Since then his comments had often come to mind. He made her think, and he sounded as if he was on speaking terms with the Lord. Several times she had wished she could talk with him again. Now that wish might come true.

Marge worked through the rest of the night in surgery and fell into bed at about ten in the morning. When she awoke it was suppertime. After eating, she returned to duty in surgery.

More ambulances arrived, but with only a dozen wounded men, instead of multiple dozens. The fighting had quieted again. When the surgeons completed operations by midnight and the new patients were stable, Marge took a break. On the way back from the latrine, she saw an ambulance pull in and brake to a halt. *So surgery isn't over after all,* she thought. The driver and his partner hopped out and removed a stretcher from the rear of the carrier. *Only one, thank goodness.* Then she noticed it was a child! A little girl with dark hair and a thin little face like Millie, the first child she had watched die of cancer.

Oh, dear God, no! Grief welled up from remembering. Four years had passed, but thoughts of Millie still hurt. She had loved Millie as if she were her own child. And Millie had loved her and trusted her and called for her when the pain was hard to bear. All she could do in the end was hold the suffering little girl in her arms until her real mother came.

Marge shook herself free of the painful memory and went to help, but two other admitting nurses reached the little patient first and guided the stretcher-bearers into the lighted tent.

Marge hurried to wash up and go to the post-op ward. To Sally, who was on duty there, she whispered, "They've just brought in a wounded child!" She almost choked on the words.

Sally muttered, "It makes me so angry when this happens. I keep my sanity by telling myself we can help. Did you get a look at the child?"

Marge shook her head. "Not much."

"Come on," Sally said. "Help me hang up sheets so we can put her in a private space for the family to visit . . . if any family shows up." She went quickly to improvise the screen.

Marge followed, but a patient called out to her. "Nurse. Water, please."

She hurried to his bedside, poured him a cupful, and held it for him.

He eased back on his pillow. "Thanks," he whispered. "You're an angel."

"Just doing what I'm here for," she said lightly. "Anything else I can get for you?"

He grinned. "A new leg? This one hurts."

She smiled, as she knew he wished. "I'll put in an order right away."

She helped Sally finish setting up the child's bed and then asked, "Do you mind if I go see how the child is doing?"

"Go ahead. Everyone here is okay for now. I can manage."

Marge hurried to the receiving tent. Two nurses were still working over a tiny girl. Whatever happened had left her hair and torn dress splotched with mud and dried blood. Mercifully, she was unconscious.

Marge helped them wash her for surgery. Medics had wrapped each of her legs and placed a compress bandage on the head wound. Her little body was covered with contusions and abrasions, which they gently scrubbed and medicated. Then Marge washed away dried blood and dirt on one leg while the other two nurses gently unwrapped the other. A red stain began to spread out across the sheet under the legs. Surgeon Bennett appeared and swore under his breath when he saw the new patient. He checked the girl thoroughly but quickly and said to Marge, "She needs orthopedic surgery. Go alert Colonel Colville.

He's just finishing up on another patient."

"Yes, sir."

In the surgical tent she found Colonel Colville. He looked up from his patient when she called his name.

"It's a civilian, sir. A little girl. Head wound and both legs."

He frowned. "How old?"

"Maybe five or six."

"Is she stable?"

"Yes. The nurses are prepping her."

"Tell them to bring her in and place her on that table over there. I'm done here." He nodded to the surgical nurse. "Go ahead. Bandage and move him out. He's going to be fine."

Marge hurried back to admitting and directed the nurses with the child to the designated operating table.

Dr. Colville was still scrubbing up, but he called, "Nurse Morris, check her vitals again. If she's still stable, start the anesthetic. Nurse Emerson, you assist me on this one."

"Yes, sir." She went to join him scrubbing up.

When they were both ready and gloved, he said, "I'm glad you're here, Emerson, no matter what quirky glitch sent you from Gilwern. When I was there, Colonel Herschel swore he'd never let you go, even if orders came through to move you."

"Thank you, sir," she said, wondering what he would think if he knew that she'd been sent to France to keep her silent and possibly safe. The latter seemed like a bad joke after last night's shelling.

Dr. Colville strode into the operating theater, and she followed. He examined and probed the girl's wounds. Finally he said, "Someone's looking out for this little one. Her head wound is flesh only—nothing short of a miracle. Looks like something cut her as she fell. The left femur is shattered, but the penetrating wound on the right leg has damaged only muscles."

As Marge handed him instruments, he worked deftly. His surgical skill amazed her as much now as it had the first time she'd assisted him in the Gilwern military station hospital. With no wasted motion, he delicately arranged and set the broken bones, inserting a small metal plate for stability. He trimmed torn flesh and sutured and finally closed the wounds.

Straightening, he said, "She's going to be all right. Are her parents waiting?"

"I don't know," Marge said.

He nodded. "Nurse Morris, have someone sit with her until she's awake. Nurse Emerson, clean up here, and I'll go look for her family."

When Marge had the operating area scrubbed down and ready for the next surgery, she went to post-op to check on the child. She found Sally sitting with her behind the sheets they'd hung for privacy. Marge went quietly to the head of the bed and studied the small face below the head bandage. Dark eyelashes curled against her colorless cheeks.

"Poor little tyke," Sally whispered. "One of the medics said her home took a direct hit from a bomb. They found her outside the house. At first they thought she was dead. The villagers haven't found a sign of her parents, but they haven't dug to the bottom of the rubble yet."

"There must be grandparents, too, and aunts, uncles ... someone ..."

"Sure, but where?"

Marge touched the child's soft cheek, feeling automatically for fever or chill. "She's cool. How about some hot water bottles?"

"Got them in place. Her BP and pulse rate are good. Doc says she's going to make it, but her left leg may never be normal."

Marge sighed. "She's hardly more than a baby."

"Yes," Sally whispered. "Rotten luck, isn't it?"

Determined not to grow attached to this Belgian girl who looked like Millie, Marge said, "Surely some relative will show up before she's ready to be discharged."

"If they fled to escape the fighting, they'll come back as soon as they can. Only I can't imagine that her mother and father would have left her alone at her home. It's more likely they died in the bombing."

"Looks that way. Are you going to stay with her until she wakes up?"

"Yes, unless we have so many incoming wounded that I can't. I'm here for the next four hours."

"Then I'll go find out where they want me. See you later." Marge left reluctantly. The child's plight tore at her. She'd be terrified when she awoke in a strange place among people who didn't speak her language. Marge never had dealt with a war-wounded child, so she was totally unprepared for the feelings of guilt that came over her, as if she had failed this child by being part of the generation that was conducting war. It did no good to tell herself it wasn't her fault, that her country had not started the war. No matter what, war should not happen to children.

She wondered if Sergeant Lewellyn had an answer to the tormenting question as to why God allows children to suffer. Even though she disagreed with his pacifist belief, she wished she could hear his reassuring voice. The fact that she longed for this stranger when she was thrown off-balance by seeing a wounded child came as a shock. She scarcely knew him, and there was little chance they could ever become friends. Military protocol forbade that. She was an officer, and he was not.

Chapter Three

Marge spent the next eight hours in the surgical ward, nursing newly admitted patients and checking in on the child frequently. At the end of her shift, the little girl still had not regained consciousness, so Marge headed to the mess tent for breakfast.

Outside, the light rain had stopped. Morning sun peeked under the east edge of the cloud cover and promptly disappeared. Two ambulances stood with doors closed near the mess tent. No others were in sight. For the moment, the flood of the wounded bodies had stopped.

Inside the tent Marge poured herself a mug of coffee, filled her mess kit with scrambled reconstituted eggs, some fried canned pork, and a slice of toast. She never ceased to be amazed at how the cooks prepared hot meals under all conditions.

Four soldiers stood to one side near the entrance to the tent, coffee cups in hand. Otherwise the place was empty. She headed for a table and sat down.

One of the soldiers approached her.

She glanced up. "Sergeant Lewellyn! Hello. At ease," she said all in one happy breath. "I hoped I might see you today. Your friend is doing well."

"That's great! Could I visit him before I head back?"

"You may need to clear that with the chief nurse or the surgeon, but I should think it would be fine." On impulse she told him about their child patient and said, "If you happen to hear of anyone looking for a little girl about five years old, send them here."

"I'll tell our captain. This sort of tragedy happens too often. People either refuse to leave their homes, or they can't. I've seen too many kids being hurt. After the war I'm going to set up a home for those who have lost their parents."

"You are?" How many more surprises lay hidden behind that quiet face?

He nodded. "Someone has to rescue the children. Our grown-up world has betrayed them. I aim to provide a loving home so they may believe that God loves them. I'll see that they're educated for good jobs and have fun too. Kids need to have fun." His lean face became handsome with a rugged kind of beauty as he spoke of his plans.

"Please sit down, Sergeant, and tell me more about your idea."

"I should get back to my buddies, and if you'll excuse me, ma'am, your being an officer and me not, I shouldn't sit with you. Thanks anyway."

She decided to pull rank. "Sit down, Sergeant. That's an order."

He hesitated, then grinned and obeyed.

"Tell me more about your children's home. How will you finance it?"

"I hope to get support from my church denomination. The Friends do a lot of charitable things like that."

"Will you come back to Belgium then?"

"No. I figure I'll go to the children of Germany. They'll need to be learning about the love and forgiveness of God. You know, some of the dead Germans we bury are just kids. They haven't even shaved yet. I calculate Hitler will use a lot more children for cannon fodder before we finally get to Berlin. Those who live to tell about it may be too old to be in an orphanage, but my home will welcome any young person who needs a friend or a home and family, no matter whether they're big or small."

This man consistently surprised her, but the idea of an orphanage in Germany sounded like a lost cause. "Why Germans? Why not kids from the occupied countries? You might have a fine kettle of sauerkraut working with young ones the Nazis have warped!"

"I figure the greatest need will be in Germany for the very reason you just expressed. Lots of folks will feel inclined to help French or Belgian or Dutch kids. But I figure God loves those who have been betrayed and deceived inside of Germany just as much as those outside who've been hurt by Hitler's gang."

She couldn't say a word against that. "Do you speak German?"

He nodded. "A little. I've always had a knack for languages. They come easy to me. Since D day I've learned enough French to get by, and I've learned some German already from talking with prisoners we've taken."

"Can you speak Belgian?" she asked, growing excited.

"Actually, here in southern Belgium, people speak French. Sure, I talk with the Belgians."

"Could you take time to see the little girl I mentioned? I know she'll feel better if someone can explain things to her."

"Well, sure. I can try right now if you want." He stood up.

Excited, she jumped to her feet. "I don't know if she's awake yet, but let's go see."

When they entered the post-op tent, Sergeant Lewellyn stopped to greet his buddy and then followed Marge to the end of the long row of beds. She pulled back the curtain and peeked in. Her tentmate Amelia had her arm around the little girl's shoulders, trying to get her to drink some water. The child looked up at them hopefully and then began to sob.

Gently Amelia eased her back down on her pillow and turned to greet them. "Hi, Marge. Did you come to relieve me? Maybe you can get her to drink."

"I haven't received my assignment yet, but Sergeant Lewellyn here may be able to help. He speaks her language."

Amelia brightened. "Well, come on, Sergeant. Give it a try. Anything you can do to help her understand may calm her."

Sergeant Lewellyn went to the head of the bed and eased himself onto a chair so that he was on eye level with the child.

The minute he greeted her in French, she burst into rapid speech.

He raised his hand, as if he were director of an orchestra signaling adagio. Then, holding her hand, he spoke in French with careful pauses.

The knot eased in Marge's stomach as she saw the girl begin to relax. When the sergeant's voice went up as in a question, the child gave a trembling smile and said, "Oui."

He stood up, patted the child's shoulder, and turned to Marge and Amelia. "I told her she's in a hospital where everyone will help her get well. I explained that she must stay here in bed for a while. I also promised to look for her mama and papa and two little brothers. Her name is Isabelle, and she is six years old."

"Tell her that she must let us know if she's in pain so we can give her medicine to make her feel better," Amelia said.

He turned and spoke to the child again. Then he said, "She will call you Nurse and point to where she hurts or to what she wants."

"Thanks. We'll teach her English words as fast as we can, but in the meantime it will help a lot to have her point."

He turned to Isabelle, spoke again in French, and then said, "She says her legs hurt, and she wants to move them. I explained that she must stay as she is for a while." Her left leg was in traction.

"I can give her a shot for pain," the nurse said. "Will you tell her I'll give her medicine?"

Resting a reassuring hand on the girl's shoulder, he talked quietly to her while the nurse uncovered her hip and administered the shot. Isabelle cried but held very still.

Marge stepped to her bedside and rested her hand on the girl's forehead. "Good girl," she said hoping her touch and tone of voice communicated encouragement.

"Tell her she's a brave little soldier," Amelia said.

He did.

Isabelle bit her lip, nodded, and clung to his hand.

Marge willed the lump in her throat to go away and smoothed Isabelle's short locks above her head bandage. They'd had to cut her hair short all over before suturing the long laceration on the left side. "I've got to go now. Thanks, Sergeant. It was swell of you to come see our youngest patient. You've been really good for her."

"Glad to help. If I can, I'll drop by again. And I'll try to find out about her family." He stood up and said good-bye to Isabelle, who gave him a trembling smile.

Marge steeled her heart against the flood of emotion Isabelle's little face recalled. Millie had looked at her with that same fear and pleading, but now she knew better than to become attached to a patient. Anyway, Isabelle would not die. And if she truly had lost her parents, she'd be placed somewhere with compassionate people, someone like David Lewellyn. Marge turned away.

Outside, she thanked Sergeant Lewellyn again and then headed for the nurse's tent to look for Chief Nurse Louise. As she crossed the muddy space between the wards and the nurse's quarters, she wished Lewellyn were an officer so they might become better acquainted without violating army rules. On the other hand, it really was wiser not to get to know him. He intrigued her too much. As Chief Nurse Louise had once said, falling for a soldier in the midst of war never helped a nurse to do her job better. In fact, she'd said, it often hampered one. Marge was inclined to agree, but she found David Lewellyn impossible to ignore, unsettling or not.

In Paris, Em stayed the night with Vivienne, waiting for word from Father Joseph. In the morning, having heard nothing, she said, "I'm sorry to leave you, but I need to go back to Hotel Scribe to finish an article and send it to London."

"I know you must. I will call a friend for driving you to the hotel." Vivienne went immediately to make the phone call.

Returning, she said, "He will be here shortly." After pouring herself another cup of coffee, Vivienne sat down at the kitchen table across from Em. "Will you come back and stay with me tonight? If Joseph doesn't call or come, I don't know what I'll do."

"Surely he will telephone, but I'll call you about four o'clock to let you know when I'll be back. If you hear from him before that, will you please call me?" She gave her the hotel room number.

Vivienne wrote it down. "I'm so glad for you to be here, Em. I am frightened. I don't know what's wrong with me. I've faced danger so many times these past few years without fear like this. It's just . . . I thought the worst was over."

Em shook her head in sympathy. "I don't know how you've endured all you've been through. Look, I'll work as fast as I can and try to be back here before dark."

A brief smile flickered across Vivienne's face. "Thank you."

When the driver arrived, Em hugged Vivienne good-bye. "I hate leaving you. Do take care, and try not to worry."

The gray-haired driver spoke no English, but on the way to Hotel Scribe he smiled and gestured with great expression.

Em was glad for the quiet. She had almost forgotten about her appointment with the OSS man, so she now made one last effort to calculate how her life would change if she were to sign on with the secret service. Since she couldn't imagine what changes might occur, she decided that when Mr. Cummins arrived she would know for sure or would ask him more questions.

The driver turned the corner and pulled up at the curb in front of Hotel Scribe. He insisted on helping her inside before driving away. Despite the language barrier, Em caught enough from his gestures and the few words she recognized to understand his good wishes. She returned them as best she could.

While she was crossing the busy hotel lobby, someone called her name. She turned to find three men strolling toward her from the front door. The windows back-lighted them, so she couldn't see their faces but knew they were fellow correspondents.

"So you made it to France," one exclaimed.

A familiar voice said, "Good to see you, Em."

Her heart gave a happy bounce. Bob Mansfield came to her side. Of these three men, he was the oldest. Near as Em could guess, he must be near thirty-five. She supposed his maturity had something to do with his kindness. He had championed her from the first day she'd wandered into the press hotel in London, and he'd done so without trying to make any passes at her. The younger men, until they got to know her, had treated her like some girl to be picked up in a pub.

Charlie and Al both worked for newspapers in the Midwest. They usually wore large chips on their shoulders, especially when they were around the New York correspondents, but apparently they felt comfortable with Bob. At least they gravitated to him whenever he showed up.

"Bob! Hello. Hi, Charlie ... Al. How long have you guys been here?"

"Came in the day after the city was secured," Charlie answered.

Al gave a slow smile and in his Oklahoma drawl said, "I came in with the commander's staff the day they entered. Took photos. Sent some to AP, but my own paper got first pick."

"Loyal Okie that he is," Charlie teased. "So, Em, what will you find here for the women readers of your mag?

Em laughed and shrugged. "Only the good Lord knows."

"You see much of this war up close and you may not believe the good Lord even exists."

She quickly studied Charlie's face. He looked worse than tired. "You sound as if you've had it up to your ears."

"I landed at Omaha Beach June seventh. Been with the GIs ever since—all the way to Belgium. I don't mind telling you I am sick to death of being scared every second of the day and night."

Em knew he didn't want sympathy. Taking a tack she'd learned from the men, she teased. "You and Ernie Pyle. You trying to get your head blown off?"

He grinned. "Nah, not me."

"Are you staying here, Em?" Bob asked.

"Yes, but not all the time."

"Oh?" He always managed to convey concern without sounding parental. She loved the way his eyes seemed to change color depending on the light and how he was feeling. Right now they had the dark sapphire look. She hoped she stirred his emotions as much as he roused hers. However, no matter how warmly he addressed her, she felt he always kept her at a distance, almost as if he were married, but she knew he was not. Despite his puzzling moments of reserve—or retreat—he was a sympathetic, staunch friend.

She realized she had been staring when he said, "Are you free for dinner tonight?"

"I'd love to join you, but I have this friend who needs me. . . ."

"Oh."

She saw his surprise and felt his withdrawal.

"Yes. Vivienne and I became friends before the war. I stayed at her apartment last night, and she's not feeling well. She wants me to come back tonight."

"I see. So how are your assignments going? Finding enough material to please your boss?"

She nodded. "So far. Look, Vivienne may feel better by evening. Could I call you if it turns out that I could join you for dinner?" She was sounding like a stammering schoolgirl. She hated the feeling. *Don't blush again,* she ordered her normally cool face.

He gave her a close-lipped smile. His eyes had turned sky blue. "Lucy-Em, I have no plans but to work. Give me a call any time before seven."

She'd never needed to keep a secret from Bob, and she didn't want to now. She suspected he would see through any lies she might attempt, but she had promised to keep quiet about the murder. And of course, she couldn't tell him about the visit from the OSS man. With all her being she did not want to hide anything from Bob. She did not want to add to the invisible barrier—whatever it might be—that already separated them. "I'll call as soon as I know anything. I'll call you one way or the other, so you'll know."

His eyes crinkled at the corners before the smile touched his lips. "That'll be fine."

On close inspection Bob looked very tired.

He returned her lingering gaze and smiled. "You're a sight for sore eyes, Lucy-Em."

She hated her real name, Lucille, and always introduced herself as Em. From the first day when he read her real name on her press card, he'd called her Lucy-Em, and the way he said it was okay. His look, his voice, and his thoughtful manner made his personal nickname for her sound special. Such was the charm of Bob Mansfield. "If I can come, shall I dress formally?"

He laughed. They both knew she preferred her army fatigues, boots, and an Ike-style jacket to dress uniforms with skirts. She'd once read that Katharine Hepburn preferred wearing slacks and sandals. That idea suited her too, so whenever anyone remarked about her casual attire, she came back with, "What's good enough for Hepburn is good enough for me." Some smart aleck always said the obvious—that she was no Katharine Hepburn. But not Bob. He usually made her feel beautiful and smart.

"Come as you are, Lucy-Em. You'd wow even a priest."

After he and the other two men left, she went up to her room to bathe, change clothes, and edit an article on the WAACs that she had been avoiding because it seemed dull.

She worked through lunchtime, and at two-thirty the phone rang. It was Vivienne. "Em, Joseph called. He is all right! He assured me he knows who wrote that note. It was one man, not a group. The man blamed Joseph for his brother's arrest and death at the hands of the Gestapo. Joseph had hidden the man and then passed him on to what he thought was another safe house. I can tell you more later. I just wanted you to know not to worry or feel you have to hurry back here."

"How does your brother know he is safe now?"

"The man, he has been killed. Not by Joseph. By Laurence's older brother."

"He just killed a man? What if it was the wrong man?"

"It was not. Em, it is better if you do not know any more about it. Joseph is safe, but he says he does need to leave Paris and continue on his journey."

"How are you? Do you feel safe?"

"Yes. Now that I know what has happened, I am fine. I trust Joseph, and he says there's no danger."

Vivienne did sound self-confident and strong. So Em told her about her attraction to Bob and how she hoped something might come of it. "Would you mind if I stay here to have dinner with him? I may not see him again for days."

"But of course you must dine with him! You didn't tell me you were in love! Do go, Em. It makes me happy just to think that you will be with the man you love this evening. Do not bother to come here tonight. I am fine."

Em laughed. "You French romantics. I didn't call it love. I'm afraid this man doesn't love me. So it won't be exactly the way you may imagine."

"But he will, *chèrie*. He cannot help it. Just be patient and be yourself."

"Me patient? I'm not sure I know the word."

Laughing together, they rang off.

Em immediately called Bob and told him she was free for dinner. Then she attacked the WAAC article with fervor. The prospect of an evening with Bob energized her.

When someone knocked on her door a short time later, she jumped. She had forgotten her appointment with Mr. Cummins! She hurried to let him inside and offered him the one extra chair by the desk.

She didn't sit, however. She paced to the window for one last thinking time. She'd been inclined all along to say yes, but now that the moment had come, she felt uncertain. For one thing, signing on with the OSS would separate her from everyone she loved. She wouldn't be able to discuss it with Marge or Bob. Her first obligation would be to the OSS. Was she really ready for this?

Mr. Cummins waited quietly while she stared out her window and then fingered the papers beside her typewriter before sitting. Then like a mind reader, he said, "Better you should say no now, than want to back out after you get in."

Then for some reason the thought came to her that this could be her chance for the one big story she always was looking for. Would the trade-off be worth it?

The murder of the young man behind Vivienne's apartment building had made Em feel urgent again about getting into wartime action. She made up her mind and spoke in the same instant. "Mr. Cummins, I do want to work for the OSS."

He nodded but remained intent and watchful. "The OSS is fighting on many fronts and in many ways. If you join us, you will not know what you are accomplishing. You won't know how you fit into the big picture. Are you willing to commit to this kind of operation?"

His warning galvanized her. "I was willing two years ago, and I still am."

He pulled papers from his briefcase and handed them to her. "Fill out all pages of the personal information, and then sign them. We never trust the security of the postal service, so I will wait and carry them to our safe. Your OSS salary is stated on page two. It will be deposited in a U.S. bank and held for you until the end of the war. I will give you cash for your assignments. As I said earlier, you will continue working for *USA Living & Review*, and your employer must not know you are working for us."

"I understand." She picked up her fountain pen and began filling out the forms. The third page was a form for a life insurance policy. She hesitated only long enough to read it before filling in her parents' names as beneficiaries. When she finished and blotted the wet ink on her last signature, she handed the papers back to him.

He smiled.

Almost friendly, she thought.

Slipping the papers into a manila envelope, he sealed it and placed it back in his briefcase. "You will receive your assignments from me and will report to me. Tell no one—no family member or friend—that you're working for us." He pulled a small piece of paper from his briefcase and handed it to her. "Here is your first assignment. Memorize the information, then destroy the note. Go visit the man and ask to interview him for your magazine. Do not telephone first for an appointment. It is important that you show up without warning."

"What is it you want me to do once I get in?"

"Just conduct your normal interview. I understand your magazine has asked you to gather stories about how the French people survived the Occupation. I am certain that Monsieur Jacques Marchant will give you a good story. That's all you need to think about. Get your story and write down every detail you observe about the man. When you get back to your room, call me. I want to debrief you as soon as possible." He reached into his briefcase again. "Here. Memorize my phone number, and then destroy it with the other note. If I am out, leave a message with my secretary. Tell her only that Elena called. Then I will contact you."

"Is Elena my code name?"

"Yes, use it whenever an assumed name is necessary." He stood up and headed for the door. "Best of luck, Miss Emerson. You will be a strong asset to us." He held out his hand.

She wasn't sure she liked being called an asset, but she grasped his hand and shook it. "Thank you."

When he opened the door, he glanced both directions before stepping out.

She closed the door behind him and leaned against it. When she first had applied in the States for espionage work, she'd been an idealistic twenty-year-old. Now she had no illusions about romantic adventures. It was enough that this job would help win the war.

By six o'clock that evening, Em had committed to memory the

brief history of Jacques Marchant as well as his address. Cummins had given her enough information about the WWI veteran to conduct an intelligent interview. She burned the notes about him over the toilet and flushed the ashes.

After freshening her lipstick and her hairdo, she went to the lobby to meet Bob. She saw him before he saw her. Watching him enter the lobby, she wondered how she ever could have felt he was too old for her. When he saw her, his obvious pleasure made her face turn warm. He strode toward her, not taking his eyes from hers.

"I was afraid you might not be here after all."

Keep your voice carefree, she cautioned herself. *If he suspects your real feelings, he will hide behind carefully impersonal comments.* "I thought we agreed I'd call if I couldn't come."

He grinned and nodded. "So we did. How did your afternoon go?"

"Fine." It had been her custom to share colorful bits of information she'd uncovered in her interviews. This would be her first test. She had to say less, yet not act differently.

Bob held out his arm to her with a show of exaggerated gallantry. She tucked her hand under his elbow and playfully matched his mood and his steps as they marched out the door.

Outside, he gestured toward a parked pedicab. "Would madam care to ride?"

She tightened her hand on his arm. "I'd rather walk, if you don't mind." *Anything to extend our time together.*

He bowed slightly. "M'lady's wish is my command."

Oh, Bob, if only that were so. With a melodramatic wave of her hand, she said, "Then let us stroll down the avenue."

The restaurant, lighted with candles, served a single menu—real beef, sliced thin and sautéed to a gourmet's pleasure, with just the right touch of wine in the light gravy. Vegetables done to a tender turn decorated the plate. As they finished with a tiny individual cake, Bob began to talk about his hometown and his parents. He'd never before revealed much about his personal life, so Em listened eagerly, hoping nothing would stop him. He'd gone to a country school, a small-town high school, and then had won a scholarship to a local college in Kansas. He'd worked on a small newspaper before packing and moving to New York.

"How did your family feel about you moving so far away?" Em asked.

At her question, an instant look of reserve shuttered his expression. Then he answered quickly, "My mom and dad were glad for me.

They both knew how much I'd always wanted to work for a large newspaper. And they still had my sister living nearby with her children."

"You weren't an only child then."

"No, but I just have one sister, five years older." He ate the last of his simple French cake and said, "What about you? Are you an only?"

"I have one sister, Marge, who is two years older than I, and a baby brother who was born when I was five. Marge is the army nurse who gave me the idea for my articles on combat fatigue."

"Oh, the series you wrote while in Wales. So is she in Wales?"

"Right. At a station hospital. Our mom and dad now have all of us overseas. My little brother, Billy, is in the navy in the Pacific."

He nodded. "War is tough on families." Then he seemed to slip away, lost in thought.

"Do you hear from your sister and your parents often?"

He jumped. "Uh, yes. Often. They write regularly. More than I do." He drank the rest of his coffee in one gulp and said, "I see you're finished. Shall we go now?"

"Okay." Again Em felt as if she'd touched on something that sent him reeling away from her. She had seen this abrupt change of subject before, as if he were hiding something.

On the way back to the hotel, she slipped her hand under his arm again and made small comments meant to draw him back to his previous playful mood, but his laughter never regained that earlier carefree note.

He walked her to her room and waited while she unlocked the door. Opening it, she turned to him. "Thanks, Bob. I had a lovely time."

"So did I. You're a gem to put up with me, Lucy-Em. That good food made my sleep deprivation suddenly catch up with me."

To her surprise, he bent his head and kissed her on the forehead. Before she could respond, he backed away. "Sweet dreams, young'un," he said lightly and left.

She glared after him. *Young'un?* Did he really think of her as a child—a daughter figure? If he had physically shoved her away, she couldn't have felt more rejected. This first date probably was also their last.

Em stomped into her room. So much for the great evening of romance Vivienne had presumed.

Chapter Four

The next morning at the Hotel Scribe reception desk, Em asked for directions to the area where Jacques Marchant lived.

The woman shook her head and exclaimed, "Ah, but you don't want to go there! Is not a nice place. See our beautiful city, instead. Go to the Seine—a lovely walk for you."

"I want to look up an old friend," Em explained.

The woman's eyes widened. "Your friend lives in Armagnoc? Too bad. But if you must go, it is too far to walk and not safe with bicycle. You must hire an auto. I will try to locate one for you." She picked up the phone receiver and dialed, then spoke rapidly into the mouthpiece. To Em, French always sounded like a floodtide of words flowing together and running over each other.

The woman paused to address her. "You have good fortune. My cousin can take you. He has only old auto, but he will get you there. Do you wish to hire?"

"Yes. That will be fine."

"When will you want him?"

Em glanced at her wristwatch. "As soon as he can come."

The woman spoke into the phone again, nodding and waving her free hand as if her listener could see her. Then she hung up. "He will be here at the desk in thirty minutes. I shall introduce you."

"Thank you so much! I'll be ready." With nothing better to do, Em went to the mess hall the army had set up for the correspondents and got a cup of coffee, then she returned to the front desk a few minutes before her driver appeared.

The cousin couldn't speak English. He read the address she had written, and a short time later delivered Em to the place. She had no idea how long she would be here. She tried with sign language to ask him to wait until she came back, but either he didn't understand or didn't want to. In the end, she paid him and waved good-bye. It would take a while, but if she had to, she could walk the six or seven miles back to Hotel Scribe.

Standing on the sidewalk in front of her destination, Em understood what the woman in the hotel had meant about Armagnoc. If she saw this place in a movie, she would be expecting to witness a murder, or at the very least, a mugging, even in the daylight. The ancient buildings had suffered neglect and abuse for a long time. So much for "gay Paree."

The narrow front of the hotel where Marchant was supposed to be living was stained almost black. Its door retained only a hint of paint. Garbage and broken glass lay scattered both directions from the steps. Two old men in shabby clothes and worn berets sat on the steps staring at her with red-rimmed, watering eyes. In the States she would have expected them to be accompanied by cheap wine bottles. Apparently they had no such thing to ease their day.

One gazed at her overly long and made a remark to his friend that Em was glad she could not translate. She said without hope, "Do you speak English?"

They shook their heads and leered at her, exposing broken brown teeth. One gestured at the door and nodded.

She went inside. The entry was dark, dusty, and smelled of a latrine. On the first door a stained placard said "Concierge." She knocked firmly on the old wood.

A stooped, gray-haired woman opened the door and squinted up at her. Her eyes widened as she took in Em's army uniform with the big *C* on the armband of her right sleeve indicating she was a war correspondent and not a WAAC officer. The woman's attitude instantly changed. "Oui, mademoiselle?"

"If you please," Em said, "Monsieur Marchant's apartment?"

The woman's expressive face became unreadable. She motioned with one hand and said in reasonable English, "Number eight, that way."

The passageway was so dark Em could barely read the numbers on the doors. The stench of urine grew stronger.

At number eight, she knocked. Monsieur Marchant, having lost parts of both legs in WWI, probably would need time to get his wheelchair to the door.

In a moment, however, the door opened a crack, and a young woman, tall like herself, peered out at her. "Oui?" she asked.

"I'm sorry. I only speak English. I'm looking for Monsieur Jacques Marchant. I am a correspondent for an American magazine."

The door opened wider, and the young woman studied her from head to toe. Then she said in very good English. "Why do you wish to talk with him?" she asked.

"I learned from another correspondent, Bob Mansfield of the *U.S. National Tribune*, about Monsieur's service to France during WWI, and I wanted to talk to an honored veteran about Paris now that it is free again."

"You have identification?"

No slouch, this young woman. Em, in uniform with her obvious correspondent's armband, had not expected such suspicion. She fumbled in her briefcase and retrieved her press card.

The young woman studied it and finally said, "One moment, please." She closed the door, and Em heard a key turn in the lock.

So much for a welcome from Monsieur Marchant. Who was the young woman? The atmosphere of the neighborhood suggested a woman of the night, but from the little Em saw of her, she sensed this was not the case.

Several minutes ticked by. Finally she heard the key turn again, and the door swung open to admit her. "My father says come."

"Thank you!" Em entered a dark, sparsely furnished room with a narrow window at one side. It was spotlessly clean and emanated no bad odors. She wondered how they'd managed such cleanliness in this old monster of a building.

"This way. We live in the back rooms."

After the dark first impression, the kitchen came as a shock. It was large, with high ceilings. The white walls, although obviously not painted in a long time, remained a cool white. The doors, cupboards, an armoire, wooden chairs, and table had been painted a sunflower yellow. This cheerful space apparently served as dining room and sitting room as well as kitchen.

Beside a window, in a wheelchair, sat a stocky man with a beak of a nose and a lion's mane of iron gray hair that refused to lie down. Em's first thought was of Joseph Stalin, disguised by a large nose. She stepped forward and said respectfully, "Thank you for seeing me, Monsieur Marchant. It's very kind of you."

The dignified face softened into a smile. "Mademoiselle, most welcome. I wonder . . . what can American . . . magazine wish from me."

His fragmented English made her wonder how well he would understand her questions.

Then he said, "My Jeanette, she help. Good English . . . from school." He smiled and patted his daughter's hand, which rested on the arm of his wooden wheelchair. He leaned forward. "Come." He nodded. "Sit, *si'l vous plait*? Jeanette—" He switched to French.

His daughter listened, nodded, and said, "Father wants to know what you would like to drink while we talk."

Em didn't know what to say, guessing they didn't have much to offer.

Jeanette helped her out. "Would you care for tea, mademoiselle?"

She nodded, relieved. "Tea would be just right, please." She sat down on the chair Monsieur Marchant indicated, facing him.

Jeanette brought a small glass of wine for her father and a pot of tea and a teacup for her.

Marchant sipped his wine, leaning back with a pleased sigh. "Ah, good French wine. Now tell me"—he gave her a shrewd look—"why you choose me for talk."

Before coming, she had determined the line she would take. "My friend Bob Mansfield of the *U.S. National Tribune* learned your name from someone previously in the Resistance. Mr. Mansfield thought your work, despite your WWI war injury, would fit my assignment to interview survivors of the Occupation."

He turned to Jeanette who supplied a translation in French.

Then she translated his answer to Em. "My father says we barely survived. The second year of the Occupation my mother fell ill and only lived a few weeks. We moved into this apartment in Armagnoc because the Boche did not come much to this place."

Em found herself watching Marchant as if he were speaking. "Father says losing Maman, that was our greatest loss to the enemy. After that, he and I wanted to fight the Boche with our bare hands."

Marchant was able to follow reasonably, for he raised his large hand in a fist and shook it.

Jeanette interjected on her own, "Maman, she suffered from the weak heart, and then winter influenza took her. Papa, he could find not a doctor or medicine. The Germans took many of our doctors as prisoners with our army. Before the war Maman had best of care." She frowned.

The big man spoke abruptly. "Jeanette—she is my legs and feet. We did make things—how you say . . . ah, *difficile* . . . for *les Boches*." He slipped back into French, chuckling and obviously pleased with the memory.

Jeanette translated. "He says, after all, who would suspect an old man in a wheelchair and his poorly clad attendant?"

"What did you do?" Em asked, taking out her pad of paper and a pencil.

Jeanette repeated Em's question in French.

He frowned for a moment and then nodded to Jeanette. "No hurt now for speaking." From that point on, Marchant talked through Jeanette without being questioned.

Em wrote furiously as a story of underground rebellion emerged. The disabled father and young daughter, at the risk of death, had kept a shortwave radio from the beginning of the war. They became a contact for the British and published an underground newspaper.

Then some of Marchant's old buddies introduced him to a ring of saboteurs. He and Jeanette became couriers for them. As he had hoped, the Germans never suspected them. They carried messages all over Paris for the Resistance, under the very noses of the Gestapo. To the British they reported which German divisions were represented in the city and gave the names of German officers.

He paused, and Jeanette went on, seemingly for herself. "I played the part of a collaborator a few times, but Père soon forbade me. Not even for the allies would he allow our neighbors to think I liked the Germans."

Marchant reached out and clasped his daughter's hand. The obviously close bond between them made Em homesick for her own father.

It seemed to her that Jacques Marchant understood English quite well but was not skilled in speaking it, just as she was with French, understanding more than she could speak.

Marchant began his narration again, and Jeanette translated. "Père can walk on wooden legs, but in public he leaves them off. That secret alone helped us. No one guessed where he could go. He fought in every way he knew, and I always went along." She launched into a detailed description of one night when they helped other resistants free an Englishman from a prison hospital.

Jeanette, standing beside her father, rested her hand on his shoulder in an expression of both affection and pride. "Père fooled everyone. All I had to do was go along and obey him. He always seemed to know what the Gestapo was planning."

Marchant shook his head, spoke quickly, and she translated. "He says it's not hard to read their unimaginative minds. Their training makes machines of them. An observant man needs merely to watch."

Marchant smiled, sipped his wine, and smacked his lips. "Good wine! From my brother . . . in Burgundy." He set down the glass and folded his hands in his lap. "So, Mademoiselle Emerson, is enough now . . . for magazine?"

Em laid down her pencil. "Yes. Thank you!"

"When will the story be published?" Jeanette asked.

"I can't be certain, but soon I hope. I'll mail you a copy if the editors accept it. I can't control what they finally decide to print, you know."

"It would be nice to have a copy for my father. He will be happy for Americans to know we did our part to free France."

Em smiled, wishing she had more time to get to know these two. "I will make your efforts very clear. Thank you so much for telling me. Now if you'll excuse me, I must go and begin the writing while my memory is fresh."

"Do you have an auto?"

"Not now. Someone brought me. I didn't know how long I would be here, so I sent him away. I can walk."

"Oh, no," Jeanette said. "You should not to go alone. This is bad area. I will walk with you."

"Oh, I'll be all right if you just give me a few directions."

She spoke to her father, then gave his answer to Em.

"He apologizes for our city, but Armagnoc is not a safe place for a young woman who doesn't know the area. He agrees I go with you. I know the ways of this neighborhood. Also I have made friends who watch out for me."

Em couldn't prevail against the two of them without sounding rude, so she agreed.

Jeanette went to fetch her coat. When she returned, she looked twenty years older—gray-haired and stooped. In one hand she held a cloth shopping bag and in the other a cane. Worn wooden sabots completed her costume.

"I can't believe it's you," Em exclaimed. "Have you done this often?"

"Many times. Now shall we go?"

Em intercepted a furtive glance that passed from father to daughter, an expression that suggested, *Be careful, we've said enough.* So they had their secrets too.

Despite the genial behavior of the father and daughter, a whisper of danger set Em on alert. She couldn't ignore her odd reaction, but she also couldn't identify a valid reason for it. Nothing about these two could rationally inspire fear.

She must be edgy because of all of Vivienne's warnings. She could go directly to Vivienne's apartment if it was closer than the hotel. She gave the address to Jeanette and asked.

"But yes, it is much closer! A short walk, really. I will show you."

Again Em intercepted that quick look between father and daughter. Em started to ask if they knew Vivienne, but a protective instinct kept her from mentioning her friend's name. Maybe her new position with the OSS was making her imagine risks. At any rate, when she talked to Vivienne she would ask if she knew the Marchants. Actually, Father Joseph might have met them. The Resistance had no doubt created strange bedfellows.

Em thanked Monsieur Marchant again for his time and followed his daughter out into the dismal street.

Jeanette walked like an old woman and chose not to talk much, so Em followed her lead. Not many people walked these streets, and those who did seemed not even to notice the American accompanying an old woman. After a couple of hard-faced men passed them without a glance, Em said in low voice, "I am very glad you came with me. I had no idea it was this bad." She glanced at the tall vacant building beside them. It seemed more threatening than the people. Windows had been boarded up on the ground floor, but the door to the street hung ajar.

"Even I do not often come this way," Jeanette murmured. "But it is the shortest route to your friend. I shall walk home another way."

The scrape of a shoe against the cobblestones made them both whirl around. The two men who had passed them were upon them. Em screamed and fought back. Jeanette fought fiercely but silently. In a few seconds the men had them both on the cobbled sidewalk. The one who grabbed Em, twisted her arm behind her, jerked her to her feet, and forced her toward the door of the vacant building. She struggled. Searing pain ripped through her shoulder. He would tear her arm from its socket. A flash of nausea warned her she was about to faint, and she didn't want to pass out in the hands of this monster.

The moment she eased in her resistance, he shoved her inside the dark hallway. She heard Jeanette still fighting outside. *Oh, God, help us!* The thought of being alone inside with this brute terrified her. His grip on her twisted arm tightened. She could not keep from crying out. She could smell his foul breath over her shoulder.

The door behind them crashed open, casting light down the dirty hall in front of Em.

Jeanette's shout in French cut the dank silence.

The grip on Em's arm eased.

Jeanette yelled again. The man whirled around and shoved her toward Jeanette. She stumbled and fell. At the same instant a shot nearly shattered her eardrums.

Her assailant did not fall. Instead, he darted into a dark doorway. She heard his footsteps as he ran, then silence.

Jeanette was beside her, helping her up. "Come. I won't pursue him in this place, and he knows this. Come quickly out."

Em hurried out to the sidewalk, dizzy from the pain in her shoulder. She grabbed the wall to keep from falling. "What happened to the other man?"

"When he saw my gun, he ran. You are hurt?"

"My shoulder. It may be sprained."

"Can you walk?"

"Yes."

"Then come. We must to hurry."

"Do you always carry a gun?" Em asked, remembering the impressive weapon she'd glimpsed in Jeanette's hand.

"Oui. I must for so long. I cannot go without now." She made no effort to keep up her disguise. She kept hold of Em's good arm and tugged her along.

"Shouldn't we report to the gendarmes?" Em asked.

"I'm sorry to say, for this type of crime it is no use to try. We are not back to peacetime order yet."

"You are sure?"

"Oui. This is how it is."

After several blocks the slum appearance eased. Soon they entered a neighborhood of modest apartment buildings. A few blocks more, and Em recognized the pleasant street where Vivienne lived.

"The address you said—it is over there." Jeanette pointed across the street.

They had come from a different direction than Em's approach last night. The courtyard gate to the apartment building gave a whole different appearance. "Yes, that's it. Won't you come in and meet Vivienne?"

"Vivienne?"

"My friend. Vivienne Hugo."

"Oh." A fleeting expression of surprise crossed Jeanette's face but passed so quickly Em wasn't sure she'd seen any change.

"Do you know her?" Em asked.

"Non. Hugo is a common name, and for a moment I thought yes. But non. I would like to meet your friend, but I must return to my father. He will need me."

"I don't know how to thank you. I think you saved my life."

"I am so happy to be there. Now I must go. Au revoir."

"Au revoir. God bless you."

Jeanette smiled, nodded, and with a wave of her hand turned back toward home.

When Em closed the door of Vivienne's apartment building behind her, she sighed in relief. Her shoulder throbbed miserably. She couldn't wait to bathe and lie down for a while. The climb to the second floor apartment left her panting. She was suddenly very tired.

When Vivienne opened her apartment door and saw Em's face, she cried, "What happened? Did you have an accident?"

Only then did Em realize how dirty and disheveled she was. In the hall mirror she saw an angry red welt on her cheek.

"Come let me clean you up! Whatever happened?"

Em sagged against the wall and closed her eyes. "I was attacked. Fortunately a courageous French girl saved me with a gun big enough to kill a bear."

Vivienne led her to a chair and in seconds returned with medicines and bandages. "Did you or the girl report the crime?"

"She said not to, that no one would investigate."

Vivienne frowned. "Unfortunately, she may be correct. Do you want to try?"

"I think not. It would involve her as a witness, and I believe she doesn't want that to happen." Actually Em didn't want to get involved in an investigation either. It would be the worst possible way to start her career as a secret agent.

"Sit down here near the light." Vivienne held her arm until she was seated beside the kitchen table. Then as she gently soaped Em's cheek, she asked, "Who was this guardian angel who saved you from the attack?"

"She's the daughter of the man I interviewed—Jeanette Marchant."

All expression left Vivienne's face as she stared at Em's wound.

"What's wrong?" Em exclaimed. "Is it really bad?"

"Oh no. I was thinking about what to put on it to prevent scarring. Did that woman with the gun see you safely here then?"

"Yes. She came with me to show me the way."

Vivienne patted Em's cheek dry with soft cotton. "Did you mention my name?"

"Why, yes. I invited her to come up and meet you, but she said she had to get back to her father. He's disabled. He was active in the Resistance. Maybe you heard of him. Jacques Marchant."

Vivienne shook her head. "No. I have never heard of Monsieur Marchant."

Despite Vivienne's outward calm, Em felt her tension. "Should I not have mentioned your name?"

"Why do you think this? It is fine. Now hold very still while I use a little alcohol, and then I'll apply a soothing salve."

Em obeyed. Her shoulder hurt so much that all she could think of was getting into a hot bath.

CHAPTER FIVE

Safe in Vivienne's apartment, Em began to relax under her friend's ministrations.

Vivienne heated large pans of water on her kitchen stove to add to the tap water for Em's bath. Then Em eased herself into the luxury of a hot soak. Her shoulder ached seriously, but she didn't think it required a doctor's attention. As the heat seeped into her muscles, the hard pain eased. Then the loud jangle of Vivienne's phone brought Em upright in the tub. She could hear Vivienne talking, but as usual, she couldn't capture much meaning from her rapid flow of French.

In the silence that followed the phone call, Em tried to relax again, but she couldn't ignore a persistent uneasiness. "Vivienne!"

In a moment the door opened, and Vivienne poked her head into the steamy room. "Do you need something?"

"You were so quiet. I heard the phone, and then it seemed like you weren't even here."

Vivienne stepped into the bathroom and sat on the vanity stool. "It was a friend of Joseph's."

"I'm ready to get out. Will you hand me that towel, please?"

Vivienne passed her the towel. Then, unlike her usual chatty self, she said no more.

"Is your brother all right?" Em reached for the towel bar to steady herself as she dried one foot. Forgetting her injury, she used the wrong arm. "Ouch!" She grabbed with her other hand, barely avoiding a fall.

"Careful!" Vivienne leaped up to steady her.

"Thanks." Her careless action had undone the healing touch of the hot water. Her shoulder screamed and then maintained a throbbing ache.

Empathy twisted Vivienne's smooth face. "Maybe you should have a doctor examine your shoulder."

"It really is not that bad. Back to your brother. Did he get out of Paris?"

"Yes. He's fine, but our friend wasn't as confident as Joseph about my safety here."

"Why?"

"He thinks there may be more than one man after Joseph and that they may very well know who I am. He thinks I could be kidnapped to force Joseph out of hiding and back to Paris."

"Oh, Vivienne, you ought to report this to the authorities!"

"You don't understand how it is. Only weeks ago traitors had to be annihilated for the sake of survival. Even now threats cannot be resolved in a normal way. No gendarmes. I must obey Joseph and his friend. They will know when to call in the authorities. Right now I have to think where to go."

Em rubbed herself dry, taking care not to flex her sore shoulder again. "Come to the hotel and stay with me."

Vivienne's lips parted as if to say yes, but then she shook her head. "It is too public."

"The whole first floor is being used for press offices and the censors. Everyone is working, heads down, or on the telephone. We can sneak in a service door at the rear and go right up to my room. No one will know."

"You are sure you can get me in without notice?"

Em nodded vigorously. "I'm sure."

Vivienne's eyes narrowed as she considered. "This might be right. Then I will leave Paris as soon as possible."

"Where will you go?"

"To friends on a remote farm. Joseph can send word when it is safe to return."

Em put on the robe Vivienne had loaned her. "Shall we walk to Hotel Scribe?"

"It is about ten kilometers."

"Ten—that's about six American miles. No problem."

"I do think we disappear most easily walking like everyone else. You can wear some of my clothes. Your uniform will make you noticeable and easy to follow."

"You think they may be looking for me too?"

"If they saw you come here. And after all, someone already accosted you."

"He was just a common criminal type. I was in a bad section of the city."

"You can't know what he had in mind. Someone knows that I am Joseph's sister, and if so they probably know where I live. Maybe you were seen last night coming here with him."

Em caught her breath. "You're making too much sense. Let's get out of here."

Vivienne nodded. "I'll put a change of clothes in a small bag." She stopped. "But your shoulder. Can you walk that far, hurting as you do?"

"I'll be okay. My shoulder feels much better after the hot soak," she lied.

Vivienne disappeared into her bedroom and returned with a skirt, sweater, and woolen coat. "Here is clothing for you. It is good that we're near the same size. I'll be ready in a few minutes." Vivienne was so upset Em didn't question or argue anymore.

Em dressed and felt very French in Vivienne's clothes, which included a black beret and black coat. The coat was old, worn thin on the seams and edges of the sleeves, yet still it gave her a stylish air.

They left the building by the back entrance, and seeing no one about, they hurried down the alley. For a long time Vivienne led Em through alleys. At last they came to a thoroughfare crowded with pedestrians. They blended in and headed toward Hotel Scribe.

When they finally neared the hotel, they watched from across the street to see if anyone was paying undue attention to them. Seeing no one suspicious looking, they hurried to the service entrance. Inside, a closed door separated the stairs from the mess hall and the transportation storage area where gallons of gasoline and oil were stored for the press corps.

"I'm on the second floor," Em said. "Come on."

At the second level they waited until no one was in sight and then hurried down the hall and into her room.

Em collapsed on the edge of the bed with a sigh of relief. The pain from her wrenched shoulder extended from her neck to her tailbone. "I don't think I've been this tired since haying season on the ranch." She pulled off the beret and ran her fingers through her hair to smooth it back behind her ears.

Vivienne sank into the chair by the desk. "I believe we escaped notice."

"Yes. Thanks to you. You must have had a lot of practice in disappearing."

Vivienne chuckled. "Not exactly. However, everyone in France has learned ways to avoid attention. Right from the beginning of the Occupation, we learned that being innocent did not save us from the Gestapo. So we tried to be invisible."

Pain from Em's shoulder was making her head ache. She leaned back on the bed pillow and closed her eyes. Tired as she was, she still had to contact Cummins and do it without Vivienne's knowledge. The hotel had a bank of public telephone booths at the back of the lobby. That would have to do.

She sat up. "I'm hungry. I'll go downstairs and find some food. I'm sorry I can only offer you canned army rations. If I'm lucky I'll include some D rations. They have a chocolate concentrate for dessert."

"I can eat anything."

"Good." Em put on the uniform she'd left hanging in the closet. She hoped Brad Cummins could pull strings and quickly replace the uniform she'd left at Vivienne's apartment. Normally, she'd be in trouble for losing so many articles of clothing at one time.

She tried to conceal the mark on her cheek with makeup, but she didn't have a good blemish cover. With a shrug she gave up. "Unfortunately, I didn't come prepared to hide bashes on my face," she said. "Be back in a few minutes."

Downstairs, before she reached the phone, she met Bob. His eyes immediately locked onto her cheek. Hoping to distract him while she thought of a credible lie, she said, "Bob! I didn't hope to see you again today. I thought you were on your way to join General Devers in eastern France."

"I am. Turned out that we leave tomorrow morning. What did you do to your face?" With a finger under her chin, he turned her face to the light. "Did you have a doctor medicate that?"

His touch made her giddy, but she lied convincingly, she thought. "Yes. She also put on some good healing medicine."

He frowned. "She?"

"A French doctor. She was good . . . knew her stuff. It felt better right away. Whatever she used took all the burn out of it."

His eyes had taken on a greenish blue hue, and he didn't step back from her as she had come to expect. Instead, frowning, he studied the scrape. "You didn't say what happened."

"Would you believe I fell over my own feet and with my hands full? I actually hit the ground with my face before my elbow."

He shook his head, still watching her closely. Without smiling, he said, "I can almost believe that."

"Well, good luck on your assignment tomorrow." She backed away.

"Will you have dinner with me again tonight?"

Em almost cried aloud in frustration. She had to say no and tell him more lies. "I'd love to, Bob, but I'm so tired. And I have to write up today's interview before I can go to bed. May I have a rain check?"

He studied her again with his blue-green questioning look, but he assented. "Sure. Anything for you, Lucy-Em."

"Let me know when you come back to Paris."

"I will."

He wasn't in a hurry to leave, so she excused herself. "I have to make a phone call to check on some facts. See you later."

"Yeah. See you later." At last he walked away. She hurried to a phone booth and made her call. She prepared herself to say she was Elena as she'd been instructed, but Brad Cummins himself answered.

First she told him about the attack she had suffered on the way to Vivienne's.

"I see," he said. "Are you all right?"

"Yes. I just have a wrenched shoulder."

"You must see a physician then. I'll have a military car pick you up at the main entrance of the hotel at eight tomorrow morning."

"What shall I tell my friend—" Too late she realized not even the OSS was supposed to know that Vivienne was with her, in case it would make any difference for Father Joseph.

"What?"

"My friend, Bob Mansfield. I was going to meet him for breakfast."

"Tell him the truth as far as you can, that you need to see a doctor. Nothing more." Abruptly he returned to the subject of her interview. "What was your impression of Marchant and his daughter?"

"Nice folks. They make an amazing team, and they're devoted to each other. Jeanette may have saved my life. They gave me excellent material for my feature story."

"Have you told anyone besides me about the attack?"

"No, of course not. Well, my friend Vivienne, but not the police. I was on my way to stay with Vivienne, so I had to tell her." She decided she must tell him the whole truth after all. "Vivienne ended up coming to the hotel to stay with me." She explained about Father Joseph, and his warning to Vivienne.

He swore under his breath. Then she could hear him sigh. "Okay. You've done well for a beginner. I didn't expect you to run into anything of this sort, though, of course, one never knows. As soon as our doctor finishes his exam in the morning, I want to meet you for a thorough debriefing. Your driver will drop you at the Louvre. From there walk past the Temple de l'Oratoire. Turn right on Rue St. Honoré and walk on until you see on the right the Café Cleremont. Ask for Monsieur Pierpont's table. In case I am detained, wait at least an hour."

"Café Cleremont on the right. Okay."

"You'll have to conceal our rendezvous from your friend Vivienne. And make sure that no one follows you."

"I will."

"Tomorrow, then. Be downstairs by the door at eight. Your driver will call you by name and identify himself by saying he is picking you up for Monsieur Paul Osgood—one of my assumed names."

"All right."

When she came out of the phone booth, there sat Bob, as if waiting for his turn to use the phone. He stood up. "Em, are you really okay?"

"Right as rain in a monsoon," she said.

"You don't look all right, and you're not acting like yourself."

He reached out and gripped her shoulder. His fingers sent dagger signals through her injury. She winced and groaned.

He let go as if he'd touched a hot stove. "You are hurt!"

She sucked in a deep breath. The pain waned. "I injured my shoulder when I fell. That's all. It's sore, but I'm okay"—she made herself smile—"as long as no one grabs me."

His eyes narrowed. "And your French doctor said you are fine."

"Yes."

"You should have an army doctor look at it. I'll run you over to the military hospital."

"No. I'm all right."

Through tight lips, he said, "You obviously are not all right."

She had to steer him away from this subject. Throttling an overwhelming wish to fall into his arms and let him pamper her, she blurted, "Since when are you my boss?"

The hurt expression that crossed his face gave her a pain worse than the one in her shoulder. She wanted to snatch back her words—especially the way she'd said them. Of all people, he never before had tried to dictate to her. She started to apologize, but in the next instant he gazed back at her without emotion. It was too late. Anything she said now would be useless. Without moving an inch, he had retreated from her again. No, this was different. She had chased him away. She tried to console herself that this was for the best. Best thing now was just to leave. She turned to go upstairs.

She hadn't taken more than a step when he called, "Lucy-Em."

She hesitated, and he was beside her.

This time he gripped her good arm as if fearing she would run away. "I'm sorry. It is none of my business. You are fully capable of taking care of yourself. I just—lost my head, I guess. I hate seeing you hurt." He leaned forward and kissed her firmly on the lips. Before she could respond, he hurried toward the front of the lobby.

With a racing heart she stared after him. If it were not for her work in the OSS, she'd be running after him.

The next time Marge saw David—now she thought of him as David more often than as Sergeant Lewellyn—he had brought in four more wounded men from the aid station and was about to return for more.

Seeing him beside his ambulance, she detoured to speak to him. "Your buddy will be sent to an evacuation hospital tomorrow, and little Isabelle is learning English almost as fast as you learned French."

He brightened. As before, his smile transformed his face from ordinary to handsome. "Tell Isabelle hello from me. I hope I can get time on one of these runs to see her again. So far no one knows about anyone missing a little girl. It's tough. If she has relatives, they may not find her until after the war."

Her spirits sagged. She had feared this might be the case. She'd tried so hard to avoid loving this little girl, but often when she passed the child's bed, she found her needing some small attention. "I'd so hoped that someone would come looking for her."

He shook his head. "I'm afraid it's not likely."

"Well, thanks. I just wanted to tell you about your friend. I see you brought four men this time."

"Yeah. We're advancing. Snipers hit all these men. We're almost to the Hurtgen Forest. It's a black place that spills all the way from here in Belgium on into Germany. The trees meet overhead so low in places a man can't stand up. Getting through that dense growth will be a tough go. When we move into it, I'll be back on the front line, and the less experienced medics will do the ambulance runs."

For an instant Marge felt as if an elevator had dropped out from under her. *This reaction is crazy!* "How soon do you think that will be?"

He shrugged. "No telling. You'll know when the big push begins." He glanced at the surgery tent and jerked his head that direction. "In there you'll know."

"We'll be ready." She had seen so many torn and destroyed bodies. She didn't want David to be the next. Was that being selfish? "Take care of yourself and your men," she said lightly.

"I will—me and the Lord," he said.

Since she was the officer, it was up to her to end the conversation, but she didn't want to. She had to make herself say the words, "Good day, Sergeant," and walk away.

She headed for surgery, wishing she had a sustaining faith like his. Her nursing experience had taken her a long way from her childhood belief that God would say yes to all her prayers of concern for others. She'd seen so many people die despite her prayers.

Chapter Six

A few minutes ahead of schedule the next morning, Em stood at the door of Hotel Scribe, waiting to go with the driver Brad Cummins had promised. Em smiled to herself. In her mind the name Brad did not fit her boss. Cummins, yes, but Brad conjured up the image of a bulky football player she'd known in high school. She decided that she would privately call him Cummins, but she would have to remember to add Mr. whenever she addressed him.

Vivienne had agreed to stay at least one more night at the hotel. As far as Vivienne knew, Em was going to see an army doctor and then interview someone.

Promptly at eight o'clock, an auto pulled up in front of the hotel. Em stepped out the door and waited. He came directly to her. "Miss Emerson?"

"Yes." She didn't move.

"Mr. Osgood sent me. I'm to take you to your appointment with the doctor." He unobtrusively extended his hand, palm up. In it, she saw a small card that identified him as army personnel with special clearance.

It looked on the up and up, but she studied his face again. Either he was a great actor or he had nothing to hide. She nodded. "Let's go, then, Sergeant."

A French general hospital had been turned into an Allied military hospital. The building was old, ornate, and very clean. The doctor who examined her said, "No bones fractured, Miss Emerson. However, a sprain can take longer to heal than a broken bone. The shoulder is attached, as you are feeling, to muscles that extend over your chest and around your back. Today, alternate hot and cold packs on it. After today, do whichever feels best. You might want to wear a sling for a few days. The nurse will give you some exercises for later. For pain, take these APC tablets according to the directions. If any stiffness remains after six weeks, work harder on flexibility. Any problems, check in again with one of us."

She stood up. "Thank you, Doctor. If it's okay, I'd rather not wear a sling."

He grinned and nodded. "Slings aren't very glamorous."

Inwardly she bristled. Why did men, especially military men, automatically think of some stereotypical female who thought always about how she looked? Just barely she kept irritation from her voice. "That's not what I was thinking about. I have a job to do, and a sling gets in the way."

He raised his eyebrows. "Do as you wish. It won't likely slow the healing."

He excused himself, and in a moment an army nurse came into the examining cubicle. "I'm to show you how to apply this sling," she said, smiling in a genial manner.

"I told the doctor I didn't want to wear one."

"He's sending one with you in case you change your mind."

"Okay. But I took first aid, and I do know how to apply a first-aid sling."

"Then you know enough. You might try wearing it for a while when you get back to your hotel room to see if it eases your discomfort." The nurse folded the cloth to fit in Em's briefcase. Handing it to Em, she said, "Shoulders can freeze up if you don't give them as much gentle motion as you can. I want to show you a few exercises. First, lean forward from your waist, let your arm hang and then swing it in circles, like this." She demonstrated. "As your shoulder heals make wider circles." Then she demonstrated a couple more ways to regain strength and mobility.

Watching the nurse reminded Em of Marge. "My sister's an army nurse. She's in Britain in a military station hospital. I wonder if your paths ever crossed. Her name is Marge Emerson."

The nurse shook her head. "No. I came straight to France right after D day."

"Oh. Marge enlisted right after Pearl Harbor. She's hoping someday to become a physician."

The nurse raised her eyebrows. "That will take a long time and hard work."

Em laughed. "That's what I keep telling her."

"Medicine is still a man's world." Then the nurse looked at Em's war correspondent insignia. "But then so is being a war correspondent, isn't it?"

"You could say that. I guess Marge and I have a similar masochistic twist in our psyches."

The nurse laughed. "More power to you. Me, I just want to get married, have a family, and maybe do some nursing on the side."

"Thanks for showing me the exercises. As soon as I can, I'll do them."

The nurse smiled. "Don't push yourself. As long as you do what you can each day, you'll be okay." She walked Em to the reception area.

Obeying Cummins' orders, Em told her driver to take her to the Louvre. From there she walked the remaining blocks to the café. Cummins was waiting for her in a shadowed corner at the back of the small restaurant. The waiter brought food immediately.

"They don't have a menu—they're lucky to have any food at all to serve," Cummins said, "but I didn't want to have you drive all the way to my quarters outside of Paris. Nor did I want to meet you at Hotel Scribe. I already ordered for both of us."

"Fine. Almost anything would look good after days of K rations at the hotel." From somewhere the chef had acquired mushrooms and had created a chicken and mushroom concoction with a tender top crust. She took a bite and sighed. "Wonderful."

He nodded. "Not bad. The doctor called me and said your shoulder may mend quickly, depending on whether it is strained or sprained. Apparently he could not be sure which. How does it feel?"

She shrugged and flinched from the effort. "Sore. I wish I had some of the liniment my dad used to put on the horses."

He grinned. "I'll see what I can do. Now tell me all you can remember about the Marchants."

She described the visit in detail—from the first moment Jeanette had greeted her to their last good-bye. Cummins nodded and asked questions while he ate. When she finished, he said, "Good. I think you've given us exactly what we needed to know."

His questions had seemed disjointed and gave no clue as to what he had in mind. He obviously had no intention of revealing anything. "Next, I want you to interview this man." He leaned forward and slid a note across the table.

Em read the first line of neatly printed information—*Hubert Espe, Macon.*

He gave her a wad of tightly folded bills. "Travel money. Slow as the train is, you'll have to take it. Memorize the information, and then destroy the note." He reached into his breast pocket and produced a locket-sized gold pocket watch on a thick gold chain.

"Put this around your neck, and in case anyone is watching, do some oohing and aahing of surprise and pleasure. My gift to you, you see."

She obeyed with ease. The watch made a lovely pendant.

"In fact, the watch is a gift to give Hubert. Don't let it out of your possession for an instant." He leaned toward her, making them look intimate and murmured, "If you were to lose this, and it fell into the wrong hands, many men would die."

She swallowed hard.

"Nothing to be nervous about."

"Am I that transparent?"

He gave her one of his rare smiles. "Only to someone like me who is only inches away." Abruptly he covered her hand with his. "Excuse me, but we need to look like lovers meeting secretly. People may think so even if we don't play the part. This will cover the times I have to see you in public. I assure you, I have a wife at home whom I love. And we will not meet this way frequently. Do you mind?"

She smiled, as if in response to a lover, and murmured back, "Would it matter if I did?"

He squeezed her hand and leaned closer and whispered in her ear endearingly, "No. And you followed my lead very well."

While their heads were bent together, a man strolled past their table and took a seat a few tables away.

Cummins whispered, "It's time to go. I want you to leave first. I'll watch to be sure no one follows you."

"Do you know that man?"

"I've seen him before. Get up and leave with a show of reluctance. When you get outside disappear fast. Can you walk the distance to your hotel?

"Yes."

"I meant to drop you off near Hotel Scribe, but now it's better if I stay here and you go ahead. Watch your back, and guard that watch. It is best that you give me back the note. I don't want you caught with it. I will call you soon with complete instructions."

Em played the part of a woman in love who hated to leave her lover. Once beyond sight of the windows of the café, she hurried to the next corner and darted down a side street. From there she took a zigzag course. At each corner she looked back and saw no hint of anyone following her. After she crossed the Seine, she walked more easily, pausing only to drop the watch inside the neck of her shirt, where it rested cold against her skin. In moments it had taken on warmth and faded from her attention.

As she walked, watching all directions but trying to look as if she were not, she thought of Vivienne, almost a prisoner in her hotel room. She would be expecting her back by now. Em had left enough food in the room to last until supper, but she hated leaving her friend alone this long without calling. She began to look not only behind to see if she were being followed but also for a public telephone.

When Em finally reached the hotel, the afternoon light was fading. She had not seen any available pedicabs. Neither had she found a telephone. Her feet hurt, and her shoulder made her whole upper torso ache. Not wanting to have to chat with other journalists, she entered the hotel by a side entrance and hurried upstairs. She tapped on her door. When Vivienne didn't come, she slipped the key in the lock. As soon as she opened, she called, "It's only me!"

Vivienne didn't answer, and she wasn't in sight. The bathroom door was open.

Em raised her voice. "Vivienne?"

The silence seemed to scream *Vivienne is gone!* Then Em spied the paper propped in the roller of her typewriter. She hurried over and ripped it from its mooring. Vivienne had typed a note.

Dear Em,

I have to leave. I decided to go while you are out so that I won't involve you more than already you are. Please do not worry. I will contact my brother, and he will tell you when I arrive at my friend's home.

I am so sorry I didn't show you my city yet, but soon I hope I shall. Do take good care of yourself.

Your friend,
Vivienne

Em sank into her chair at the desk. How could she not worry? She would miss Vivienne. However, Vivienne knew her way and what was best, and Em could not deny that having one less person to lie to made her own work a little easier. All she had to do now was finish her article on the Marchants and send it to London. By the time she completed that, maybe Cummins would call with the remaining instructions for her new assignment for the OSS. All she knew at this point was the man's name and the town to which she was to go.

She snacked on a D ration she'd left for Vivienne and, ignoring her aching shoulder, typed furiously. Sometime later her phone rang.

Picking up the receiver, she leaned toward the mouthpiece. "Em Emerson speaking."

"It's me, Em. Brad Cummins. Did you have any difficulty? Any hint of being followed?"

"No one that I saw. When I got to my room, my friend Vivienne was gone, though. She left a note."

He met that with a few seconds of silence. "You didn't see any signs of foul play?"

Icy fear engulfed her. She wanted to deny the possibility, to yell, no, of course not! Instead, she looked around again and then said unsteadily, "No."

"I had to ask, you know."

"I know."

"All right, here's the agenda. I'm sending a woman to bring you the details of your assignment and a ticket for Macon. You will be on the train that leaves at ten in the morning."

"Tomorrow?"

"Yes. And Em, from now on, always watch your back. That man in the restaurant did nothing today, but I'm sure he was there to watch me. I want you out of Paris for a while now that he has seen you with me. At nine-fifteen tomorrow my driver, the same man who drove you today, will pick you up at the hotel, take you to the train station, and stay near you until you get on board."

Cummins' courier, an older woman, arrived just before dinnertime and handed Em a small cloth shopping bag. "Our friend wishes you well," the woman greeted her.

"Thanks." Em took the bag, intending to ask her inside, but before she could, she heard a quiet au revoir, and the courier hurried away.

Em closed the door, locked it, and opened the bag. Inside was a bottle with a note tied around it. She took it out. The herbal odor suggested liniment. She saw nothing else so she pulled the note from the bottle and read, *I don't know anyone who has horses, but a Frenchman in my office swears by this liniment for himself. I thought you might try it.*

Aren't these French shopping bags wonderful? Room for everything a shopper could want to carry.

There was no signature, but Em had no doubt the courier was from Cummins. She opened the bottle. By the smell of it, it ought to cure anything. Wrinkling her nose, she screwed the lid back on and looked again in the bottom of the bag. Cummins must have concealed her instructions. A search revealed no pockets. She felt all over the bag and finally noticed clean thread on a seam on the bottom. She ran to the bathroom, came back with her nail scissors, and clipped the telltale thread. Pulling it out stitch by stitch, she found a thin sheet of paper and a train ticket wedged into a secret pocket.

On one side of the note Cummins had written instructions explaining how to find the man in Macon, in case he could not meet her at the train station. On the other side was a map of the town and the area across the river Saône, where Monsieur Hubert Espe lived on a small farm. Because Madame Espe knew nothing about her husband's cooperation with the OSS, Em was to interview them in the same manner as she had interviewed the Marchants. From what Cummins said, it would be a viable interview for *USA Living & Review*.

That night after a hot bath, Em rubbed the odiferous liniment on her shoulder and wrapped the sling over it to keep it warm and also to protect her pajamas. The fragrance was mostly herbal, like rosemary, but on her skin it heated up as if it contained red pepper.

She turned back the covers on her bed and reached for her directions for tomorrow. She always remembered better if she studied material before falling asleep.

The phone interrupted her. She stretched to pick it up, glad that this hotel had placed its phones on the bedside table, instead of on the wall. "Em Emerson speaking."

"Em, this is Bob. I'm sorry to be calling you so late, but may I see you before I leave tomorrow? Will you meet me for breakfast?" His voice, usually easy and relaxed, sounded strained.

"Is something wrong?"

"No. What made you think that? I just wanted to see you."

"Fine, but you could come to my room right now if you want."

"You know what the guys would think if I did that."

"I don't mind."

"I do. Em . . . don't ever invite even the most trustworthy men to your room at night."

His assumption that she would invite anyone else irritated her. She wanted to snap, "Do you really think I need you to tell me this?"

Instead, she said, "You are not just anybody."

"Sorry. I didn't mean to tread on your independence again. You just seem too trusting at times. Am I forgiven? Will you meet me in the mess hall at seven?"

"Yes. I'll be there."

"Thanks. See you then."

"See you." She hung up and leaned back on her pillow. He was worried about something. It showed because anxiety was so out of character for him. She'd seen him face air raids without a blink. What could make him so anxious? She was glad she'd held her tongue when he irritated her. If she minded her manners, she might learn the answer in the morning. A niggling fear ran through her. Maybe she didn't want to know. She really didn't want to hear anything that would make him unavailable or less desirable.

She closed her eyes and pulled her blanket up to her chin, hoping for sleep, but her mind would not lie down.

She'd never meant to fall for Bob. She and Marge had promised each other they would avoid wartime romances. They had big plans for after the war that did not include early marriage. Neither of them wanted to fall into a life of scratch dirt for survival as their parents had done. They planned to get good educations that would set them up for earning as much as any man.

Em wished she could talk with Marge right now. In their shared bedroom on the ranch, bedtime had been confiding time. Marge always had a way of helping her think more clearly.

She hadn't even had a letter from Marge in weeks. It wasn't like her to go so long without answering Em's letters. Could she be ill? Well, if so, she'd surely get good care, being already in a hospital with access to whatever she might need.

Em punched her pillow, which seemed to have turned into solid rock the way it made her neck and shoulder ache. Then she allowed herself to imagine that Bob had no secrets except that he loved her and wanted to marry her. For him, she might be willing to change her postwar plans.

Chapter Seven

The next morning Em woke up tired. After Bob's phone call, she had slept fitfully. However, despite her lack of sleep, her shoulder felt noticeably better.

She washed off the liniment, dressed quickly, and slipped the watch with its thick chain around her neck and under her blouse. Then she hurried downstairs to breakfast.

In the mess hall Em spied Bob at one of the small tables. She picked up a cup of coffee, made her way past the larger tables with groups of men and women already eating, and slid into a chair across from him.

His eyes looked as tired as hers felt, but he brightened when he saw her. Smiling, he glanced at his watch. "You're early."

"I aim to please. You said you had to leave early. Which direction will you be going?"

"South to meet General Devers in Marseilles. Our troops have made rapid progress going up the Rhône and Saône Valleys, but the Germans are entrenched in the north in the Vosges Mountains. I'm hoping the general will be visiting that combat zone."

"If you get as far north as Macon, we may meet." She sipped her hot coffee.

"Really? It hasn't been long since the Germans left there. I know you usually land on your feet, but I wish you'd stay away until that area's really secure. When I get back I'm sure I can get you a ride with me right to Hitler's West Wall up by Belgium."

She grinned. "You have no qualms about bribery, do you? You know how badly I want to go to the West Wall. And I'd love to go with you, but in the meantime I'm going to visit Macon."

"You're not traveling alone, I hope."

"As a matter of fact, I am."

His smile faded. "I don't know why I try to change your mind when it's made up. You are one stubborn woman." He drank his coffee and set down his empty mug down with a thump.

Now she had made him angry. Suddenly her shoulder throbbed, and she shifted uneasily in her chair. She certainly had a talent for saying the wrong thing to this man.

He averted his eyes, studying his plate.

Cautiously she broke the silence. "I suppose I am stubborn, but I've had to be in order to get this far as a journalist."

He raised his chin, glanced at her, and looked away. Without meeting her eyes, he seemed to search for words. "I'm not angry at you, Em. I'm upset about my own problems, and I took it out on you. I apologize." He stood up. "Excuse me while I get a refill on coffee?"

"Surely." Trying to relax, she followed him with her eyes as he went to the common pot on a makeshift counter.

When he returned and sat across from her again, he said, "I picked up my mail last night and found a letter from my sister and—Em, what would you think of a man who didn't want his own child?"

Obviously this was not a rhetorical question. Her mouth went dry. "I guess I'd need to know the circumstances to give an opinion."

"I . . . have a child. And I have not been a good father."

The words hit her like a boulder. *A father? Is he married after all?* Em sucked in a deep breath and let it out slowly. No wonder he had walled himself away from her. He was still talking—rapidly now. She pulled herself out of her personal shock to listen.

". . . and I couldn't stand to look at the baby. I felt as though she had killed Marion. I just couldn't handle losing Marion. At least that was how I felt at age nineteen. I know being young is no excuse, but—"

You're right about that, she thought. She struggled to incorporate his confession into what she knew about him. *How could he not stand to look at his own baby?* A wavering queasiness gripped her.

He went on. "After Marion died, I was so broken up. . . . Then later, seeing the baby reminded me that I was the one who killed my wife. We both knew she wasn't supposed to have a baby because of her diabetes. In fact her parents had begged us not to marry." He blinked and closed his eyes.

The throbbing pain was creeping up the back of Em's neck again.

Still reeling from his admissions, she straightened, seeking a more comfortable position. Sure he was young, but would a decent young man behave this way? Would her brother, Billy, do such a thing? Then her eyes met Bob's, and the obvious grief that made him clamp his mouth into a tight line of self-control ripped her anger to shreds. "How long ago did your wife die?" she asked, her voice barely audible.

Bob looked at her squarely and through stiff lips said, "Twelve years. Susie was twelve October fourth."

"Then yesterday was her birthday!"

He nodded. "Sis's letter arrived on Susie's birthday. She'd enclosed a new snapshot of my little girl. Then yesterday I saw a French girl who looked so much like Susie, and when I chatted with her, I realized all over again how much I've missed. Can you imagine how it feels to know you've made the worst mistake in your life and there's no going back?"

Almost in a daze, Em murmured, "I really can't imagine. Where is Susie now?"

"She's with my sister. She believes I'm her uncle, whom she's only seen a few times. When she was a year old, I let my sister adopt her."

"What about your parents? What did they think?"

"They didn't like the idea. They had offered to baby-sit while I worked, but there just wasn't any work in the area. Finally they agreed that Ruthie could take better care of Susie than I."

"Sometimes adoption is the best choice, so why do you feel you're such a bad father?"

He frowned, fidgeting with his coffee cup. "Because of the way I felt after Marion's death. In the beginning I really did not want Susie under any circumstances."

She cringed again before his honest admission. She had been relieved to learn he wasn't married after all, but the man she married would have to love children. The man she married could never give away his own child. Then, still thinking these hard thoughts, she met his gaze.

Unshed tears glistened in his eyes. His unguarded pain filled her with a choking rush of compassion. Who was she to judge? At seventeen, she had not loved anyone enough to sacrifice herself or her career plans. Had he been any more selfish than she? She drew in a shaky breath. "It's not too late to make amends. It's never too late to try."

His bleak expression eased. "I wish that were true."

The knot in Em's back relaxed a little. Maybe she could think of something positive for him. "Does Susie have a happy life with your sister?"

"I think she does. I didn't visit them for six years. When I did, Susie was so much like Marion, I had to leave for fear I would snatch her up in my arms and tell her who I was. I saw her again when she was eight, just before I came overseas."

"Is your sister against having you visit Susie?"

He gave an uncertain shrug. "She doesn't want me to upset Susie, so I've kept my distance. But lately I've been thinking that if anything happened to me, I'd want my daughter to know about me someday—more than what my sister knows about me. I'd like her to know what I think is important in life. I'd want her to know how sorry I am for giving her away and that I love her. Lucy-Em, if anything happened to me, would you ... could you tell her about me?" His eyes were overbright again.

The desire to wrap her arms around him and comfort him welled up inside her. She really did love him. However, in this crowded room she could only say, "I'd count it an honor if it was okay with your sister."

"Thanks, Lucy-Em." He pulled out a card from his breast pocket. "Here's my sister Ruthie's full name and address."

She looked at him long and hard before taking it from him. Had his concern over his daughter come from some kind of a premonition? That thought chilled her. On impulse she said, "Bob, why don't you start writing letters to Susie?"

"I can't start sending her letters just like that!"

"Then write them but don't mail them. Save them. If anything should happen to you—heaven forbid—someday Susie would have your own words to read."

His eyes narrowed thoughtfully as he stared at her. Slowly he began to look like himself again, confident and calm. "Letters. A journal for Susie. Why didn't I think of that myself?"

Em struggled to assimilate his newly revealed vulnerability. He'd always seemed so independent and unflappable. She followed a sudden urge. "Bob, guilt is an intolerable burden. I'm sure God doesn't want you to go on feeling guilty. Have you talked with a chaplain about this?"

He grinned. "Lucy-Em, are you preaching to me?"

"I hope not! I just thought I should suggest it."

"Okay. Thanks. In fact, I have talked with a chaplain here in Paris, and I will see him again."

"I'm glad." *More than glad,* she thought. Things were looking better and better. Bob had never mentioned his faith before. Although Em loved him, down deep she'd always known she couldn't marry an unbeliever. "Next time we're both in Paris, will you show me the city? I always dreamed of coming here, but I haven't yet seen any of the places I've wanted to visit." She kept her manner light but watched his face closely. She was asking for a date, something she'd never tried before.

"I'd love to show you Paris." A smile softened his face. "I should be back here in about a week."

She grinned. "Me too."

"Will you be staying with your friend Vivienne?"

"No. Actually she's gone to visit family for a few weeks, somewhere outside the city. I'll miss her."

"However did you meet her?" He raised one eyebrow in the teasing way that meant he expected a good story.

"It wasn't especially exciting. I was covering an embassy party for my magazine, and her husband, a lesser person in the French embassy, introduced me to his wife who liked to write. For a few weeks after that, I showed her America—at least the part around Maryland and Virginia. She had planned to show me her city and country too, but I guess that will have to wait until after the war."

Bob gave her one of his steel-eyed looks. "I'm glad you are keeping in mind that the war is not over. I still wish you weren't going to eastern France just yet. Even here in Paris there are places where you shouldn't go alone. Why do you suppose they put the press all in the same hotel?"

"To keep a finger on us," she challenged. "When General Eisenhower lets us women go to the combat zones as the men do, I'll stop sneaking around on my own."

Both of his eyebrows went up. "So you are sneaking," he accused. "That's why you're going alone. I don't suppose I can change your mind, but please consider that being under house arrest really inhibits one's ability to get the news. You'll accomplish a lot more by cooperating. Besides, the restrictions on the women are easing. Some are getting out to the front now."

She wondered if any other women had accompanied him. Much as she hated envy and jealousy, she was on the edge of it with her wonderings. "When I get back to Paris, I'll try again for a ride to the combat zone. In the meantime, my interviews with civilians will give me a few good stories that won't need heavy censoring. Some of my pieces have ended up not making sense to my editors after the London censors removed portions."

"That's tough. It's not fair that you don't get to read your work and repair the damage. Still, you'll accomplish more by working within the rules."

She smiled at him with the most saccharin look she could muster and said, "Well, what Ike doesn't find out won't hurt him . . . or me. I guarantee no one will be the wiser, not even my publisher. I aim to cover the war from a woman's viewpoint, and I will. Anyway, all these precautions to protect women are ridiculous. The military is simply denying us access to the news. And except for you, the men of the press are glad to get rid of competition."

His dark blue eyes had turned greenish again. "Look," he said, "I really will work to get you permission to go with me on my next trip to Belgium."

Even if he did, she'd have to clear it with Cummins. She squelched a sigh. "I'd love to, but first I want to finish my interviews with French civilians. I have a good feeling about it. You know how it is when you discover a fresh angle that no one else has touched? That's how I feel about this. I have to finish these interviews."

"I wouldn't worry so much if I thought you understood the risk."

If you only knew, she thought. Good thing he'd never guess how she'd spent yesterday. "I understand enough to be careful."

"Pardon my skepticism." He glanced at his watch and exclaimed, "I'm sorry, but I have to be on my way. Excuse me?"

"Certainly. I have to get moving too."

When she stood, he didn't step back to make room for her. His intimate gaze held her motionless. As if he forgot they were in the middle of the mess hall, he murmured, "I don't know what I'd do if anything happened to you, Lucy-Em."

She could see desire in his eyes and thought for an instant that he was going to kiss her again. Abruptly he stepped back and teased, "I don't know what I'd do without a kid reporter at my heels to keep me alert."

Still, the longing lingered in the softened lines of his face. A flutter of excitement filled her chest, reminiscent of the way she'd felt the first time a boy held her hand. *Take it easy,* she told herself, but her heart didn't hear.

"Thanks, Lucy-Em. I'll be seeing you." His eyes caressed her lips, and then he strode away.

Never say good-bye. That was an unspoken agreement between friends and family ever since Pearl Harbor. "See you when you get back," she called after him. He half turned and waved.

Back in her room Em mentally tallied what she had to do and tried to push her emotions out of the way. Automatically she put together her travel kit, including some American powdered coffee to give to anyone she visited. That was something she'd learned from Bob—people loved powdered coffee after having had no coffee at all during the Occupation.

Her arm was sore but not aching. Dutifully she did her arm swinging exercise. Then, although it was early, she grabbed her typewriter, her steel helmet, and her small bag. Bob should be gone by now. No matter how she tried to stay focused on what she was doing, everything drew her mind back to him. *Concentrate,* she told herself.

Before stepping out the door, she checked the clasp on the watch chain and decided to tuck the watch under the edge of her bra for safety. Descending to the lobby, she felt prepared as well as possible for her trip to the Saône Valley. In the lobby with a few minutes to wait, she wrote a brief letter to Jean Kagawa in Wales, asking for news about Marge. As she dropped it in the mailbag for Britain, she thought about Bob writing to his daughter. She was glad she'd persuaded him to do that. All in all this day had begun on many good notes.

Everything Cummins had planned moved like clockwork. Em's driver showed up exactly on time and stayed with her until she boarded the train. When the train finally left the outskirts of Paris, she took out the card Bob had given her and memorized his sister's name and address. She did so with a silent prayer that she would never be called upon to keep her word to him.

The train ride seemed endless. Besides stops at towns along the way, several times the train waited on sidings for another train to pass. Detours around destroyed sections of track and sabotaged bridges took them miles and miles out of the way. France would have a huge job getting its railroads repaired after the war. This journey, formerly a two or three hour jaunt, was taking all day.

At last, rolling hills, striped with rows of yellow-leafed vineyards, led to the river Saône, gleaming in the autumn sun. The train slowed and huffed into a small town where a cathedral towered over modest business buildings—Macon, at last.

Em quickly gathered her gear and climbed out onto the boarding platform. A tall figure stepped forward. "Miss Emerson!"

With his priestly robe and collar concealed by a topcoat, she hadn't recognized him at first glance. "Father Joseph! What are you doing here?"

"I'm a close friend of Monsieur and Madam Espe. When Hubert mentioned that a certain American journalist was coming to interview him and that she was arriving on this train, I quickly offered my services. My auto is somewhat more comfortable than Hubert's farm truck."

He had not answered her question, so she persisted. "But you don't live in Macon."

"Come." He took her typewriter and overnight bag. "We can talk as I drive."

She followed him to his car without further questions, but once they were on their way, she said, "You're the last person I expected to see after your message to Vivienne to get out of her apartment and hide. Is she still in danger? Are you? Am I?"

He grinned. "One question at a time I will try to answer." Heading down the hill from the station, he stopped at a highway that separated them from the bridge across the Saône. While U.S. Army trucks passed in front of them he responded to her questions. "First, you are most certainly not in danger. I don't think Vivienne is either. Our mutual friend insisted she should go into hiding anyway. Myself, I am as safe now as anyone else in France. I will be going back to my home in St. Hilary as soon as the Germans are thoroughly routed from Epinol. In the meantime, I will stay with friends south of here, where support for the Resistance was very strong. I can assure you that the man who shot Laurence was motivated by personal vengeance, purely focused on me. He had no known accomplices to carry on a vendetta."

"You're sure?"

"Yes. He had a reputation for vengeance. He was a violent man before the war. Then the war and underground activities made him more brutal."

"What does your church think of your work in the Resistance?"

"I've been careful not to violate my vows. For this reason my activities in the Resistance have been quite limited. Because I've kept a low profile, providing sanctuary for fleeing people and occasionally delivering messages, I'm not worried about any more reprisals for imagined crimes."

The convoy passed, and he drove over the bridge. The river was wider and deeper than she had expected.

He stopped for a horse-drawn farm wagon to cross an intersection. Turning to her, he reiterated, "Although Vivienne will remain in hiding for a while, you yourself should have no worry."

"Good." She glanced at his strong profile, wondering how his parishioners felt about their often-absent priest. Just beyond the outskirts of the east bank portion of town, he turned onto a winding road and then into a lane, which ended at a small stone farmhouse.

He stopped in the yard where chickens and a few ducks roamed free. "This is the home of the Espes," he said. "I have business elsewhere now, so I will leave you in their care. Hubert will take you back to the train. Mademoiselle Em"—he held out his hand to her—"may God watch over you."

She took his hand and felt a workingman's strength in his grip. "Thank you, Father Joseph. May God also watch over you."

He nodded. "He has and He will."

He walked with her to the door and knocked. A young woman opened the door. She spoke to him in rapid French and smiled warmly at Em.

Father Joseph answered the woman as rapidly as she had spoken. Then he turned to Em and spoke in careful English. "Madame Espe is delighted to welcome you and regrets her husband was called away for a short time. She speaks enough English words that you will be able to communicate. I really must leave now, but you will do fine." Without waiting for her answer, he bid them good-bye and left.

Em turned to her hostess, who had not yet said a word of English. She could only hope Father Joseph had not exaggerated about the woman's language skills. "Thank you for welcoming me, Madame Espe." She held out her hand.

The woman took it and said carefully, "Please call me Estelle. My English, I hope you will forgive. I hope you . . . speak slowly . . . if you please."

Em smiled. "Yes. You must stop me, if I don't."

"Please to come in. I take your bags." She picked Em's overnight case as she spoke.

Em carried the typewriter, which, although smaller, was the heavier of the two. She followed the woman inside and to a bedroom beside a small kitchen.

"Would you like for a rest?" Estelle said. "The toilette is next door to your bedroom. I have soup cooking. We soon eat, if you wish. Then talk, yes?"

"Yes. Very good. Thank you."

Estelle smiled, nodded, and left. Em washed up and changed into a fresh uniform shirt. Then she lay down on the narrow bed, intending to rest a few minutes. She must have fallen instantly asleep, for in the next moment, she awoke with a start to the sound of knocking on the bedroom door.

"Mademoiselle, are you awake? Supper it is ready."

Em jumped up and opened the door. "I'm so sorry. I dozed off."

"Is nothing. Good for you. My husband, Hubert, he has come home. You will like to talk to him. He has much to tell you."

Em ran a comb through the back of her hair and fastened the sides up again with a couple of bobby pins. Her sore shoulder felt stiff. She'd have to try those exercises before bedtime.

As she stepped out into the kitchen, a very lean man with black hair, thick black brows, and gentle brown eyes rose from the table to greet her. "Mademoiselle Emerson. How do you do? You are so welcome. I'm happy to speak with you, but first, Estelle she says we must eat."

"Thank you. I'm pleased to meet you. May I share some of my army supplies with you? One moment, please." She hurried to the bedroom and came back with chocolate bars, powdered coffee, and a bar of facial soap for Estelle. She would have to get Monsieur Espe alone to give him the watch from Cummins. Cummins had warned her twice that Madame Espe should not know about it.

After supper Hubert sat in his favorite chair with a cup of real coffee made from Em's gift.

Em took a nearby chair. Without prompting he told how he and Estelle had helped people escape into Switzerland. He described incredible journeys right past German border guards.

When he paused, Em said, "I don't see how you were able to get people through such a dangerous area."

"I didn't do it alone. If you would care to stay over another day, I could take you part of the way to meet some of the real heroes—the ordinary people who risked their lives to help us get our people out. We had safe houses and people who warned us of danger. It was like what I have read about America's underground railroad in your civil war—many people caring and helping."

While he talked, Em made notes and framed more questions. When he finished, he said lightly, "If you should wish it, now that the border is open, I could take you all the way into Switzerland on one of the routes we used."

On impulse Em asked, "Could I do it just as you did? Bicycling and walking?"

He grew serious. "The bicycling, it would be very tiring. It takes two long days just to get to the border. Have you bicycled such long distance?"

"Not for a while, but I'm in pretty good condition." She ignored her sore shoulder. This had the makings of a great story. Surely Cummins would not frown on this. Besides, so far she had not delivered the watch.

Estelle broke into the conversation. "Hubert, do you think you should?"

"The Occupation is over, *ma chérie*. No harm to go now."

"Still I do not feel good for it. Such a short time since we were nearly killed. . . ."

"Estelle, Zone Rouge is gone. The dogs and guards are gone. For you to go again would place a happier memory over the old." He spoke carefully in English, as had his wife, so as not to leave Em out of their conversation.

Estelle nodded, but her expression remained guarded.

Em hated to see her upset, but she didn't regret it enough to turn down the offer. She waited quietly for husband and wife to reach an agreement.

Hubert said gently, "I think you would feel better to go. Wouldn't you like to see the Charbonneau and Lafayette families again?"

"Yes, of course. I just wonder if it is too soon."

At the sound of the fear in her voice, Em capitulated. "Don't do anything you don't feel right about. I don't have to go. I can write the story from what Hubert has told me."

Estelle straightened and studied her husband. Slowly the tension left her face. "Hubert is right, I know. And better for you to see first and then to write. I want to go."

Hubert was nodding his approval.

"All right," Em said. "Thank you both for this unusual opportunity." She could imagine how Bob or Marge would react to this adventure, but she was delighted. She hadn't supposed working for the OSS would give her a great story so soon. Now all she had to do was get the watch into Hubert's hands and concentrate on the writing assignment.

CHAPTER EIGHT

At the field hospital, Marge was learning to hate mail call. She went, hoping she'd suddenly get the pile of mail that would signal an end to her secret hiding. When her name wasn't called, she slipped away as unobtrusively as possible. She worried about how her family would be taking this long silence from her, but wounded men arrived daily, and in the end her nursing responsibilities took priority over personal concerns. She was glad the field hospital had not received another flood of casualties like the day when she'd first met David here in the combat zone. Even so, most days she and other nurses worked twelve-hour shifts and ate on the run.

The weather was growing colder. As long as Marge kept moving, she stayed warm despite frequent rain. But the hours she spent standing still in surgery chilled her feet until she wondered if they'd ever get warm again.

Isabelle began to learn enough English words to carry on a conversation of sorts. Marge found it all the more difficult to keep an emotional distance. After all, a six-year-old in traction needed support, so Marge paused to talk with her whenever she passed her bed. All the nurses did. Isabelle talked about her family and expected them to come for her any day. Marge prayed they would.

At the request of several of the wounded men, the nurses moved Isabelle's bed closer, so they also could talk to her. Slowly the worst of the child's pain eased. Color returned to her lips and cheeks, and the pinched look around her brown eyes faded totally when she smiled. Everyone worked to awaken that smile.

One afternoon when Marge hurried in to chat with the Babe, as she had come to be called by the men, she found Sergeant Lewellyn there. Isabelle was laughing and chattering in French with him. Neither of them noticed Marge until she reached the foot of the bed.

Switching easily to her style of English, Isabelle exclaimed, "Nurse Marge, Sergeant Dave is here. Look, look!" She held up a tiny cradle, cleverly shaped from an ammunition tin, and inside, wrapped in a GI handkerchief, lay a hand-carved wooden baby dressed in khaki.

"A baby doll! Have you named her yet?"

Isabelle shook her head and tilted her head on her pillow as if in deep thought. In a moment she said, "Sally. She is my Sally."

"A good name. Very good," Sergeant Lewellyn said in English.

Marge handed the cradle and baby back to the child. "How are you today?" she asked.

Isabelle smiled. "Good. I want up."

"Soon," Marge said. "You are better, but your leg says, 'Let me rest more.' "

As she spoke, she watched the child's face. She had learned to recognize the tightness around Isabelle's eyes when English words puzzled her. This time the Babe rewarded her with a smile.

Turning to David, Marge asked, "Did you make the doll and cradle?"

He shook his head. "No. One of your patients made them." He gestured down the long row of beds. "Corporal Hansen down there—he's from our corps—he asked me to bring him the materials. He just finished it today."

"He surely worked fast." Surgery patients were evacuated as soon as they could be safely moved. That usually left no time for handcraft projects. Em glanced at Isabelle, who was talking to her dolly and turning the folds of her blanket into an imaginary dollhouse. "Were you able to locate the farm where she lived?"

"Not yet. I put several buddies onto the search though."

"Has she told you much about her home and family?"

"She has two little brothers, one an infant and the other big enough to play with her. Her father worked outside with cows and a horse and geese. Her mama taught her songs to sing to her baby brothers. Sounds like a happy family." He sobered. "I hope and pray that somehow they're alive."

"Me too," Marge said fervently. She turned to Isabelle. "I have to go now. See you later, Babe."

Isabelle grinned and waved. "See later!"

"And you, too, Sergeant. See you later."

"God willing," he said, then added lightly, "and if the cricks don't rise!"

She chuckled and left. Whenever David mentioned God, he sounded reverent and yet very natural. If she were to say "God willing" as part of her every day conversation, people would be watching her out of the corners of their eyes. She'd grown up in a home where to vocalize your faith meant you were trying to act holier than others. Dad, kind as he was, felt religious talk was for preachers, not for him or his wife and children. This had not inhibited Em, but it had throttled Marge and made her uncomfortable around people like David. She found herself wishing she were more like Em.

Outside the post-op ward Amelia called to her, "Marge, Dr. Colville wants you in surgery. We just got in another full ambulance. Two went to the shock ward, and we've got the first of the others prepped. Abdominal wounds."

"Thanks. I'm on my way." Marge ran to the surgery tent and scrubbed up.

Dr. Colville was standing by while Nurse Mills administered anesthetic. He nodded at Marge, and his eyes above his mask flashed a smile message. She stepped into her place and waited for his signal to begin.

The soldier was horribly wounded. He looked as if he'd stepped on an antipersonnel mine, a nasty little contraption that could eviscerate and—the great fear of the men—castrate. When the hair-trigger mechanisms were touched, they threw metal fragments upward to waist height.

Dr. Colville held out his hand. "Clamps." She slapped the clamps into his hand, and he set to work—searching, clamping bleeders, searching more, and finally began the delicate task of suturing. He worked silently, intently. Assisting him always started Marge thinking about Wales, where she first had worked at his side. It had been a month since she'd left the Gilwern military station hospital in the middle of the night, a month since anyone had received any communication from her. By now her mother and father would be growing anxious. So would Em.

Then the moment when she could think anything other than the surgery passed. She focused totally on her job.

In the evening before falling into bed, Marge pulled out the pad of stationery with the Army Nurse Corps insignia at the top. Early on, she had decided to write to her family. Though she knew the letters could not be delivered, she needed to feel in touch with them. Writing helped. Someday her letters would reach their destination, and everyone would enjoy the catching up.

Dear Em,

I keep hoping to hear from you. In the meantime, I'll write anyway. In this field hospital we work twelve and sometimes sixteen hours a day. By the end of a shift I feel cross-eyed, or maybe the better term is cross-brained.

We live in arctic boots, those things with buckles up the front, not because of the cold, but because of the mud. Once it starts raining, we live in mud, mud, mud. This is unnatural for a kid born in the dust bowl! At least we have a couple of stoves for heat in our nurses' quarters, one at each end of our long tent.

She couldn't reveal details of where she was and not a lot about what she was doing. The censor would cut out anything about numbers of wounded or even the types of wounds that determined her duties. So she told about Isabelle and about David, then brought her letter to a close.

I keep wondering if you are in France by now, and if so, whether you may be accredited to the Army Nurse Corps. I would so love to see you, but then it would be safer for you to be accredited to the WAACs.

She started to write about being under fire twice and then crossed it out. For all she knew, that could be information for the enemy.

Take care, sis, and if you come over, look me up! With your nose for news and your talent for getting into places others can't, we may meet. As David says, and which I'm beginning to believe more and more, "Lord willing" we'll find each other, even in this chaos and mud!

Love ya, kiddo,
Marge

Wearily she pulled on extra socks and went to bed. Outside, the big guns to the north crashed like thunder. They had been hammering steadily for several minutes. From what David said, they must be pounding Aachen in the push against the Siegfried Line. Taking Aachen would open the door on Hitler's impregnable West Wall. She dreaded what that would mean for the infantry and their medics. She closed her eyes. Fatigue mercifully beckoned her into sleep.

As the days went by with no mail Marge began to feel her isolation more and more. Most of the time she was too busy and too chronically tired to think about it. Then daily mail call would remind her.

The other nurses became obvious in their concern, overly eager to share their packages from home with her. Marge was grateful but uncomfortable being the object of charity or curiosity, so she looked for excuses to avoid mail call.

One day during mail call an ambulance drove in, giving Marge a valid reason to hurry away. When she spied the familiar lanky figure of Sergeant Lewellyn climb out, her spirits lifted.

She helped him and the other corpsman get the two wounded men inside and began preparing the first one as the examining doctor had indicated. Wanda hurried in and took charge of the second. They snipped away the dirty clothing and began to clean wounds. Both men were unconscious. Marge read their tags and confirmed that they had received morphine at the aid station. One had been given plasma. While she worked swiftly, Dr. Colville came in and checked them. "I'll take this one, and give the other to Dr. Nelson. Hello, Sergeant Lewellyn. You going to give us a double duty night again?"

"Hello, sir. I hope not. These men were caught in a small conflict."

"Good." Dr. Colville turned to Marge. "I'm having Nurse O'Neil assist me this morning. I want you to take a long overdue rest. Today you're off duty. I can't send you anywhere, but maybe extra sleep and a leisurely meal will help."

"Sir," Sergeant Lewellyn said, "I have a break myself for the rest the day. With your permission, I could drive Nurse Emerson to the village where that little girl, Isabelle, was found. Maybe we could locate someone who knew her parents. I've been trying, but a woman can sometimes deal with village folks better than a man in uniform."

Dr. Colville turned to Marge. "You're free to go if you want, but your primary mission is to get some rest."

"I'd like to go, sir."

He nodded. "Very well." To David he said, "Get her back here before dark, Sergeant."

"Yes, sir."

"Dismissed then," Dr. Colville said and strode off to surgery.

"I'll fetch my driver," David said. "He went to grab a cup of coffee and flirt with any nurses he could find off duty."

Marge grinned. "I'll go get into my fatigues and meet you back here in a few minutes." She hurried to her tent, feeling like a kid about to go on an outing. Her weariness miraculously lifted. One by one the nurses had been ordered to take rest days. Sometimes they rode on supply trucks to nearby towns, but she had worked nonstop since she'd arrived. She'd almost forgotten a day off existed. On the way to her tent she saw Louise and told her the doctor's orders.

"Good for him. I told Dr. Colville when I arrived that he'd do better to work with one nurse short all the time so we could take turns resting. I'm glad he's trying to ease up when it's possible."

"What about you?" Marge asked. "When will your turn come?"

"After a while. Got to groom several of you to fill in for me. We'll talk about that when you get back. In the meantime, it's your turn. Dismissed, Nurse Emerson," she said with a smile.

Marge went to her tent and changed quickly from her rumpled hospital uniform to fatigue pants, shirt, and jacket. She grabbed her raincoat and her steel helmet, and at the tent door, buckled on her arctic boots again. Then she hurried back to the ambulance. The driver, a corporal, saluted smartly, as did David. She returned their salutes and then said, "Please, let's forget about rank today. Who's to know anyway?"

"Yes, ma'am," the driver said.

She laughed. "That's an order, Corporal . . ."

"Corporal Vance McKinley," the young man supplied. Then he obediently dropped formalities. "At your service, mademoiselle."

"Okay, Vance," David said, "it is convenient, but don't go too far while we're around others, or we'll get our nurse in trouble." He turned to Marge. "Call me David and him Van, and we'll pretend this is someone else's war for today. Van and I were headed for Liege, just for a change of scene, when I came up with this idea to search for Isabelle's family. Van, do you want to go with us, or would you rather go to the city? We can take you there and then pick you up at the end of the day."

Van raised an eyebrow. "What's in a town besides the Red Cross canteen and a hot meal? Sure, I'll come with you. Sounds like an interesting chance to play detective." He circled the ambulance and opened the driver's door. "Tell me where to go."

David opened the other door and said to Marge, "You get in the front. Unless you prefer to sit in the back."

Marge didn't argue. His suggestion was practical more than chivalrous. Three in the front seat would be uncomfortable and would not look good to any officers who might stop them. "Thanks," she said and as an afterthought added, "Call me Marge, please."

"Short for Marjorie?" David asked.

"No. Margaret."

"I like Margaret better than Marge," he said without hesitation. He held the door for her, so she climbed up into the ambulance, which was really a small truck. David slammed the door and in a moment was kneeling behind her seat where he could see and direct Van. "Go straight out to the main road, cross over, and take the first left onto an unpaved road. We'll head away from the combat zone. From the first crossroad after that you can see the village church spire. It's not more than two or three miles—the first village you come to on that road. Since they found Isabelle there, it's got to be where her home was. The village took a lot of shelling and bombing, because the Germans holed up in the school. It had stone walls two feet thick."

Van raced down the narrow drive to the main road, then stopped for a long convoy of supply trucks. Near the end of the convoy fresh replacement troops peered out the back of the personnel carriers. It seemed longer than a month since Marge and the other nurses had been part of just such a convoy. A few of the soldiers soberly eyed the ambulance with its big Geneva red cross on a white circle.

Most, however, grinned and waved as if they were on their way to a football game. Marge waved back.

As David had said, the village came into view after the next crossroad—a huddle of homes in the midst of trees and surrounded by acres of farmland. Stone farmhouses, which had probably been in families for generations, dotted the fertile plain between them and the village. The few houses close to the road lacked not only occupants but windows, doors, and in some cases roofs. In a few farmyards burned-out German vehicles sat. What had looked from a distance like a nostalgic pastoral scene, up close became a graveyard of farms. She turned to David. "How long since the fighting passed through here?"

"The day our men found Isabelle, the Germans moved out. But they had held on for a long time in almost every building in the village. It took tanks and heavy artillery to blast them out. Now there's little left standing, so not many people have come back. If one of our boys hadn't spotted Isabelle, she may not have been discovered in time."

In a sudden turn they entered the village. It was tiny, about the size of Gilwern, Wales, with only a few businesses, a church, and a school. Homes of farmers whose land abutted the edge of the village formed the rest of the village. Shelling had stripped limbs and leaves from the trees. Marge sighed. She asked David, "Have you talked to anyone here? Looks like a ghost town."

"A few people have stayed. Pull up by the church, Van. The priest is still here, and he will know about others."

Indeed the priest did know. He directed them to the edge of the village beyond the school, where five homes remained undamaged.

Van parked at the edge of this island of life, and they got out.

"I already looked around here and talked to a few people," David said. He pointed to a shuttered stone house with a mansard roof, quite elegant for a village home. "Let's try that one. I see smoke coming from the chimney. Last time, the house was vacant."

"I'll wait by the ambulance so they won't think they're being invaded again," Van said.

David clapped him on the shoulder. "Good idea."

Marge headed for the door. "Come be my interpreter, David."

"Sure." He strode beside her, his shoulder above the top of her head, and when they reached the door, he did the knocking.

They waited and waited. Just as he reached out to knock again, the door slowly opened. A thin, gray-haired woman with tired blue eyes peered at them. Her glance went from their faces to their armbands with the red crosses. She grabbed David's arm and spoke rapidly in French. He responded in his rudimentary French and pointed at Marge.

"Her husband is ill, and she thought I was a doctor. I told her you're a nurse. Would you mind looking at him and advising her on his care?"

"Of course I'll look."

The woman caught her hand, and whatever she said, Marge understood her gratitude. Marge stooped to remove her muddy boots before entering, but the woman shook her head and, with urgent gestures, beckoned for her to follow.

So Marge did. The dignified old home showed the benefit of years of loving care. Marge wondered if many of the destroyed homes had looked like this one.

At last they came to a bedroom where tall windows let in light and fresh air. A man of robust build lay propped up on pillows in a sitting position. The woman addressed him and pointed to Marge. The man nodded.

"They want you to examine him and hope we may have medicine," David interpreted.

"Tell her I'm not a doctor, but I'll do what I can."

Through David, she questioned the man about how he felt and

took his pulse, noting that he didn't feel feverish. His pulse was rapid with an occasional irregularity. His breathing was very rapid and shallow. She wished she had a stethoscope. "Ask him if I may place my ear on his chest."

David asked, and the man consented. As she leaned over to do so, she said, "Everyone be very quiet, please."

David translated.

She held her own breath while she listened. In a moment she heard a wheezy squeak characteristic of asthma.

With more questioning she learned that he'd passed out in the midst of the shelling, unable to get enough breath. When they got him home he acted as if he were coming down with a bad cold, but it never materialized. Since then he'd had this weight on his chest.

"I think it's a form of asthma. The fresh air is good as long as he doesn't chill. There's not much we can do to help him. Bed rest is good, but if he can, he should get up and walk a little each day to get his strength back. I'm sorry we can't send a doctor, but maybe they can go where there is one now that the fighting here has ended."

David relayed the message.

Even though Marge felt she had little to offer, they seemed to feel she had been a great help and wanted to do something for her in return.

"Tell them about Isabelle, that we are trying to find her family."

The old people began to talk between themselves, and Marge recognized one word, Isabelle.

When they stopped, she asked David, "Do they know her?"

"They know the family and where the house used to stand. They said the neighbors who dug there found no survivors and no bodies. Everything flammable burned before the total collapse."

Marge shuddered. With her few French words, she excused herself and said, "Merci."

Still hoping that a search on their own might turn up clues about Isabelle's family, she hurried back to the jeep. "Which way to Isabelle's home?" she asked David.

Chapter Nine

Marge stared at the rubble that once had been a stone home as sturdy and as large as the one she had just left on the other side of the village. "This must be Isabelle's home. There's the portion of the fireplace that lady mentioned."

"Yes, I'm afraid so," David said.

"No one inside that house could have survived." Van voiced what Marge was thinking.

On this side of the village, houses had stood adjacent to their farm fields. Now an indiscernible number of homes had been erased from the village by the bombardment that had preceded the advance of the U.S. Army.

"Aerial bombs as well as tanks and heavy artillery hit here," David said. "I can't imagine where Isabelle was that she survived this."

Marge moved cautiously over and around broken and scattered stones until she reached the fireplace. On the other side of it, she saw nothing but a bomb crater.

David came up behind her. "Looks like a direct hit. They'd have died instantly. We can search in neighboring villages for relatives, but there's nothing here."

Marge sighed. "I didn't think it would be this bad. A small village—I didn't think it would be an important military target."

"It only takes an entrenched pocket of Germans to turn anything into an important target. Sometimes I have nightmares about what it will be like for civilians in Germany as we move toward Berlin with door-to-door fighting in every city and burg." His voice conveyed a shudder.

Marge had never wasted much sympathy on the Germans. Now she turned and stared at him, surprised at his obvious grief but also disturbed that she, in a healing profession, did not feel that much compassion for the enemy. It was sad, but the German people had empowered Hitler, and most of them followed him fanatically.

His eyes narrowed and his jaw tightened. "Children like Isabelle, Marge. Women and babies and old folks and youngsters who have been taught to kill for Hitler, so they will be killed. Many are innocent—they should not have to die. War is a terrible thing."

She nodded, catching only a hint of his vision before pulling back from the sympathetic images he brought to her mind. The German people would have a large debt to pay to the world when this was over. If they paid some of it before war's end, they deserved what they got. *How can David, who has seen more killing and suffering up close than I, how can he really forgive the Germans? Maybe I'm not a Christian after all. I can't forgive them!*

As she glanced down at the rubbish at her feet, a bit of color caught her eye. Stooping, she cleared away the splinters of timbers and bits of rock. Tucked in the shelter of the base of the fireplace chimney lay a small baby doll. She picked it up and shook off the loose dirt. Though the fabric body was torn and soiled, the composition head, arms, and legs were intact, its baby smile and painted blue eyes unmarred.

She held it up. "Could it have been Isabelle's?"

"I'll bet it was. She was the only girl in her family." He took the doll from her. "Let me get it mended and cleaned up. I met a seamstress who's doing some mending for me. She can mend the body and make a new dress. Then I'll take it to Isabelle. Even if it's not hers, she'll love it."

Marge had thought to mend it herself but was glad to let him take charge. "Good. Isabelle will need all the comfort she can get if her relatives don't turn up soon."

They returned to the ambulance, and this time David stationed himself closer behind her so they could talk easier. He directed Van to three nearby villages where he questioned people and translated for Marge. No one had heard of Isabelle's family or of anyone who was searching for a little girl.

As they headed back toward the field hospital, Van gestured to another village. "What about that one?"

From behind her on the backseat, David answered, "I don't recall the name of that one. It's close enough to be worth a try."

So they turned onto the road that went through the village. As they rolled into the main street, Marge saw no one walking about. She supposed the rainsquall had chased people indoors. Suddenly the rapid fire of a machine gun sounded over the noise of the jeep engine. Mud sprayed up in a line beside them on the road. David shoved Marge down and threw himself across the back of the seat and over her. She struggled to breathe as his weight crushed her.

Van skidded the ambulance in an about-face and raced away. When they stopped, David slowly straightened but held her down with one hand. Then he helped her sit up. Van had parked beside a stone storage building of some kind. It had no windows on this side.

David kept his hand on her shoulder. "Stay low."

"They shoot at ambulances?" she gasped.

"Might have been a mistake, but it happens," he said.

More gunfire erupted, but she could tell by the sound that it was somewhere on the other side of the building—rapid fire and then single shots. They apparently had driven right into a battle. She peeked over David's shoulder and saw that they were still in the village.

"Can we get out of here?" she asked.

"If we can calculate which way to go. We may be in the midst of Germans. I'll reconnoiter on foot and try to locate our men. Van will stay here with you and get you out of town if he sees an opening."

"We can't leave without you!"

"Lieutenant, out here, I'm the expert. It's my job to get you back to the hospital safely. So you'll do what I say." To Van he said, "I'll make my way back to the action and try to contact our men. They'll know the safest way out. I'll be back in fifteen minutes, whether I find them or not. You know what to do if I don't come back."

"Don't go!" The words literally burst from her. She caught hold of his arm.

David put his hand over hers on his arm. "Margaret, I've been in worse spots. I don't aim to be foolish."

The warmth of his touch spread through her, leaving her speechless. Surprisingly his confidence reassured her. She nodded.

He hunched down as he slid out of the ambulance and crouched beside it. Then, still bent low, he darted to the corner of the building and disappeared.

She could still feel the pressure of his fingers on her arm. Her instant responsiveness to his touch dismayed her. She'd always thought instant affinity between two people was a romantic myth. Now she wondered.

Minutes ticked by. Gunfire rattled sporadically. Van began to check his watch more frequently. Then a rattling, creaking, rumbling sound came from a distance and grew louder.

"A tank!" Van gasped. "Pray it's one of ours."

He started the ambulance and inched closer to the road. Then he switched off the engine to listen again. "There!" He pointed, and Marge saw the armored front of the tank with its long cannon turning into the road they sat beside.

"It's ours!" he cried. "It's a good old Sherman!"

The tank clattered down the narrow lane, and when it came abreast of the parked ambulance, it stopped. David appeared from behind it. The tank rolled forward again. He ran to the ambulance and jumped in beside Marge. "Step on it, Van. We can leave the way the tank came. Move!"

Van squirreled into the road and gunned it. His maneuver threw David onto Marge again. When he straightened, he hesitated a few inches from her face. "I'm sorry I got you into this. Are you doing okay?" He seemed unaware that he was literally holding her in his arms with his lips so close to hers that she could kiss him without stretching to reach. The shock was, she wanted to.

"I'm okay," she answered, without trying to extricate herself.

Abruptly he let go of her, straightened, and faced front.

She silently lectured herself for reacting like a schoolgirl. Simple biology explained her feelings. She was female and he was male. This was why mothers warned daughters not to get into clinches with boys. But she never had liked to be touched by anyone she didn't like. She'd had her share of kisses that had left her impassive and sometimes revolted. David was different. David . . . Why, she loved David.

Van called over the jeep's engine, "What did you find when you left us in the village?"

"Our boys were being held down by a pocket of Germans who had sneaked in during the night to take back the village. The guys said they'd been promised armored support, but the tank had not shown up. I figured if I could spot the tank, I could direct it to them, kind of like we do when an ambulance is looking for the wounded. I was lucky to see the tank. It would have found them all right, but this road is a better approach than the one they had in mind."

Marge made no comment and asked no questions. She couldn't think of anything beyond the fact that she loved David. No wonder it was called falling in love. Her feelings for him had surfaced as abruptly as a fall. When she thought about it, she realized her love for him had been growing for some time. Then, when he was in danger, it just poured out. He had risked his life for her. She was astonished to realize she would do the same for him. With all her heart, she wanted to know him better and to be with him. And it was impossible.

Thickening clouds were closing out the setting sun by the time the ambulance pulled up beside the mess tent. Marge caught herself about to thank David for a good time. How ridiculous. Nearly getting killed and searching war ruins for a lost child's family could scarcely qualify as fun. Yet, it had been a beautiful day. "David, if we can get another day's leave at the same time, I'd like to go out again—prepared to help the villagers. I could scrounge up a few simple medicines, soap, chocolate bars, and maybe even some real food. You know what I mean?"

David's smile would have lighted an operating theater. "I sure do. It doesn't look possible right now, but maybe we can do that. I'll look for you when I get another day off."

She didn't have David's faith about things working out right, but she instantly accepted his offer. "Then I'll be planning for it."

He climbed out and offered her a hand down. Then he saluted.

Smiling, she returned his salute.

Then he folded himself back into the front seat beside Van.

With a wave of her hand, she said, "Be seeing you guys. And now back to the routine. Good-bye, Corporal McKinley. Good-bye, Sergeant Lewellyn."

They grinned and responded in unison, "Good-bye, ma'am."

It was past suppertime, but Marge went to her tent for her mess kit and then to the mess tent. Two doctors and three nurses sat at tables. She picked up her food, hot chili with corn bread and canned peaches, and sat down beside the nurses.

"So how was your day with the medics?" Carolyn asked. "I was surprised Louise let you go out with noncoms."

"We didn't 'go out,' as you put it," Marge said. "We went looking for Isabelle's family."

"Find any traces?" Dorothy asked.

"No. Nothing except the ruins of the house where we think she lived. It took a direct hit from a bomb."

"Poor little tyke," Carolyn said. "She's so spunky and cute. Too bad if she has to go to an orphanage."

"On the other hand, she may be lucky if she can," Dorothy said. "I wonder if there are any orphanages back in operation yet."

"I imagine the village priest may know," Marge said. "We talked with him today, but I'll try to talk with him again. We met an elderly couple in the village, and the old man could hardly breathe. I don't know if it was asthma or his heart, but asthma, I think. I wish we could help some of the civilians who need medical attention."

"Fat chance," Carolyn announced. "There's no time and no medicine. The Red Cross ought to be out here for that."

"Red Cross," Marge repeated. She hadn't thought of help from the relief agency. "We can tell the Red Cross about Isabelle! They will have ways to search for her family. I don't know why I never thought of that."

"Yes, you've had so much spare time to meditate on Isabelle's problem," Dorothy said, laughing. "However, I think Colonel Colville has reported her case to the Red Cross already. I heard him tell Louise he couldn't let her stay here in the field hospital for as long her recuperation may take."

"I hope the Red Cross can find a relative soon. I'll tell David they're searching."

"So it's David now?" Carolyn raised her eyebrows. "Not that I'm against it, but since when do we call sergeants by their first name, Marge? You know Louise won't like that."

"I'm not fraternizing," Marge protested. "We were together for business." She didn't care what the nurses thought, but wisdom was on the side of appearing to follow protocol carefully. After all, if she had any hopes of working with David on another expedition of charity, she'd have to play the protocol game. And she fully intended to work with David whenever possible.

CHAPTER TEN

Before breakfast at the Espe farm in Macon, Hubert took Em outside to adjust one of their bicycles to fit her. While they were alone, Em removed the watch from her neck and handed it to Hubert. "From our friend in Paris," she said.

He quickly tucked it in his pocket. "Good. Before we go to the train, I'll take it to be deciphered. You keep Estelle busy with questions for your writing."

"Okay."

He smiled. "I do like that American word *okay*. Okay, we go back in the house."

After breakfast Hubert arranged with a neighbor to care for the animals while they were gone.

Half an hour later, they bicycled to the train station and waited for a northbound train to take them and their bicycles to Dijon. Although trains were running, most had been conscripted by the military for moving supplies and for the evacuation of the wounded. Em began to worry that she'd lose too much time by trying to follow Hubert's underground route into Switzerland. After a couple of hours, just when she was ready to give up the whole idea, they finally boarded the train.

When they reached Dijon, the three of them got off with their bicycles and knapsacks.

As the crow flies, Macon was about the same distance from the Swiss border as Dijon was. Traveling first to Dijon looked to be sixty miles out of the way, so Em asked, "Hubert, why didn't you go straight to Switzerland from Macon?"

"I had to find the least populated area possible for entering and crossing the Red Zone. Also my research indicated I could cross the minefield and fence most easily here."

"Ah, I remember you mentioned Zone Rouge to Estelle. What was it?"

"Hitler set up an area across the northeast of France so that no one could get near the border of Germany or Switzerland. To enter Zone Rouge one had to have official permission and carry the proper identification cards. I had a forged permit, of course, because even to request permission made one suspect.

"A high wire fence with guards and dogs separated Zone Rouge from the rest of France. As much as possible the fence followed natural barriers. I decided the safest place to enter the forbidden zone lay at a village northeast of Dijon where I only faced crossing a narrow canal . . . if I could get over the fence. Then I had about eighty of your miles to travel—two days on bicycle—before I reached the Swiss border. Although starting near Dijon meant backtracking a bit for my border crossing, the route promised more safety. Along the way I knew some farmers I could trust. I also established safe quarters in Dôle for a first night's rest.

"Come. We can bicycle to the canal in less than an hour." He mounted his bike and led the way out of town.

A few miles outside the city, they came to the village, and not far beyond, the Canal de la Marne à la Saône. Hubert pointed at the barbed-wire fence still standing between them and the canal. Portions had been torn down, but it was easy to picture the original barrier.

Em gasped. "You climbed that?"

"No. I found a gate," he said.

They passed several bridges that spanned the canal. He said, "Imagine in your mind, that these bridges are heavily guarded. We could swim or wade across where the fence opens for the bridges, but armed guards could see us. I found a better place. Follow me."

From his words she imagined they would wade across, for it wasn't very wide and maybe not deep. However, he soon stopped in an isolated place beside locks in the canal. "Here. You see, closed locks make a bridge. The spike fence around it has been removed and so have the mines. Nevertheless, step where I step." He proceeded cautiously pushing his bicycle close at his side. Em and Estelle followed, copying his every move.

Over his shoulder, Hubert said, "I was lucky enough to observe German guards when they crossed the mined area. I watched where they pushed on the fence to make it open. Then I walked where they walked and pushed on the fence where they pushed. On the other side the man who controlled the locks discovered me, but he was French. He whisked me into his private quarters, gave me a glass of wine, good advice, and directions for my return."

On the other side Hubert went to the lockkeeper's door and knocked. A man threw open the door and exclaimed, "Hubert! Estelle!" With much backslapping and laughter, the two men greeted each other, both talking at once.

At last the man paused for a breath, and Hubert turned and introduced Em. The locksman bowed slightly and said something in French in response to her greeting.

Hubert translated. "He wants us to have lunch with him, but I have explained we have a long way to go, and although we will not be delayed by having to dodge Germans, still it is many of your miles to our first night's lodging, and you will need to stop and rest along the way."

Once on the road again, Estelle spoke. "Em, you must tell me when you need to stop for the toilette, and I will find privacy. I have done this for many others, so you must not be embarrassed about speaking your need."

Em, much relieved that Estelle was frank about the necessaries, said, "Thank you." Hopefully there would be enough privacy. As she peddled behind Hubert with Estelle at her side, she grinned to herself. Marge, to whom no bodily function was embarrassing, would get a kick out of her anxiety over no rest rooms, if Em ever dared to tell her about this trip.

As the hours ticked by, Em's legs grew heavy with fatigue, and then an amazing thing happened. Her muscles came alive again with renewed energy. Pedaling became almost effortless. As they journeyed on and on, she thought about Hubert and his refugees being surrounded by Germans and guard dogs. "How did you manage to take people with you?" she asked.

"We had to hide often, especially if we brought more than one person." After that he pointed out side roads, small wildwoods, old farm buildings, and sometimes even ditches where he'd hidden his charges while Germans passed by. "When I couldn't hide, I brazened it out. I had a forged permit to cut trees for fuel for gazogene autos. Although several times the Germans stopped me, my false identity satisfied them. I told them I was searching for timber sources, since it was obvious I hadn't brought tools. The hardest times were when we had women and children along."

Estelle chimed in. "I always come with him. I know places for hiding them. We pray to keep children quiet."

"I couldn't have managed without Estelle," Hubert said. "When possible, I took a wife with her husband. The women all wore men's working clothes."

The hours passed, but so did the miles. They stopped only to eat and drink and take care of nature's calls. Hills became foothills and foothills became small mountains where the road wound through narrow valleys.

Near the end of the day, Em began to regret her decision to go on this journey. She moved only by sheer willpower. Her shoulder was aching, and she was saddlesore. Finally at dusk they entered the town of Dôle. Hubert stopped outside a small inn. Em dismounted from her bicycle and almost fell. Her legs had turned into nerveless jelly.

Hubert grabbed her arm. "You've done very well. Estelle was worried that you might not survive the whole way."

Em leaned on her bicycle and tried to laugh. "I'm not sure I have! I feel ruined."

"Well, a good hot meal will revive you. Can you walk now?"

She moved one foot tentatively. Her thigh muscles trembled but responded. She nodded. "Yes."

"Then let Estelle park your bicycle and come with me. We'll get you food and a room, in that order. You should have a hot soak in a tub before you go to bed tonight."

Inside the inn Em listened through a haze of pain and fatigue while Hubert and Estelle talked with the owner of the inn. Between the men there was the backslapping, exuberant gesturing with every word, and much laughter. Estelle said little, and Em caught her watching her with a concerned expression.

Once the greetings were over, Hubert introduced Em to Monsieur and Madame Lafayette. Then he explained, "Our supper will be ready soon. I need to see a man, but I won't be gone long. I leave you in Estelle's good hands."

The two men left, and Madame Lafayette led Em to a small rustic bedroom that had space only for the wonderful bed that looked like a giant sled filled with a plump feather mattress and covered with a down comforter. Em resisted the urge to collapse into it and never move again. With concentrated discipline, she followed Estelle to the bathroom where she supposed they could wash up for supper.

Instead, Estelle filled a metal tub with hot water and said, "For you. Better you soak now. If you sit through supper first . . . you grow stiff."

"Oh, thank you. It looks wonderful!" She fetched her soap and clean clothes from her knapsack.

The old-fashioned hip tub was just big enough for a good soak. Even her shoulder felt better. When Em's eyes refused to stay open, she reluctantly climbed out, toweled herself dry, and dressed.

Returning to the inn's dining room, she found Hubert back and enjoying a glass of wine with Monsieur Lafayette. Hubert beckoned her to the table and offered her wine.

"No, thank you. Coffee maybe?"

Hubert translated her request, and Madame Lafayette brought something hot and black.

Hubert grinned. "That will put you in the spirit of the Resistance. It is the best they can do. It's been our substitute for coffee all through the Occupation."

She tasted it. Nothing she could remember ever had tasted so vile. She must have shown her reaction, for both men laughed. She set down the cup and laughed with them. "Did you really get used to this?"

"No," Estelle said.

Food and drink revived Em briefly. After supper Hubert translated for her while she conducted an impromptu interview with Monsieur and Madame Lafayette. She took a few notes. Then suddenly her eyes refused to focus. "I'm sorry, but I can't stay awake. Will you please excuse me?"

From her tiny sleeping room she could hear the two French couples still talking. This day certainly had given her an appreciation for the resilience of the resistants. Tomorrow she'd make more notes.

She snuggled into the cloud of feathers under her, trying not to think of the fact they'd only come half the distance to Switzerland's border.

The next morning Em's legs complained at first, but gradually the exercise worked out the soreness.

They reached a small mountain village near the Swiss border in time for a late supper. When they got up in the morning, Hubert informed her the rest of the journey would be on foot. The border lay only two miles away. As they hiked along the graveled road, Em began to limber up, but her legs let her know she had abused them.

"We are going to a farm right on the border," Hubert said. Then he told her about previous trips. Once, when he returned to get his bicycle from the inn they'd just left, Germans had requisitioned all the rooms and the small dining room rang with German voices singing over their beer.

To travel after curfew invited immediate arrest, but he didn't dare to go back over the border of Switzerland. Tired or not, he bicycled the forty miles more to Dôle. He reached Dôle by sunrise and was afraid to linger all day and night in Zone Rouge, so he pedaled straight on to the canal and the friendly gatekeeper. By the time he reached Dijon, he was literally staggering. He slept for a day in the home of resistants before taking the train back to Macon. After that he set up two alternate locations where he could cross the border with the help of French farmers whose land paralleled the border.

The narrow road they were now following led them through a deep valley, then up a long hill. "My friends, the Charbonneaus, live a kilometer or less from the border." Hubert said. "I'll take you to meet them. Then we'll walk on into Switzerland. Although we don't have to worry about German patrols, we shall not be entering Switzerland in the usual manner, so we'll have go to the nearest customs to report. The distance is only about two of your American miles from the Charbonneau farm. Then we'll go by train to meet another of my friends in Geneva."

"I'd like that very much. I don't know how to thank you for letting me do this. You have my word that I will write nothing that you don't want people to know."

"I knew I could trust you, or I wouldn't have offered to bring you. As long as you do not use real names for either the people or the towns, the story can be told. France will need friends among the nations as we rebuild. I believe it is to our advantage that the world knows how we never stopped fighting, even while under occupation." He gestured to the left. "See through the trees on that rise? That is the home of the Charbonneau family. Just beyond the house, at the top of that grassy slope, the Swiss border lies in the forest."

She gazed up the slope at five hundred yards of open land with no place to hide once a person began the climb. Glancing back at Hubert, she said, "Did the Germans patrol here on this isolated farmland?"

He nodded. "Yes, regularly. Georges Charbonneau and I, we had a prearranged signal. His barn midway in the field has a door facing the forest above. He always watched to see that the regular patrol had passed. When I returned, if the Germans were due, he left the barn door open. When I could safely cross his field, he would close the door."

"Then he had to know exactly when you would return."

"No. He had to always watch and set the signal."

"It sounds chancy."

"It was, but trust grows. We began to expect success. Of course, I planned every detail every time. I made certain unbreakable safety rules for myself. And I watched and moved like a cat."

"Was it difficult to get the people with you to keep quiet?"

"They were frightened enough to do anything. For groups, I took them to the other crossing locations. The Charbonneau farm was better for only one or two refugees."

Estelle had grown quiet as they approached the farm. Now she said, "If only we had gone the other way for the Gaudet family."

Hubert sighed. "Oui. A disastrous mistake. Never a day goes by that I don't regret it. But we thought this shorter route would be safer."

She didn't respond, and he didn't continue.

They turned up the slope on a graveled drive to an alpine farmhouse. A barking dog bounded down to meet them.

Before Em could ask if it was friendly, it stopped barking and approached Hubert with wagging tail.

He scratched its ears and ruffled the shaggy fur on its neck. "Hello, Napoleon. Good dog."

Inside the farmhouse, the Charbonneau family spoke some English. They had seven children. The four older sons were in De Gaulle's Free French Army. Em asked if they had not been afraid for the younger children when they had helped Hubert. Both father and mother shook their heads, smiling.

"Afraid, but more we wanted France to be free for our children," Monsieur Charbonneau replied.

"I think you are all very brave," Em said.

Both parents smiled and gave a typically French shrug. So did the oldest boy, who looked to be about twelve. The oldest girl, on the verge of becoming a woman, did not. She only watched Em with sober eyes.

After a short visit they said good-bye to the Charbonneau family and climbed the slope to the woods. In the forest beyond the pasture, the climb grew steeper.

"From here the trail is uphill all the way to the border," Hubert said. "Once we reach the crest, it will be easier, more gradual ups and downs for the rest of the way."

Em had to stop to catch her breath several times.

The higher they climbed, the quieter Estelle grew. Finally she said, "We come near to the border now. It was here that—" Her voice choked off.

"You did as much as you could, dear one. Try to forgive yourself," Hubert murmured, pulling her into his arms.

A shot split the air.

Grabbing Em's arm, Hubert pulled her with him as he shoved Estelle to the ground and threw himself down beside them.

CHAPTER ELEVEN

The echo from the single shot rolled away. No birds sang. Not even a breeze stirred. Hubert whispered, "Do not move." He carefully rolled away from them and then lay still. Finally he whispered, "Stay here. I'm going to look."

With her cheek pressed against the ground, Em watched him move like a panther to the shelter of a large evergreen tree. She grabbed Estelle's hand. Estelle, shaking, held on fiercely. Clinging to each other's hands, they waited for what seemed like forever.

At a rustling noise Em held her breath. Cautiously she turned her head. Hubert beckoned from behind a tree. "Stay low," he hissed. "Follow me."

Copying Estelle, Em rose to a crouching position and darted over the soft pine needles to the shelter of the tree trunk where Hubert waited. Following the bed of a small stream, he led them straight up the mountainside. When they reached the timberline, he pulled them behind a large boulder. "Rest," he whispered. "We must stay away from the trail and be very quiet. I saw a man with a rifle. He did not look like a hunter. I can't believe any Germans or collaborators are still in this area, but we must assume the worst."

"But aren't we in Switzerland now, in neutral territory?" Em whispered.

"In Switzerland, yes. Neutral, no. Whoever has the power breaks the rules. This small nation has been a hotbed of secrets and espionage since the beginning of the war. All the Swiss government asks is that everyone be discreet." He put his arm around his wife and murmured something in French. She answered in French. Then he glanced at Em. "Please excuse me. For what I wanted to say, she needed French."

Em nodded. "Sure. How are you, Estelle?"

"I'm . . . I have asked Hubert . . . that he tell you what happened . . . last time I came here."

"You don't have to do that. Don't make it harder for yourself."

"I want for you to know . . . to write it."

Em gave the woman's shoulder a pat. "Thank you for trusting me."

Hubert cleared his throat. "We brought Estelle's sister and her husband on this route. Border guards saw us. We ran. Jocelyn, seven months pregnant, she could not move fast. We held her hands and pulled her. Just before we reached cover, they shot her twice. She lived a moment to say good-bye. It was obvious . . . the bullets had killed her baby too. To save ourselves we . . . we had to leave her there. For Estelle, it was so much pain. Nightmares come to her. I went back with Georges Charbonneau, hoping to give Jocelyn a Christian burial, but her body was gone. We never found a trace. . . ."

Em gasped. "I'm so sorry . . . so sorry you had to go through that."

Silent body-wracking sobs shook Estelle. Hubert held her close and rocked her in his arms.

Em found herself crying with her.

When Estelle finally quieted, Em rubbed away her own tears but couldn't speak.

Estelle whispered, "I will be better . . . from coming here. . . . My dear sister . . . I so miss her. Maybe you can tell her story, for remembering her."

"I would love to try."

"When we are far from this border you may tell her about Jocelyn," Hubert said. "Right now we must go quiet and quick." He stood up and helped her to her feet.

As they traversed the mountainside and finally returned to the trail, Hubert pointed out landmarks—tall tree snags, unusual rock formations, bends in the creek and canyon walls, and jutting cliffs—that he had used to mark the way in the winter when snow obliterated the trail.

Finally, in a normal voice Hubert announced, "I think we are safe to talk now. If the man with the gun was not a hunter, we have lost him."

As Em followed Hubert and Estelle, she decided this was the longest two miles she'd ever hiked. However, even while she was aching with fatigue, the alpine scenery awed and delighted her.

After a while, Estelle began to tell about her sister, who had been the first in the family to become active in the Resistance. The longer she talked, the steadier her voice became. Jocelyn had worked as a cook for a German officer when he took up residence in a large chateau that had been the home of a prosperous wine merchant. Jocelyn listened and observed, and for two years she fed information to resistants. Her messages helped them destroy transportation and communication lines repeatedly and enabled them to rescue some of their captured comrades. Then Jocelyn overheard the plotting of her own entrapment and arrest. She and her husband, a leader in the Resistance, fled to Macon, and Hubert and Estelle guided them into Switzerland.

"And to her death," Estelle said in a carefully controlled voice.

"Your sister was so brave," Em said. "When we get to a town, I'll write what you've told me. Where is her husband now?"

"He joined General De Gaulle's army," Hubert said.

"Someday I'd like to talk to him too."

"May it be so," Hubert replied.

They walked for a while without conversation. When Estelle spoke again she sounded composed and looked more at peace.

At last they descended to a small Swiss town named Bonnedeux where Hubert reported to the customs office, explaining they had hiked over the border and planned to take the train to Geneva for an overnight visit. He did not mention that someone had shot at them near the border. They each showed their identification papers.

The agent welcomed Em in English. "We are neutral, as you know, and we do remain watchful to protect our neutrality. I must warn you not to engage in any nationalistic activity while you are in Switzerland."

She laughed. "I assure you I will not. I only came to see your beautiful country and to rest, if I may, from the war."

He nodded and gave her a slight bow. "May you find rest here. Good day to you. The railway station is down this street about a kilometer in distance. I believe a train for Geneva is due in soon."

Out in the street, Em asked, "Did you check in with customs when you entered the country secretly?"

"Yes. The Swiss like for everything to appear legal. I'm sure they suspected I came for more than just business, but they chose to not question me. Their neutrality is skewed in the favor of the Allies, though they never dare to let the Germans think so."

At the train station they had no difficulty purchasing tickets and soon boarded the train to Geneva. As they descended toward one of the picturesque valleys where most people lived, Em wished she had brought a camera to record her first visit to Switzerland. The train took them through the city of Neûchatel and along the shore of an immense lake, Lac Neûchatel.

Switzerland looked tidy and serene until they reached Geneva. There, after such peaceful pastoral scenes, the hubbub of the city abraded Em's senses. However, the afternoon sun gentled the first impression, and the air felt clean and brisk.

"We can walk from here, unless you really want to ride," Hubert said.

"Walking again feels good. Lead on!" After sitting on the train, her sore muscles had begun to stiffen.

"Come this way." With Estelle on his arm, Hubert guided Em down the sidewalk. Shortly they came to a wide thoroughfare. As they walked, Em gazed into luxurious store windows filled with merchandise she hadn't seen the likes of since the beginning of the war. So this was neutrality.

"Here we are," Hubert announced. He entered the lobby of an office building and told the elevator operator they wished to be taken to the fourth floor.

As they went up, Em raised her eyebrows questioningly at Hubert. She had expected to go to an apartment building or to someone's home, not to an office. He shook his head slightly and rolled his eyes toward the other men, so she didn't voice her question.

When they got off on the fourth floor, he whisked them down the hall away from their elevator companions. Or was she imagining he hurried her? He stopped at an office door that was labeled *Bremer, Hayes, Blackwell & Krieger*. Inside, the office was furnished simply. The receptionist looked up. "Monsieur and Madame Espe! I'll announce you."

Hubert nodded. "Thank you, Mademoiselle Allred."

She spoke into a telephone and then nodded. "Mr. Blackwell will see you immediately, sir."

Sir? Em thought. *Have I missed something here?* She glanced up at Hubert, but he was already a step ahead of her, opening the door for her to enter an inner office. Estelle showed no surprise.

A stocky man rose from behind a wide desk. "Hubert, it's good to see you! And how are you Madame Espe?"

"I am fine, thank you," Estelle replied.

Hubert said, "I've brought a friend of Father Joseph."

Em noted the fact that this stranger in Geneva also knew Father Joseph. He surely did have a large parish, larger than he had suggested.

Hubert introduced her. "Mademoiselle Em Emerson is an American war correspondent. She wanted to follow the route we used to come secretly into Switzerland. She is writing articles for her magazine about how we survived the Occupation. As long as we are here, I wanted her to meet you." To Em, he said, "Monsieur Andrew Blackwell has been a good friend to our work."

"How do you do," Em said.

"How do you do, Miss Emerson? You surely did not bicycle and walk the way Hubert used to come."

She laughed. "Yes. I'm afraid so. It was incredible. He says he made that trip at least once a month."

"I can attest to that, but surely you must be worn out, not being used to such primitive travel." He pulled out a chair. "Do sit down!"

"I'm tired, all right, but it was more than worth it. Hubert says I can write about it all as long as I don't give real names or exact locations."

He glanced at Hubert. "Right. The war is over as far as that part of it goes, but we've still got a long way to go to get rid of Hitler . . . and his cronies."

"I had a touch of realism," Em said. "Someone shot at us at the border."

Mr. Blackwell frowned and turned to Hubert.

Hubert shook his head. "He got away."

"I see." Mr. Blackwell pursed his lips. "Estelle, that must have been terrible for you. I'm so sorry."

"Yes, but I do all right."

"Hubert, I want to hear more about this later. No point in disturbing the ladies with it now. Did you bring me any news from Father Joseph?"

"As a matter of fact I did." He produced a thin envelope from his inner jacket pocket.

Mr. Blackwell took the envelope and, without opening it, placed it in a drawer. This piqued Em's curiosity more. He turned to her. "Miss Emerson, I'd like for you to be my houseguest. You surely can't go right back after such an arduous journey. My wife and I are both displaced Americans. She would never forgive me if she heard that an American woman came to town, and I did not bring her home."

"Is this all right, Hubert?" Em asked.

"It is very okay. The rest you need. Your story cannot be complete without a visit to the Blackwells. Estelle and I have friends to visit, so we will meet you tomorrow. Andrew will bring you to us at the train station."

So Em went by private car to a chateau on the shore of Lac Leman. Mrs. Blackwell treated her like royalty, and so did Mr. Blackwell when he came in for a late supper. After he finished, they took their coffee to the broad porch overlooking the lake and watched the moon rise.

Mr. Blackwell seemed eager to hear about Oklahoma and how she became a war correspondent and what it was like to be a woman in a man's profession. His enthusiasm loosened Em's tongue. For a change she was answering, not asking, the questions. She enjoyed the change of roles.

As darkness fell over the silver lake, Lydia—Mrs. Blackwell already had insisted that Em call her Lydia—yawned and excused herself. "Please forgive me. I was up most of last night. And I rise early. Em, do make yourself completely at home. You'll find a robe and your choice of gown or pajamas on your bed. We keep a supply for guests who come unprepared to stay. We do love company, you see. Sleep well." She leaned over and kissed her husband. "Andrew, please don't keep her up forever, as you are inclined to do."

"I'll be along in a few minutes," he promised.

After she was gone, Andrew fell silent, sipping his coffee and gazing at the lake. Finally he spoke. "Miss Emerson—Em, if I may?"

"Please do," she said. The Blackwells were considerably older, maybe as old as her parents, but first names seemed natural with them.

He nodded and smiled. "And I prefer to go by Andrew. Em, would you be willing to take Father Joseph a message from me?"

Just in time she kept surprise from her voice. "I'd be glad to, but I don't know where he is or when I may see him again."

He turned from studying the lake and studied her. "He is returning to his home parish near Epinal in a couple of days. I received a phone call from him just this morning. It would be important that you tell no one I sent him a message. Do you mind keeping a secret?"

She wondered momentarily whether her service to the OSS would be compromised by this secret, but she respected and trusted Father Joseph. "My work as a journalist requires me to keep confidences."

He nodded. "Good. I'll have it ready for you in the morning. I don't want Hubert or even my wife to know. Does that bother you?"

She would have to check out all this with Brad Cummins before acting, but she said, "Not if it's important to Father Joseph and his work."

"It is."

"Then I'll do it." First she would call Cummins. She knew nothing about Andrew Blackwell and his business in Geneva, but she wanted to see Father Joseph again. He was her only contact with Vivienne now.

Near the field hospital in Belgium, the battle to take Aachen, Germany, intensified. The city was surrounded by the Siegfried Line fortifications. The battlefront still remained too fluid to move the field hospital closer. As it was, shock waves from the bombing and shelling reverberated over the low hills of the farmland. Marge had learned to recognize the difference between artillery shells, bombs, and the raucous repetition of antiaircraft ack-acks. Despite the barrage, the field hospital received no more casualties than usual. Then after the sixth day of bombardment, the gunfire and shelling quieted.

A post-op patient who was a history buff explained to Marge the value of seizing this historical city. Germans considered Aachen their Imperial City. From the days of Roman rule, it had been a wealthy city. Charlemagne had ruled Europe from there and was buried there. Thirty-two German emperors and kings had been crowned in Aachen. Many world leaders had made pilgrimages to its healing hot springs, including Frederick the Great, Bismarck, Peter the Great of Russia, and even Franklin Roosevelt. Hitler personally prized Aachen as the symbol of German superiority and the German right to rule—his historic sign that the Third Reich was destined to bring Europe a thousand years of peace.

Although the amateur historian had bandages from his waist to his feet, he concluded his impromptu lecture with, "Now we're gonna show those Krauts what-for!"

"It'll be a tough battle," another patient chimed in. "The terrain around Aachen is against us. It's hilly and wooded, so there's no clear approach for tanks. That always makes it harder for us infantry guys."

Marge hated listening to dire predictions.

Sally, however, murmured, "Yeah, that's right," and headed for the receiving area.

Marge followed.

Sally began breaking out boxes of fresh bandages, and Marge helped her, working feverishly, hoping the battle would not be as brutal as the last soldier had suggested. Other nurses, taking advantage of the lull in new arrivals, began to open extra packages of medicines and morphine in preparation for the next onslaught of patients.

Before long the firing commenced again, and soon wounded men began to arrive—first in a trickle, then a flood of injuries. Even jeeps were used to bring in stretchers strapped across the back while those with lesser wounds sat propped up on the front seats. The war was on again.

"It's always this way when the soldiers jump off on a big offensive," Sally said. "After all the shelling comes the rush here."

"So even without that soldier's opinion, you knew what to expect?"

Sally shrugged. "Only a guess. You learn after a while. Come on. Help me break out more surgical supplies. We're liable to have even more wounded by evening."

Since Marge was off duty from surgery, she worked with Sally and some orderlies to line up extra cartons of bandages, medications, and plasma within easy reach. Some men tinkered with the generators and the lights to make sure they would stay on when they were needed.

When Marge and Sally finished, they went in search of Louise and found her near some ambulances that were loading men for evacuation. Seeing them, she beckoned. "Here's a list of the rest of the patients to evacuate. Get them ready, and soon as they're out, prepare the beds for new patients."

"Yes, ma'am," Marge said in unison with Sally.

They hurried into the tent and began to make sure the patients' medical charts were complete, that injured heads, legs, and arms were stabilized, and bandages were clean and secure.

"What's happening, Nurse?" a patient asked.

"You're on your way to a hospital ship." Marge checked his temperature, pulse, and blood pressure. As she recorded the results, she said, "You're doing fine, soldier. We're going to get you out of here for the rest of your recuperation."

"I wanted to get back to my buddies," he said. "All that bombing means they're softening up the Krauts to go into Germany."

"Your orders for now are to rest and heal up."

He sank back onto his pillow. "I just hate to think of the guys going on without me. You know what I mean?"

"As much as I can, I know."

"You've been swell. You and all the nurses working out here right beside the troops. The Krauts ain't always respectful of that cross on your tent or on your arm either. One of the medics bought it the same day I got hit. There wasn't no doubt but that the dirty bum shot him on purpose."

Oh, God, don't let it be David! As casually as she could, she said, "Did you know the medic?"

"No. He was with another battalion. I just heard about it. Made everybody mad. They went after the sniper who did it and got a whole nest of Nazis in the process."

She tucked his blanket around him, ready for the orderlies. "I wish you a safe trip, soldier."

"Same to you, ma'am. For wherever they send you."

"Thanks." She hadn't thought about being moved, but the hospital would follow the battle. Right now, though they were close to the German border, they were nearly ten miles south of Aachen, much farther than ideal for a field hospital. They'd been due to move closer for some time. Would she see David in this growing chaos? Was he still alive?

No, she wouldn't question that. He had to be alive. He just had to be.

As Marge went from patient to patient on her side of the ward, preparing the men for evacuation, she glanced at Isabelle at the opposite end of the long tent. When the field hospital moved closer to the front, the child surely could not go. And yet, with her leg in traction, it would be days before she could be up. And then she'd have to learn to walk again. What would happen to her?

If only David were here. Remembering that a medic had been killed, she clamped off the fear that it could be David. Surely the casualty was someone else. Wouldn't God protect a good man like David so he could do more good? Then she chided herself. Thousands of good men had not been spared, and thousands more would be lost before the war was over.

Turning to the next patient, she set to work. Speculation was a waste of energy.

Within two hours the incoming wounded began to fill every sheltered area. Prepared as the field hospital was, each doctor could treat only one man at time.

Colonel Colville assigned Marge to assist him and took all the orthopedic cases. A visiting surgeon, Colonel Marlin, took head injuries and neurological cases. The rest went to the general surgeons.

Each time Colonel Colville had to amputate a mangled limb, Marge heard him swear under his breath. Though swearing wasn't part of her vocabulary, she felt the same frustration. He worked on, doing what had to be done and hating it all the while. She slapped instruments into his gloved hand as soon as he reached for one.

During a pause, he said, "I've got to find a way to save more arms and legs."

"You're doing the best you can, sir."

"The best is not enough! Somehow if they come in with arms and legs attached, I've got save them!"

Marge knew he had no other choice when he amputated. Blood supply, nerve connections, enough bone for regeneration—what could he do lacking these factors? She worked on. Sometimes she felt like a machine functioning mindlessly, handing him the instruments the instant he needed them. "If there's a way, you'll find it, sir," she said.

His eyes above his mask turned toward her, and she could tell he was smiling. "You're a gem, Emerson. You know that?"

She smiled back. "No, but I know you always do your best. Been watching you, sir."

When Marge went to wash up between patients, she stretched her back and had a cup of much needed coffee. Then she stole a peek into the admitting area. Seeing the men ready for surgery and more coming all the time, a phrase popped into her mind like the title of a book. There was the Siegfried Line, the Maginot Line, and here in the field hospital they had the Long Bloody Line. She dared not dwell on this gruesome observation. She hurried back into surgery where Colonel Colville's next patient was being anesthetized and took her place beside the instrument tray. In a moment the doctor was there, probing leg and groin wounds that were still bleeding.

She watched Dr. Colville work to put the damaged tissue into a healing position. Then, seemingly for no reason, a vision of Em the day she'd mounted that unbroken mustang flashed into her mind. After all these years, thinking about her sister, bleeding and limp on the ground, still made Marge shudder with dread. She had run to rescue Em from those flying hoofs, fearing her little sister was dead. *Is this a warning that Em is in danger, like the occasional warnings Em claims to have? Where is Em now? Is she okay? Oh, dear God, please keep her safe.*

"Nurse Emerson, sutures please!" Dr. Colville ordered, snapping her out of her reverie.

She jumped and handed him the sutures, ready to apply. She must not let her mind wander. Em was the one to follow hunches and react to inner nudges. A nurse could not afford to dwell on the illogical. All the same, she felt unsettled. The vivid memory reminded her of Em's proclivity to believe she could do anything she set her mind to without considering the risks.

Chapter Twelve

For the journey back into France, Em met Hubert and Estelle at the train station. Hubert had tickets for her and Estelle but said, "I am going back the way we came. I shall arrange to bring back our bicycles."

"Oh, please!" Estelle cried. "Do not go there again. Come with us."

"I will be very careful. You know that. I must know more about the man who shot at us. I do not think it was an accident."

"Yes, but—"

He touched a finger to her lips. "I won't be long, I promise. Em, will you stay with her until I come?"

"I'll be glad to. I'd like to write your story while Estelle is available to answer questions."

Privately, while Estelle went to the rest room, Hubert told Em he might return with information for her to deliver to Cummins.

"You mean a secret agent may have shot at us in the mountains?"

"Not at us. At me. I may have lost my cover."

At the very thought she felt as if a breath of something cold and evil passed over her.

He looked at her steadily. "I must check."

A few minutes later, as the train left Geneva, Em sat by the window at Estelle's suggestion. "The view for you will be lovely," she said.

"Thank you. Where I grew up, we could not see mountains. They are so beautiful."

Although Estelle leaned back and appeared calm, Em knew she wasn't. She was still jumpy from having been shot at. Her eyes moved nervously from person to person in their railcar. As Em observed

Estelle, she began to imagine how frightening train rides must have felt when the ever-present Gestapo had been in control.

Even now Hubert had warned Em against talking freely on the train. Reaching across the space between them, Em silently squeezed Estelle's hand.

Estelle responded with a brief smile and returned her gesture. Then she gently slipped her hand from Em's, and Em understood that their actions should not reveal any nervousness. Estelle's reaction further illuminated the years of fear she had faced during the Occupation. Obedient to the French woman's signal, Em said lightly, "The valley is so beautiful, even though winter is coming."

Estelle smiled. "Yes. The Rhône River and the vineyards are lovely any season."

They chatted about the weather and small things until Estelle said she would like to nap and leaned her head on the back of the seat.

Em pulled out her notepad and wrote more of her memories of the trek on foot over the Swiss border. If nothing else, someday her adventure would be part of her family history. She'd made copious notes last night at the Blackwells before falling asleep. For fun she had even sketched some of the landmarks Hubert had pointed out. Now, if she closed her eyes, she could remember clearly how the mountains and the trail looked.

When they reached Macon, Estelle awoke fresh-eyed. They gathered their small bags and headed for the farm on foot. Em's legs were a far sight more painful and stiff than her shoulder. She wished she had some of Cummins' odoriferous liniment for her thighs and calves.

"It will take us most of an hour to walk to our farm," Estelle said. "I hope Hubert comes quickly. Once he reaches the Charbonneau farm, they will take him in their truck to the train."

"Surely he will hurry. He knows you are worried."

Estelle gave her a fleeting sideways glance. "With the Germans gone, it is still so difficult, when I thought it would be easy." She seemed more confident in her use of English, a good thing, Em thought. After the war English could be helpful to her. As it was, she could get more practice now with the U.S. Army traveling back and forth through Macon on their way to the battlefront. The Germans still held the mountains between France and Germany.

Em had a yen to get into the Vosges Mountains' combat zone. That part of the war had been underreported because the largest troop movements continued to be in Belgium and the Netherlands.

But once the American and French armies drove them from the Vosges Mountains, the Allies would have a clear shot into the heart of the Rhineland.

Approaching the farm, Estelle asked, "Must you leave tomorrow?"

"Yes, as soon as Hubert returns."

The women walked in silence for a few moments.

"I can't thank you enough for taking me on your underground route," Em said as they proceeded through east Macon. "I know it was hard for you."

"I feel—how shall I say?—relief for going. The bad dreams, they did not come last night. I went to help you and—" Smiling, she threw her arms wide. "*Voilà!* I helped me!"

"I'm so glad!"

That night Em wrote as much as she could about their journey and ended up with a series of anecdotes, impressions, and lists of story ideas. Then, with her shoulder aching again and too tired to think any longer, she collapsed into bed.

The next morning Em worked over her notes and typed them into a first draft of an article. In the background, Estelle caught her attention as she flitted from one household task to the other, apparently unable to sit and relax. By afternoon Em, too, grew uneasy about how long Hubert was taking.

She could not leave Estelle until he returned, but she dearly wanted to telephone Cummins about Andrew's message for Father Joseph. She had promised not to confide in Hubert, and that seemed wise. After all, Cummins had made a big point that only from him would she receive orders. She was beginning to wish she had simply said no to Andrew's request. Now that she was away from him, she didn't know why she'd said yes. She supposed the appeal to help Father Joseph had captured her.

The way things were progressing, she probably would miss her date with Bob in Paris. When she called Cummins, she would call the hotel and leave a message for him.

Unable to sit still any longer, Em closed up her typewriter and went to help Estelle. She was doing the laundry on a scrub board. Happily she had a mechanical wringer, which Em cranked while her hostess neatly fed the dripping garments and sheets into it. Then they hung the wet things on lines inside a floorless stone building that Estelle called a carriage house.

After supper Em returned to her typewriter and polished her first article about the underground route into Switzerland. She used fictitious names for people and locations. When she finished, she knew it would impress her boss. Unfortunately she couldn't send it from Macon.

She went to bed hoping Hubert would show up soon.

In the morning when Em got up, he was there, eating breakfast at the kitchen table as if he'd never been gone. She realized this must be the way he came and went during the Occupation.

Estelle looked radiant. "Hubert arrived after midnight." As she poured coffee for Em, she said more soberly, "Tell her, Hubert, what you discovered."

"First," he said, "I want to thank you for staying with Estelle. It relieved me much to know you were here."

Em sat down across from him and sipped the hot, bitter liquid in her cup. "I was happy to stay. Did you have any trouble on the trail back through the mountains?"

He shook his head. "No. The Charbonneau family, they had heard the shot. Georges went up the hill immediately to see if we were all right. Fortunately he is a good shot—"

"He shot our assailant?"

Hubert nodded. "Shot and buried him."

Em tried to swallow and couldn't. She cleared her throat and still couldn't keep a squeak out of her voice. "So someone really meant to kill us, and Georges killed him just like that?"

"Yes, though it was in self-defense. He recognized the man as a collaborator we had tried to capture. He had posed as a friend to the Resistance and then betrayed us."

"I see." Em's voice was working again. She turned at Estelle. "You were right about being afraid to go back there."

Estelle nodded. "But I do feel better to know the betrayer is killed."

"You said Georges buried him," Em said. "Did he mark the grave?" She couldn't help thinking that even a traitor must have a family who would want to know where his body lay.

Hubert frowned. His dark eyes narrowed. "In many cases to mark enemy graves is dangerous. Georges took the man's papers. He will turn them over to the government."

Em met Hubert's hard gaze and detected a silent warning to let the matter go. She said no more.

Estelle, however, took up the questioning. "Hubert, do you think that man killed Jocelyn and her baby?"

"*Ma petite fleur*, I do not know." He wrapped his arms around her, held her close, and murmured something in French. When he let her go, her eyes were wet with the remains of tears, but she nodded.

Then she excused herself. "I must go and feed our chickens and goats. Please, Em, sit and eat with Hubert."

"Sure. Thank you." Em sensed that Estelle needed to be alone, or she would have offered to help. She filled a bowl with porridge, added some goat milk and honey, and sat across from her host who was savoring some of the powdered coffee she'd brought.

As soon as the door closed behind Estelle, Em looked Hubert in the eyes. "Was the gunman working alone?"

"So it seems. Charbonneau found no trace of another."

"Does Charbonneau know you work for the OSS?"

"No. He only knows me as a Resistant."

She wished she could ask him if Andrew knew, but she sensed that she should not. "Estelle will be coming in soon. I'd better pack. I need to get back to Paris. Excuse me, please." She stood up and headed for her bedroom.

She'd only taken a few steps when he called, "Wait. Andrew thought we could trust you, but I wasn't sure until now. I work for Andrew as well as the OSS. His business depends upon exchanges of industrial secrets. I help him by delivering data and plans that his operatives in Paris acquire. They don't steal, understand. They buy information, but all must be done discreetly."

"Why are you telling me this?"

"Andrew needs you. He says that you, as a war correspondent, can go places that I cannot. A woman correspondent would not be suspected as readily as I. If you are willing, Andrew wants you to return to Geneva to talk with him."

Aware that her mouth was hanging open, Em closed it and clamped her teeth together. What an insane idea. How could Andrew Blackwell think she would go into spying for him? Was he really serious? He should know she was under the control of the U.S. Army, even though he couldn't know she was already a courier for the OSS. Was this what came of agreeing to take a message to Father Joseph?

"I can't get into some covert action in industry. I don't even believe in buying information."

"I must tell you that what he does is of great benefit to the Allied cause. Through him, they have acquired some of Hitler's most precious secrets."

"You mean an American businessman can buy secrets from German businessmen?"

"Andrew's people have contacts. They trade information, even go into Germany."

His words flew past her in a blur. She shook her head and gasped, "Into Germany?" Nothing horrified her more than the thought of a non-German entering Nazi Germany. But even worse, he could be betraying the United States. "Does he trade American expertise for German?" This was beginning to sound like a situation Cummins should know about.

Hubert lit a cigarette, watching her over the flare of the match. He snuffed the match and inhaled. Leaning back on the kitchen chair, he exhaled through tight lips. "If you will even consider hearing about his work, I have a train ticket for your return to Geneva. He will answer your questions. But now we must hush about this, or Estelle will wonder when she comes in. She has endured too much grief and worry already."

Em wanted to yell, "Then why do you have to get into more danger when your country is virtually free now?" But she didn't. She knew that if she were he, and if America were France, she'd never give up fighting until the enemy was totally defeated.

Estelle entered the kitchen at that moment, so Em went to pack her things. When she came out, it took every ounce of self-control to act as if she didn't know anything about covert activities. "Hubert already has a train ticket for me," she said casually. "The only thing is, I have to leave right away."

"Must you? So soon?"

"Yes. I've so enjoyed getting to know you both. Thank you for telling me your story and for all you have done to help me."

"Now you go to Paris?" Estelle said.

"Yes. If your story is published, I'll mail you a copy. I do hope to see you again. Thanks so much for all you've done for me."

"Is nothing. We are so happy to have you," Estelle said.

Hubert stood up and handed her the train ticket to Geneva.

"Thank you." She handed him money, so it would look like he purchased the ticket from his own funds.

He pocketed the cash. "You are welcome."
She put the ticket in her purse.

When Em arrived in Geneva, she went straight to Andrew Blackwell's office. Upon finding him in, she realized she'd taken a chance. He might have been off anywhere. She didn't know anything about his business except that he habitually went home late in the evening.

His secretary announced her, and he invited her into his inner office. Closing the door, he asked her to be seated.

He looked so little like a plotting industrialist that she found herself wondering if somehow she had misunderstood Hubert.

Andrew sat down and leaned his elbows on his desk. "Hubert called to say you were coming. He told you what he is doing?"

"Not what, but for whom."

Andrew nodded. "Since you came back to see me, I assume you may consider working for me."

Believing honesty was the best policy, even when dealing with intrigue, she said, "I'm not free to join anything, so credit my being here to a journalist's insatiable curiosity. I had to come and find out as much as you're willing to tell me."

"Off the record?"

"Of course. You have my word."

"Before I tell you anything, I assure you I can obtain permission from the army to allow you to join me."

A little alarm bell went off amongst her neurons. He was too confident, and this sounded really shady.

He grinned. "I see that I have your undivided attention, so I will tell you a little. But I must have your promise that you will not speak or write a word about what I divulge. Your silence will protect many lives. Were you to leak any information, I would be forced to ruin your reputation as a journalist. Will you give me your word on this?"

His manner as well as his words left no doubt that he would and could do exactly as he said.

She thought hard and fast. "Why would you trust me at all when you scarcely know me?"

His mouth quirked into a tight-lipped smile. She thought she saw a glint of approval in his eyes.

"Your first recommendation came to me from Father Joseph Dupre and his sister Vivienne. I trust them."

"Vivienne! You know Vivienne too? Do they work for you?"

"They are only old friends."

"Good enough friends to know you are into buying industrial secrets?" She was remembering the young man who had been killed and how Vivienne had fled to hide. She frowned. Was Andrew's unsavory work involved with getting her friends in trouble? She didn't want to suspect everyone she met, but maybe that was the way it had to be in wartime Europe.

Andrew was watching her with the detachment of a scientist. "Right after we met, I ran a check on you. The types of articles you've submitted to your magazine have been unorthodox and courageous. When I contacted your editor, he spoke glowingly of your honesty. He indicated you might be trusted to fulfill an assignment, despite your talent for getting into risky situations." He stopped and opened a package of cigarettes. "Do you smoke?"

She shook her head impatiently. "You did all this in the short time since we met?"

"Getting information is part of my business." Without asking permission, he lit up his cigarette. "Even the fact that you don't smoke tells me something about you. A young woman in your profession who doesn't smoke has standards of independence that we value." He inhaled and blew smoke above his head and didn't say anymore. He just sat smoking and watching her.

After a long silence Em spoke. "You said you could get permission for me to participate in your ... ah ... activities. How can you do that?" She was leading him on, not intending to do anything but find out as much as she could about his so-called business.

"I have contacts. I can get official permission. I can get it in writing. I can arrange for you to go anywhere and even provide good transportation. No more walking for miles in Paris to get an interview, no more plodding train rides. You could have your own driver. You'd be a press woman with special permission to go anywhere."

That sounded good, if she were not already in the OSS. "What would you want me to do?"

"You would function as a journalist. You would continue to submit your articles to your magazine. But you would make regular trips to Geneva or to Hubert. You would take my messages to certain people in Paris and would bring their messages to me."

He wanted another courier. What was it about her that attracted people to offer her undercover jobs? This could be an opportunity to learn something for Cummins if she appeared interested. She'd better not burn any bridges until she talked to Cummins. "I have to tell you,

I don't like buying and selling industrial secrets, but Hubert said you are helping the Allied war effort."

"Until I have your word about secrecy, I cannot tell you more."

She decided to test her ability to lie. "You have my word."

He tamped out his cigarette and leaned forward. "Have you heard anything about Hitler's secret underground defenses in the Bavarian Alps?"

"Yes. I've heard talk, especially since D day."

"It's not a rumor. He also has established factories underground in the mountains. It's almost impossible for the Allies to damage his hidden forces and factories with bombing. Germans who are disillusioned with Hitler are willing to risk their lives to stop him. They have given us many details. We know he's producing bigger rockets. He plans to arm the warheads with deadly gas."

As he talked, a vision of a neighbor back home flashed into Em's memory. The poor man had died slowly from breathing mustard gas, leaving his wife with three children to raise alone. One of the girls had been Marge's best friend. "You have confirmed that Hitler is planning to deliver poison gas with rockets?"

"Yes. It's only a matter of time. The new rockets will have guidance systems and will reach London and Paris much faster than the V–2. If we don't find ways to destroy those underground factories, conceivably Hitler could win the war."

"So this is why Hubert continues to expose himself to danger," she murmured.

"Yes."

"But why me?" She didn't think they'd send an English-speaking presswoman into Germany.

"As I said, we need a new trusted courier in Paris—one such as you, whom no one would suspect. All you would have to do is pick up messages at a given time in a given place and deliver them as soon as possible to Hubert or me."

"I would only deliver messages?"

"Correct."

She thought quickly. She could give Cummins definite information if she made even one run for Andrew. And Andrew did say he was helping the Allied war effort. She couldn't believe both he and Hubert were lying. It did not fit anything she had observed in them, and she usually could trust her instincts about character in people.

"If I were to agree to act as a courier once, could I quit if I wanted out for any reason?"

"Yes. Remembering, of course, that you never could speak or write about it, or . . ." he paused. He might as well have made a slashing gesture across his throat.

She finished for him. "Or you will ruin my career as a journalist." She smiled. Telling Cummins didn't count as far as she was concerned. She'd never publish anything. "I can live with that. Give me my first assignment."

"You have my message for Father Joseph."

"Yes."

"Deliver it to him in St. Hilary. He will tell you what I want you to do in Paris."

"Father Joseph? But you said he's not working for you."

"He's not. He will explain." Meeting his piercing gaze, Em wondered how she'd gotten an impression while in his home that he was a genial softy. At this moment he looked quite unapproachable. Question time was obviously over.

"Okay," she said.

Chapter Thirteen

Andrew reached in a desk drawer. "I'll give you cash to help you on your way. Father Joseph will direct you to my next assignment for you. I will leave it to him to brief you on that when you see him."

She hadn't thought about the cost of getting to St. Hilary. She still had cash from Cummins, but she wasn't about to refuse this help. "Thank you." She put the money in an inner pocket of her uniform jacket.

"You'll no doubt have a lot of questions by the time you reach Father Joseph. Even though he's not in my employ, you may trust him for as much as he does know. If you can't get permission from the army to go to Epinal and St. Hilary, go on to Paris and give me a call so I can change my plans accordingly. So"—he held out his hand—"until we meet again. I wish you the best. I'll be in touch."

"Thank you," she said again and almost added, *sir*. His seriousness made her feel as if formality fit better than first names.

He escorted her to the door.

On the way to the train station Em glanced into a dress shop window and saw her reflection in her army dress uniform. She didn't know how Cummins had managed to arrange for her to stay in the press corps while serving the OSS. And now Andrew was offering something similar. The whole situation should interest Cummins.

She thought about what Andrew had said about the threat of Hitler's plans. She would run that by Cummins too. The thought struck her that if she could work for Andrew as well as the OSS, she might be able to make a big difference in the war effort. Her mind buzzed with the possibilities. She had no doubt about her ability to provide whatever Andrew wanted.

Before boarding a train for France, Em located a public telephone in a quiet corner of a plush hotel. She dialed the operator and gave her the phone number to Cummins' office. When Cummins' secretary finally answered, Em identified herself by her code name, Elena, and asked for Cummins.

In a moment his voice came on. "Where are you?" he asked abruptly.

"In a hotel in Geneva. I'm on a public phone in quiet corner."

"Don't say any more than you have to."

"I wanted to ask your opinion. An acquaintance here has offered me an unusual opportunity to help him in his business. I wondered what you might think about it. His name is Andrew Blackwell."

"Of Bremer, Hayes, Blackwell & Krieger? Big name in all types of fabrics, including nylon for parachutes. If you are wondering if you can trust him, I'd say yes."

"My little errands for him will not interfere with your business?"

"If they do, I will tell you."

"In that case I will go to St. Hilary before returning to Paris. Is there anything you want me to do in that direction while I am doing him this favor?" She didn't think she should come right out and ask if he wanted her to gather information on Blackwell. When she got to Paris, she would tell him everything.

"No. Just call me when you return."

"Okay, I will. Good-bye."

"Good-bye."

She hung up wondering what she had accomplished. She wasn't good at clandestine messages. Did he understand what she had meant to communicate? Well, it would have to do. She walked on to the train station.

The ride to Dijon went deadly slow for Em. Twice the train waited on sidings for other trains to pass. She had a lot of time to think about her decision to carry a message to Father Joseph. She was eager to see him and eager to visit the area around Epinal.

That part of northeastern France had been freed only recently. Father Joseph's parish was about seventy-five miles from the Rhine River in Germany. Between Epinal and the border, the rugged Vosges Mountains were still stalling Allied progress. She hoped her OSS assignments still might place her in a position to cover the American troops crossing the Siegfried Line by the Rhine. Maybe Bob was there right now, if he still was with General Devers.

At last the train steamed into the station in Dijon. Along an adjacent highway, Em noticed a convoy of army trucks parked in line on the side. The soldiers remained in the back of the trucks. Only a few officers and drivers stood lounging beside the vehicles.

As the train pulled into the rail yard, she watched the convoy. If she couldn't get on a train to Epinal immediately, maybe she could hitch a ride with the army. Two command cars approached from the rear of the convoy. Everyone, even the men in the backs of the trucks, straightened to attention as the two vehicles passed. When the first cars came closer, Em saw the insignia of a general and several other high-ranking officers. Then seated in the second car with more officers she spied Bob Mansfield.

She willed him to look up at the train, but he didn't. He was talking to the man beside him. The cars passed and moved to the head of the convoy. She wanted to jump off the moving train and run waving after Bob's car.

So Bob was in Dijon! She'd supposed that by now he'd be back in Paris. She bit her lip as the train slowed into the station. Jumping up, with typewriter and small bag in hand, she positioned herself at the railcar door. At last the train stopped. Pushing her way through the crowd, she rushed outside. The convoy was gone. Disappointed beyond reason, Em reminded herself this was the way it would be if they were to marry—Bob off on his assignments and she tied to her own. Her self-administered lecture didn't help her to feel better.

She'd planned to stay the night in Dijon. She remembered an inn that Hubert said he'd used when he stayed in Dijon. It was in a humble area, very close to the station. She picked up her bag and typewriter and headed for the first cross street. The walk would have been pleasant if it were not raining. For some reason she never thought to prepare ahead for rain in France. England, yes, but not France. She would be soaked to the skin by the time she reached the place Hubert had used.

Without much difficulty she found the small inn. She stepped into the shadowed lobby and stood dripping a puddle on the faded old carpet.

A woman of undeterminable age came from a room behind the desk. "Oui, mademoiselle?" She stopped and smiled. "Américain, are you not? You wish a room?"

"Yes, please. Hubert Espe recommended that I come here. I'll be staying only one night."

She smiled. "Yes, of course. For a friend of Hubert, I would give my own bed." She reached for a key hanging on the wall behind her. "But come. I have a room."

Em followed her down a dark hallway to a room at the end where a hall window looked out on a small garden. The woman turned the key and opened the door. "Will this satisfy?" she said.

Em stepped into a spotless little sleeping room. "Yes. It's fine. I'll leave my things and come back to the desk to pay."

"No need. Just knock on my door later. I am always in. Here is your key."

"Thank you . . . I wonder, do you know where army headquarters is? I would like to check in with them."

"I do not know, but my husband may. I will send him to you. He may also drive you. We have a car of sorts." She smiled. "I will send him right away if that is your wish."

"Yes, please. That would be good."

Em went to the bathroom down the hall and washed her face. Back in her room, she applied fresh lipstick and combed her hair. A tap on the door announced the arrival of the concierge's husband.

When she opened, a gray-haired man with a neatly trimmed beard greeted her. "Mademoiselle wishes to drive to the army headquarters?" he said carefully.

"Yes, please. Can you arrange it?"

"I will take you. We offer this service to our patrons when the car cooperates. Today it cooperates." When he smiled, his brown eyes nearly disappeared in wrinkles. He seemed a good deal older than the concierge. Although her hair had silvered, her skin was almost without lines.

"I'll get my coat," Em said. She had hung it over a chair, hoping to dry it out quickly.

"Ah, the rain. I shall find an umbrella for you. The car, she is out this way." He opened a side door on the hall that opened, to a covered walkway skirting the edge of the garden. In a garage that probably had housed horses and carriages in the old days, he produced a large black umbrella and then opened the door of an ancient vehicle. She knew nothing about French cars, but this one looked like a touring car from the First World War.

However, it ran. Her host backed out of the carriage house and into the circle driveway. By the time he pulled up to the curb beside a downtown hotel, Em knew she was in good hands. "I will wait," he said.

"Thank you. I really won't be long." She grabbed the umbrella and hurried across the sidewalk.

Inside, the usual military personnel, intent on their duties, did not even greet her. She had hoped she might ask someone about Bob Mansfield's whereabouts. She even had hoped he might have stopped here.

She approached the main desk and waited for a lieutenant to look up from paper work. When he did, his surprise at seeing her made her a bit nervous. She did not want to be sent back to Paris.

"Yes, ma'am?"

"I was looking for the rest of the press corps, namely correspondent Bob Mansfield." She handed him her press card.

"Well, I don't know, ma'am. We can't keep track of the press."

Good, she thought. *Then you won't know I don't have official permission to be here.* Aloud, she said, "Of course. The last he said to me was that he might be with General Devers."

The man stared at her for a moment. "Well, General Devers could be anywhere from Marseilles to Epinal. If you wait here, you may see him coming or going or you may not. Can't say."

"Epinal? Has Epinal been secured? May I go on there to wait for my friend to show up?"

He scratched his head thoughtfully. "I guess you could, ma'am. If you can get clearance from our CO."

"May I talk to him?"

He hesitated, and she thought she'd lost the chance to go legally. Then he said, "I'll ask him, ma'am."

He disappeared into a room across the lobby.

When he came back, she couldn't tell from his face if the answer was yes or no. Behind his desk again, he said, "Colonel Meyers will see you. Right over there." He gestured to the room he'd just left.

Em marched to the door and knocked. A brusque "Come in," didn't sound too promising.

A stern man with a bristling crew cut motioned her forward without even looking up at her. Around the cigar in his mouth he said, "Why do you want to go to Epinal?"

"To report on the battles near there, sir," she lied.

He looked up from under bristling brows. "You prepared for observing mountain fighting?" His eyes moved over her dress uniform, wet shoes, and soggy topcoat.

"I hoped you'd outfit me. I just need fatigues, boots, and a steel helmet."

He sucked on his cigar a moment. "You'll need . . . ah . . . a lot more than that." He scribbled something on a sheet of paper. "Take this to the commissary in the morning and wear what they give you. You got your own transportation?"

"No, sir. I came on the train."

He wrote again and handed her a second piece of paper. "That'll get you a ride with a convoy going north. It will be up to you to flag them down and get on."

He sure wasn't making it easy, but he wasn't standing in her way either. "Thank you, sir."

"No problem. We need some reporting on this campaign. Folks need to know what's going on, and our boys need to know they're important enough to be interviewed. You'll do that, won't you?"

"Yes, sir. Thank you, sir." She saluted.

He saluted, and his lips twitched toward smiling. "On your way then."

She nearly ran from the hotel, feeling she'd better hurry before he changed his mind.

On the return drive to the inn, she realized she had forgotten to ask about Bob. She'd meant to find out if he had gone to Epinal. Well, maybe she fared better by not mentioning him. Obviously the colonel didn't know that a veteran correspondent for the *U.S. National Tribune* was reporting eastern France. She wasn't about to test her good fortune by going back to ask after Bob.

From the inn she telephoned Andrew and told him she had gotten permission to go to Epinal, so the rest of the task would be simple.

When Em hopped off the army personnel carrier at Epinal, a corporal pushed his way through the soldiers and few civilians and introduced himself as her driver. Thinking he'd mistaken her for someone else, she asked to see his written orders. He produced them.

She couldn't guess what kind of strings Andrew had pulled, but if having one's own driver came with the job, she highly approved. It had been raining hard all day, and she'd been dreading the thought of searching for her lodging on foot. Her driver also knew where St. Hilary, Father Joseph's home village, was located. He said his battalion had driven through there right after it fell to the Allies.

As Em placed her portable typewriter in the jeep, some army trucks stopped across the street. Em glanced at the men peering out of the back of the covered personnel carriers. Asian eyes in tanned faces gazed back at her. *The Nisei Combat Team!* She hurried across to the back of the closest truck. "Do any of you fellows know Sergeant Tom Kagawa?" she asked.

One man called from inside the truck. "I know Tom."

"Oh, good. He's married to a friend of mine."

The men shifted as the speaker moved to the tailgate of the truck. "Tom will want to talk to you. I think he's about three trucks ahead of us."

"Thanks! I'll try to find him. In case I don't, will you tell him Em Emerson said hello? Maybe I'll see him later, one way or another."

"Sure, I'll tell him, but if you hurry you may get to say hello yourself."

"Thanks!" Em waved as she hurried on. At each truck she asked for Tom, and several men knew him. At last in the fourth truck, a soldier at the rear of the covered truck yelled, "Hey, Sarge! You're wanted." Everyone shifted to make room, and Tom appeared at the tailgate.

"Em!" He leaned down and grabbed her extended hand. "How long have you been in France?"

"Seems like a year, but the calendar says a month."

"Have you heard from Jean?"

"Not since I left Abergavenny. I haven't stayed in one place long enough to pick up my mail. Hey, it's good to see you! Any idea where you're headed?" She forgot in the excitement of finding him that she shouldn't ask.

He shook his head. "No."

Unbeknownst to her, a signal had been given because the truck started up and began to move. "When you write, tell Jean hello from me, and I'll do the same for you."

He nodded and waved back until the truck turned the corner at the end of the block.

When Em returned to her jeep, the driver, standing beside the jeep exclaimed, "You knew those guys? They look like Japs!"

"They're Americans," she snapped. "The man I talked with is married to a good friend of mine."

He shook his head. "I heard tell of a Japanese division in Italy but didn't really believe it."

She climbed into the jeep seat and motioned for him to do the same. "So now you know." She hated the condescension in his voice. Maybe she could get a new driver when she got back to Epinal. "Okay, Corporal, get going. Take me to the church in St. Hilary."

As they pulled into the village of St. Hilary, Em hoped that Father Joseph was at home. The houses and shops along the narrow street bore only a few battle scars. The impression of the town, however, gave the same picture of deprivation that marred all of France. Most noticeable always was the fact that it was a community of women, children, and old people, who watched with curiosity as the jeep passed them. A few children waved.

The old church, more properly called a cathedral, stood solidly on stone paving that matched the gray cobbled street. No shrubs softened the lines of the structure. To the rear, off a small courtyard, she spied the parish house.

A nun answered Em's knock and a few moments later led her down a dark hallway to a room where bookshelves lined the wall and a heavy desk occupied the bright space by a tall window.

Father Joseph rose from the desk and came to meet her. "Ah, Mademoiselle Em. You've come at an auspicious time. I only arrived home the day before yesterday, and I must leave again in a few days. I received a message from Hubert saying you went into Geneva with him." He glanced at the nun. "Sister Clarice, please bring us a small repast. And please bring Mademoiselle Emerson's driver into the kitchen for lunch while she and I chat."

Sister Clarice nodded, smiled, and left.

"Thank you!" Em said.

"You're welcome. It's a pleasure," Father Joseph said. "Sister Clarice and two other sisters who grew up in St. Hilary have stayed on here to keep house for me and also to help with my charities." He gestured toward an upholstered chair facing his desk. "Please be seated. We shall eat in here, because it is the only room other than the kitchen that we try to heat. The rain, it comes early this year." He glanced out the window where the steady patter had begun with renewed insistence. "Here, sit close to the little stove."

"It does feel good." She sat down and eased her wet feet closer to the grate.

"If you will excuse me, I'll just finish one little task while we wait for lunch. Then we can speak freely."

A few minutes later the sister brought hot soup and dark bread on a wheeled cart.

Father Joseph pulled his chair closer to the stove, so they faced each other across the little portable table. He bowed his head, said a brief blessing, and then served Em from the soup tureen and bread platter.

"If you please," he said, "tell me about your travels so far. Have you found the people willing to talk to you?"

"Oh yes." She told him about walking into Switzerland with Hubert and Estelle and how someone apparently had tried to kill them.

"A collaborator," he said with no hint of doubt. "Still out for blood."

"That's what Hubert thought. He went home that way to investigate, and his friend confirmed that the man was a collaborator. Andrew Blackwell said he told you about me being a courier for him. He said although you don't work for him, you could answer some of my questions."

"So you did agree to serve in his effort?"

"Yes. I agreed to do one assignment for him. I hope you can clarify my task. Andrew said you would."

"I can only tell you about this next assignment. The reason he left it to me to tell you is that he felt you would trust me more than him. I am to assure you that his work, unsavory as it may sound, has helped to shorten the war. Your first, and he hopes not your last, assignment for him will be to carry a message from me to a man in Paris."

"Well, that sounds easy enough. Is this anyone I can interview too, so my contact will look innocent and maybe even serve two purposes?"

"Yes. He is German but speaks English well. In fact, until recently he lived in England. Now he is in Paris. He will tell you his story when you interview him, but you need to know that he has volunteered to go back into Germany as a spy."

She gasped. "Am I to interview him about that?"

"No. You must not mention spying at all. I'll write you a note of introduction and explain that you want to do a human-interest feature on how Germans who fled to England felt about the war and what they did in Britain. He escaped to Britain shortly after Dunkirk and had a time persuading the English he was not a German spy. That is an interesting story of itself."

"Sounds like it. So what is Andrew's connection with this man?"

"That I can't tell you. Just give the message that I am sending. Then interview him as you would any other person, if he is agreeable."

She shook her head wonderingly. It sounded too easy. "Is this all? May I send the story to my publisher?"

"With his permission, by all means. Outwardly everything must seem that you are only writing your stories as usual."

"So I can go to Paris right away." She had expected this little adventure to take more time. "Have you heard from Vivienne? Is she back in Paris yet?"

He shook his head. "I have word from friends that she is well and safe, but she won't be going back to Paris for quite some time."

"Can you send her a message that I miss her? I can hardly wait for her to show me Paris. Remind her that she promised!"

He laughed. "I will tell her, but I can never show her that glint of determination in your eye!"

She chuckled with him. "Vivienne and I had so much fun when she was in America."

"And you will again in Paris. Believe that," he said with passion.

For the first time she saw his priestliness. She could picture him giving a challenging homily to his parishioners.

"Thanks. I will."

"Em, I think you should know you are replacing Vivienne for Andrew."

Stunned, she cried, "What do you mean?"

"Vivienne was Andrew's courier all through the Occupation. Now that she's retired, you will take her place."

"But why didn't he tell me?"

He sighed and nodded. "He saw no need for you to know. I'm not sure Andrew expected me to tell you this, but I feel you need to be very careful. I have begun to wonder the longer Vivienne remains in hiding if she was in more danger than I ever suspected. It was Andrew Blackwell who called Vivienne and sent her into hiding and then told me what he'd done."

"He is the one who called?" she repeated. "Not you?"

"Yes. Vivienne couldn't talk about Andrew's work, so she told you I called. You must not hold it against Andrew that he hasn't warned you of possible danger. He risks so much himself that he forgets how it is for others. And then, with France free again the risks are certainly less. I think he assumes you would know to be reasonably careful."

"But you think I need to be warned."

He nodded.

Em chewed her lip. She was lost in another consideration. Cummins had given no indication of knowing that Andrew was conducting dangerous espionage missions. How could he not know? And if he did, why had he not warned her?

CHAPTER FOURTEEN

Marge longed for a glimpse of sunshine. For days rain had poured and pounded without letup against the tents that formed the field hospital. Wounded men arrived wet and muddy. Nurses worked fast to get them cleaned up and warm. The sodden cold was a new hazard. Crippling trench foot brought in dozens of soldiers who had no way to keep their feet dry or warm.

At least the First Division was making progress in the battle to take Aachen. U.S. troops were on German soil and inside the revered Imperial City at last. The ambulance drivers told her that the fighting was house to house. German soldiers hid in every conceivable place. Tanks blasted holes in the buildings so the Yanks could advance block by block, but snipers lurked even in the manholes in the streets.

The Siegfried Line, Hitler's West Wall, actually surrounded the historic city. So, although the troops had breached the city's formidable fortifications on one side, a second line of bunkers, as solidly fortified as the first, awaited them on the other side of the city. When Aachen fell to the Allies it would be a severe blow to the morale of the German army, but in the meantime, the cost in lives and crippling disabilities was mounting hourly.

Despite the news that the U.S. troops had entered the city, the fighting went on and on. Each ambulance arrived carrying its maximum load. As soon as the men had necessary surgery and had been stabilized, more ambulances evacuated them. Now that trains were running, the wounded didn't have to endure a jarring ambulance ride for longer than fifty miles.

Finally on Saturday, October 21, the crashing of distant guns faded, and the arrival of newly wounded men slowed. The bloody battle for Aachen had been won. The nurses took turns sleeping around the clock.

For days after the fall of Aachen, whenever Marge closed her eyes, sleeping or awake, she saw soldiers in muddy, blood-soaked clothing lying in patient rows and sheet-draped bodies on the operating table, revealing mounds of torn flesh that looked beyond repair, and too often it was.

The tired eyes of Chief Surgeon Colville above his surgical mask, intent on his job and filled with grief and anger when he lost a patient, had been burned into her brain cells too. She wished she could have grown numb but knew that would be the first sign of an emotional breakdown.

When it was Marge's turn for twenty-four hours off duty, she thought she would never wake up if she allowed herself to really sleep. But she awoke after twelve hours. A quick bath in the makeshift shower the engineers had rigged up for the nurses refreshed her, and she found hot coffee in the mess tent.

Taking her cup to a table, she sat down. She'd eaten standing up for so many days it felt good just to sit. Staring into her cup, she paused for a thank-you prayer. She gave thanks more conscientiously each day. With her silent amen, she drew in a big breath and let it out slowly. *At least the battle for Aachen is over.* Then she pushed away all thought of battles. She had a theory that it helped a lot to pause and celebrate any victory, whenever one could. At times like this her inborn ability to concentrate on the present moment helped a lot.

She lifted her cup, inhaled the aroma, and sipped more coffee. Today she was free, like a kid let out of school. No place to go, but free for twelve more hours. Time to write letters, do some laundry, and spend some time with Isabelle. She'd make her a picture puzzle or some paper dolls. And maybe David would come, now that the hard fighting had subsided.

Whenever she'd thought about him, she'd said a prayer for him. Surely he was all right. He had to be. The ambulance drivers she'd questioned hadn't seen him. The troubling thing was, there were other field hospitals he might have been sent to if he were injured. And if he'd been killed, would she ever learn of it? *No! I won't think such a thing!*

She finished her coffee, now cooled and flat tasting, and returned to the kitchen counter for more. One of the cooks handed her a thick sandwich.

"Thanks, Max." Looking at it she recognized good beef, instead of canned pork. "Thanks a lot!"

The cook grinned. "Late breakfast." He saluted playfully and tried unsuccessfully to sound like a French chef. "Enjoy!"

Just laughing with him lightened her weariness. "Good job! Say, would you have any plain wrapping paper? I want to make paper dolls for the Babe."

"I think I can find something. Be back in a jiffy."

By the time she finished her sandwich, he had brought her several pieces of manila packing paper in one hand and a box of colored pencils in the other. He smiled shyly. "My mom sent me these pencils because I like to draw. Maybe you can use them and then give them to Isabelle to keep. I'll ask Mom for more."

"Are you sure? It will take a while for her package to get here."

"It'd make me feel no end of good if Isabelle likes them. And who knows, I may find more art supplies for myself right here in Belgium." He scrunched the cap he wore into a semblance of a French beret over one eye.

Marge laughed. "Thanks, Max. I know the Babe will love them."

With a casual salute, he said, "So back to slaving over my hot stove. See you later."

When Marge finished the paper dolls and delivered them to Isabelle, the little girl giggled, delighted. "The boy is Edouard and the girl is Anne-Marie," she said and immediately began a conversation with her dolls.

Marge stayed to show her how to make new clothes for Edouard and Anne-Marie and gave her the colored pencils. Before she left, Isabelle dictated a thank-you note for Max.

On the way to her tent, Marge delivered Isabelle's thank-you. Judging by Max's reaction, the note made his day. What a blessing that child was despite the sadness of her plight. She shouldn't even be here, but so far no one seemed to know what else to do with her.

Seated at the makeshift desk in her tent, she picked up the writing tablet. She'd been in Europe going on two months and still had not received any mail. Surely her wait would soon end.

In the meantime she continued to write as if her letters were being delivered, trusting that someday they would be. This time, she wrote first to her mother and father. That was the most difficult. She didn't want to say anything that would worry them, and she couldn't say anything about where she was. That pretty much left something like, *I'm fine, how are you?* Well, anything was better than nothing. She knew that from experience. She filled three pages, falling back on recalling happy home memories.

Then she wrote to Em. This was easier. No need to explain anything to Em, at least not much.

When she finished, she glanced at her watch. The day was still young. She went out to the mail drop. Automatically her eyes turned toward the receiving tent.

An ambulance had just pulled up and two men were getting out. When the taller one climbed out, her heart did a flip-flop. *David? Yes, it is David!*

He glanced up and, seeing her, discreetly waved.

David was safe, not even wounded! David was here! A whispered, "Thank you, Lord," escaped with her breath. Trying not to hurry, she dropped her letters into the mailbag and went to say hello.

After greeting him, she helped move the newly wounded—thankfully only three this time—into the tent, where the nurses on duty took over. Then she stepped outside to find David standing under the shelter of the awning beside the tent. He looked so tired, but his whole face brightened at the sight of her. The pleasure she felt at the sight of him startled her.

"I brought you something," he said. "Well, it's not for you. It's for you to give to Isabelle. Wait here." He hurried back to the ambulance and returned with a small bundle wrapped in a piece of army drab fabric. He handed it to her. "Open it."

She unfolded the material and uncovered the doll they'd found in the ruins of Isabelle's home. Caring hands had fashioned a dainty baby dress and bonnet out of women's lacy prewar handkerchiefs. "It's lovely! Your seamstress did a wonderful job."

He grinned. "I thought so."

"Why don't you take it to Isabelle?"

"I want you to give it to her. I saw that look on your face when we found it. You wanted to give it to her. I just figured I could save you the work of dressing it."

"Oh, David, thank you. You did the right thing. I haven't had a bit of time to sew."

"Good."

"I prayed for you." Her words came out as awkwardly as she'd feared they might, but she wanted him to know.

"Thanks. I'm glad. You look tired."

"So do you." She wanted to touch his face, to smooth away the lines of exhaustion with her touch. She made herself look away.

Focusing on the muddy ambulance, she said, "I don't suppose you'll have a day off soon. I still hope to find some trace of Isabelle's family before she is taken from here. If they send her away, her relatives may never find her."

"As a matter of fact, I'm headed for a short leave now. Thought I'd go into Liege for a few hours." He stood there smiling down at her, almost as if he wanted her to go along.

"Why that's great!" Should she invite herself? She was sure Chief Nurse Louise would let her go with him. She could use the excuse of searching again for Isabelle's family. Cradling the doll on one arm, she looked up at him, hesitant but eager. "I wonder if you would care to take me out again? I have the day off too. We might come across someone who knows Isabelle." Her proposition sounded weak, once she said it. Since no one had asked for the child by now, a further search probably would be in vain.

He straightened. "I'd much rather do that than go alone to Liege. You think you can come? Out with me alone, I mean?"

"I'll go request permission. I'll give a good reason. Be right back."

When she found Louise, she proposed another mission for finding a home for Isabelle. She was even thinking about friends of the family, since no relatives had been located.

"Dr. Colville said a Red Cross woman would come by and do what she could," Louise said. "She'll probably take Isabelle to an orphanage."

"Surely the Babe won't be well enough for a while. I really hate to see her go to an institution."

Louise frowned. "Me too. But with the war going on, that's the best anybody can do. There are quite a few civilian casualties in Aachen. They're being cared for in the hospital there. If we have to move the field hospital, as I'm sure we will any day now, Isabelle may have to go there. About this jaunt you want to take with the medic, it's okay with me. I'll give an official reason to Dr. Colville."

Caught off guard by Louise's frankness, Marge stammered, "I really meant it to be an official reason!"

"Okay. But if it's not, just play the protocol game. I don't want you to get caught, and I don't want to be on the carpet for letting you fraternize with a noncom." Despite her stern words, Louise was smiling.

Marge grinned back. "Thanks. Really this is not a date or anything, but I do like him. I'll be careful."

Louise shook her head in sympathy. "Girl, you are a goner already."

Marge formed the word no, but it never came out. No point in arguing. "I'll be back in time to work tonight if I'm needed." She held out the baby doll. "Look what he did for Isabelle. We found this where her house had been, and he cleaned it up and had it dressed for me to give to her."

Louise touched the dress. "What a nice thing to do."

Marge couldn't stop smiling. "I'll take it to her right away."

Inside the ward tent, she hurried to Isabelle's bed. Before she could say anything, Isabelle saw the doll in her hand. Her eyes widened. "Marie!"

Marge placed the doll in her outstretched hands. "We found her, and Sergeant David had a friend make her a new dress."

"Did you see my maman or my père?"

Her question caught Marge unprepared. "I—no, we didn't see any of your family. We found Marie waiting for you where you used to play." How could she explain that the family home was gone?

Isabelle was so glad to have her doll, she asked no more questions. She began to talk to the doll in French.

Marge squeezed her arm and said, "I have to go now. You have fun with Marie, and I'll be by later."

"Oui! Merci! Thank you, Nurse Marge. Thank you."

Marge ran to her tent to grab her oilskin poncho, and then ran to the waiting ambulance.

David was sitting inside behind the wheel. He leaned across, an easy reach for him, and threw the door open for her. "I'd get out to let you in, but I thought I'd better stay out of sight so as not to rouse questions."

She laughed. "Sure. I'm driving this thing myself!"

He laughed as he put the muddy vehicle in gear and slithered out to the main road. "Did you give the doll to Isabelle?"

"Yes. I couldn't leave without delivering it. It is her doll. She's in seventh heaven talking to her Marie in French. I'm so glad we found it, and that you had it dressed so nicely."

He grinned. "What good fortune we had that day." When they reached the paved road, he turned away from the battlefront. "Do you have any inspirations about where to search today for Isabelle's family?"

She turned sideways to face him. How honest should she be? She only wanted to be with him, anywhere. He glanced at her, one eyebrow raised, a gentle half-smile brightening his tired face. She blurted, "David, I lied just to get to spend some time with you."

He slowed the ambulance and pulled to a stop on the edge of the road. With the engine still running and windshield wipers slapping, he faced her. "I'm right proud that you should want to be with me," he said softly. "I didn't exactly dare hope that might be the case." He threw back his head, laughed, and faked a punch against the rainy roof of the ambulance. "Who would ever have thought today could be so bright without the sun! Where would you like to go, Margaret?"

She laughed with him. "You choose! I don't know anything about anywhere."

"Well, we sure can't go to Aachen to forget the war. It is so battered, that would be no vacation. Let me think. . . . There's a small town west of here about fifteen miles that hasn't been damaged much. There's more than one church and a lot of shops. Maybe something is open for business there."

"Let's go see!" She felt as if she were embarking on a treasure hunt. At last she would get to know David better, no matter where they went.

The town, when they reached it, was picturesque, filled with many quaint stone homes and small shops. As she had hoped, many shops were open to serve the residents, despite the fact they had little to sell.

David parked the ambulance on the main street. She struggled into her poncho before stepping out in the rain. He hadn't bothered to put his on, so they walked fast from sheltered doorway to doorway. When they came to puddles in the cobblestone sidewalks he slipped his arm through hers and lifted her up and over with a swinging motion. She quickly learned to lean on him and leap. With each landing on the other side, they laughed like kids.

Unfortunately, they found no public eating establishment. At the bakery, however, there was still some of the day's fresh baked bread. "Let's go in," she suggested.

He opened the door and followed her inside. The small shop, warmed by the ovens, smelled of good bread. David took charge of the purchase, conversing in hesitant French. The man gestured as if asking a question. David answered in the negative. That much she understood. Then to her surprise David took a long loaf of bread, unwrapped, and handed it to her. "Since we have no shopping bag, you can put it under your poncho to keep it dry."

He paid the baker, and they hurried back toward the parked ambulance.

Marge hugged the loaf. It was still warm. At the ambulance David opened the door and gave her a lift inside. It was basically a truck, when it came to getting in or out.

The rain was still steady but lighter. When he was settled in the driver's seat, he said, "I'll light a can of Sterno and heat water for coffee, and we have K rations too. Shall we dine?"

"Right here?"

"Why not? We're not going to stop traffic, because there is none. We can sit on the benches in the back. Are you game?"

"Okay. I'm sure hungry, and this bread smells like the real thing." She had heard of bread being part sawdust during the Occupation.

"It is. The baker had hidden his last store of flour when the battle approached. He says they prayed for protection, and God saved their town. I agreed it sure looks that way. They sustained no damage. The Germans rushed past, and then the Allies." While he talked, he lit a kerosene lantern and the canned candle for heating water. Over the flame he set a small aluminum pan and filled it with water from his canteen. In minutes they had hot coffee.

Breaking a chunk of the crusty loaf of bread, he said, "We owe the Lord a big thank you for today." Without a pause, he bowed his head and said, "Thank you for this good bread. This is great! Thank you."

Marge barely had closed her eyes before he was done. A tingling delight passed through her. This man was so natural, so surprising . . . and loveable. Why had she been put off by the way he talked about God? For him it was right.

As they ate in the back of the ambulance, the hot coffee and bread and K rations erased the outdoor chill and gloom. Marge told David about how she'd grown up on the ranch and finally decided to become a nurse.

And he told her about the rolling hills of Pennsylvania and his father's farm. "I have three sisters and two brothers. I'm the only one who didn't want to take up a gun in this war. My brothers are in the navy. My sisters are married to servicemen."

This surprised her. She'd supposed his family all felt the same way as he. "Then you mean they're not Quakers?"

He sobered. "No. They don't believe as I do." Even in the dim light she could see the flash of sorrow. His look tore at the brightness of their time together. Gently she asked, "Did they give you a hard time about your pacifism?"

"One of my brothers did, as did my sisters' husbands, until they learned more about what I'm doing as a medic. Now they all accept my independent ways." He chuckled. "One of these days, I pray they'll accept the Lord too."

Then he sat staring at her. Maybe he was thinking and was unaware that he was staring. She started to speak, to break the silence for her own comfort, but he spoke first. "Margaret, do you have a boyfriend, someone you plan to marry?"

She shook her head. "No. I've always planned to become a doctor. Maybe ranch life made me too independent for marriage."

He gave her a sideways glance. "Too independent? I think not. When I think of marriage, I think of working together. But there are things a man likes to do for a woman, helping her and protecting her."

His words touched off an incredible longing inside her. She wanted that kind of caring! Her intense reaction so shocked her, she mentally fled from her feelings. To break the spell he'd cast, she teased, "Like when you nearly crushed me a couple of weeks ago when the Germans shot at us?"

He grinned. "I did overdo it that time, didn't I? Sorry. Did I hurt you?" The last he said seriously.

"No. I knew you were looking after me."

"Well, I forgot how small you are. I flopped on you like I would to protect my buddies. . . ." From his low seat facing her, he leaned closer. "Has anyone ever told you how beautiful you are?"

This was getting out of hand. Marge tried to come up with a smart remark and couldn't. "I don't think so."

"Well, they have now. You are the most beautiful woman I have ever met."

"I—well, thank you." She could hardly think of herself in this way. She'd always felt plain.

"May I just once kiss you?"

"David . . ." she meant to straighten and increase the distance between them, but she could only gaze at his rugged, beautiful face as he moved closer.

Then without a word, she leaned forward. His kiss was gentle, searching, passionate, and honorable all at the same time. *Oh, dear God,* she found herself praying, *what is happening to me?*

He pulled back and touched the tip of her nose with his forefinger. "Thank you," he whispered. Then in a normal tone he said, "Now I'd best be taking you back to the hospital." He put out the lantern and went forward to the driver's seat.

By the time she settled on her own side of the ambulance, he had the engine going. Before putting the vehicle in gear, he said, "I know now is not the time, but someday, Margaret, I'd like to ask you to marry me."

Her mouth fell open, and she turned to him.

He was facing her, not the road. He set the brake and switched off the ignition and said, "I know it's presumptuous for me to warn you that I want to ask in the future, but I wanted you to know I have honorable intentions. And if you find someone else by the time we get this war done, I'll never bring it up. I just wanted you to know . . . how I feel."

Breathless over this unexpected revelation, she said, "How *do* you feel?"

"I feel like maybe I've died and gone to heaven when I'm with you. Margaret, I dearly and truly love you. And I will for all eternity."

"David!" She felt near tears. If it weren't for the war, maybe—no, they were too different. She would hurt him too much in the end. She should never have invited his interest. Desperate to protect him, she said, "Don't say things like this! We can't. We're too different. We hardly know each other."

He reached over and took her hand. "Don't be afraid of love, Margaret. It's a gift from God." He squeezed her fingers, then released them and turned on the ignition again.

He drove in silence. For Marge it was a very heavy silence. Her emotions pulled her toward this man, but her reason said *no, never*. She had not followed her feelings for a long, long time. She didn't trust them.

Suddenly he turned off the paved road. They had reached the lane to the field hospital. He pulled up by the mess tent and parked. She didn't want to leave him, and at the same time, she couldn't get away fast enough. "David, I'm honored that you love me, and I'm ashamed that I'm afraid to love you. No, I'm not saying this right. I do love you. I'm ashamed that I can't offer you any hope, and I'm ashamed that I pursued you the way I did. I did lead you on. I was thinking only of myself."

He caught her hand again. "Don't you ever be ashamed or think you played games with me. I knew the first minute I saw you that I loved you. Why else do you think I've showed up here whenever I got a few hours' leave? This time my buddy told me you had a day's leave and traded days with me. We've had six wonderful hours, Margaret, a gift from God. Now you better get out before someone wonders about us."

She sat for a moment, half dazed, longing to kiss him good-night, and at the same time wanting to run and hide. *I'm feeling and acting like a kid!*

The wind blew a gust of rain into the open ambulance door. She quickly climbed out and waved him good-bye. *For the good of both of us, I should try never to see him alone again.*

But she did see him. The very next day he was in the mess tent having coffee when she entered at midmorning. He strolled over when she sat down with her coffee and a doughnut.

He saluted. "Good morning, ma'am."

She returned his salute. "Good morning, Sergeant Lewellyn." She didn't ask him to sit, but she couldn't take her eyes from his face. Just looking at him filled her with pleasure.

"I came from Aachen. We're to take some of your trench-foot patients to the hospital there. Dr. Colville says it will help to get them into a dry building."

She had to think of something to say to keep him here and not give the wrong impression. "Does the hospital have good heat now?"

"It's not bad after what they've been through." He shook his head sadly. "I wish I could have seen that city before the war. It must have been beautiful. Now it's a mess. Fortunately a lot of the people got out before the siege. They say the population used to be a hundred thousand."

"But now at last our men are inside Germany."

"Yes, and it'll be all uphill from here on." His ragged tone made her flinch. His sorrow became hers.

Without meeting her eyes, he said, "Old men and children—that's who we fought in Aachen. Oh, there were some regular army men, strong and well trained, but they were in the minority. Most of the wounded Germans were boys as young as fifteen and gray-haired grandfathers who should have been home by their firesides."

"That's sad, but doesn't this mean we'll defeat Hitler faster than if he still had thousands of crack troops?"

David's eyebrows came together in a rare frown of anger. "I suppose it does, but the price makes me sick."

She never had seen him angry, and she didn't know what to say.

He straightened. "Got to go, ma'am. Thanks for your prayers."

"You're welcome. Bye."

He paused a few feet away and looked back. For a minute she thought he was going to salute and be formal. A smile gentled his face again. "Good-bye, Nurse Margaret," he said softly. "You take care now." Then he beckoned to his partner, and they left together.

Marge gulped her coffee and headed for her tent, fighting tears all the way. The war was painful enough without being in love with a medic.

CHAPTER FIFTEEN

From Epinal, Em called Cummins and left a message saying that she, Elena, was on her way to Paris. The train stopped a lot, but she arrived at Hotel Scribe in the evening before suppertime. When she checked in at the lobby desk, the clerk handed her mail from home and an envelope with only her name on it.

In her room she dropped her bag by the bed and set her typewriter on her desk. She opened the note first. A single sentence stared up at her. *Call as soon as you arrive. BC.*

As if I wouldn't, she thought. He had some explaining to do if he had known that running errands for Andrew Blackwell could endanger her as it had endangered Vivienne. She plopped onto the edge of her bed to make the call. Hoping he would be in his office this late in the day, she gave the hotel operator Cummins' phone number.

He answered.

"This is Elena," she said.

"I'm glad you're back."

"I need to talk to you," she said.

He cleared his throat. "I'm the one who gives the orders."

"Well, I have a problem, and I need to know what I've gotten into."

"Go to Le Chapeau Neuf, a small hat shop a block south of the hotel. Be outside by the door. I'll have my driver pick you up in thirty minutes."

"All right." At least he wasn't putting her off until tomorrow.

She left her unpacking for later and refreshed her face and hair. Thirty minutes later, she was window-shopping at the hat shop. When a car paused by the curb, she easily recognized Cummins' driver.

Besides, there weren't that many civilian autos in Paris. She hurried over and let herself in the rear door, and he drove off without having to park. Then he drove, and he drove.

Finally she called, "Are we leaving the city?"

"Yes, ma'am."

"Where are we going?"

"To a chateau outside of Gennevilliers."

She leaned back. Might as well relax. He also was obviously taking the long way. She'd seen two different views of the Eiffel Tower so far.

The chateau, when they arrived, looked more like a museum or palace than a home. The driver let her off at a side door. She didn't even have to knock. A woman in a WAAC uniform opened the door. She must have been watching for her. "Miss Emerson? I will show you to the study."

As Em followed her down the dark palatial hallway, she saw more military personnel moving about at the other end. Her escort didn't take her that far. "In here, please," she said, holding a door open for her to enter.

The room had once been a library and was still lined with books, but now army desks and file cabinets filled the space. Each desk had a phone. Only one person was there. Brad Cummins stood up from a desk at the far side. "Come have a chair, Em. We'll be a while. Private Nelson, would you bring us some coffee?"

"Yes, sir," the WAAC said and left.

After she left, Em asked, "Are you an army officer?" He wasn't in uniform.

"To her, I am."

"Do you live here?"

"I have a room here. I also have a hotel room in Paris."

"Am I supposed to call you sir?"

He laughed. "No. Because of our irregular activities, you must not do so in public, and I don't wish it here."

That made sense. "I see," she said and settled into her chair.

Before she could get to her questions, he said, "I know you have questions, but I think if I tell you first what I have to say, that may take care of your concerns."

"All right."

The WAAC came back with hot coffee and left again. Em gratefully sipped hers. She needed a lift right now.

Cummins left his cup sitting to cool and said, "You have just completed a test that Colonel Jennings requires of recruits hired in the field."

"A test! Am I only in training then?"

"Not exactly. You did deliver an authentic message to Hubert Espe, which he then turned over to his contact. You also delivered another important message to Father Joseph Dupre."

"You mean"—she nearly choked on half-swallowed coffee—"that Father Joseph and Andrew Blackwell are in the OSS?"

"Not exactly. Let me get to that later. Back to the test. We had to know you could hold your tongue, deceive an intelligent observer like Andrew Blackwell, and not act on your own without consulting me. I'm glad you passed the tests."

"So you didn't trust me after all."

"Trust must be earned. Let's say we were willing to place our bets on you."

"I don't think I like that."

"But you're more intrigued than ever by the work."

She glared at him. She hated for people to assume they could read her mind, but Cummins did understand her inclinations. "You're right," she conceded with irritation.

"Let me tell you what you've already accomplished for us. I told you that Nazi spies remain in France. We know who most of them are, and we're glad they stay in Allied territory where we can watch them and use them. You have already interviewed one double agent. You know him as Jacques Marchant. I sent you to him because we had to confirm that Marchant had not changed his residence. We also hoped you might find out a few details from him and his daughter that would assist us. Your first assignment revealed several facts we found useful."

Stunned, Em leaned back. "But Jacques lost his legs for France. Why would he turn against his country in this war?"

"Because he was born into a French family of German descent. The trench warfare embittered him. He became an ardent socialist, convinced that Hitler has the answer for peace in Europe. From the beginning of the Occupation he worked as a double agent. He did so well that the Germans left him here to continue to report straight to Berlin on everything he can observe in Paris. His daughter learns many details from unsuspecting soldiers she meets at the canteens and cafés."

"Jeanette is a double agent too?"

"She could hardly live with him without knowing his passion for the Third Reich."

Em did not want to believe this, but she remembered the covert look that had passed between father and daughter just before she'd left with Jeanette. "If you know his duplicity, why don't you stop dealing with him?"

"He's more valuable to us if he trusts us." Cummins rose from his desk, went to his office window, and seemed to have forgotten she was there.

She wasn't done yet. "But Jeanette saved my life!"

"My agent told me that was a setup to demonstrate their loyalty to the Allied cause and to make sure you wrote favorably about them. Your life never was in danger."

"How could your agent know this?"

"He was the man who accosted Jeanette. While the other one forced you into the building, he simply left the scene."

"The man who grabbed me injured me and would have done more. I saw it in his eyes."

"He might have gotten out of hand, but more likely he had orders to make the attack convincing. When you came to the Marchant's door asking for an interview, they must have decided an American journalist on their side could prove valuable. They intended to charm and disarm you. I'm very sorry you were hurt. I did not expect them to behave so radically.

"Another thing," he said, "my agent is still trying to win their complete confidence and didn't know at the time that they had learned about Vivienne's work for Blackwell. Assisting in the effort to frighten you was only the second time they had trusted anything of him. He thinks he satisfied them.

"But you," he said almost accusingly, "you handed them an unexpected plum when you showed Jeanette where Vivienne lives. Fortunately for Vivienne, Andrew had once shown her photos of Jacques and Jeanette and told her not to trust them. So when she saw Jeanette out in front of her apartment the very next day, she called me."

"She called you!" Em grappled with the impossible coincidence that her friend knew Brad Cummins.

"Vivienne works for me as well as for Andrew. But her brother Joseph, of course, doesn't know this. She and I agreed she must call Andrew, whom Joseph does know, and have him tell Joseph that she was being stalked and needed to go into hiding."

Em hoped she didn't look as shocked as she felt. "Apparently being a good liar is a prerequisite to success in your business."

"Precisely. As I told you in the beginning, working in the OSS means you don't reveal anything to anyone. I would not have told you about Vivienne's work for the OSS, but I need your help with the Marchants. Now that they know you are Vivienne's friend, they may contact you."

"Were they planning to kill Vivienne?" Em asked. Cummins' continuing revelations were beginning to daze her.

"No, I don't think so. But they could have given her away to men who would kill her for the sake of what she knows. My agent says that Marchants only gather information. They report regularly to agents in Germany. If you met them, at most they would want to find out whether you knew where Vivienne went."

"Good thing I don't know."

"Yes. They must never suspect that you know me or that you are in touch with me. They know the press corps stays at Hotel Scribe, so they know where to find you. From now on, don't ever leave there without making certain no one is following you. Don't ever telephone me without making certain no one nearby is listening." Cummins stood up and went to the window, as if to give her time to digest the matter.

She needed time all right. That Vivienne worked for the OSS was a surprise, but somehow not as much of a shock as the news about Jacques Marchant and Jeanette. While Cummins stared out the window, she tried to make sense of the Marchants' defection to the Nazis. They had seemed genuinely patriotic to France. *It could not have been all an act. They must believe that Nazi socialism is what France needs.* Finally she let go of the enigma and called to Cummins' back, "Why do you leave the Marchants free if you think they have orders to track down Vivienne?"

He swung around and faced her. "It serves our purpose for the time being to let them think we know nothing about this. Watching them gives us information we need. We'll bring them in at the proper time." He returned to his desk and sat down. "Have I answered any of the questions you wanted to ask?"

"Yes. I wanted to know whether you knew that Vivienne was in danger when she worked for Andrew Blackwell. I was upset that you let me go ahead without warning me."

He peered at her through his thick glasses and sighed. "You are in danger working for us, just as Vivienne is, but not more so from working for Andrew. We need you to cooperate with Blackwell and to keep an eye on him. That's what Vivienne did."

"If you wanted me to do that, why didn't you tell me?"

"You had to make a natural, innocent contact. You had to appeal to him as someone whose presence would enhance his parties and who also could do the work Vivienne had done. We didn't want you to have to act a part on this one."

She gave that a moment of thought. Okay, so they didn't know how well she could act. Neither did she. She moved on to her next question. "Hubert says Andrew has turned over several of the German's top secrets to the Allies. Why don't you trust him?"

"He's a man of many sides. His patriotism may be self-serving. His business has grown to international proportions since the war began, with many connections in South America where the Nazis also are setting up bank accounts. He has developed close connections with some German industrialists whom he entertains in his home. Even though he delivers the goods, we cannot trust anyone without reservation. Spying is an ugly business, Em Emerson. Do you want out now?"

She chose not to answer that one yet. "So is Andrew a double agent?"

"He's a high-powered American businessman who tries to serve his country by maintaining close ties with longtime friends who are German. That's a risky position, with many temptations for a man who loves power as much as he does."

She pondered this for a moment. "You're saying you don't trust him. Why did you trust me in the beginning, before I earned your trust?"

"You are a less convoluted person than Andrew Blackwell. Your record of honesty has shown in your writing. So has your dedication to your country."

At this she laughed. "Less convoluted? Are you telling me you can trust me because I'm too simpleminded to cheat?"

He smiled and looked very likeable for a second. "Not quite. Your life may depend on how devious you can be. I think you will make the right decisions, or I never would have enlisted your help. Now school is over, and we're in business. That is, unless you've changed your mind and want out."

"We're in business. Give me my next assignment."

"Okay. Go ahead and interview Father Joseph's German friend. I'm as interested in him as Blackwell is."

"I'll try to see him tomorrow."

"When you finish the interview, call me." He reached for a button on his desk and pushed it. "And now that you know about the Marchants, keep an eye out for them. Let me know if they approach you for any reason. You are now part of our surveillance crew."

Em wanted to shake her head in doubt. She hadn't seen any hint of the Marchants since she'd interviewed them. Nevertheless, she nodded in agreement. "Okay. I'll be watching."

The WAAC who had escorted her in appeared almost as if Cummins had rubbed a lamp for a genie. She walked Em to the door, where the car, engine running, was waiting to return her to Hotel Scribe.

She was in her room, removing her coat when her eyes fell on the interview notes she made on the Marchant interview. She really didn't want such a misleading story to be published under her name. And yet she couldn't wire her editor at *USA Living & Review* and ask him to kill the story without giving a good reason. Maybe her next interview would provide something good enough to crowd out the Marchant story. There was a slim chance if she sent it right away.

The interview with Hermann Doenitz went well and supplied a viable story for Em's editor. When she finished, she reported to Cummins and got the debriefing over in a couple of hours. Then he ordered her back to Geneva with a message for Andrew.

Back at the hotel she wrote her article quickly, went over it, and by bedtime had it ready to send to London.

She still had not seen Bob or anyone who knew where he was. As she had feared, her OSS work promised to keep them apart more than ever. Before going to bed, she wrote him a note explaining her absence with a series of believable lies. Then she ran downstairs, dropped her article in the courier bag to London, and left his note at the hotel desk.

The next day, remembering Cummins' warning about the Marchants, Em tried to have eyes in the back of her head from the moment she left the hotel until she boarded the train. She never caught a glimpse of any attention from anyone. *So much for being followed,* she mused.

Once out of Paris, she began to think about her previous journey into Switzerland, the walk over the border with Hubert and Estelle, and the traitor who had shot at them. Hubert had lived on the edge of death for such a long time. No wonder he despised collaborators and double agents.

She wondered about Hermann Doenitz, whom she had just interviewed. He'd been born in Germany and had volunteered to spy for the Allies. Could he be a double agent too? Was this the reason Cummins had asked her to interview him? The man who had debriefed her had given her no clue.

She hated suspecting everyone now, but she'd been totally fooled by Marchant and Jeanette. It looked as if suspicion went with her OSS job.

When Em reached Geneva, she went straight to the hotel and telephoned Andrew Blackwell at his office. Since it was late in the day, he said he'd come by and take her to his chateau for dinner. "I have other guests I'd like you to meet. Did you bring a dress uniform?"

"Yes."

"Good. That will be suitable." Without further explanation he said, "I'll come by for you. We can talk on the way. Be downstairs at the door at six-thirty."

"I'll be there."

He rang off. She hung up and went to the window to check the weather. It was still raining.

Nevertheless, she visited a couple of fancy department stores, and then took a short nap before doing her nails and hair.

Andrew picked her up at exactly six-thirty. After greeting her and ordering the driver to go on, he said, "Did Father Joseph clarify what I hope you will do for me?"

"He explained that you obtain useful information for the Allies, and that you need someone to take his sister Vivienne's place as your courier."

"Yes. You did very well delivering my message to him, and he has passed it on to the right party. He only did so this once because, as you know, Vivienne must stay in hiding for a while. I'm encouraged by the fact that you returned to report. I was afraid that after hearing about the danger to Vivienne, you might not want to work for me." He paused, obviously wanting her agreement or denial.

"I'm willing to be your courier as long as it does not jeopardize my work as a war correspondent."

"Good! I can assure you I will be careful that it does not." He leaned back on the leather seat of the sedan. "I do hope you can frequent my home, as some of my other close friends do. And as Vivienne did. It will be important to keep up a front of friendship. I'll introduce you as the daughter of an old college friend in America. Can you handle that?"

She smiled. "You'd better tell me about this friend in case someone asks."

"We both graduated from Columbia University in New York. What does your real father do?"

She laughed. "He's a dirt poor rancher in Oklahoma."

He smiled. "All right. My friend gave up business to follow his dream and become a rancher in Oklahoma. I lost touch with him, and now you have looked me up at his request. Whatever you tell me about your real father will be about my old friend. Sound feasible?"

"Yes. Very easy and clever."

"Then I think we are set for tonight."

When they reached Château Bleu and he escorted her into his gracious salon, Em instantly felt out of place. All the women present were wearing formal gowns. She felt as if she had stepped onto another planet, one that hadn't seen war for ages.

Lydia Blackwell, in a slimline gray chiffon gown, glided to her side and squeezed her hand. "Em, I was so pleased when Andrew called and said you were in the city. This is one of his typical business associates parties, but some of our dearest friends are here too. I want them to meet you."

Andrew laughed. "All right, dear. You may have her first, but only for a while. I have some people I want her to meet too."

Lydia raised her neatly plucked eyebrows. "Thank you, husband dear. You and your cronies can have her later. Please come along, Em."

Lydia led her from one couple to another. Em remembered as many names and faces as she could but finally decided she was out of her depth and gave up. One couple remained memorable, not only because they were siblings instead of a married couple, but also because they told her about their parents and brothers who lived in Germany. They'd been in universities in England and France when war broke out and had decided not to return to Germany. Now they worked for a Swiss manufacturer of textiles, she in design and he in sales.

Em found she had many likes and dislikes in common with them. They laughed over their similarities and asked if she had any German ancestors. "Yes," she said, "a lot of us in America do. Maybe we're distant cousins."

Andrew appeared at her elbow. "Excuse me, Gunther and Elsa. I want to steal our American presswoman for just a few minutes to meet another journalist."

He led Em across the room to a tall blond man with a straight Nordic nose and regular features. "Werner, my friend, I'd like you to meet Em Emerson, an American war correspondent. Em, meet your counterpart, Herr Werner Koch. Werner is a German war correspondent."

Em supposed she must have visibly gulped. This was the last thing she expected, to meet a German pressman. She nodded formally. "How do you do, Herr Koch?"

He bowed just as formally, in what she'd come to think of as a typically Prussian acknowledgment. She almost expected him to click his heels, but instead, he smiled and said in a friendly tone, "Miss Emerson, a pleasure to meet you."

Believing forthrightness covered a multitude of social inadequacies, she said simply, "Thank you."

His mouth turned up at the corners in a wry smile. "I think we may find much in common to talk about."

"Perhaps we may." She had no idea what to expect from Hitler's press and wondered what he was doing in Geneva.

As if guessing her thoughts, he said, "My family owns a textile factory. That business brings me to Geneva. The Fuehrer has been gracious about letting me manage the business, as well as serve him as a correspondent."

"Really." Was he here to spy? Was he one of Andrew's useful German contacts?

They chatted at length about writing and about his wife and children, but as far as Em could tell she never learned anything of use to the OSS. Neither did Andrew question her later about her conversation with Herr Koch, so he must have been simply playing the thoughtful host when he introduced them.

Em was surprised to find that Herr Koch's remarks about freedom of the press kept nagging at her. When she had asked him how he could feel like a reporter when he had to report only what the Fuehrer allowed, he'd pointed out that no journalist has any more freedom than his editors and publishers permit. She thought, however, that she detected a certain wistfulness in his pronouncement, and she found herself hoping she'd meet him again at one of Andrew's soirées.

Chapter Sixteen

Marge left surgery after ten hours of assisting Dr. Colville and headed for her tent. The rain had stopped, and early dawn revealed a sky full of charcoal clouds. She pulled her coat close. The breeze carried the prophecy of early winter. She could hardly wait to shower and go to bed. A few hours of sleep, and she'd be ready to go again.

Stepping inside her tent, she tiptoed so as not to awaken the women who were still sleeping, but Amelia raised her head anyway.

"Sorry," Marge whispered.

"I was awake already," Amelia whispered back. "Wanted to talk to you."

"Okay. Meet me in the mess tent in ten minutes."

Marge swiftly gathered her towel and clean clothes under one arm and, with her soap and shampoo in her other hand, slipped out to the shower tent.

She turned on the water, praying the orderlies had lighted the little water heater in anticipation of morning. It was cold. She undressed and dodged under the low-pressure stream, spun around to get wet, turned off the water, soaped, and then rinsed in microseconds, quickly towel drying to warm her skin. Once she put on her clean fatigues, she began to stop shivering.

In the mess tent Amelia sat at a table with steaming coffee, pancakes, and what the cooks called scrambled eggs—the best they could do with powdered eggs. All the other tables were empty.

Marge picked up her own tray of food and joined her. She sipped the black coffee, found it too hot, and said, "So what's on your mind, girl?"

"Last night after you went to surgery, Louise informed me that Isabelle will be sent to the Aachen hospital today. I packed the few things she's accumulated, but she was already asleep, so I couldn't talk to her. I thought you'd like to go be with her since you're closer to her than I am."

Marge nodded. "Sure. Thanks for telling me. I . . . really hate to see her go." In fact, she had dreaded this day. The ache in her chest at the thought of maybe never seeing Isabelle again made it hard to breathe. "I always knew she would have to go, but she's so little to be alone!" She cleared her throat. "It wouldn't be so bad if some of her family would show up." She stopped, swallowing hard.

"Would you rather have me go and see her off?" Amelia asked. "I just thought you'd be best for her. She talks about you more than any of the others—and Sergeant Lewellyn, of course. He has popped in to see her every time he could. Maybe he will be able to do that in Aachen too."

David—his name twisted Marge's heart into a new knot. She'd missed many of his brief visits with Isabelle because he'd come when she was in surgery. "I'm sure David will visit her if he can." She'd often wondered how he could stay so tenderhearted when he had to endure so much violence and pain on the battlefield. Usually a person had to toughen to survive.

For herself, Marge had begun to feel that strength might come from not caring too much. Somehow she had to learn to carry on without having her insides ripped up by each new casualty. Right now the thought of sending Isabelle away to an unknown future was an agony almost as bad as when she'd watched Millie die. And try as she might to avoid negative thoughts, she lived in continual dread that David would be wounded or killed. She wished she could turn off her feelings.

Amelia was saying, "Will you excuse me, Marge? I need to go and relieve Dorothy in the triage tent."

"Yes . . . sure. I'll eat quickly and be off to help Isabelle."

Amelia stood up and squeezed her shoulder. "Give my love to the Babe, and if I can, I'll run in before she leaves."

"Sure." Marge cleared her throat and said firmly, "She'll be okay. She's a courageous little girl."

Amelia nodded. "Yes, for sure." Then she hurried away.

Marge finished her coffee and pancakes, then headed for Isabelle's bedside.

She dreaded the task. She simply could not stay objective, yet she must keep her distress to herself. Isabelle needed a hopeful, cheerful send-off.

She found the Babe still asleep, looking cherubic in her halo of short dark hair. Although they'd had to cut it almost as short as a boy's, no one would mistake her for one. Her left leg still hung in traction. Marge sat on the stool close to the head of her bed, hating to awaken her. *Dear Lord, watch over this little lamb. Please don't let her be frightened. Help me to find the right words to keep her brave.* If David were here, he'd know better what to say. *Please help me . . . to help her.*

Louise came down the aisle and halted at the foot of Isabelle's bed. "Better wake her now, so she'll have time to eat," she whispered.

"Yes, ma'am."

"You all right? You want me to get someone else to prepare her?"

"No! I'm fine," Marge whispered.

"Okay," Louise walked on through the ward.

Marge stood up. "Isabelle," she called softly.

The child stirred and opened her eyes. As soon as she saw Marge she smiled.

"Good morning," Marge said, stretching her own lips into a cheerful smile.

"Good morning."

"It's time to wake up." Marge picked up the washing basin. "I'll get warm water. Be back in a minute."

"A minute," Isabelle repeated, holding up her forefinger and shaking it like the proverbial schoolmarm.

Marge laughed. "Yes. I promise." *What a little sweetie,* she thought for the millionth time. Hurrying to the heated water tanks, she drew enough water for bathing Isabelle. She flung a couple of towels over her arm and went back to the child's bedside.

She made quick work of the bath while Isabelle chattered in fractured English. Then she dressed Isabelle in a clean GI T-shirt, cut down to her size. "Today is an important day. You get to go to a real hospital with plastered walls and glass windows. And soon you will get up out of bed and walk again. Won't that be nice?"

"Is everyone going to the real hospital?"

"Everyone? You mean the soldiers? Yes, but they must go to different hospitals."

"Will you come, and Nurse Amelia?"

Marge tucked the covers up over the small chest and smoothed her hair. "We have to stay here to take care of more soldiers. You will have new nurses to help you."

"I don't want new ones. I want you and Nurse Amelia and Sergeant David."

Marge sat down on the side of her bed and held her hand. "Sweetheart, we can't go with you, but your new nurses will take very good care of you. You will get well faster in a real hospital. Some nice ladies will try to find your mama and papa. Here we have so many soldiers to take care of that we can't go out to look for your family."

Those wide gray eyes seemed to probe Marge's soul. *God, this is so hard!* She willed herself to smile calmly. "It will be good. You'll see," she assured the child.

"I want to find Mama and Papa," Isabelle said. "How soon can I go?"

"After breakfast."

"Will you go with me . . . for a while?"

Marge shook her head and fought the constriction that grabbed her throat. "I'm sorry. I can't go. None of us can go with you, but you will not be alone. You'll have a soldier nurse in the ambulance and then nurses like me when you get to the hospital. Remember how Sergeant Lewellyn said God is always with you, and you can talk to our Father God and ask Him for help?"

Isabelle nodded. "He said talking to God is praying."

"Yes. And God loves us and answers our prayers. I'll be praying for you, and so will Nurse Amelia and Sergeant David. We'll pray for God to keep you safe and make you well very soon."

Isabelle nodded. "Sergeant David asked me to pray for him, and I do. God is taking care of him."

"I pray for Sergeant David too, and I've been praying for you," Marge said.

"Can I take my dollies and my colored pencils?"

"Yes, you certainly may. I'll pack them for you."

"Marie must go beside me, so she won't be afraid."

Marge picked up the baby doll that David had mended and dressed and tucked it in beside Isabelle. "She will stay right with you. Now I'm going to bring you breakfast."

By the time Isabelle finished her oatmeal, orderlies appeared with a stretcher. Amelia was with them, and beside Amelia stood David.

"Nurse Amelia, Sergeant David!" Isabelle cried. "I'm going to a real hospital."

"Sergeant David heard you were taking this trip today so he arranged to ride with you," Amelia said. "Isn't that nice?"

"Oh yes! Look! My Marie is going with me." She held up the baby doll.

David stepped forward. "I brought a new quilt for your Marie. Here, you can wrap her to keep her warm." He held out a quilt made of squares of bright fabric.

Isabelle cried, "Oh, so pretty!" and wrapped the doll.

Marge pushed down her tears again. "Wherever did you find that?"

"Same lady who made the dress. She's been working on it ever since and just finished it in time for this trip to the hospital today."

"Wonderful," Amelia said. "Well, look, I have to get back to work." She bent and kissed Isabelle. "Good-bye, Babe. You keep that smile. Before you know it, you will be up and walking." She backed away, waving.

Isabelle waved back, hugging her doll in its new quilt.

Marge's spirits lifted at seeing the child so happy. She looked up at David. "She will be all right, won't she?" she whispered.

"You bet!" he whispered back. He smiled down at her until her cheeks grew warm. "And so will you, Margaret. Everything will be okay." To Isabelle he said, "How's the Babe today?"

Isabelle giggled. "I am not a baby!"

"I know. I just like to make you laugh," he said. He kept her giggling while telling her about her ride in the ambulance.

The orderlies stepped forward and moved Isabelle to a stretcher.

Marge said good-bye to Isabelle after she was snug and kissed her cheek. "Remember to say your prayers," she whispered.

"I will. When Mama and Papa find me, we will come see you."

"That will be nice. Bye-bye, sweetie."

She watched David walk beside the stretcher. At the tent door he glanced back and gave her a lingering look and mouthed the message, *She'll be okay,* with a little salute before he disappeared. She couldn't guess how he'd managed to come at this time, but he'd made a difficult time turn out gentle.

Marge stripped Isabelle's bed and readied it for a new patient. Then she went in search of Louise, who informed her that the field hospital had been ordered to move to Elsenbourg, a village closer to the Hurtgen Forest, on the border of Belgium a few miles south of Aachen. The Hurtgen was the treacherous black forest David had mentioned. The West Wall of bunkers that enclosed Aachen also ran a double fortification through the center of the Hurtgen Forest.

If the campaign to take the Hurtgen Forest turned out to be as difficult as David expected, no one would have had time in the field hospital to care for the Babe. Also, being closer to the action could have put her in danger. It was easier to give her up, knowing she would be safe in an Aachen hospital.

As a child, Marge had once watched a circus set up and had marveled at the roustabouts' efficiency. Now she was part of just such a move. By midafternoon the hospital tents, supplies, and personnel had been packed and moved to the new site.

As before, they set up the tents outside the village in an orchard beside the main road. Of course it was raining all the while, and heavy clouds made it twilight by four o'clock. The nurses unpacked medical supplies while the orderlies set up beds in the wards. They had just finished securing the tents when ambulances began to arrive. The majority of the wounded had to be treated for shock. In addition to their injuries, they were wet, cold, and exhausted from lack of sleep. Everyone on staff pitched in to fight for their lives, but still some were lost.

Many men suffered from trench foot. One soldier lay with the sheet propped up to avoid touching his swollen purple toes while Marge gently placed wads of iodine-soaked cotton wool between his sausage-shaped toes.

He didn't complain, but when she finished, beads of sweat stood out on his face. She went to the head of the bed and said quietly, "I can give you something for pain."

Through pinched lips he said, "Okay." His chart indicated he'd had no morphine. She gave him a shot, and his face began to relax.

"How long since you slept, soldier?"

"Can't remember. Couldn't make a trench in the rocks. Shells bursting in the trees. . . . We had to cover our trenches with logs and sod or get killed by fragments. Had a hard . . . time . . . finding logs. . . ." His voice trailed off, and his eyes closed.

"You made it, though," she said. "Whatever it took, you made it. Sleep well, Sergeant."

She'd heard the GIs call Hurtgen Forest the Green Hell, because once a soldier went in, he was lucky to find his way out. The deck was stacked, they said, in favor of the Germans. The enemy had the advantage of being able to set up effective ambushes and hide plenty of snipers.

She marked her present patient's chart and moved on to the next to repeat the careful cleansing and medicating. The endless rain could disable a man for life if he couldn't get out of his boots and take care of his feet.

The next man—boy, that is—looked up at her with a haunted expression. "Can you give me something for the pain like you did him?"

She checked the tag the medics had placed on him. He had not been given morphine. "Let me have a look first," she said gently. His feet were only beginning to swell, so he had a better chance than the last man of walking on his own feet the rest of his life. "I'll give you a shot before I start."

The morphine erased some of his fear as well as the pain. After she had cleansed and dressed his feet, he asked, "How do they look, Nurse? I sure feel better. Didn't know cold feet could hurt so much."

"You're going to be okay. Keep your feet uncovered. The air helps the healing."

"Thanks," he said, and she could tell he, too, was falling asleep.

Moving on through the ward, Marge treated feet and tried to cheer the men. Some were tough as nails and either endured in silence or joked, in spite of incredible pain.

Although she liked assisting in surgery, she was glad for the change that tending patients gave her. Colonel Colville rotated the nurses so they'd be competent in any position when a rush came. Marge believed that changing jobs prevented the type of exhaustion she'd seen on the faces of her last patients.

Near noon she had time to eat sitting down, so she went to the mess tent early. She picked up a tray and received the hot stew and chunks of French-type bread the cook served her.

"Hey, Emerson."

Marge turned to see Carolyn just inside the door of the mess tent beckoning for her to come. Her voice and stance suggested bad news. Marge left her tray and went on the double. Up close, she definitely saw trouble on her tentmate's face. "What is it? What's wrong?"

"A new batch of wounded. Your friend—Sergeant Lewellyn—is one of them."

Marge froze. "David?"

"Kid, I'm sorry. He's pretty bad. They're prepping him for surgery, and I thought you'd want to see him in case he wakes up . . . you know. . . ."

Stunned, Marge muttered, "Yes. Sure. Thanks." She pushed past Carolyn and ran to the receiving tent. The familiar odor of blood suddenly sickened her. She fought a wave of nausea, took a deep breath, and went quickly to look at the four wounded men. She spotted David right away and hurried to his stretcher. Dorothy was administering plasma. Wanda was cutting away his coat and shirt. He had lost a lot of blood. As Wanda lifted the clothing away, Marge saw a gaping wound in his side. *Oh, God, save him! Please save him!* "How are his vital signs?" she asked.

"A bit of touch and go, kid." Wanda worked while she talked. "The next hour or so will tell. Dr. Colville says he has to have surgery immediately. Dr. Ames will operate because Dr. Colville has three orthopedic cases." She paused and looked at Marge. "Look, I think you'd be better off to go help with one of the others. We can handle this."

Marge couldn't move. Something had happened to her legs. Then she heard Dr. Colville call her name.

"I want you to assist me, Emerson."

She wanted to stay with David! Automatically, she said, "Yes, sir. I'll wash up."

"Try not to worry," Dorothy said. "We're doing our best for the sergeant. All hands are here. We'll let you know how he is if Dr. Ames finishes before Dr. Colville."

"Thanks. Please do." She couldn't leave without even touching David. She lifted his limp hand. It was cold. She gripped it firmly. Leaning close to his face she said, "David, you're going to be all right. You're in good hands. You're going to be all right." She made herself let go and stand up, then without looking back, she hurried to scrub for surgery.

She felt wounded herself. While she lathered her hands, she prayed desperately for David. She'd seen enough to know his chances were not good. *Oh, God! Oh, God!*

Once in the operating theater, her training took over. She focused on Dr. Colville's needs and watched his skilled fingers trim, set, repair, and suture. At last he said, "Ready to close, Nurse," and she slapped the next instrument into his upturned palm.

"This man will walk again," he said, "maybe with a bit of a limp when he tires and maybe a touch of arthritis when he grows old, but he'll be able to do most things. When I get this last stitch in, you finish up." His eyes met hers above their masks. "Good job, Marge."

She put a smile in her voice and said, "Thank you, sir."

She bandaged the wound and called for ward men to move the patient to recovery. Then she went to wash up for the next surgery.

When Dr. Colville finished with the orthopedic cases, Dr. Ames was still leaning over David with frowning concentration. Marge went to the receiving tent. Four more wounded had arrived. Dr. Nelson was examining them. Hurrying over, she set to work with two other nurses, glad that she could keep busy. Then she realized how selfish it was to be glad that men had been wounded so she could stay busy. Surely she was losing her mind as well as her heart.

Chapter Seventeen

One of the newly admitted men required orthopedic surgery. His shoulder and arm had fractures in addition to the penetrating wound in his chest. Dr. Nelson told Marge to alert Dr. Colville. She found him in the surgery.

"Okay. Let's go again," he said.

For an instant her thoughts flipped to David. She'd rather be assisting Dr. Ames.

"Nurse Emerson, is the new patient ready?" Dr. Colville's voice called her back to his orders.

She jumped. "Yes, sir."

He strode into the receiving area and looked at the chart she had begun.

Scanning it quickly, he said, "He's stable. Looks good." His eyes met hers, and for the first time he focused on her. "You okay? Things have slowed to where I could ask someone else to assist me."

She shook her head. "I'm fine. I want to work."

"Good. Orderly, take this man in while we wash up. Nurse Hooper, start the anesthetic as soon as he's on the table." He headed for the scrubbing area, and Marge followed.

A few minutes later when she entered the operating theater, her eyes moved instantly to the far side of the tent. Two surgeons were at work, but the table where David had lain was empty. It was all she could do to keep from running to find him. Surely he was all right. Dorothy would have told her if he wasn't. Painfully she moved to her station at Dr. Colville's side where his tray of instruments awaited her.

He examined the patient's wounds. "I've got to take care of these chest wounds first. How's he doing, Hooper?"

"Pulse steady, 85, blood pressure 110 over 70."

"Okay. Let's go."

Marge worked automatically. The scene before her—the clamping of bleeders, the deft movements of the surgeon's hands—did not screen out the percussion of heavy gunfire. A new stream of casualties would soon arrive. This would be an all-nighter by the sound of it.

Dr. Colville worked swiftly. At last he closed, nodded for her to place the bandages, and went to scrub up for the next patient.

By 1:00 A.M. all the wounded had been cared for. At last Marge could go look for David. A couple of nurses were tending the post-op patients. Marge went down the line, peering at sleeping faces in the dim light. David wasn't there!

"Marge," her tentmate Dorothy called in a stage whisper from the next bed where she was taking a temperature, "they took Sergeant Lewellyn to the shock ward."

The scene in front of Marge began to recede. *Oh, Lord....* She sucked in a deep breath and said, "Thanks. I'll go see how he is."

Her heart raced faster than her feet. The specially trained nurses were good, but— She hurried out into the dark and headed for the shock tent where a dim light glowed through the canvas walls.

Two nurses were tending half a dozen patients, administering plasma and whole blood and checking vital signs frequently. David was easy to spot because he was almost longer than the bed.

Marge went to his side and, in the guise of checking his pulse, held his hand. His skin was cold, his face bloodless. Gina, one of the trauma nurses, paused beside her and whispered, "We're doing all we can. You know him? They say he's a medic."

"Yes, I know him. Is there anything I can do to help you?"

"You can sit here and check his pulse and blood pressure every fifteen minutes or so. I've left the cuff on his arm until we know he's out of danger. Ellen and I are working with two other guys who are too weak for the surgery they need."

"Sure. I'm glad to help." She sat down on the stool beside the bed and pumped up the blood pressure cuff. His blood pressure was 100 over 60—his pulse was weak and racing. She double-checked and counted it at 130. She recorded the time and the numbers on his chart. Then she checked his IV line and the plasma bag. Sitting beside him again, she tried to pray. To think that David could die was so monstrous she could barely dredge up words to address to God. After an awkward attempt, she lapsed into a continuous cry, *Please, God, please. Please. . . .*

The third time she checked David's vital signs, his pulse had slowed to a stronger beat, and his blood pressure had moved up a few digits. *Oh, thank you, God!*

A few minutes later Gina came and read his chart, then checked him herself. "I think he's going to make it. If he keeps improving we can move him to post-op by morning."

"Good," Marge said.

Gina laid a hand on her shoulder. "How long since you slept? You sound fuzzy."

Marge squeezed her eyes shut to clear them and shook her head. "I'm not sure." With effort she said, "Maybe twenty-four hours by now. . . ."

"Go get some shut-eye. Most everyone else is. You've got to be ready for tomorrow."

"Right." But Marge didn't move. "You really think he's out of the woods?"

"Yes. He will still be with us in the morning. He's a fighter. I can tell."

"Do you mind if I stay a few minutes longer?"

"Not at all. I was just thinking of you. Stay as long as you want."

When the nurse left to see to her other patients, Marge took David's hand again. Bending close to his ear, she whispered, "David! Can you hear me? Please fight to get well. I love you so much, David." He gave no indication of hearing. After a few minutes she checked his blood pressure again. It was higher. Barring an unforeseen complication, he would make it. She stood up and discovered she could barely walk in a straight line.

"I'm leaving now," she called. "See you in the morning!"

"Thanks for the help," Gina answered.

In her tent Marge fell into bed half-dressed and pulled the covers up around her neck. *David is out of the woods,* she assured herself, but the real woods, the Green Hell of the Hurtgen, would have one less medic. David had paid enough toward winning the war.

The next morning Marge went first thing to the shock ward and found that David had been transferred. She hurried to post-op and found him still unconscious but with color in his face. Picking up his chart, she read the record of his battle back to the living. He'd had morphine a short time ago so would probably sleep awhile. She checked his pulse. It was strong and steady now. Most of the other men were still asleep, and the nurses assigned to post-op had everything under control, so she headed for breakfast.

Out of doors a sheet of cold rain hit her. Stretching to ease the taut muscles in her shoulders, she drew in a deep breath and let it out slowly. For the moment, now that David had survived his wound and the surgery, the world looked hopeful. She strode to the mess tent for a cup of good strong coffee.

After breakfast, the morning again turned into a procession of ambulances bringing in men disabled from trench foot, combat fatigue, and wounds characteristic of shells bursting overhead. They were more exhausted than the previous patients, if that were possible. Most had been awake longer than they could remember.

Marge assisted in surgery again for six hours nonstop. Then suddenly the line of patients waiting for surgery ended. She washed up and helped orderlies scrub down the operating theater. Then on the way to the mess tent, she went to see David.

She found him awake. His expression brightened, almost like his old self, when he saw her. He smiled, started to raise his head, and then grimaced with pain. "Didn't know I could hurt my insides by smiling," he said, when she reached his bedside. Still he smiled again, but with care.

"So how are you?" she asked, resting her fingertips on his wrist.

"Now I call that unfair. You walk in here, pretty enough to stop a guy's heart, and then you check up on his reaction."

She grinned. "I didn't know you've been to Ireland, Sergeant."

"Ireland? What do you mean?"

"I mean you must have kissed the Blarney Stone." With a little laugh, she let go of his wrist. "Your heart is fine. Strong as a healthy racehorse. But I think the morphine has you a little dopey."

"Yeah, I guess it does. From what they tell me, I'm lucky to be here. But I'll be up and out in no time. I've got work to do."

She didn't contradict him or tell him he'd probably be on his way home once his body began to mend. "Sure," she said instead, "you'll be back in no time."

He smiled again, taking care not to move the rest of his body in the process. "I wanted to hear that from you. Figured you'd be honest. . . . I'm awfully sleepy. . . ." He closed his eyes, and in a few seconds he was in a drug-induced sleep.

Taking advantage of his sleep, Marge lifted the blanket and checked the bandages to be sure he wasn't bleeding. Then she looked at his chart to see when his temp had last been recorded. *Not long ago. It's up a little, but that might just be reaction to the trauma.*

When she left the tent, she met Dr. Ames, who had performed David's surgery.

"You were chatting with my miracle patient, I see," he said.

"Sergeant Lewellyn, you mean?"

"Yes. I don't know how he lived long enough to reach the field hospital, let alone make it through the surgery. I've never seen a man survive with the kind of tissue damage he sustained. We'll have to watch him for a few days, especially for internal bleeding. Is he a friend of yours?"

"Yes. When will you be sure he's going to be okay?"

Dr. Ames looked down at her quizzically. "You can probably make as good a guess on that as I can. He shouldn't have survived the surgery, but he did. That's in his favor. He's a fighter."

"Actually, he's a crusader. He has a mandate to live."

"You getting religious, Nurse Emerson?"

"If you want to call it that. I think God wanted him to live. As you said, he shouldn't have survived transport, but he did."

"I don't want to fault God, but I think the difference between living and dying out here is a matter of skill, happenstance, or luck. Maybe all three."

She liked Dr. Ames, and she was much too tired to discuss theology, so she simply said, "You may be right, sir," and left.

But all the way to the mess tent, she felt as if she had failed David. He would have said unequivocally that God was in control, that God knew whenever a sparrow fell and had numbered every hair on each person's head. God . . . She longed for a faith like David's.

Twice that afternoon Marge looked in on David. The second time his eyes opened when she stopped at the foot of his bed. "Hi," he said.

"Hi, yourself." She went to his side and checked the flow of the saline solution dripping into his vein. She hoped he would be able to drink water soon. It would be a good sign.

He was watching her as she worked, so she kept close guard over her expression.

"Say, what about our little Isabelle?" he asked. "Has anyone been to see her since we transported her into the city?"

Marge shook her head. "We're all too busy. I plan to go as soon as I get a day off."

"Yeah. That's what I thought too. Didn't expect to be laid up like this. If I could just get up out of this bed we could go together. Guess the Lord has other plans for right now." He sounded at peace, as if he truly didn't worry.

"David," she burst out, "how did you learn to trust God the way you do?"

He came alert, gazing up at her with such a tender look that it took her breath away. "How I came to faith wouldn't necessarily mean much to anyone else. From what I've seen, the Lord leads each person according to that person's need. For me, I was like the Prodigal Son in the Bible. I headed out to prove Christians were foolish and wrong."

He fell silent, staring into space, maybe into his memories. Then he looked up at her with the intensity of a well man and said, "I nearly died from remorse and guilt when I nearly killed my best friend while driving drunk. By that time I had the good sense to run to God. I can't really put into proper words what happened. God's love was so real that I've never slipped back to blaming myself or doubting or complaining."

"You didn't hear or see anything?"

"Nothing. It happened inside me. Like Jesus said, the kingdom of heaven is within us."

What David had revealed was not a lot different from messages she'd heard in church all her life. No one seemed able to tell her how to make that spiritual change.

David must have seen disappointment on her face, for he said, "Don't you be worrying about not feeling the way you think you should. Feelings are not reliable. When the time is right, God will touch you in a special way, just for you, and you'll know it's Him. You'll never be the same." He closed his eyes. She thought he was going to say more, because his lips moved briefly. Then she thought he was going to sleep, but he opened his eyes again and said, "You will find your own answer. You can count on it." He closed his eyes again, and in a minute his breathing told her this time he was sleeping.

She returned to duty and did not see him again until her last rounds before going to bed. He was awake, looking brighter, more alert. His color was good and so were the reports written on his chart.

"You're looking so much better. You'll be out of here before you know it." She was careful not to reveal that out meant to an ambulance ship and a general hospital in England.

When she checked his pulse, he murmured, "Nurse Margaret, I will sorely miss you when that time comes."

"You sure you've never visited Ireland?" she said, smiling.

"Sure am. Lovely, tender Margaret. I love you, Margaret."

"Please. Someone will hear you."

He made a humorous face of horror. "Oh, I forgot. Love is not permitted. I am dearly fond of you, Margaret." He gave her a wicked grin. His eyes were overbright.

She smiled and touched his forehead, feeling for a fever.

He caught her hand and kissed it. Then he looked up innocently. "Now how could I not do that when it was right there within easy reach? And anyway, what's a kiss between friends?"

"You know what the army calls it."

"Okay. I'll take back the kiss." He grabbed for her hand again.

She snatched it away but had to laugh. *Oh, if only we were free to love each other.*

"Will you marry me, Margaret?" he whispered.

She was glad for the dim light. It concealed her start of surprise. After their earlier talk, she supposed he would not mention marriage again for a long time. "I don't think we should talk about it right now."

He caught hold of her hand again and held on. "We don't have to talk about it, not unless you know the answer will be yes."

She felt a tremble in his fingers that telegraphed hope. "It's so hard for me to think about this now."

He let go. "Okay."

She leaned close and whispered, "David, I love you. I want to say yes. It's just that . . . we scarcely know each other. I don't want us to start something that we'd be sorry about later. We need to let time test our feelings. We need to go home after the war and then see how we feel."

"You're right, I suppose," he said. "It's just that I believe we're better suited than we can even guess right now. I've loved you ever since I saw you on the beach at Normandy. But with you being an officer, I couldn't say a word. But now I suspect I may be going home, and I hoped you could tell me yes before they move me out." He smoothed the back of her hand with only one finger, as gently as she used to touch spring flowers in Oklahoma. "Is there a chance for us, Margaret?"

Yes, her heart cried, but she said, "I want to say yes, but I can't trust my feelings right now." Being honest made her totally miserable.

His hand dropped back onto his blanket, but his eyes didn't leave hers, and he showed no hurt feelings. He smiled. "I guessed you'd feel that way, but I had to ask. Anyway, I love you, and I'll be waiting. But I won't bother you anymore about this now."

"Okay." Marge's spirits sagged, sad that she'd had her own way. *How childish can a grown woman be?* she chided herself.

Chapter Eighteen

After Em's interesting conversation with Werner Koch, the German war correspondent, she returned to Paris and delivered Andrew's message. Then on orders from Brad Cummins, she interviewed several more people.

Remembering she had returned to "Marchant territory," she paid close attention to whether anyone seemed to be watching or following her. She saw nothing to arouse suspicion and said so to Cummins. He told her to keep watching.

Bob Mansfield's friends hadn't heard from him in days, so Em assumed he was still in eastern France. Hoping to see him, she lingered in Paris until Cummins telephoned her one evening. "When does Andrew Blackwell expect to hear from you again?"

"He didn't say."

"We've tightened surveillance on two of the people you just interviewed. I want you out of Paris in case anything transpires that could draw attention to you. You've been too valuable to us for you to lose your cover now."

She straightened and rubbed her neck. It had been more than two weeks since she'd seen Bob. She sighed and tried to set her mind on her present assignment. Surely he'd be back in Paris when she returned. "Okay. How soon must I leave?"

"In the morning. I'll send over your train ticket tonight. Can you get to the station on your own?"

"Sure."

"Good. You'll be less noticeable without an escort."

She hung up and started packing the few things she'd need. By the time she finished, Cummins' messenger arrived with her ticket and also with a sealed message for Andrew. Now that was a surprise, but Cummins had hinted that Andrew had cooperated with the OSS in the past.

The next day, as Em prepared to board the train, a young woman stepped forward beside her, also ready to board. "Mademoiselle Emerson," she exclaimed, "How nice to see you again! You do remember me—Jeanette Marchant? You interviewed my father for your magazine."

"Yes! Yes, of course. How is your father?"

"Very good. We have been hoping to hear from you that our story has been published."

"I'm sorry to tell you that it hasn't." She tried to sound sympathetic and cordial, while thinking, *How do I get away and call Cummins without arousing her suspicions?*

"Are you going on this train?" Jeanette said, motioning to the waiting car.

Oh, now I'll have to go back to the hotel and start all over. "No. I was meeting that train." She gestured toward one that had arrived a few minutes earlier. "My friend did not get off, and I was just standing here trying to decide what to do. I guess I may as well go back to my hotel. Are you boarding or meeting someone?"

"I am going to visit my uncle in Troyes. I was hoping for your company if you were boarding, but au revoir then." She gave a friendly wave and climbed aboard.

Em smiled, waved, and went back into the station. Well, at least the occasion had given her an opportunity to test her acting ability. She waited inside until the train to Geneva with Jeanette aboard pulled out. Then she found a secluded public phone and called Cummins.

He was out, so she left a message and hired a pedicab to take her back to the hotel.

Cummins, when he returned her call, was not happy. "That was no innocent encounter. We picked up the two German agents I mentioned. I'm positive the Marchants are connected to them. We don't dare arrest Jeanette and Jacques right away, or the fact that you interviewed all of these suspects might come up. Conceivably you could be called on to testify. I need for you to remain our best-kept secret. I'll send you new train tickets immediately. Stay in your room until my courier arrives. And remember, Jeanette might be back in Paris by the time you board."

"Okay. I'll be waiting for your instructions."

He remained silent, and Em wondered if he had hung up. Then he said, "I'm sending you to the Riviera."

"What?"

"It's too bad the season is wrong and the transportation horrendous, but it will get you out of sight for a few days and mislead anyone if they see you boarding the train."

That afternoon, after Em had been on the dirty crowded train for five hours and they had traveled about fifty miles, she understood Cummins' remark that the journey south would get her out of sight for a few days. The train stopped and started, parked on sidings, and traveled at a slug's pace. At this rate she'd be two days just getting to the Riviera.

In the end her wild estimate was nearly correct. The train ride took twenty-five hours. Tracks had been destroyed and bridges blasted away in so many places, she wondered why the French made the effort to run a train. At the Riviera she went immediately to the hotel where a room had been reserved for her, washed off the grime, and located a place to eat. A glimpse of the aqua sea beckoned her to walk to the beach and kick off her shoes. With effort she marched back to the hotel and took a needed nap until she could board a northbound train.

By this exhausting circuitous route, she reached Geneva three days later than she had anticipated. From the hotel where she'd stayed before, she called Andrew.

"Em, let me pick you up and take you home to dinner with me. It's one of Lydia's soirées this time. Much more social. She will have some single young men she'll try to pawn off on you, but you mustn't succumb to her matchmaking. I have to screen anyone you spend too much time with, not because I don't trust you, but for your own safety."

"Do you really? Because of how it went for Vivienne?"

He didn't answer instantly. Then he said, "Yes." Maybe he hadn't really hesitated. His voice sounded reassuringly normal. "But don't worry. Mainly I want to be sure someone hasn't decided you may be useful to his own agenda."

"You mean you have unfriendly friends at your soirées?"

"It's just that Lydia has no knowledge of my varied contacts to help the war effort. And she enjoys all kinds of people."

"Sounds risky."

"Not greatly. You just have to be aware of possibilities. Other than that, you'll have a good time."

"Then, thank you. I'd love to come."

That evening the soirée was all that Andrew had promised. Em met so many interesting people she wished she could have carried her notepad. Only once did she detect a look from Andrew that suggested she should move on to someone else. Then, in the midst of a conversation with a Bulgarian countess, she noticed Werner Koch standing alone in the arched doorway of the salon. He must have just arrived. When he saw her, he nodded and smiled. She returned his smile.

A few minutes later when she went for more punch, he strolled to her side. "Good evening, Miss Emerson. I've been hoping we would meet again."

"Thank you, Herr Koch." She didn't know how to respond to his suggested interest. "How is your textile business?"

"Busy. I find my trips here a great help. And you? I trust your work is going well."

"My publisher seems to like the stories I send."

"And does he let you write as freely as you want?"

Her hackles went up. He was deliberately baiting her. "Herr Koch, you know all editors have the final say. And I'm sure you know that during a war, journalists are on their honor to obey certain restrictions. But our newspapers and magazines do report what's really happening in the war."

At that point Andrew came and reached for the cupful of punch the waitress poured for him. "Only in Geneva and at one of Lydia's soirées could the U.S. press meet the German press."

"Andrew, I have longed for a chance to question Miss Emerson about certain procedures in the American press," Herr Koch said. "Is there a place we may chat undisturbed for a while?"

Em hoped Andrew would get her out of this, especially after his warning about not spending too much time with any one man. Instead, he placed a fatherly hand on her elbow and said, "Certainly. I have just the place." He guided her, with Herr Koch following. His attitude gave Em the feeling that he wanted her to talk again to this Nazi. She would stay alert, just in case her chat with Herr Koch turned into an assignment.

In a small sitting room a log burned in the ornate marble fireplace. Andrew gestured toward comfortable chairs near the fire. "Shall I send you coffee, or tea perhaps?"

Herr Koch smiled. "Some of your good coffee. Thank you." Then he made small talk until the coffee arrived. When at last they were alone, he said, "I have very much wanted to meet you again."

"Why is that?"

"You talked about honor and integrity in your free press. I have thought about all you said, and I believe I can trust you to publish a message to the people of your country."

Em straightened and looked him in the eye. Was he hoping to use her for propaganda purposes? "As I said, I really have no control over what my editors choose to publish and what they reject. Also they're interested in facts, not ideas."

"I understand. Is it true that you have an honor system that allows you to keep your source a secret?"

Every nerve in her body went on alert. "Yes. We do practice that principle."

"Would you be willing to protect me if I tell you . . . what I can tell you?"

"Herr Koch, I am not open to spreading propaganda." She rose to her feet.

"Wait! I am speaking of facts. But I must have your word. If the Gestapo were to suspect me, I, as well as my family, would be executed. This has been the law since the attempt on the Fuehrer's life last summer."

"How awful!" The risk to his family made her realize his information must be of great importance. "Are you sure you should be seen with me? There are others who can deliver your information to the right people more directly than I."

"I dare not approach any person of consequence. I have thought about this for days. Forgive me if this offends, but with you, no one will suspect. You are scarcely more than a girl. If you are willing, we can make it appear as if I am infatuated with you. Many men have affairs or mistresses in Geneva, and no one frowns on it. The charade would make it easier for me to get my family safely out of Germany. If they believe I am in love with you, they will assume I would never want to bring my wife here."

Em gaped at him, stunned by the idea. "Me? In love with a . . . with you?" If such a farce reached the ears of Bob or Marge, what would they think?

"Even if you don't wish to pretend to love me, still you are the best choice. As a correspondent, you may take information to your leaders with more dispatch than someone confined to official channels. Will you take a message to Eisenhower himself?"

She thought fast. "I don't think I can!" But Cummins probably could deliver information to Supreme Allied Headquarters, possibly to Eisenhower in person. "Did you tell Andrew any of this?"

"To do so is too dangerous for both of us. The Gestapo knows that I have known him for a long time. They would connect me immediately with anything he leaked. Furthermore, although I like Andrew, I suspect he is more than an aggressive American businessman. I dare not send intelligence information through him. If he is an agent, our double agents have access to anything he learns. You see, Germany has infiltrated the secret services and underground movements of the Allies from the beginning. No, I cannot trust anything to Andrew."

Em considered the situation and decided what he said so far made sense. If she truly had won Werner's confidence, this could be of great value to the OSS, even if they did only want her to be a courier. "Okay. If you think I can help, I'm willing to try."

He leaned forward in his chair. "I cannot tell you how much this means to me." He pulled a photo from his pocket and handed it to her.

A pretty dark-haired woman with little two girls smiled up at her.

"My wife Frieda and our children—Maria, thirteen, and Anna, seven."

She studied the faces, then handed the photo back. "They are lovely. Are you sure you should go through with this?"

"I must. It is for them. I wanted you to see them, to help you remember why I so desperately need secrecy."

"I will remember."

He carefully placed the photo back into his wallet and then leaned his elbows on his knees, clasping his hands together loosely. As he began to speak, his laced fingers tightened. "If you will bear with me, I want to tell you how I came to my decision. For my newspaper in Berlin I go with the Fuehrer whenever he permits. I have done this from the beginning of the war. I know the leaders of the Third Reich well, and I have shown them I will be discreet and say only what they want the people to know.

"That is why I was permitted to see the Fuehrer's plan for the survival of the Third Reich. He took me, with a few others, to the salt mines where he has the airplane factories, and then we went further, underground again, into the Alps. I was allowed to see the V–3, a rocket far superior to our present V–2. This did not surprise me. We all knew something like this was being developed. It's what I saw next that made me decide I had to let the world know.

"Hitler plans to control these superior missiles with guidance systems to take them accurately to London and Paris. He will arm them with poison gas."

This confirmed what Andrew had told her, but hearing it from Herr Koch made the information even more chilling.

"You do not look surprised."

"I've heard rumors."

"Did you hear also that he has scientists producing colonies of bacteria? He plans to unleash plagues via the rockets. He has become insane. He will kill millions of innocent people if—" His words caught in his throat.

Em recoiled at the image his words conjured in her mind. Looking at Herr Koch, she no longer saw an enemy but rather a decent, horrified man who was risking his life and the lives of his loved ones to expose a heinous plan.

Herr Koch cleared his throat. "The Allies must stop him. I can supply maps, even blueprints of these factories. Air raids won't touch them. Saboteurs must get into the heart of the mountain caves. Once my family is safely in England, and as soon as the Allies permit, I want you to write the full story for all the world to know."

"But if the information is published, the Gestapo may guess it comes from you," she said, finding herself as concerned for his safety as for his family's.

"This is so. I have made careful plans. I do not intend to die. My wife and daughters already have left Munich to stay with her brother in the mountains. In three weeks she will meet me at the Swiss border, and I will bring her here. I have obtained permission from the Fuehrer to have a Swiss specialist examine and treat little Anna. Her heart condition requires more treatment than our overworked and aging physician can provide. I will return to Munich after placing her in the doctor's care here, but my wife and our Maria will remain with Anna.

"Then Dr. Schneider will find it necessary to send Anna to Paris to save her life. From there I want the Allies to hide my family in England. Anna's heart condition, it is real. She may die without better medicine. Already we have lost our little son, Frederick, from a similar heart condition following the same terrible illness.

"Once Frieda and the girls are safe from the Gestapo, then you may deliver the maps and blueprints to Allied headquarters. It must all be done very quickly. As soon as your military leaders allow, you should write the story. I hope I shall live to give you more details.

Write it so the whole world will know what horror Nazism has brought." He stopped and studied her. His intense need, escaping from the control of his German discipline, burned in his eyes. "Will you do this? It is what I would do as a journalist if I were free like you."

"I'll do my best," Em said. "But surely you will write your own story."

"Someday in German for the German people, yes. You must write it for the English-speaking world."

Em wondered if Andrew Blackwell had any idea what Herr Koch had wanted to discuss with her. Werner had suggested he didn't, but Andrew seemed to know more than his friends would ever suspect. "I'll deliver your information to Allied headquarters, and I will write the story when it is safe to do so." She stood up, and so did he. "Also, I agree with your earlier plan. When we leave this room, we should look as if we have become . . . very interested in each other."

"Thank you," he said in such a sober manner that she felt her first doubts return. His plan sounded workable, but in agreeing to flirt with him, she might be flirting with death.

Outside the sitting room she tucked her hand under his arm, and he folded his fingers over hers. Looking down at her with a warm smile, he could have fooled her if they hadn't planned this scene. They strolled out to the salon, giving a good impression, she hoped, of two people newly entranced with each other.

Werner Koch spent the rest of the evening attentively at Em's side. Despite her inner reservations, she found him a charming partner. As far as she could tell, no one raised an eyebrow over their sudden attachment to each other. Just as he'd said, in Switzerland no one asked questions. The fact that she was American and he was German would be an affront to her compatriots, but it caused no stir here other than envious glances she caught from a couple of men. Their attitude disgusted her, but she was too serious about playing her part to let that distract her.

At the end of the evening, Werner—she made a point of calling him by his first name—told Lydia and Andrew that he would take her to her hotel in the city. Andrew flashed her a look of concern but quickly covered it with a smile and gracious thanks to Werner. Em suspected Andrew would have questions and warnings for her in the morning.

"Good night," she said to both Andrew and Lydia. "I had such a lovely time. Thank you for inviting me."

Lydia smiled and took her hand. "I insisted that Andrew invite you when he said you were back in Geneva. I'm having an afternoon tea tomorrow for ladies of the Red Cross and several of the embassy wives. I'd love to have you join us for that too, if you can."

She glanced at Andrew, received a slight frown, and took it to mean no. "I'm sorry. I'll be working all day tomorrow, but thank you for asking."

"Another time then, I hope," Lydia said. "And Werner, as usual it is a pleasure to have you with us. Thank you for seeing Em to her hotel."

He gave her his Prussian bow. "Thank you for such a pleasant evening. Your hospitality always makes my trip to Geneva a treat."

"You are most welcome." Lydia turned to her husband and said, "Darling, I see Madame Grolier looking a bit lost with no one talking to her. Will you all excuse me, please?" Not waiting for a reply she said, "Good night."

"Take care, both of you," Andrew said. "Good night."

Em went out with Werner and waited for him to bring his auto. Standing alone on the wide steps of the chateau with the moonlight glittering off the lake and the mountains illumined by their snow, Em thought fleetingly of winter back home in Tuttle, Oklahoma. *What am I doing here, consorting with the enemy?* She almost ran back into the chateau to beg a ride from Andrew.

By the time Werner's black sedan pulled up to the steps and he got out to open the door for her, she had regained her courage. As a journalist, she had fallen into the opportunity of a lifetime. This could lead to her big story. She hurried forward, making a show of eagerness to leave with him, in case anyone was watching.

On the way to the hotel Werner didn't seem inclined to converse. Maybe he was having second thoughts about his plan. She almost hoped so. Yet if what he said was true, the Allies needed the information he claimed to possess, and quickly.

He cleared his throat. "I've been thinking. I must be sure nothing is revealed until my family is safe. Tomorrow I will confirm the date of Anna's appointment with Dr. Schneider and set a date for delivery of the maps. Will you be in Geneva tomorrow? I will surely know by the end of the day."

"I can stay until you call."

"Frieda and the girls must be utterly safe before I can hand over the maps. This could place the time of delivery near Christmas." He turned to her sharply. "You understand it is imperative that you tell absolutely no one anything until my family is safe?"

"Yes. Your concern for your family will be my concern." Marge would think she was jumping into trouble, and she was pretty sure she was. But this time she had the best reason in the world. If all went as planned, she'd be saving lives.

Beside her, Werner said a quiet thank you and grew silent again.

The next day Em dressed and ate early. While awaiting a call from Andrew, she made notes from her most interesting conversations of the night before without, of course, any mention of Werner Koch.

Immediately after eight o'clock the phone rang. It was Werner. "I have a problem. I was able to reach Dr. Schneider at his home, but he says he cannot possibly work out details for hiding my family until January. He insists Anna will be fine and told me what to do to build up her health for the journey. If I had known she must wait that long, I . . . would not have talked to you so soon. You must keep everything I said to you utterly secret. Have I your promise?" His question came across as a command.

"Yes. I won't say a word to anyone."

"Dr. Schneider insists Anna will be all right. . . ."

She sensed a tremble of anxiety for his daughter. "You said he's the best heart specialist in Europe. Surely you can trust his word. When shall I return to Geneva to pick up the information from you?"

"Can you meet me at your hotel the fifth of January? That will fit my normal schedule for visiting my textile business. As long as Anna is strong enough, the delay may work for the best. Frieda can tell friends she is going to stay through Christmas with her aunt and uncle."

"It's only a few weeks. Surely Anna will be fine."

"According to Dr. Schneider she will be stronger for the journey from the vitamins and tonic he is sending with me."

Em felt acutely sorry for him but knew he didn't want an expression of sympathy as much as agreement. "You have trusted a great deal to me. Trust him too."

There was a long silence on the other end. They had not been disconnected, for the line remained open.

Finally he said, "I think we were meant to meet. Do you believe in God, Em?"

"Yes."

"Then I am certain we were meant to meet. Frieda and I have prayed for help like this. And I do trust you to keep my secret. As things stand then, with this delay, I will come to your hotel on the fifth of January. You must not have the maps in your possession for long. If my defection were discovered, you could be killed for them. I shall find a safe place to leave them and let you know where. Then after my family is safe, if I don't escape from Germany, your people can pick them up."

"All right."

"Then for now, good-bye."

"Good-bye." She hung up the receiver. Why had this man singled her out? Had God led him to her? Who could know? Mysterious things had happened in this war, such as the way Hitler had let the whole British army escape from Dunkirk and the way the Germans did not move in force to stop the invasion of France until the beachhead had been strongly established.

Turning, Em walked to her hotel window and gazed at the mundane activity in the street below to assure herself she was not dreaming. She really was in Geneva, and she really had agreed to help a former Nazi. She felt very much alone with her new secret.

Chapter Nineteen

Right after Em hung up from talking to Werner Koch, her phone rang again. She ran back and picked it up.

"Em? I've been trying to reach you," Andrew said.

"I was saying good-bye to Werner Koch."

"Em . . . I wanted you to meet Werner, but you aren't . . . He's married, you know."

"Yes. He just needed the ear of a friend. He dearly loves his wife. I assure you, we only became friends." She wished she could tell him why they had become friends, but her promise to Werner stopped her. His family was in more danger than ever since his plan for escape had to be postponed.

"Good. I'd like you to take a message to Paris. How soon can you leave?"

"In about fifteen minutes. I ate early, so all I have to do is pack."

"Make it an hour. It's better for you to wait in your room than in the train station. I want you to stop over in Macon to see Hubert. He will have a second message for you to take to Paris."

"Oh." She smiled to herself. "I've been wanting to see the Espes again."

She thought she heard him sigh. "Sometimes I regret enlisting you. You act as if these assignments are a lark. There's a possibility of danger. You need to remember that. Certain people may be watching you just because you've been in my home, which leads me to ask again, how involved are you really with Werner?"

"I told you. We just struck up a friendship based on the fact that we're both journalists." The lying came so easy she shocked herself.

"And about danger, you said in the beginning that I wouldn't be taking any risks by helping you. That was before I knew that Vivienne had worked for you."

"I was wrong not to warn you. Also, I didn't calculate on your making friends with Werner Koch. Will you meet him again?"

How much should she say? "I may if I happen to be in Switzerland when he is."

"But you made no plans."

"Not a one," she lied. "You need to know that besides the fact he is happily married, I'm in love with an American correspondent. I hope to see him when I get back to Paris." She found it odd to say this to a stranger when she had not said it aloud to Bob, but speaking the words felt good. Soon she would find a way to tell Bob.

Silence lingered between them so long that she wondered if they'd been cut off.

Finally he said, "It's only fair to warn you that Werner may be a marked man. You could become a target if you are seen meeting him again."

"What do you mean? Who wants to kill him?"

"His own people. He as much as told me. He avoids meeting me anywhere but inside my home. There was a time when he gave me bits of information for the Allies, but that dried up long ago. He became too frightened. I was very surprised that he accepted my invitation last night and that he openly spent time with you."

"You mean the poor man can't even make a friend without being suspected?"

"In this city everyone watches everyone. The real business in Geneva is not what you see on the surface. I've tried to protect you by telling people you're the daughter of my longtime friend in America. But Werner cannot protect you. I hope you won't see him again."

The lie came easier than ever. "I'll do my best. After all, it would be unlikely for our paths to cross again, unless we would meet in your home."

"Good."

All the way to the train station, after Andrew's emphatic warning, Em glanced over her shoulder to see whether anyone seemed to be following her.

Once on the train she relaxed a little. The journey gave her time to think about what she had gotten herself into. In the end she decided that, if she had it to do over again, she still would agree to help Werner.

By the time she reached Macon, she felt more confident surrounded by the French people. Then her concern faded, because she saw the Nisei Combat Team. Several of the unit's officers were standing near the station beside parked army trucks. She grabbed her two small pieces of luggage and approached the closest man.

"Sir, I wonder if you might know Sergeant Tom Kagawa?"

"Yes, ma'am. He's down there in that truck at the head of the convoy."

"Thanks. I hope I'll have time to talk a minute."

"We're going to bivouac outside of town. Be here overnight. The boys will have evening leaves to come to town."

"Thanks! I'll go ask him out for dinner."

Tom saw her coming. After a word to the officer at his side, he hurried to meet her. She dropped her suitcase and held out her hand.

Gripping it tightly, he exclaimed, "Em! I can't believe my luck—seeing you twice like this."

"Me too. How are you? Where have you been? Near here all the time?"

"I'll say not. We were up north in the Vosges Mountains. We helped take Bruyeres and then fought our way into a trapped battalion of Texas Rangers." His expression turned serious. "It was rough. We've been released for rest, and then we head back south."

"Will you be in Macon for long? Can we have a real visit?"

"Let me go ask. Maybe I can come into town tonight and meet you for supper or something. Wait a minute, and I'll be right back."

She watched him stride back to his CO. Even his rumpled fatigues and bulky army coat couldn't make him look slouchy. There was something tireless and graceful about his easy walk. She'd noticed this about him even while he'd been recuperating in the Gilwern hospital in Wales. His previously injured arm didn't seem to be bothering him.

Tom jogged back with a broad smile. "I can come into town for supper. Where shall we meet?"

"How about here at the train station? It's the only location I'm sure of. I don't know any restaurants."

"It's a small town without many options, but my buddies can probably suggest something. Say, it's great to see you. We'll have a lot to talk about."

"Shall we aim for 1900?"

"Good. See you then." He gave her a jaunty salute and marched back to his truck.

Em headed down the hill, intending to walk to the Espes' farm, but before she got to the river, an old farm truck pulled up beside her. Hubert himself called, “Em! I’m sorry I’m late. Andrew called and said you’d be on this train.” He started to get out to help her with her luggage.

“I can do it,” she said, quickly loading them onto the back and then climbing into the front. “I didn’t stop to think that Andrew might have telephoned. I’m glad for the ride. And before I forget, this is for you.”

She handed him the envelope bearing his name that Andrew had given her along with her train tickets.

Hubert pocketed it. “A long convoy held me up. It is difficult to cross this highway—as if we were in a big city. The trucks, they never stop coming.”

“How is Estelle?”

“She is fine. She will tell you.”

“Then she’s over the shock of being shot at again? I’m still sorry I asked you to do that.”

“Don’t worry yourself. I think she needed to go, maybe even needed to face danger again and walk away safe. You know?”

“In a way. I got a hint of how it feels to be trapped quarry, but it wasn’t anything like what she experienced, having to leave her sister.”

He glanced at her. “May you never know this.” He turned his attention back to the road. “She still does not know that I serve as a spy for the OSS. Please be very careful that you don’t say anything that could reveal this or your work for Andrew. She only thinks of him as someone sympathetic to the Resistance.”

“I will be very careful.”

Hubert turned into the dirt drive leading to their farm home. The dog ran to meet the truck and escorted them to the door.

After greetings were over, Em told them about her dinner date with Tom. “I hope it’s not too much of an imposition, Hubert, to ask you to drive me back to the train station tonight.”

“Not at all, but there are so few places to eat in town, and his buddies will no doubt fill them. Why don’t you bring him here for supper.”

“Oh, I am sure we will find something. And I’m counting on him to get me a ride back out here.”

“But you must dine here with your friend,” Estelle insisted. “I have a nice chicken and vegetables from the root cellar. Much better than anything you will find in town. Please to come here. We haven’t had guests for such a long time. Please.”

Estelle finally convinced Em she'd be doing them a favor to bring Tom to dinner, so at the appointed hour, she and Hubert met him at the station and brought him out to the farm.

Estelle's cuisine, chicken in a wine sauce with real butter and shallots from a flowerpot in the kitchen window, left them all with happy stomachs. Finally they sat around the kitchen table with their coffee and talked.

Hubert asked Tom about the campaign in the Vosges Mountains.

"The battle had been going on for a while before they brought us in from northern Italy. Rugged mountains, the Vosges."

"Yes, and the rain, it hasn't stopped for weeks," Hubert said.

"We had only two days in all of October that cleared enough to permit air support."

"The Vosges," Hubert mused. "They befriend whoever is there first. Never has an attacking army crossed over the Vosges. That's one reason the Germans attacked France through Belgium in this war as well as the last. So our armies are making progress against the Germans holed up in those mountains?"

Tom nodded. "It's slow. Like house-to-house fighting, only it's tree-to-tree. We can't get tanks in on the narrow roads, and the Germans ambush our jeeps and small artillery. Still, we are advancing. We've taken St. Die. That's what the Texans were aimed for when the Germans surrounded them on a ridge. But we broke through." He sat lost in his own thoughts, and for the first time fatigue lined his face.

Em wanted to draw him back from the memories that tightened his mouth to a grim line. She remembered Jean had said that Tom wanted to become a journalist. "Do you ever try to keep a log about where you go and what you do?"

His face relaxed. "Yeah, whenever I get enough of a break, I write. We don't even have a company photographer, so I figure after the war the guys may want a book, a history of the 442nd Division. Only thing is, I have to carry my notes everywhere I go. If I tried to send them home in letters, they wouldn't get past the censors."

Em laughed. "I know about that. I'd love to read your notes, but I don't suppose you'll be here long enough for me to do that."

"Not likely. . . . The Bruyeres campaign has been one of our toughest. We went in with about four thousand men. We are leaving with closer to two thousand. We had memorial services for the one hundred forty men who died in the twenty-five day campaign. Twelve hundred are in hospitals. Near the end of the campaign buck privates were directing some of the fighting. They'd lost their officers and noncoms and just kept going. One rifle battalion went out twenty-eight strong, and only two men came back. Both were privates.

"I made a special effort to document the actions of men who performed far beyond the call of duty. I don't aim to let anyone forget."

"Good for you," Em said. "Hubert, these guys, whose parents or grandparents came from Japan, are serving over here after being stripped of their homes and possessions and placed in U.S. prison camps. Many still have families in those camps. That's why I'm especially awed by their actions."

Hubert's mouth fell open. "I did not know! Did your country do the same with the children of German immigrants?"

"No. Only a few German immigrants were held under suspicion. You see it wasn't so easy to see who had ancestors in Germany."

Hubert turned to Tom. "Man, why did you let them conscript you to fight for them?"

Tom grinned. "No one in the 442nd Regimental Combat Team was drafted. We all volunteered."

"But why?"

"To show we were good Americans. To defend freedom—even though a few people wanted to take that freedom from us. The restrictions on us grew out of fear, and fear wipes out justice in any nation or community. Like you and everyone else, we're really fighting for a better world for our kids."

Hubert nodded. "That's what it always comes down to when you have to fight."

Estelle had been listening attentively. "Monsieur Kagawa, if you please, I would like to hear about your family."

"Well, there's my wife, Jean, who is serving in the Red Cross in Wales. Em knows her. Then my mother and father are in war work in a factory in Michigan. After the first year of the internment, families were allowed to leave if they could obtain employment away from the West Coast. My sister, Helen, is a schoolteacher in one of the internment camps. I have a small brother, Peter, who is still in elementary school."

"You have much to fight for then," Estelle said.

He smiled and straightened on the rustic kitchen chair. "I certainly do, Madame Espe. I'm a lucky man."

Em couldn't keep quiet any longer. "Tom, would you be willing to let me interview you and write a story about the combat team—about how it feels to fight for a country that rejected you?"

"You really think anyone would publish such a story?"

"I think my magazine would. Maybe you can tell me from memory about the individual sacrifices of some of your buddies. It's a story that people need to hear."

He shook his head. "I don't know. I think people back home want to hear about their own sons and neighbors, not about 'little yellow men.' "

Em swallowed. He was partly right. "They're not all like that. After all, you saved their sons when you rescued that trapped battalion of Texans."

He leaned back on his kitchen chair. "You're as much of an idealist as my wife." Then he chuckled. "That's not at all bad. I miss her like my right hand. Well, okay. If our hosts don't mind, fire away."

Hubert said, "Do go ahead. We will like to hear."

"Yes, please," his wife said.

"Well," Em said, "I'd like a view of the battle situation in general, and then give me the human specifics, including the names of some of the men. Can you do that?"

"Sure."

Estelle filled Tom's cup with fresh coffee from the supply Em had brought on her last visit.

"Thanks," he said. "Our orders were to move in and take Bruyeres and then go on to take St. Die. The Texas 100th Battalion had moved ahead, and suddenly the Germans cut them off. The top of a ridge where they were trapped may as well have been a desert island. They held on for days, but the weather was ceiling zero. Planes couldn't drop them food or medicine. They were running out of supplies and ammunition.

"We had to get to them. We couldn't get artillery in to soften up the enemy, so it was tree-to-tree, mud, rain, cold, and no sleep. The Germans had taken over houses and could sleep dry at night. None of us wanted to sit waist deep in foxholes half full of icy water, so we stayed awake. For one eight-day stretch we got no sleep. After twenty-five days trench foot disabled a lot of men, and some fell out from combat fatigue.

"Well, I'm getting ahead of my story. I could tell you of dozens of heroic actions, but I'll try to focus on a few examples. Early in the fight to reach the lost battalion, fifteen German machine-gun nests pinned down the 100th. At nightfall, when fog began to rise in the little valley, the Germans decided to counterattack. They had artillery, mortars, self-propelled guns, and a platoon of tanks. Our field artillery broke their back, but just after dawn they tried again. We formed bazooka teams and resumed attack, but our men came under fire from Germans who were hiding in houses on the hills.

"Well, that's the background. Lieutenant Masanao Otake went out with a patrol to try to take care of the machine-gun nests. His group knocked out one and took possession of the house. Then Lieutenant Otake went on alone to check out the next farmhouse. While he was inside, the Germans discovered him. He fought and held on until his patrol came to his assistance. The Germans finally killed him in a burst of machine-gun fire, but the number of the enemy he killed cleared the way for our advance the next morning.

"Staff Sergeant Yoshimi Fujiwara, with a bazooka, stopped two German tanks from making a breakthrough. He lived to fight again.

"In another deadlock to take a hill, one of our men was wounded, and Technical Sergeant Abraham Ohama went to his aid. Sergeant Ohama was not a medic. He was also hit. Litter bearers were able to get to both men. As Sergeant Ohama was being carried away, the enemy fired again, killing him on his stretcher. Without a word the entire unit rose to its feet and charged at point-blank range. They killed fifty Germans, took seven prisoners, and the hill was ours.

"Our division slogan is Go For Broke! and to a man that's what my buddies did. Another example, Staff Sergeant Robert Kuroda led a squad to knock out a machine-gun nest. When they got close, he took it out with grenades. Then when he spotted a lieutenant who had been killed, he grabbed his tommy gun and knocked out another machine-gun placement before a sniper killed him."

Tom stopped and gestured with a hand palm up. "The list could go on and on. Have you got enough?"

Em blinked back tears and looked at her watch. "I hate to stop, but it's near midnight. When is your curfew?"

"I was supposed to meet my buddies at the train station at 2300." He glanced at his watch. "Too late now."

"I'll run you to your camp," Hubert said, and went to fetch their coats.

"Will you be in trouble?" Em asked. "Should I come and explain?"

"No need. I'll be in trouble one way or the other, but not too bad. We're taking it easy on the way back south. Look, Em, let me know if you need more information." He scribbled his mailing address on a scrap of envelope from his pocket and handed it to her. "If you get the story in your magazine, Jean and I will take you out for a special celebration after the war."

"Promise?" she said, smiling as cheerfully as she could after the stories that had made a lump in her throat.

"Absolutely."

After the men left, Estelle said, "What a nice man, and how brave his friends were."

"Yes. Like you and Hubert. You also risked everything. Now you can start working for peace."

"Oui. So I hope."

Em's energy level abruptly sank below sea level. She covered a yawn. "Excuse me! I can hardly keep my eyes open."

"Ah, let me turn down your bed for you." Estelle hurried to the small guest room ahead of her.

No bed had ever looked more inviting. Em quickly undressed and sank into featherbed comfort. Tomorrow would be soon enough to sort out all that had happened these past two days.

Chapter Twenty

Marge could no longer refuse to think about how she would feel when David left. Today was the day. The doctors decided he would be able to return to active duty after two or three weeks' recuperation in a Paris military hospital.

When she saw the ambulances lining up to transport the stabilized wounded, she hurried to post-op to tell him good-bye.

She wished she'd had more time to talk with him. Their visits had been sporadic and brief. Sometimes after twelve hours in surgery she'd found him asleep when she went to see him. Today his eyes sought hers the minute she entered the tent. She hurried to his side.

"Good morning," she said. "I hear you're going to Paris for rest and recuperation!"

He grinned, easy and slow. "That's what they tell me. Have you been to Paris?"

"No."

"Someday I'd like to take you."

She kept her voice light. "That would be nice. In the meantime, mind the doctors. Concentrate on getting well, and maybe they will let you go out on the town before you come back."

"If they do, I'll bring you some French perfume."

She laughed and looked down at her muddy boots. "That would raise my morale."

"Margaret, I'm right thankful I made it, and when this war is over maybe we can be more than friends."

"Yes, I'm thankful, too, Sergeant David." She meant to sound light and friendly but realized too late that mentioning his rank, lower than hers, could be taken as a put-down. She quickly tried to undo that possibility. "I didn't mean that the way it might have sounded. If you were a general, I couldn't respect you more."

He grinned. "Don't you trouble yourself about that. Of course I understand. One thing troubles me though. What about Isabelle? Have you had time to visit her?"

She shook her head. "No. I'm due for a day off, but you know how that is. And Aachen has been off limits to nurses."

"Well, look—" He handed her a penciled map. "If you can get permission, here's the location of the hospital where we took her, the best I can remember. You might need to ask for more directions, depending on who drives you into Aachen. When you see her, would you give her this from me?" He handed Marge packages of hair ribbons and chewing gum.

She put them and the map in her uniform pocket. "She'll love those. Wherever did you find the ribbons?"

"Bought the ribbons from a woman in a village we went through. I don't know what Isabelle's nurses will say about the gum. Here." He reached in his robe pocket again. "Give them some too." He handed her two more packages.

"You're very well supplied for not being able to get to a PX."

"I've got buddies."

"Yes." He had a lot of buddies. So many men from his outfit had asked about him. They called him Doc.

The stretcher-bearers came to David's bed, so she backed out of their way. "Take care, David."

"Yeah." He placed his hand dramatically on his chest. Reminiscent of General Douglas MacArthur when he'd been forced to retreat from the Philippines, David proclaimed, "I shall return!"

She laughed. "Not as a patient, please."

"Right. Bye, Nurse Margaret." He caught her hand and gave it a squeeze that went right to her heart. Then they carried him out to the waiting truck.

Amelia walked up and stood beside her. "Well, your favorite medic is on his way."

"Yes." She tried not to think of the times that trucks marked with red crosses had been strafed, shelled, or bombed. David had demonstrated a charmed life, but a sudden overwhelming fear filled her. *Please, dear God, watch over him and keep him safe!*

A few days later, Chief Nurse Louise gave Marge and Carolyn a twenty-four hour leave. With a plea to visit Isabelle, Marge obtained permission to go into Aachen. Carolyn jumped at the chance to get out of the field hospital, even to visit a war-devastated city. Dressed in boots, pants, winter coats, and scarves—with rain ponchos over the top—they hitched a ride on an army supply truck.

Marge was surprised at the size of Aachen, even though David had described it as large. They got out of the truck, supposedly close to the hospital. Wind slapped heavy rain in their faces and sent them to the shelter of a bomb-gutted building. Under its undamaged arched entrance, Marge unfolded David's map. He'd noted the location of some major buildings and named main streets. Still, she couldn't tell which direction to go.

"I don't see how we can find the hospital on foot," Carolyn said. "Why don't we go to a restaurant or canteen and ask for directions."

"Good idea," Marge agreed. So they walked down the street past piles of broken masonry and stones. A few buildings that hadn't been damaged suggested the former beauty of this historic city. Soon they found a small eating establishment that was open.

At least we're out of the rain, Marge thought, looking around at the few tables and customers who all seemed to be dining on some kind of soup.

A woman greeted them. "You wish for lunch?"

Marge glanced at Carolyn who shook her head no. "Please, can you direct us to this hospital?" She held out the piece of paper, hoping it would make sense to the waitress.

The woman looked at it. "I ask." She walked away with David's crude map in her hand. It was all Marge could do to keep from following and snatching it back.

"I hope she knows someone who can figure it out," Carolyn said.

The woman returned with a man wearing a cook's apron and cap. He inclined his head in a stiff little bow and said, "Hospital"—he pointed to their left—"down street past church. One more street to right." He handed back the map and gave his little bow again.

"Thank you," Carolyn said.

"Yes, thank you," Marge echoed.

Following his brief directions, they found the hospital. The name on the front matched what David wrote. Inside, they went to the registration desk, where a sister greeted them.

Marge smiled at the woman. "We're looking for a little girl who was treated in our field hospital. She was brought here when she was well enough to transport. Her name is Isabelle Moulton."

The nurse looked through some papers and a card file. "Yes. She was here, but she has been released to a small orphanage run by the Catholic sisters in Bovigny."

"Bovigny. That's on the edge of the Ardennes Forest," Marge gasped. The only thing she knew about the Ardennes was that her childhood friend's father had been gassed there. The name Ardennes still conjured up a black feeling. She couldn't help wishing that Isabelle was somewhere else.

"Can you give me the name of the orphanage?" she asked.

"Yes, Hollard Farm Home. It's an old farm that the Hollard family donated to the church. It's about sixty kilometers south, almost to the Luxembourg border."

"Thank you," Marge said, writing the name on the back of her map and calculating it must be about forty miles. If she could get transportation, it wasn't too far for a visit.

Outside in the rain again, Carolyn said, "Now what? It's not much of a day for sight-seeing here."

"I agree. Too nasty cold. Let's look for an army headquarters and find a ride back to the hospital."

They trudged on down the street between piles of rubble and silent buildings. Marge was determined to locate Isabelle, one way or another, before David returned from Paris. How hard could it be to find a farm that had been converted to an orphanage near a small village?

Em stayed an extra day with Hubert and Estelle, hoping Tom's battalion might linger a day too. It didn't, so Em used the time to type out a detailed draft of the story she'd gleaned from Tom's stories.

Then she took the night train to Paris. From time to time, between dozing, she pondered on her improbable alliance with Werner Koch. In retrospect the situation seemed utterly unreal. Bleary-eyed, she arrived just before dawn, not an overly lengthy trip considering the damaged rail lines. She'd heard it would take several years for France to bring back good railroad service. Tonight she could heartily agree.

When she reached Hotel Scribe, she tried to put Werner out of her mind. For the moment there was nothing she could do about her agreement to help him. But what he had revealed frightened her.

What if Hitler completed the V–3 missiles before Werner could get the information out? She wished he had turned over the papers right away. Yet she couldn't fault him for wanting to save his family first.

Heavy clouds the next morning made it look like twilight in Paris. Rain slanted between the buildings. Em telephoned Cummins and answered a few questions that he worded cryptically so that no one else would understand who or what he was talking about. Then he told her she was to go to Belgium. A courier would deliver details to her hotel room. For a moment she forgot the OSS for the joy that at last she would be allowed to report from the front lines.

The rest of the morning she stayed in, waiting for the courier. Before starting her writing project, she ran downstairs to the mess hall and grabbed some coffee and toast, a treat today, as their cook had acquired fresh bread from a French bakery.

Back upstairs, with the rain sloshing in sheets against her window, she penciled in final changes on the Nisei Combat Team story, then typed a clean copy.

Shortly before noon Cummins' courier arrived, gave her an envelope, and left without conversation. Em quickly read where she was to go and whom she must see in the Aachen area. She still was more excited about her writing possibilities than by her undercover assignment. As Cummins had warned in the beginning, what they asked her to do made no particular sense to her. She was glad, however, that in each case so far, she had acquired exciting stories for her publisher.

When she went to lunch, she asked several correspondents if they'd seen Bob lately. Al Thompson volunteered that Bob was off again with the Seventh Army in eastern France. She sighed. Just her luck. She wished she could have gone to the Vosges Mountains with him. Being in that combat zone would have given her 442nd Division story more authenticity.

However, if she'd been with Bob, she probably would have missed seeing Tom, and she would not have been able to fulfill these last OSS assignments in a timely manner.

She hoped Bob would understand why she'd had to miss their date to see Paris together. But then, he might not have given it a thought. After all, the idea had been hers.

On her way to her room after lunch, the hotel clerk called, "Mademoiselle Emerson, you have mail." He held up a bundle of envelopes.

"Thanks!" She hurried to take it. "I was afraid it would never catch up with me."

"Ah, but we would find you," the fatherly old man said. "Here. Enjoy."

When she took them, she noticed the top one was a large fat envelope from her editor. "I will, I'm sure. Thank you!"

In her room, ensconced in a soft chair by the window, she hungrily thumbed through the envelopes—four from her mother and father, one from her kid brother, Billy, one from Jean Kagawa, and one from Nella Killian. But none from Marge. That was a surprise. Ever since they left home, Marge had written weekly, as regularly as Monday follows Sunday. She'd nagged Em to do the same. By now there should be at least eight letters from her.

Well, she'd better take care of business first. She opened the envelope for *USA Living & Review* and pulled out published copies of several of the articles she'd submitted. At her request, they automatically sent copies for her to give to the people she interviewed. She thumbed through them and came to a halt at the sight of her story about Jacques Marchant, "WWI French Hero Serves Again." She scanned it quickly. They'd published her piece with little cutting. She bit her lip in frustration and tossed the article onto the bedside table. She'd have to take time to mail all the others as she'd promised, but certainly not that one.

Next she ripped open Jean's letter, hoping she'd have word about Marge.

30 September, 1944
Dear Em,

I hope you have heard from Marge. She was shipped to France the week after you left Abergavenny.

The next three lines had been blacked out by a censor's pen.

My uncle Al says Marge is surely all right, and I can't bear to think otherwise. I know it's a big war, but maybe you can visit field and evacuation hospitals whenever you see one and look for her. Do let me know if you find her.

Now that I've probably sent you into a tizzy of worry, I hope that you are fine and are getting lots of great stories. I pray for your safety and Marge's too.

Nella has joined the Land Army and is working on an estate not far from Abergavenny. Actually it's at the village where Peggy teaches. I'm busy with the usual but missing Tom more than I dreamed possible.

Do take care of yourself.

Your friend,
Jean

So Marge was in France! Em read the letter again, alarmed over what had been deleted. Marge had been dead set to provoke an investigation into the death of young Private Johnson. Em had worried about her at the time, because it had sounded risky. Now somehow she must find Marge. As Jean said, surely her assignment to a field hospital was an ordinary military decision, but all those blacked-out sentences made Em uneasy.

She read Nella's letter next. It had been censored to the point that it gave little real news, but it was obvious she, too, was worried about Marge.

"What on earth is going on?" Em murmured. Her anxiety ballooned into fear. *Where is Marge that she can't write? How can I find her?* Em laid the rest of the mail aside and called the hotel desk. "Please, can you tell me if Mr. Mansfield has returned?"

"One moment, please."

She held and waited impatiently.

The voice came on again. "I'm sorry. I'm not certain if he's in, but he hasn't picked up his mail. Do you want to leave him a message?"

"Yes. But I'll come down with it. Thank you."

She hung up the receiver and returned to her desk. She wrote quickly.

> *Bob, I need to see you. Please call me no matter when you get in. Of course, if you don't return to Paris by tomorrow, Sunday, I may be gone myself. I'll be heading for the combat zone in Belgium.*

If she saw him, she'd have to come up with credible lies about how she'd broken free of the army regulations that had kept her out of combat zones until now. She signed her name, sealed the note in an envelope, and put his name and room number on the outside.

It took only a minute to run downstairs, hand the note to the concierge, and hurry back upstairs to read the rest of her mail. She enjoyed the letters from her mom and dad and brother, but she couldn't get Marge off her mind.

When she finished reading her mail, she couldn't sit still. She paced to the window several times. One way or another she had to find Marge! On the way to Aachen, she'd stop at every army hospital she saw.

She forced herself to sit down again and put the final touches on the combat team story. Darkness settled over the city by four o'clock. She flipped on a desk light and kept writing. At last the piece was ready. Just as she opened her door to go down to dinner, her phone jangled. She ran back and picked it up.

Bob's welcome voice greeted her. "Em? What's wrong?"

"Oh, I'm so glad you're back! I can't tell you on the phone. As soon as you can, please come by my room. I have something I'd like you to read."

"I'll be right over." The receiver clicked, and the line went open.

She hung up and ran to the mirror to comb her hair and apply some lipstick.

His knock sounded on the door almost immediately.

She opened, and one look at his concerned face erased all she had meant to say.

He took her by the shoulders. "You okay, Lucy-Em?"

The concern in his voice nearly undid her. She nodded, unable to speak without her voice trembling.

He studied her for a second and then wrapped his arms around her and held her close. The feel of his arms tight around her slowly overpowered her fear. She pressed her face against his shoulder. When she stopped shaking, he slowly let go of her. "What happened?" he asked.

Surely it was love for her that softened the tired lines around his eyes as they searched her face. To move away from him took all of her willpower. She sensed that if she clung to him he would kiss her, but this was not the time for love. Too much depended on her being able to move and act independently without having to explain anything to him. And if there should be danger, she did not want him involved. Once Werner Koch had delivered his information, then maybe she could think about love.

She stepped back. "Please come in. I want to show you a couple of letters I received."

He followed her to the desk and leaned against the wall by the lamp to read. When he finished, he said, "You think some shady dealings sent Marge to the Front?"

"I don't know. I'm not even sure she—" her voice cracked. She swallowed and started again, telling him about the way Marge had tried to have a soldier's death investigated in Wales, and how the evidence had pointed toward murder. "I keep thinking, what if someone wanted to silence her? What if she never got to the Front! She always has written to me every week, and I haven't received a single letter from her. Good grief—it's been over eight weeks!"

He frowned. "Eight weeks doesn't mean too much with the way things are here. In fact, it might be evidence that she is at the Front, working so hard she doesn't have time to write. The army nurses I've seen have been grossly overworked."

His words broke through some of the dread Jean's letter had triggered, but she argued, "Marge would write. She always has."

"Well, how about you? Have you written to her weekly since you've been over here?"

"No. I— Things have been happening so fast. I guess you have a point." Remembering her manners at last, she said, "Won't you sit down?"

"Thanks, but I won't stay. I have your reputation to think about."

At this she smiled. Among the journalists, Bob had a reputation for avoiding romantic liaisons, and so did she. "You know gossip goes on around here for any reason and for no reason, so what difference does it make?"

"It matters to me. Let's leave it at that. Please don't create situations that some men might misunderstand." Without explaining further, he headed for the door. With his hand on the knob, he turned. "The note you sent me mentioned going to the combat zone. I'm glad you broke through the red tape, but I was wondering if you might be able to delay for a day. If you remember, we had a date to do the town."

"I need to go as soon as possible, but how about going out tonight?"

"Sure. I heard of a new little place where we can get a real meal. Probably black-market meat, if any, but Al told me the food is better than the K rations here at the hotel. We might even find a concert or stage show of sorts."

"Dinner and a show!" She sighed. "I'd almost forgotten such things exist."

"Then come on," he urged. "You need a bit of a break."

"Okay. What time?"

He checked his watch. "In half an hour? Meet me in the lobby?"

"I'll be there."

As she washed and put on a clean uniform, Em's anxiety over Marge eased a little. Surely Bob was right. Marge was just overworked. She'd write soon. In the meantime, whenever Em saw a military hospital, she would check it out. For a few hours, she would try to forget the war. She wished she could really dress up, in a gown even. Oh well, being with Bob was special, gown or no.

She brushed her hair into an upsweep behind her ears, pinned it into a French twist, and then perched her service cap on her head at a jaunty angle.

Downstairs in the lobby Bob was already waiting. Seeing him freshly groomed and pressed decidedly took her thoughts off the war.

He came to meet her and held out his arm for her to take. She suddenly felt pampered and cared for, and found she liked the feeling. She slipped her hand in the crook of his arm. With the back of her hand against the warmth of his side, she felt like a schoolgirl again. For want of any clever words to cover her quick pleasure, she exclaimed, "I'm really hungry. I hope your friend is right about the café's food."

"I trust his taste, but we shall see."

When they reached their destination and said good-bye to the soldiers with whom they had shared a ride, Em was pleasantly surprised. The small restaurant smelled of freshly baked bread and herbs. It had candles on the tables and Impressionist paintings on the walls. There was no menu. Only one dinner existed. Chicken came in a wonderful wine sauce with lightly sautéed vegetables and some real butter for the crusty bread. Dessert was a French type of pudding. She savored its smoothness on her tongue before swallowing.

When they finished, Em leaned back satiated. "I can't believe that feast after finding only bread and some substitute for wine offered in places that are labeled café."

He shrugged. "No doubt we ate some black-market foods, but they may have family connections with a farm." He leaned back with a pleased sigh. "Not bad, no matter where it came from. Did you get any good stories from your friend Vivienne's contacts? You never said."

"Oh yes. Great stories. My editor was pleased. He already sent the tear sheets on several. I have another one ready to go, plus a story I happened upon just before returning to Paris. Do you remember my telling you about my Red Cross friend, Jean, who married a Japanese American?"

He raised his chin and tipped his head slightly, a gesture she recognized as his most attentive, considering look. "Yes. I thought about her when I met some of the Nisei Combat Team. They were on the way north from Marseilles with the Seventh Army when I first joined General Devers."

"Did you interview any of them?"

"No. I wanted to, but they were on the move to a combat zone, and I never caught up with them after that."

"Well, I did. I met Jean's husband in Macon after the Bruyeres campaign. We spent a whole evening together. I have a marvelous story from him ready to go. I sure hate having to send it to London first. They'll mangle it and delay it." She told him about the Bruyeres campaign and the actions of the combat team.

When she finished, he said in a thoughtful tone, "Maybe I can get the censors to work on it here and then send it with my story."

"You can do that?"

"I said maybe. One of the guys owes me. If he will clear your story with mine, I can send them both to my office with instructions to forward yours to your publisher."

"They'll do that? That would be wonderful!"

"Your eyes are big as our plates. Would you like to get it off tonight? It would mean we can't look for a stage show."

She laid aside her napkin and stood up. "There will always be another stage show. Bob, this will be a scoop. I don't think anyone else has covered the 442nd Division. It would really make me feel good to showcase the courage of those guys who were imprisoned at home as if they were spies. People need to know the truth."

Bob signaled the waiter for the check, and in moments they were outside looking for a ride back to Hotel Scribe.

When they reached the hotel, Bob said, "Bring me the story, and then wait in your room. I don't want you involved if anything goes wrong."

"Well, my name will be on the story. That does make me involved."

"Sure, but I think I'll get more cooperation if no one sees you in person."

"Well, I like that! Talk about prejudice."

"Just do as I say, and change your by-line to your initials. L what?"

"L. M."

"Okay, L. M. Emerson. Can you fix the by-line fast, like already?"

She grinned. "I'll be back ten minutes ago." She ran upstairs, put a new piece of paper in her typewriter, and retyped the first page with her new by-line.

When she returned to the lobby he was waiting.

"Okay. Now be a good girl and make yourself scarce. I'll come tell you when the deed is done."

"Thank you, thank you! How long do you think it will take?"

"Not long if I can reach the right guy."

She hurried upstairs, feeling like the night before Christmas. Getting her story in quickly, while the news was hot, would be wonderful.

But she was more excited by the fact that Bob was going to such unexpected lengths to help her.

She was much too wakeful to go right to bed, so she composed brief notes to her interview subjects and put their published stories in envelopes to mail to them. When she finished, she saw the Marchant story lying where she'd tossed it. She sat down on the edge of the bed and read it. She decided she'd written a captivating story despite her wish not to submit it. As she read, every detail of the interview came back to her. The father and daughter certainly were masters at deception.

She started to throw the clipping away but suddenly remembered a look in Jeanette's eyes when she'd asked whether the article had been published. Wistful, that's how she was when she said the story meant a lot to her father. She'd expressed a disarming concern for her father, like a normal loving daughter.

Em sat poised to crumple the article, and then on impulse, she grabbed an envelope and addressed it to Jacques Marchant. She folded the article neatly, placed it inside without a note, and sealed the flap. It surely should not cause a problem to mail them what she'd promised.

CHAPTER TWENTY-ONE

Em paced the floor of her hotel room, waiting for Bob to come and tell her whether he had successfully submitted her story with his. The more she thought about it, the more she regretted letting him try. She had no idea what kind of trouble he might be risking just to get her story to her magazine by a faster route.

The expected knock on her door sent her flying to answer.

He stepped inside, closed the door, opened his arms wide, and announced, "Voilà! It is done."

"I've been thinking about how much trouble you could get into. You're sure it's okay?"

"Positive. I took the liberty of reading the censored version and placing a few connecting words. It's a great story, Em. Beautifully written, and the censoring didn't diminish what you wanted to say."

"Thanks. I hope my editor agrees."

"I sent a wire with it to tell my editor where to send your story. So you should know in a few days."

"I really appreciate your help, Bob. I can't thank you enough."

"I know one way," he said.

For an instant she thought he was going to say what she wanted to hear, something like "How about a kiss?"

Instead, he said, "Take me with you to Belgium. It would make up for our cancelled date tonight."

She supposed it should be easy for him to get permission for himself but not necessarily for them to ride together to the same location. Would his presence hamper her secret mission to interview the peasant family on the border south of Aachen? She decided it would not.

"I'll talk to the man who cleared me for the trip and ask permission for you to come also. I don't know why he'd say no."

"Good girl." He stood looking at her with a bemused expression. "Would you do me one more favor?"

"You have but to ask." She raised her hands in her most grandiose imitation of a fairy godmother.

He grinned. "Come to chapel with me before we head out."

She made no effort to conceal her surprise. "Chapel?"

"Sure. I have a friend who is an army chaplain. He makes more sense than anybody I've heard. You'd like him."

"I didn't know chapel was important to you."

"I don't go around broadcasting my beliefs."

He didn't go around broadcasting anything personal. She wished he would.

"Some days," he said, "my faith is the only thing that holds me together. Are you shocked?"

"No. Just surprised."

He studied her. "Surprised good or surprised bad?"

"Good." How blind she had been. She should have known this was why he had never made passes at her or at other women.

"If I can't go north with you, will you still take time to come with me for Ben's early chapel message?"

"Well, sure." She'd made the effort to attend church regularly in England, but somehow not here.

Again Em sensed he was about to kiss her, but he stepped back into the hallway. "Good night, Lucy-Em."

"Good night."

Alone in her room, she thought of all the times he had seemed close to making a romantic advance and then had retreated. She had wished more than once that she were the flirting type so she could break through his cautiousness. Now she knew that flirting wouldn't likely work with him any more than it would work with her. Funny, she hadn't thought about that before. She had never trusted a flirting man.

This fresh insight relieved her but also frustrated her. Even though she did not want romance to blossom between them right now, she treasured hopes for the future. What lay behind his careful reserve toward her? Had his marriage made him unwilling to marry again? Did he have a girl back home? He had dated several of the press corps women in London, but never showed an attachment to anyone.

If he came with her to Belgium, or even while she was with him in chapel service tomorrow, she might learn more about him. She hoped so.

When Marge returned to the field hospital with Carolyn, she placed David's small gift for Isabelle in her footlocker. No telling how soon she could get another day off to go searching for the Babe. She sighed with frustration. She had so hoped she'd be able to reassure David about Isabelle—that she had found her happily settled into a good home. The orphanage could be a good one, but it was not like being with a family.

Marge took the remainder of the afternoon to do her hand laundry. Just as she was finishing, she heard Amelia yelling, "Marge! Marge! You've got a pile of mail!"

Her friend burst into the laundry tent waving a handful of envelopes. Marge just gaped for a minute. Then she rinsed and dried her hands and took the letters from Amelia. "I can hardly believe my eyes!"

At last her own letters to her family and friends would be delivered too. What a relief that the secrecy was over. Quickly she thumbed through them—two from Em, six from her parents, one from her brother, several from nurse friends in Wales, several from Jean and Nella. "Good thing I have the rest of the day off. It will take me an hour to read all these," she exclaimed.

Amelia grinned. "I'm sure glad for you. I worried, you not getting any mail for so long."

"Me too, actually," Marge said, which was half true. She'd worried that she wouldn't know if her loved ones fell ill or worse. "But here we are!" She held up the envelopes.

"Hey, I'll hang your things with mine. You read your mail." Without waiting for an answer, Amelia snatched up the wet socks, panties, and bras and carried them to the makeshift clothesline at the end of the tent.

"Thanks!" Marge called. She sat down on her cot with her wealth of news. Which one first? She decided on Em's and learned she had indeed come to France. Then her curiosity about what had happened in the Gilwern hospital after she left led her to read the nurses' letters next. They all expressed shock over her sudden departure, but otherwise things sounded as if nothing had changed in the station hospital.

Marge finished the pile by opening the most recent envelope from

Nella. She glanced at Amelia still hanging laundry. "Guess what! One of my Welsh friends is engaged to marry a lord's son!"

Amelia stopped. "No kidding. Is he wealthy?"

"I don't know, but for Nella that wouldn't be important. She's a very young war widow who never planned to marry again. I'm sure she's been surprised by love."

"Sounds wonderful," Amelia replied. "I could be green with little effort."

Marge laughed, pulled off her boots, and sat cross-legged on her cot, hoping to warm her feet. Then she opened the earliest letter from her parents. Her mother's homey letter had nothing removed by censors. As she read, she could imagine her petite mother sitting at the kitchen table, writing before doing the breakfast dishes, just as the letter said. A sweet affection flowed from the paper. Her mom and dad were doing well. Now if her brother was okay, her fears from waiting so long for mail would be totally erased.

Yes, he was fine, in the navy somewhere in the Pacific. His breezy letter made her grin.

"Good news, I see." Amelia was back beside her.

"Very good news," she replied.

The rest of the day, whenever she had a quiet moment, she remembered what Nella had said about Rufe, that he was a hero. She'd known from the beginning that he had a special quality of strength, despite the fact everyone else said he was mentally ill. He'd been a good actor . . . and a good boy.

In Paris, before Em went to bed, she telephoned Cummins at his quarters in Gennevilliers. He agreed to arrange for Bob to go along. He said Bob's presence might assure anyone watching that her journey involved only journalism. He ordered her to stay in a hotel in Aachen, leave Bob there, and go alone to her contact in the St. Vith area. It was imperative that Bob not know exactly where she would be going. "Despite the destruction in Aachen, you'll find the best accommodations there and also plenty of reporting opportunities to conceal your real mission."

"Okay," she agreed.

As soon as he rang off, she called Bob in his room. "I've arranged for you to go with me to the Front. A jeep will be waiting for us at 0900. Does that give us time for chapel service?"

"Sure does. Can you be ready at six-thirty? Service starts at seven."

"I'll be ready."

"See you then. Thanks, Em. I appreciate this."

"You're welcome. I'm glad it worked out." She rang off and quickly packed for the next day.

The chapel service was held in one of the dining rooms of a nearby hotel that served as a U.S. Army headquarters. Em and a dozen or so WAACs were the only women present. There were lots of men with brass on their shoulders and many more plain GIs. Sitting beside Bob, hearing him sing hymns she had grown up singing, gave her surprising comfort. The service was simple, and Bob's friend, Chaplain Ben Sawyer, did have insights that made Em think.

He gave her questions to gnaw on and helped her get a surprising look at herself. "If you think God created humankind and then stepped out of the picture, think again. Our hours, days, and years are in His hands," he said.

Lately Em had been feeling that God was too busy with big things to watch after her. She'd stopped praying the way she used to at the beginning of each day.

"Read again the story of St. Paul. Forget he's a Bible personage. See him as a zealous killer, perhaps no different from a dedicated Nazi. Look at him with the same eyes you use on people today. Then with your everyday eyes—not with church eyes—look at him after his journey to Damascus. With everyday eyes see his frequent doubts and remorse and worries, and consider how God led him step-by-step to living a life we now call saintly. . . ."

Hmm, Em thought. She'd never had a desire to be saintly, but she'd feel much better if she could believe God led her in the way He had led Paul.

On the way back to hotel, Bob said, "What did you think of Ben's sermon?"

"I liked it. He made me face my own sloppy thinking."

"Yeah. He does that for me too."

"Lately," she confided, "I've had a hard time believing God has time to pay us individual attention, especially in the midst of war."

"Me too, but I'm coming more and more to believe that He does. I expect someday we'll understand more clearly."

The driver pulled up in front of Hotel Scribe, and they parted to get their bags and typewriters.

When Em came down, there was still time for coffee, so she went into the mess hall and took a seat where Bob could spot her.

In a few minutes, he came in and dropped a battered case beside the other chair and sat down. "I left my bag in the lobby, but I never leave my typewriter." He fetched coffee and returned. "You were swift getting here. With all the rush, you don't have a hair out of place. How'd you do that?" He rubbed his chin. "I'm only half shaved."

"You don't look half shaved," she assured him. He looked wonderful, but she sensed she'd better not say so. Her opinion was inflated, she knew, by how she felt about him. "I've always been able to pack and run on short notice, probably because I love to take off on an adventure without a lot of falderal. I like to keep things simple."

He nodded. "I've noticed that about you—that you like to just take off. That can get you into trouble, as I've said before."

"I suppose so. But so far, I've been glad for every time I followed my nose for news."

"Is this trip one of those nose leadings? How did you manage, in the few weeks since I saw you, to meet someone who could get you into a combat zone—in your own jeep, no less?"

She made herself smile in a relaxed manner. "I met a few people who had some clout."

"With Eisenhower?"

"Well, almost as good."

"So you're not going to tell me."

She'd known this might come up. She looked him in the eyes and said, "That's right. I'm not going to tell you. And you, being a gentleman, are not going to ask any more questions. And Bob, thank you for taking me to church this morning. I'll be thinking for quite a while about Chaplain Ben's message."

"You change the subject becomingly. No more questions," he agreed. "And you are very welcome."

On the way out of Paris, their driver wove expertly through the streets, and within an hour they joined an army convoy heading north on one of the Red Ball highways reserved for transporting supplies.

Em had to shout to be heard above the jeep noise. "At this rate we should be there for supper."

"Yes. This road's in good shape."

She glanced at the countryside. Although bleak from days of rain and signs of an early winter, the land showed no battle scars this close to Paris. She couldn't see all that well, of course, with the side window shields battened down to keep out the rain. Chilling wind whipped in around the window covers, making her glad for her boots, thick socks, and the layers of winter clothing she wore. Even the steel helmet offered weather protection.

The noise inside the bouncing jeep made conversation impossible. Monosyllables and hand gestures had to suffice. Nevertheless, she enjoyed Bob's company. He had a gift for seeing the funny side of things and kept her smiling with his pantomiming long after she had become totally miserable from the cold and the hard seat. The convoy made a few rest stops, and by the time they reached their destination, it was dark. Their driver left the convoy and drove them into Aachen.

It must have once been a lovely old city, but now it contained the worst devastation Em had seen. She wondered how it could ever be brought back to life, but already the residents had begun to pile some of the debris in preparation for removing it.

Their driver, Corporal Benfield, took them to a centrally located hotel and parked while they signed in. Because Em would need him to travel about, he had orders to stay at the same hotel.

They found a place to eat within walking distance where they ordered a supper of coarse bread, sauerkraut, potatoes, and a few bites of carrot.

Em whispered, "I think we'd do better with C rations."

"I think they'd do better with C rations," Bob replied.

They left without lingering over ersatz coffee. The hotel and restaurant people were courteous but never smiled. Em remarked on this as they walked to the nearby hotel.

"I guess I wouldn't want to smile either at a conqueror," Bob said.

"They did bring this destruction on themselves."

"Yes, but you can't expect them to be friendly."

"Uh-huh," she said, but she was thinking about the Germans who were cooperating with the OSS. At least some Germans were friendly to the Allies. The woman she had been sent to interview, Clara Kertzen, had been inside Germany sending out intelligence information for the past few months. Now she was in the village of St. Vith, her adopted hometown. She had crossed the border through the Hurtgen Forest several times, but now that the war had taken over the forest, she stayed home.

And since St. Vith had fallen into Allied hands she was safe. Em's press corps interview would involve the woman's whole family, covering how they lived during the occupation, but she aimed to focus on the woman. Her husband had served in the underground, but not in the OSS. As before, Em had no idea what Cummins expected to discover through her interviewing. He had only given her a thin envelope plus an oral message she'd memorized for only Madame Kertzen.

"Penny for your thoughts," Bob said.

She laughed. "They're not even worth a half penny. I was thinking about Marge," she lied, "wondering where she is."

"Tomorrow maybe we can locate some field hospitals."

When they reached the old hotel, she said to Bob, "I'm really tired. And first thing tomorrow I have to get moving for my interview. Shall we try to meet for supper tomorrow night?"

He didn't answer right away, and as he studied her face in the dim light of the hotel lobby, she knew he wanted to question her. She braced herself to make acceptable excuses, but he said, "Sure. I want to look for army headquarters and get permission to visit the famed West Wall and interview some of the fighting men."

"If for any reason I'm not back here by seven o'clock, go ahead and eat, and I'll do the same if you aren't back."

"Okay." He glanced around the hotel lobby. "Let me walk you to your room. This place gives me the creeps with all the glowering Germans around."

"There are also American soldiers," she said, nodding toward officers who had just come in the front doors.

"All the more reason I want to escort you to your room."

"As you wish, kind sir." She tried to curtsy.

He chuckled. "Em, you'd never make anybody a proper serving maid."

"I choose to take that as a compliment."

They both had rooms on the first floor. He pointed out his before they proceeded to hers. He waited to be sure her key worked, and when she turned to say good-night, he said, "You be careful tomorrow. I ought to insist on going with you, but I can see you'd put up a big fight. If you leave the city, remember to stay away from active zones. It's dangerous enough just to be here. A lot of people think the Germans are permanently on the run, but I have learned never to expect weakness from the enemy."

"I'll be careful," she promised. She thought he was borrowing trouble to think the Germans could counterattack at this point in the war. Tens of thousands of German soldiers had surrendered, and Hitler's army had barely slowed the Allied advance. But she knew better than to argue. "Good night," she said. "See you tomorrow for dinner."

He cupped her face with his hands and kissed her. She kissed him back with all the love she'd tried to save for a better time.

He drew her into his arms and held her close. She slipped her arms around his waist and held on tight.

He didn't kiss her again. He just held her as if he would never let go. She wished he never would.

"Lucy-Em, I can't stand to think of you being hurt. I wish you weren't doing this. I wish I could go with you. I wish this war were over and we could—" He stopped abruptly and let go of her. "What am I doing robbing the cradle? I was on the way to becoming a hard-bitten newspaper man when you were still in kindergarten!"

"You never made it to hard-bitten," she said. "But I've been out of kindergarten for a very long time."

"Will you let me go with you?"

"No."

"I only want to be sure you're safe."

"Why?"

"What?"

"War is not a safe place to be. Why should you think I deserve some kind of special protection? Why do you want me safe?"

"Because I love you so much," he answered harshly. He turned away from her and stomped down the dimly lighted hall.

For the first time in her life, Em did not pursue what she desperately wanted. This was not the right time for either of them. She went inside her room and locked her door. No one ever had told her how much real love could hurt. She bit her lip and then decided to go ahead and cry.

CHAPTER TWENTY-TWO

In the morning, when Em went to the hotel café to look for breakfast, she saw no sign of Bob, but her driver hopped up from his table and came to greet her.

"Good morning, Corporal Benfield," she said. "Before we go, I need to talk to Bob."

"Morning, ma'am. Mr. Mansfield left already. Said to tell you he'd see you tonight. Some officers invited him to go with them for the day."

"Oh. Good. Then I guess I'd better eat so we can go." She beckoned to a nearby waiter, who responded with plodding deliberation.

"Sausage and a roll, please. And coffee."

Unsmiling, he said, "Only a roll we have."

"That will be fine."

He nodded and left.

"Friendly sort, ain't he?" Corporal Benfield remarked.

"Well, as Bob says, we're the invader now. So tell me, did you check out road conditions for the drive to St. Vith?"

"The fighting is a few miles to the east of the town. Roads are muddy. The rain is mixed with snow, but Antoinette can go through most anything."

She grinned over his pet name for the jeep. "Why are cars always given female names, Corporal?"

He raised his eyebrows and shrugged. "I suppose there's lots of reasons. Some do it for luck. Me, I just do it for laughs."

She smiled. "A guy needs laughs."

The glowering waiter brought her two small rolls. A minute later he sat the steaming cup of brew beside her plate. She looked up and said, "Thank you."

He nodded and his mouth moved next door to a smile.

She turned back to her driver. "Do we have clearance to go to St. Vith alone?"

"Clearance to go wherever you want. I handed the CO my orders. He read them and signed his name without any questions." He gave her a teasing look. "Funny, you don't look the sort to have such a way with the officers."

She gave him a raised eyebrow look and shrugged. "I try to make friends in high places. That's how I get my best stories." Even though he'd never guess the truth, it was safer to let him think whatever he wished.

"Well, you and Mr. Mansfield looked pretty thick to me. But I have a hunch you got connections that don't depend on hanky-panky."

She cut him off. "Is there anything you need to do to get Antoinette ready? I'll be at the front door in ten minutes."

He took the hint. "Yes, ma'am. I'll go gas up and be there waiting."

She ate quickly, paid her tab, and hurried to the main door of the lobby, buttoning her winter coat as she walked. Outside, Corporal Benfield waited in the jeep. Fastening the chinstrap of her steel helmet, she climbed in beside him. In her battered briefcase she carried paper, pencils, and the envelope to give to Clara Kertzen. She had memorized the location of the Kertzen farm.

A short distance from Aachen, they passed a field hospital—a complex of tents, boldly marked with red crosses on white backgrounds. "Be sure you can find that hospital when we return. I want to stop there," she called over the noise of the engine.

"Yes, ma'am. That should be easy, it being close to the road and all."

They drove through rain mixed with snow, as predicted. When they finally reached the little town of St. Vith, Em said, "Drive on through the town."

"You mean we ain't going to a house here in the village?"

"No. It's a farm near another small village off to the east."

"But that could lead right into the combat zone. Our men have been fighting for weeks in that godforsaken terrain—"

"Corporal." She glowered at him. She didn't need a doomsayer on this trip. "Despite how it may look, God has not forsaken any place of this earth, and I'll thank you not to use that term on this trip. We have clearance to go anywhere, so take the next right and head out that way until we come to the first left outside of St. Vith."

"Yes, ma'am."

He gunned the engine. The tires slopped a trail through muddy slush. Soon they came to the graveled road that should lead to the Kertzen farm. The route made right-angle turns along property lines. Leafless trees guarded one side of the road and then the other. In several places the jeep wallowed through and over mud ruts caused by tanks. Em began to wonder if the Kertzen family would be at home. How could they stay if it lay in a battle zone?

Landmarks told her it shouldn't be much farther. At last, after passing a large old barn, they rounded a curve, and directly ahead she saw the stone farmhouse that matched the photo she'd memorized in Geneva. She pointed. "That's it. Drive up to the house." Barren trees and mud had turned the hillside dismal. The pasture sheltered no animals. The yard revealed no evidence of occupants.

Corporal Benfield swerved into the drive, and with minimum spinning of the wheels, he pulled into the muddy dooryard that separated the old house from storage buildings and barns. A farm dog came barking from a small shed. Behind the dog a man appeared. He waved the dog back to the shed and strode toward the jeep.

Corporal Benfield switched off the engine.

Em got out. "Monsieur Kertzen?" She'd been told the Kertzens spoke English fluently.

"Yes," he replied.

She introduced herself and her purpose.

He wiped his hand on his pants and held it out. They shook, and in reasonably good English he said, "Come into the house." He glanced at the corporal. "Both of you."

Monsieur Kertzen and his wife were fair-skinned, gray-haired, and sturdy. They moved with vigor, but Em calculated they must be past sixty. She'd been unprepared for them to look like grandparents.

As they sat around the kitchen table drinking a hot brew of homemade barley coffee, she learned that their grown children had moved far away before the war. They had endured the occupation alone, obeying German orders for production of wheat, milk, eggs, and beef until the battle moved close to them.

"When the Americans pushed into this area," Monsieur Kertzen said, "we fled to the village. Fortunately the worst of the battle passed to the north of the farm without much damage, but we lost most of our livestock. Now we hang on, rid of the Germans at last."

"What was it like for you to be so near to the border during the Occupation?"

"We saw a lot of German soldiers," Madame Kertzen said. "After a while we came to know the ones who patrolled here regularly. Once they heard our German name and learned that we have many cousins in Germany, they began to look on us as sympathizers. We found it safer to let them think this."

"Did your neighbors accuse you of collaborating?" Em asked.

Monsieur Kertzen waved his hand in a gesture of dismissal. "Some did—even a friend we'd gone to school with. But we knew we could persuade them they were wrong after the Boches were pushed out. And it has been so, hasn't it, Clara?"

"Yes. People again respect us." She stood up. "Please excuse me while I tend the soup. You will eat with us, of course. Rene likes a hot meal in the middle of the day, and I have prepared plenty."

"Thank you. We'd be pleased to accept," Em answered.

Madame Kertzen turned to her husband. "Rene, please will you go fetch the nice bottle of wine Marcel promised you. It will go well with our soup and bread."

"A good thought. It won't take long, just to the next farm. Corporal, would you care to come along?"

Corporal Benfield greeted the invitation with a huge smile. "I'll drive you, sir."

"The bread I am just now putting in the oven," Madame Kertzen said. "Go now and don't dawdle on the way."

The men put on heavy coats and left.

As soon as their voices in the yard faded, Madame Kertzen said, "Mademoiselle Emerson, my contact told me you were coming, but not why. Do you have a message for me?"

"I do." She pulled the envelope from her inner pocket. "Also, I'm to tell you, 'The black cat hides in the old barn. The full moon will reveal her flight.' "

As she pocketed the envelope, Madame Kertzen exclaimed, "This comes at the worst possible moment. You are sure you have message right?"

"Yes." Em repeated it.

"Can you take a message back to Monsieur Cummins . . . soon?"

"Yes. Within three days."

"Tell him, 'Before the full moon sets, the last will be first, and the first will be last.' Write it down."

Em reached for the notepad in her pocket. "And I'll memorize it."

She wrote it and then read it back to Madame Kertzen.

She nodded. "And tell him the Kertzens are well and hope to see him before too many months. You don't have to memorize that."

"I'll tell him. Is there anything else?"

"Nothing. When the men return, remember that Monsieur Kertzen knows nothing about my work for the American OSS. You and I have only been baking bread. Ask Rene how he makes our own blue cheese. That will keep him talking for a while." She smiled affectionately.

When the men returned, Em obeyed Clara Kertzen's suggestion and not only learned how to make blue cheese but got to visit the cheese room under the house where he had several wheels of homemade cheeses aging.

Shortly after lunch, Em thanked the Kertzens and said good-bye.

The slush had piled up, turning the hills and fields a soggy gray-white. A couple of times on the road back to St. Vith, the jeep slid and spun its wheels.

"Good thing we're leaving these mountains," the corporal said. "When evening comes this slush will turn to ice. You sure you want to stop at that field hospital we passed?"

"We'll see how the roads look by the time we get there."

"Right."

They drove on without trying to talk. The wipers threw the slush from the windshield in regular thumps. Em gave up trying to look out the side and focused on the road ahead. She hated to think of soldiers out in trenches in such nasty weather.

When they reached the crest of a long hill she spied the field hospital. The snow had turned to rain so she waved her hand toward the hospital. "Let's stop. We might be able to beg a cup of real coffee."

He turned in and parked away from the ambulance driveway. "If this setup is like other field hospitals, the kitchen tent ought to be over that way."

He guessed right. Inside the mess tent, they found a large pot of coffee with mugs beside it. When the cooks saw the big C on Em's armband, they took turns coming to chat. They were friendly guys, eager to talk to the press. She wrote down their names and hometowns, making sure she spelled each one correctly.

When they learned her last name, one of the men said, "Hey, we got a nurse here named Emerson. Any relation to you?"

Em told herself to stay calm. "I have a sister who is an army nurse. What is your nurse's first name?"

"Marge," one of them said.

Em held her breath. Surely there wouldn't be two Marge Emersons in the Nurses Corps.

Corporal Benfield was looking at her with a funny expression on his face.

She exclaimed, "Where would I find your Nurse Emerson?"

"Usually in surgery, but we haven't had any new arrivals for a while. Maybe she's in post-op. You want one of us to go find her? You think our Marge could be your sister?"

"Yes! Yes, please find her. May I come along?"

"Sure," a sergeant said. "Jones, you take her to find Nurse Marge. The rest of us will hold down the coffeepot."

In a long tent with hospital beds lining each side, Em saw several nurses on duty. At the far end, she spied a petite dark-haired nurse bent over a patient. "It is my sister!"

She hurried down the center of the tent and stopped at the foot of the bed. When Marge finished giving an injection, Em called her name.

Marge whirled around. "Em!"

In the next second they were hugging each other, laughing.

"I can't believe it!" Em exclaimed. "I can't believe I found you!"

"I've been here for weeks, ever since I left Wales. I hoped I'd see you, but it seemed too incredible. Carolyn, Amelia," she called to the other nurses, "this is my sister! My little sister, Em!" She laughed and hugged Em again.

The two nurses waved and called a greeting.

"Go visit with her, Marge," Carolyn said. "I'll watch your patients."

"Thanks!" Marge gave one more shot and then hurried back to Em.

As soon as they were alone, Em asked, "Have you heard from Jean and Nella—about Rufe, I mean?"

"Yes. I just recently got all my mail in a pile. I'll let you read their letters."

Em was so happy to see Marge, but at the same time, she hated having her here. She'd heard too many times about field hospitals close to the lines being shelled and bombed.

With Em right there in front of her, Marge felt as if she were dreaming on her feet. She'd just finished ten hours in surgery after a night with only four hours of sleep. Her only reality for days had been the wounded and sick men—coming in, being treated, then evacuated. To see Em's fresh face so unexpectedly in post-op seemed almost unreal. "Em, is it really you?"

They grabbed each other again in a long hug.

"I can't believe I found you in the first field hospital I've seen," Em said, "I was going to stop at every one I could find."

"Can you stay awhile? I can set up a cot for you up in our tent."

"I'd love to, but I have to get back to Aachen tonight. I'll come back tomorrow."

"If you can stay a few minutes, I'm due for a break."

"Sure. There's only me and my driver, and I don't have to be back in the city until seven."

"Wonderful. Oh, it's so good to see you!" Tired as Marge was, seeing Em gave her a boost. By the time she reached the mess tent, she was beginning to feel renewed.

When Louise came in for coffee, Marge introduced her. "Em, this is our Chief Nurse, Captain Louise De Mille. Captain De Mille, my sister, Em Emerson."

"Your sister! No kidding! Did she know you were here?"

"No," Em said. "I was prepared to check out every field hospital in France and Belgium. I only learned day before yesterday that Marge was in Europe."

"How amazing that you should find her so quickly."

"Yes, it's pretty near a miracle."

As Em talked with Louise, Marge could tell they hit it off well. Then when Em started to say good-bye, Louise said, "Marge, you're overdue for a leave. Why don't you go stay with your sister in a real room tonight? Take off tomorrow too."

Marge gave Em a questioning look. "Do you have other plans?"

Em grinned. "Are you kidding? Nothing I can't change." She turned to Louise. "Thanks a lot. Do come, Marge. We don't have hot water for a bath, but the bed is good."

While Marge went to wash up, she let Em read her pile of mail. When she returned to her tent, Em was huddled on the edge of the cot with her coat pulled snug around her. "How on earth do you ever keep warm in here?"

"The stoves at each end of the tent ward off some of the chill. The guys who keep the fires going in the stoves in the wards keep ours burning too. At night if it's really cold, we just wear more clothes to bed."

"I hear gunfire. Do any shells come your way?"

"Not here." Marge quickly packed clean underwear, wool socks, a few cosmetics, and pajamas into her smaller canvas bag and slung it over her shoulder. "On the way here our convoy had some near misses, but the hills around this little valley shield us from accidentals. And as long as the Germans keep on retreating, we aren't in the line of fire."

"I dearly hope so. Anything I can carry for you?"

"No thanks. This," she patted the bag, "is all I need. I'm ready."

Outside, the rain had stopped, but a gusty wind threatened more to come. They climbed into Corporal Benfield's Antoinette and, with the window flaps closed, headed for Aachen.

Marge leaned close to Em's ear. "So you finally have your own jeep and driver."

"I manage," Em said with a mischievous grin. "By the way, when we get to Aachen, I may have a supper date if he has returned from the Front. I want you to meet him—Bob Mansfield."

"Isn't he the man who helped you get that story about the London dock worker during the blitz?"

"He's the one. He's been a real friend. I think you'll like him."

Marge was curious about this man whom Em often had mentioned but had insisted was not a romantic interest. She'd said that Bob was older, somewhere in his thirties. For a man to be unmarried in his thirties was not necessarily a good sign. Now was her chance to meet and judge Bob Mansfield for herself.

After cleaning up in a real bathroom at the hotel, a treat despite the cold water, Marge followed Em to the hotel dining room where she met Bob at last. Older or not, the man was handsome with regular features, striking dark blue eyes, and a thick shock of brown hair that apparently defied combing. Watching Em's face as she talked with Bob, Marge decided her sister felt more than friendship toward this man. And no wonder. He treated her, and Marge too, with concern and conveyed the flattering impression that he found them both intelligent and beautiful.

Marge personally liked the tall rangy type like David, but Bob, more compact and not much taller than Em, impressed her as someone who could be trusted. She had always worried a little about what kind of man Em would fall for. Bob would be okay.

Under Bob's interested questioning, Marge found herself telling them about Isabelle and then about David. "It was such a help to have a medic who could speak French with her. They really took to each other. Now she's down by St. Vith in an orphanage, and David is in

Paris on a recuperation leave. I had hoped to visit Isabelle and deliver his little gift to her before he returns. But it isn't that easy to get transportation or time off for the trip."

"Well, you're off now, and I have a jeep," Em said. "Let's go tomorrow and see if we can locate her."

"You can take the time?"

Em turned to Bob. "How about you? Do you have to be back in Paris tomorrow?"

"No. Actually I was hoping to stay one more day. Got an invitation to inspect the bunkers they've taken from the Germans and get a good photo of the dragon's teeth—those concrete pillars built to stop tanks."

"Good," Em said. "So! We'll go to St. Vith tomorrow and then head for Paris."

After dinner, Marge went up to Em's room first, leaving Em to say good-night to Bob. She was in bed by the time Em came in.

Em climbed in the other side of the double bed, letting in a draft of cold air when she lifted the coverlet. She snuggled close, as she had when they were girls. "Remember winter on the ranch? I always loved it when you beat me to bed and warmed the sheets for me. I guess in its way the old ranch house prepared us for now."

"I hadn't thought of that. I guess I did adjust to field hospital conditions faster than the city girls. On those icy nights at home before I fell asleep, I used to imagine the kind of house I'd have someday—with central heating in every room."

"I can't get over finding you so soon! I was going to search everywhere, and here you are. I wonder how many people meet their family way out here on the battlefront."

"Not likely many. Em, I like Bob. He's a good man."

"Yes."

"So how much do you like him?"

"A lot. He kind of grows on you."

"He likes you a lot too. He looks at you that way."

"Well, he's elusive. Sometimes I've wondered if he has some insurmountable secret hidden somewhere, like Mr. Rochester in *Jane Eyre*."

Em's cautiousness surprised and reassured Marge. "It certainly doesn't hurt to be careful," she agreed.

"So what about the medic—David? Are you in love with him?"

Marge stared into the darkness of the hotel room, then finally said, "I love him. In love? Yes, I guess I am, yet I don't want to be. Remember how Mom used to tell us we could be anything. There wasn't money for nursing school, but I got started and then made it into the army. And you got your start on the town newspaper, and look at you now. Is there room for romance, for having a family, and having a career too? I don't think so, not for me. Once I saw what a skilled surgeon could do, I decided I really do want to be a doctor. I don't know how I can get the education, but I sure aim to try. And David—he wants to be a missionary to Germany."

"A what?"

"Well, the orphanage he plans to run will be under the auspices of his church."

Em became uncharacteristically quiet, so Marge finally prodded her. "What are you thinking?"

"I'm thinking David may be on the right track. The more I hear people's stories, the more I realize that our world needs people filled with God's forgiveness to bring about healing after this war."

"I don't argue against that. It's just not for me."

Em sighed. "Me either. Not the orphanage business. But I do hope to do some good through my writing."

Marge had never heard Em sound so serious, so committed to a purpose beyond the next story. "You will. I'm sure of it." She turned over and tucked her feet next to Em's. "Well, little sister, let's go to sleep and get an early start in the morning. I sure hope we can find Isabelle."

Chapter Twenty-Three

The next morning Corporal Benfield motored Marge and Em to Bovigny, just north of St. Vith. Marge felt sure they could find the Hollard Farm Home, especially given their early start.

Before lunchtime they did find the place, tucked against a hill outside the village with a backdrop of forest. Knowing the farm was only about ten miles from the German border made Marge uneasy about Isabelle's safety, but she reminded herself that this land near the Ardennes had been securely in Allied hands since mid-September. The Siegfried Line had been breached in one place, and the Allies stood on German soil. She had no rational reason to be concerned. Obviously the Germans would continue to retreat.

The Babe still could not walk, but she did a fast hobble on her little crutches. The sight of her elfin smile and her race to be hugged brought a lump of tears to Marge's throat. But she never let them show, not in front of Isabelle. What a little bit she was. "It's so good to see you, sweetheart. How are you?"

"Okay. Fine—okay. See how I walk?"

"I saw. You are doing so well. And you have all the sisters to help you."

Isabelle pointed to the three nuns present and gave their names. "I help them," she said.

Marge laughed and hugged her tight. "Of course you do. Now that you can walk, you must be a good helper."

Isabelle nodded.

She snuggled on Marge's lap while Marge tried to communicate with the nuns, none of whom spoke adequate English.

When it came time to leave, Marge gave Isabelle the hair ribbons from David and the gum to share with the other children. Fortunately it was a small orphanage, maybe only a couple of dozen children. There should be enough to go around. "Sergeant David sends you a hug and a kiss too." She delivered them.

Isabelle kissed Marge a second time. "Give to Sergeant David."

Marge smiled. "Okay." One of Isabelle's first English words had been *okay*. "I will give him your kiss, and as soon as he is able, he will come see you too."

A few minutes later, as Corporal Benfield backed around and headed down the Hollard Farm Home driveway, Em said, "Are you going to keep your word?"

Puzzled, Marge said, "What?"

"About giving David her kiss?" Em grinned and looked altogether too delighted over cornering her sister.

Marge thought a minute. "Yes, I will."

"Good. I wish I could be there. If he shouldn't want to cooperate, that could be a challenge from what you've told me. He must be at least a foot taller than you."

Corporal Benfield was grinning but kept his eyes on the road.

Marge chuckled. "I guess David is a foot taller, but I think he will cooperate. He proposed to me."

Em whirled toward her. "You didn't tell me that."

"Well, I said no. . . ."

"Having second thoughts now?"

"No. Like I said, his plans are very different from mine."

"Marge, nothing says you have to give up your dream to become a doctor just because you marry. If you love him, follow your heart. Talk it over with him."

Maybe Em was right. Maybe. Happiness welled up inside Marge. "Thanks, sis. I may do that."

When they reached the field hospital, Corporal Benfield pulled in close to the mess tent.

"Don't get out with me in this rain," Marge ordered.

"Okay." Em gave her a fierce hug. "I don't know when I can come back."

They clung to each other. It seemed unlikely that they would meet again for a long time. Marge said, "If I ever get a leave to go to Paris, I'll let you know. Write to me." She pulled away and climbed out in the rain. With a quick good-bye wave, she ran for the mess tent.

As she ran, she noticed three ambulances had driven into the circle beside the receiving tent. *Time to get back to work.* She ran to her tent to change clothes.

After Em's surprise visit to the field hospital, Marge found herself thinking of David almost constantly. Em's remark that she didn't have to choose between marriage and a career attached itself to her thoughts like an Oklahoma beggar-ticks, those pointy weed seeds that wouldn't let go and kept burrowing deeper.

Despite her preoccupation, Marge worked quickly, but she gave her full attention only when talking to her patients. She scolded herself for woolgathering on the job, but that didn't stop the problem. In every quiet moment, she continued to mull over the kind of future she might have with David. She loved him. Was love for him enough to carry her through times when she might have to submit her career needs to his? Was her faith equal to his?

She had believed in Christ as her savior since she was ten years old, but she did not have the awareness that the Son of God was an intimate friend, not like David did. She sensed that this was a prerequisite for entering missionary service. Maybe this was what people meant when they said that God called them. She had no calling. That was it. She probably couldn't serve well with no call. Yet she loved David and wanted to be with him as his wife.

There was the other obstacle too. Right now she was an officer, and he wasn't. Would she be discharged from the medical corps for fraternizing with a noncommissioned man? The army needed nurses so badly that it might not be a problem.

Nearly three weeks had passed since David had left for Paris. Whenever an ambulance drove in, if Marge saw or heard it, her pulse picked up a staccato beat. She longed to see him and at the same time almost dreaded how she might react. Her emotions swung from one extreme to the other. Would she stay out of sight or run to meet him? She'd better not run. That would never do.

A few days after Em's visit, Marge was in the triage area when an ambulance drove in with four wounded men.

"Nurse Marge," one of the medics called. She turned and recognized Vance, David's friend. One look at his face, and she knew something had happened to David. He came quickly to her with something in his hands. "Can you come outside?" he whispered.

She followed dumbly. *No, God, no! Not David!*

Outside the tent, Vance turned to her, his face twisted with grief. He bit his lip and then stammered, "Dave—he was killed. On the way back from Paris . . . almost here. The convoy was traveling at night, but a bomb . . . a direct hit—" He choked.

Marge, stunned, gripped his arm. The words *killed* and *bomb* filled her mind with a thousand screams, but she couldn't make a sound.

Vance's voice came to her from far away. She made herself listen.

"I brought you Dave's Bible. He said . . . if anything ever happened to him, he wanted you to have it." He was holding out a small package.

"Thank you," she whispered.

"You going to be okay?" His voice cracked.

"I'm all right," she said, unable to think beyond the fact that she was still standing upright, breathing, and able to speak.

He touched her arm. "Look, you stay right here. I'll get one of your nurse friends."

She obeyed because her feet refused to move.

The next thing she knew, Carolyn was beside her. With an arm around her, she led Marge to their tent. Marge stood inside, uncertain as to why she was there. "I've got to get back to work."

"Come sit for a minute. You've had a shock. Just let go and scream if that's how you feel."

Marge sat where Carolyn placed her. David dead? He couldn't be! No, David had been wounded, but he was in Paris, recuperating, and he'd be back any day. This was a nightmare. Any second she would wake up. *Wake up, Marge!* she told herself.

Finally the book she was clutching to her chest made her realize she was awake. She lowered her hands. David's Bible was real. Pain began small and piercing, then mushroomed into crushing agony. *David is dead. And I never really told him how much I love him.*

She had even turned him away. *God! How could you let this happen? He was so good. He would have made the world a better place.*

Cold wind whipped into the tent. Louise's voice penetrated her rage. "Marge, I'm so sorry. I could swear, when I think how unfair this is. He was such a good man." She sat on the cot beside Marge and wrapped her arms around her like her mother used to hold her when she was hurt, smoothing her hair and murmuring words of sympathy. She began to cry.

Marge wanted to cry. *I should be crying. Why can't I cry?* When Louise finally let go of her and studied her with concern, Marge said, "Thanks. I'll be all right." Her voice sounded foreign to her ears.

Maybe it was. She didn't feel like herself. Marge would be crying.

"Take the rest of the day off, kiddo. We'll get along."

"I think—" Yes, she could think again. "I think I'll feel better working."

"If that's what you want. Where would you prefer to work?"

"Surgery. It will keep my mind on helping the guys who still have a chance."

"Right. I'll pull Amelia and put you with Dr. Ames. Go scrub up and be ready for his next patient."

So Marge went to work in the one place that could give her life meaning. She knew she was an excellent surgical assistant. In her mind she did each operation right along with the surgeon, analyzing what he was doing and why. Someday she would operate. She would be the one to repair the battered bodies.

By the time she finished the twelve-hour shift in surgery, she was ready to sleep. She needed the oblivion of sleep. In the tent she moved David's Bible from her cot to her footlocker. She couldn't face looking at his Bible yet. Maybe tomorrow. She crawled under the covers and pulled them tight up to her chin.

Back in Paris Em had orders to report in person to Cummins. So when Bob said he'd been invited to accompany General Bradley's staff back to Hitler's West Wall, she gave a sigh of relief. He was asking too many questions, and it was not pleasant to keep secrets from him.

She guessed that Cummins would send her on another assignment right away, and both she and Bob would be away from Paris on Thanksgiving. She didn't mind, and Bob had admitted he'd be glad to be with the troops, where he'd get turkey with all the trimmings.

With Christmas only a month away, she didn't make plans with Bob, because her promise to Werner Koch would have to come first.

After her briefing with Cummins, he ordered her back to Geneva. Once she was on the train, Em tried in vain to nap. Her thoughts lingered with Bob. He had nearly caught her in a lie during dinner last night. He'd said, "Two weeks ago you were dying to see the Siegfried Line. What has become more important?"

"A great interview that I can't miss."

"Another of Vivienne's friends?"

"Indirectly. She gave me more leads than I can follow."

He frowned and sighed.

Thankful for the dim light of candles, she met his probing look with as much innocence as she could muster.

A smile tugged at the corners. "Lucy-Em, you're a rotten liar. I guess I'm glad, but you worry me. You're so sure you can manage anything. I don't want you to find out you can't after it's too late."

She grinned and gave a casual shrug. "What can I say? You're so sure you can read my mind. I guess we're two of a kind when it comes to overconfidence."

He chuckled. "Thanks for nothing. I guess we are two of a kind. But I've had more years to learn where to draw the line."

"Am I inside the line you draw around yourself?"

He stared at her. For a second, she was afraid he wouldn't even answer. Then he said, "I don't aim to shut out people. I was only talking about assignments."

She wanted to press him for a more direct answer, but the way he had brushed aside her feeble attempt at flirting devastated her. Mostly she was angry at herself for trying to give him a come-on after she had decided against playing such games. His revelation about being a widower and having given away his daughter had not totally removed the invisible wall he kept around himself. If he couldn't trust her, then how could she trust him? For the rest of the evening she had avoided personal subjects.

Now as the train rolled through the hills of Burgundy, Em began to think about Hubert and Estelle. She wished she might see them, but on this trip she had to go straight to Geneva. Outside her rain-blurred train window the winter landscape spread out soggy and bleak, now that the trees and vineyards had lost their leaves.

When the train reached the foothills of the Alps, the rain changed to snow. In Geneva, drifting snow filled every cranny. She checked into the hotel and telephoned the Blackwell home. Andrew answered. "I'm glad you're here. We're having a few guests this evening. I'll send the car."

No asking with him. Oh well, she had agreed to work for him, and now she had to because of Cummins' orders. "All right. I'll be ready in half an hour." She hoped she'd feel more like festivities after a quick bath.

"Good." The receiver clicked in her ear.

She supposed he couldn't talk freely from home, but no doubt he'd find some way to talk to her privately. In the meantime, the thought of cleanliness, warmth, good food, sparkling chandeliers, and soft rugs enticed her. Madame Blackwell had insisted that she plan to use one of her guest gowns that she had set aside for her. So Em bathed and put on a touch of cologne, knowing she'd be changing into something glamorous when she reached Château Bleu.

Punctual as a Swiss clock, Andrew's black sedan pulled up to the entrance of the hotel at the appointed time. When Em reached the chateau, the clouds had parted. The moon turned the lake to polished silver, and the snow seemed to take on an inner glow. The chateau loomed over the luminous carpet, its warm lights inviting. Once again Em was amazed at how Andrew Blackwell managed to live so well while conducting his own private espionage. He behaved at home as if under no stress or distraction, and his wife never seemed to suspect him of clandestine activities.

Inside the chateau a uniformed maid led Em to the room where her evening clothes had been laid out. She changed quickly, enjoying the soft touch of the fabric as it fell to her feet. Red velvet and simple lines demonstrated Lydia's excellent taste. Em could wear any bright color well, but deep red was one of her favorites.

She fastened an antique pendant made of garnets and seed pearls around her neck and brushed her hair into a smooth pageboy. Glancing in the mirror, she could barely recognize the stylish young woman staring back at her. She buckled the gold strapped shoes Lydia had chosen for her and found them a good fit. The woman was a marvel. With such a glamorous beginning, this was bound to be an exciting evening.

In the great room she was not disappointed. Women in beautiful gowns and men in tuxedos stood sipping drinks and talking. Lydia, ever the perfect hostess, glided to Em's side and whispered, "You look utterly ravishing in red, my dear, just as I imagined. I'm so glad you could come right over. Our friend Werner Koch has been asking about you."

"He's back again?"

"Yes. We were surprised. Actually he's been here twice since you last saw him and asked about you each time. If he were not so utterly devoted to his family, I would wonder about this. He's never shown any personal interest in the women at my soirées before. Andrew said to tell you to be polite to him, but not so far as . . . well, you know . . . getting emotionally involved or anything."

Em grinned. "I understand. Tell Andrew not to worry."

"I already did. I said you are very wise for your age. Well, come along. The Aryan is looking our way." She tucked her hand under Em's arm and drew her along, pausing to introduce her to several couples before reaching Werner Koch, who was standing beside the stately white fireplace.

"Miss Emerson," he said, nodding formally. "A pleasure to see you again." His gray eyes, so calm before, nervously darted from her to others in the room and then back to her.

"Hello," she said. "I didn't expect to see you tonight."

"My business brings me more often to Geneva. May I get you something to drink?"

She turned to her hostess. "Do you have anything nonalcoholic?"

"Of course, my dear. Werner, the punch bowl is on the far end of the table."

Werner left, and Lydia lingered to keep Em company until he returned. Then she excused herself. "Dinner will be served in thirty minutes. Werner, will you be so good as to escort Miss Emerson?"

He gave a Prussian bow. "I shall be pleased to do so." To Em, he said, "In the meantime, have you seen Andrew's wonderful library? He has a number of original volumes from the last century housed there. Perhaps, since you are a writer, some of these would interest you?"

"Yes. I love old books."

"This way, then." He led her toward the tall doors at the far opposite end of the great hall.

When they reached the library, a gracious room with floor-to-ceiling bookshelves, Werner closed the door behind them and turned to her. "I began to fear I might not see you. Circumstances have forced me to get Frieda and the girls out of Germany sooner than Dr. Schneider planned. I dare not wait until early January."

"What about the maps and blueprints?"

"I will have them, but first my family must be made safe. Although Dr. Schneider could not provide for them at an earlier date, I have arranged sanctuary for them with a pastor here in Geneva. I have reason to believe the Gestapo is closing in, gathering evidence against me."

"Oh no!"

"The fact that I am in Hitler's favor may buy enough time. But if I am discovered trying to get my family out of Germany, that will immediately incriminate me."

"I'm so sorry. How soon can you get them out of Germany?"

"The earliest I can bring everything together is December twenty-fourth. I must secretly move my family from Frieda's brother's house to an abandoned ski hut close to the border, and this will take time. The hut is unknown to anyone other than my closest family. My grandfather built it. I will place the maps in a safe place in Switzerland, then on the night of the twenty-fourth, I will bring Frieda and the girls across the border to Hamel, a small Swiss town. I mentioned before that the train station is only a kilometer from the German border. It will be important that no one sees me. I'll have to return quickly the way I came. That is why . . . I desperately need you, Em. Please, will you meet my family at the edge of Hamel and help them board the train and come to Geneva?"

Now look what you've gotten yourself into, she chided herself. *This may be the type of inextricable situation that worried Bob.* And how could she sneak away from everyone on Christmas Eve? Still, she only hesitated a few seconds. The faces of his children smiled at her from her memory. "Okay. Tell me where and when I need to be there."

"I cannot thank you enough! You will need to be on the east edge of Hamel at one o'clock on Christmas morning. I'll give you specific written directions. By taking Frieda and the girls to the station in Hamel, they can avoid the normal customs check. Later, we will take care to make all things legal, to seek asylum."

"What about little Anna? Will she require special care or medicine?"

"Frieda will bring all that she needs. Anna may need to be carried. It will just be a matter of you being there to offer extra hands. I can't thank you adequately." He stopped and seemed to be groping for words or for emotional control. At last he found his voice. "May I ask one more favor? If anyone is watching me tonight, it would insure the success of my plan, if you could . . . act as if we are . . . really having an affair, not just a flirtation. For me to have a lover here would suggest to the Gestapo that I would never want to bring Frieda to Switzerland." When he mentioned the Gestapo, Werner's mouth tightened and his face turned defiant.

She hesitated. How could she pull such a charade off? What if Bob or Marge found out? And yet she wanted to help his sick daughter and get his information for the Allies. He was watching her with a grim expression. His angry look struck her as funny after his request to pretend they were in love. Shaking her head, she smiled. "Herr Koch, if we are to accomplish this, you must look at me with warmth and desire on your face, not as if we just had a fight."

His expression softened. "Then you will do it?"

"I'll do my part if you do yours. This will be something new to me, falling for a handsome enemy."

"Then come. Let's get started." He ran his fingers through his carefully combed hair, letting it tumble across his forehead.

When they came out into the great hall, he paused and discreetly straightened his tie and smoothed his hair. She looked up at him with what she hoped was naïve adoration and slipped her hand possessively under his arm. The rest of the evening she acted as if she could not keep her eyes from his, and he did the same toward her. The acting came easier and easier.

Andrew cast Em a number of warning looks and even tried to pry her away from Werner by introducing her to several other men, but each time Werner appeared at her side before the conversations progressed beyond inanities. When she excused herself to go with him, no eyebrows were raised except Andrew's.

At the end of the evening, while Werner went for his car to drive her to the hotel, Andrew caught her alone in the vestibule. "What are you doing? I told you not to get involved with anyone," he hissed in a stage whisper.

"I am not getting involved," she snapped. "Besides, you said Werner was one of your longtime friends."

"Not friend! Business acquaintance! Em, he's a Nazi. He's the enemy!"

Before she could respond, the door opened, letting in a gust of nippy air as Werner stepped in. "The car is ready," he said, glancing at Andrew. "I hope you don't mind my escorting Miss Emerson to her hotel. I have to go now and thought I could spare you the drive."

Andrew smiled graciously. "Thank you. Do take care. My friend would never forgive me if you lost his daughter in a snowdrift."

With a show of joviality, they parted, but Em knew she'd hear more from Andrew when they were alone again. In the meantime his words, *"He's the enemy,"* gave her a sense of relief. Surely Andrew was a loyal American, no matter what Cummins might suspect.

Without much conversation Werner drove her to her hotel and walked her to her room. At the door, he said, "May I please come in for a while? It would be natural, you see. . . ." He was clearly embarrassed.

"Yes. I think you must." She handed him her room key.

Once inside her hotel room with Werner Koch, Em wanted to call the whole thing off. It was a lot different to pretend out in public. "How long do you think. . . ?" She felt her cheeks grow warm and hoped he wouldn't notice or even think about her as a woman at this moment.

He went to the window and stood for a moment before pulling

the drapes shut. "Actually, if I could stay here several hours, that would be most convincing."

For an instant she panicked. Then she noticed that he was careful not to look at her as he spoke. *Why, he knows I'm embarrassed and doesn't want to embarrass me more!* "All right," she said. "Maybe we should order something from room service to make it look good. A bottle of champagne?"

"You are most clever." He picked up the phone and placed the order.

By the time the room clerk delivered the champagne, Werner had his coat off and shirt collar unbuttoned. He looked the part of a man in love.

Em did not even remove her uncomfortable shoes. She stood back when he tipped the man, hoping she was less noticeable.

After the door closed Werner popped the cork and said, "A sacrifice to the cause," as he poured the bubbling wine into the bathroom sink. "I can't risk drinking, and you don't drink," he added as if apologizing for wasting good wine.

She went to the armoire and pulled out the extra bedding and laid it on the sofa. "This should keep you warm."

"Thank you. I shall be gone long before you awaken in the morning. So I thank you again. I must be honest and say my plan is not without a little risk right at the border. But once my family is clearly inside Switzerland, you ought to be safe."

She wanted to say, "So now you tell me." Instead, she said, "I see." The enormity of the task scared her. She had agreed to take on a huge responsibility, escorting a family with a sick child all the way to Geneva. If anything did go wrong, she'd be on her own. She wanted desperately to confide this whole thing to Cummins, but Werner had insisted that for anyone to know might mean death to the family as well as failure for his effort to get secrets out to the Allies.

Without voicing any of her concerns, she told Werner good-night, went into the bedroom, and locked the door.

In the morning she found the down comforter neatly folded on the sofa. Werner was gone.

Andrew had told her to be at his office by nine. She hoped her meeting with him would be brief. She felt more nervous about her agreement with Werner now than she did last night. This was not a good sign. Normally things looked better in the morning. Today she wanted to flee to Paris and forget about clandestine arrangements with anyone, especially with a former Nazi. She wanted to flee to Bob.

Chapter Twenty-Four

When Em finally reached Paris, Bob had not returned. She settled down for a stint of serious writing. During their meeting Andrew had given her a message to deliver to Hubert and had asked her to return and stay at the chateau for Christmas. Em was thankful for the invitation because she wouldn't need to travel so far to meet Werner's family.

Now all she needed was to think of an excuse for leaving the chateau the day before Christmas and for staying away all night. Werner had hoped the holiday would draw attention away from his family's actions. However, it made it more difficult for Em.

In the meantime Cummins asked her to interview a Resistance leader in Paris who was an ardent communist. To pull a publishable story out of the interview would be a challenge. This time Cummins told her what he wanted to know. His questions definitely would not lead to an article for her magazine, but maybe she could find a thread of human interest to follow. He also reminded her that the Marchants remained free so she should be watchful.

It took two days for Em to find the man and two more to obtain an appointment. After completing the interview, she shut herself in her room, transcribed her notes, and wrote the article.

She kept expecting a letter from Marge, but none came. Things must be rough at the field hospital. She did, however, get a wire from her magazine. She opened it in the lobby. *Can't use the Nisei story. Get back to your beat. Leave racial problems to the experts. Albert Greenly.*

She crumpled the message into a tight ball and hurled it into the nearest wastebasket. Her article on the 442nd Division had been some of her best writing.

"Bad news?" Bob asked, as usual, appearing as abruptly as a genie from a bottle.

She jumped. "Can't you give some kind of approach warning?" Her voice came out angrier than she intended. She drew in a deep breath and exhaled slowly. "I'm sorry. I didn't mean to snap. Yes, I just got bad news."

"What is it?" He stepped closer, and the concern in his voice stirred a pleasant flutter in her chest.

"A wire from my boss. He rejected my story on the Nisei Combat Team. Told me to get back to my own business."

He frowned and shook his head. "That was a great story and well written. Did you keep a copy?"

"Of course. Why?"

"My paper might go for it. Why don't you type it up clean again, and I'll send it."

"You really think they'd take anything from me?" The Tribune was the big time in the publishing world.

"It's definitely worth a try." He changed the subject abruptly. "Heard from Marge recently?"

"No. Now that she knows I'm here in Paris, I thought I would. It's not like her to go this long without sending a note."

His serious expression startled her and then frightened her. "What's wrong?"

"I stopped at the field hospital to see Marge on the way back here, and she's had a bit of a shock. A medic she'd grown fond of was killed. Seems to have hit her very hard. I thought you should know."

"Oh no! Not David Lewellyn!"

"You knew him?"

"No. I never met him, but she loved him and he, her, I think."

"I'm sorry to be the bearer of such news, but I thought you should know."

"How did Marge look? Is she okay?"

"She looked drained and exhausted. But I don't know her well enough to judge how she's doing."

"It's not like her not to write to me about something so important. I think I'd better find an excuse to go back to Aachen. I hate to think of her bearing this grief alone."

"She has good friends among the nurses. They were the ones who told me about her loss."

"But that's not like family. I need to go." She stood up. "Look, if I type a clean copy of the Nisei story, may I give it to you at noon?

Then I'm going to get permission to head north again."

"Sure. I'll send your story, but I hate to see you go back to the Front. Things are heating up. You could stumble into a combat area."

"Not unless Marge does too. I will only go to the hospital."

He frowned. "I suppose you have to go."

"Yes."

Back in her room while she typed furiously on the Nisei story, the phone rang. She expected to hear Bob's voice, but a woman spoke. "Em Emerson?"

"Yes."

"This is Louise De Mille, your sister Marge's supervisor."

"What's wrong? Is Marge okay?"

"Yes and no. I don't know if she has told you about a medic named David Lewellyn . . ."

"I just learned this morning that he was killed. How is Marge?"

"Not good. She's worked so hard and refused to rest . . . maybe she couldn't. We've had a lot of casualties, so I didn't force her to rest. Anyway, she caught the flu. She's over it now but is not in shape to work, and now she's showing signs of the depression that goes with combat fatigue. I have to send her someplace to rest and recuperate. I don't know whether this is something you can arrange, but if she could be with you . . ."

"Can you give her a leave until after Christmas? I know a place where she may stay—in Switzerland. I was planning to go there myself. I'm sure they'd welcome her too."

"I'll get her the leave time, but she can't travel alone."

"I'll come to get her."

"You can do that?"

"Yes. I'll be there as early as I can tomorrow."

As before, Em had no difficulty obtaining permission to go where she wanted. This unquestioning respect for the private ID and orders from Cummins still surprised her. Not that the army was happy to let her go. She got looks of frustration and irritation, but they didn't argue.

She left her Nisei Combat Team story in Bob's capable hands and headed out early in the morning on the most direct route north.

By nightfall she had a room in the hotel in Aachen where she had stayed before.

In the morning she had her driver take her directly to the field hospital. While he headed for the mess tent for coffee, she sloshed through mud and freezing rain to the tent where Marge slept. With luck she would see one of the nurses she'd met before.

Her instinct had been right. Carolyn was there. "Marge is in surgery," she said. "Say, I'm glad to see you. I'm really worried about her. Did you hear about David Lewellyn?"

"Yes. That's why I came."

"Well, Marge won't talk about it. She's been so quiet, not herself at all. She's been working long hours, like the rest of us, but I don't think she sleeps much. She looks absolutely exhausted. Louise has offered her time off, but she won't take it. Maybe you could persuade her."

"I aim to. Can you let her know I'm here? I'll wait in the mess tent."

"Right." Carolyn clutched her poncho against the wind and hurried out.

Em went to the mess tent, poured coffee, and sat down at a table.

The chief nurse, Louise, came in and sat across from her. "I'm sure glad you could come. Once Marge was over the flu, I thought she would be okay. She has insisted on working, but twice she got the shakes when she was on duty in the receiving ward. She's done okay in surgery, and we've needed her so badly, I let her have her way until you could get here."

"How long will it take for her to get over this if it's combat fatigue?"

"A few people don't recover, but that's not Marge. On average if the soldiers get a few days of sleep in a dry bed, some hot food, and good hot baths, they can return to duty in a short time. A week might do it if she hadn't also had the flu. Taking off until after Christmas should bring her back to normal. We're expecting three new replacements this week, so I can assure her we won't be shorthanded." She stood up. "I'll send Marge to you the minute she finishes her present surgery."

Em poured another cup of coffee and waited.

When Marge finally came, her expressionless face shocked Em. She stood with a small bag in one hand. With no hello, she said in a dull voice, "I'm ready to go."

It didn't take a nurse to tell Em her sister was into depression, big-time.

She jumped up and went to her. Hugging her was like hugging a fence post. Marge went through the motions of hugging her back but without real feeling. Em had seen the deep depression of soldiers in Wales who were suffering from combat fatigue, but to see Marge this way stunned her. She murmured, "I'm so sorry about David."

Marge nodded as if it took all of her strength to respond. "Louise said you want me to spend Christmas with you."

Marge always had said people need to talk about their grief. With growing anxiety, Em released her. "Yes. She said you're overdue for a leave and that you can have the time off. You'll love it in Switzerland. I made friends with a couple who have a chateau on the lake. . . ."

Marge didn't say anything, so Em took her by the arm, and her driver took Marge's bag. When they reached the jeep at last Marge showed emotion. She pulled back, agitated. "I really shouldn't go. Dr. Ames needs me. Nursing is what I'm here for, not holidays."

Encouraged by this verbal burst, Em said, "Sure. But they will get along. New nurses are coming, and after this leave you'll be able to work harder than ever. Marge, you need a rest. Surely you can tell that for yourself. You look burned-out. Come on, sis. Let's go."

For a moment Marge relaxed under Em's guiding hand. Then as Marge was climbing into the jeep, she exclaimed, "Wait! Hear that? More guns than usual. I'd better go back. The wounded will be here soon."

"Marge, please. Come with me. You won't be of any use at all to the wounded if you keep on like this. Think what you're doing to yourself, for pete's sake!" The last came out in a burst of desperate anger, and then Em felt guilty. Marge didn't need someone yelling at her.

Before she could apologize, Marge snapped back, "You can't know what it's like trying to save them. No one knows but those of us who are doing it!"

Em expected her to stomp back to the hospital tents, but instead she climbed into the jeep. Her cheeks flushed with anger.

Maybe her burst of emotion was a good sign. Em climbed into the backseat and told her driver to head for Paris by the best route he could find.

They had driven only a short distance when a long convoy stopped them at a crossroad north of Malmédy. A soldier beckoned toward Em's driver, and he got out. After talking and gesturing, the driver beckoned for Em to come. She left Marge sitting silent and staring straight ahead.

"What is it?" This was the first time she'd seen anything like a traffic director in the liberated portion of Belgium or France.

"Ma'am," the GI said, "intense fighting has broken out in the Ardennes. You'll need to take to the side roads and head north to Liege and then follow the Meuse River into France."

"You mean the Germans are pushing this direction?" Knowing the course of the Allied invasion so far, this seemed improbable to Em.

"Yes, ma'am. Go back to that last intersection, turn left, and in about five miles you'll see a marker to Liege."

Her driver nodded. "Thanks, Sergeant. I'll get them around this."

On the way back to the jeep Em said, "Don't tell Marge about the battle getting worse."

"Yes, ma'am."

Other than that detour, the drive to Paris proceeded uneventfully.

Marge didn't want supper, so Em helped her into bed in her hotel room and then went down for her own meal. In the hotel dining room she learned from the other correspondents that the Germans had launched a serious offensive in the Ardennes. Everyone was seeking permission to go and cover the action. Em thought it ironic that she'd been where they all longed to go and had missed the action entirely. That had been her pattern lately.

From the lobby she telephoned the Blackwell's and asked if she could bring her sister to visit. As she had hoped, they were delighted. "May we come tomorrow, please?" she asked. "I'd like to get Marge there before she hears about the German breakout in the Ardennes. She's got to be protected from war news for a while."

"Oh, do bring her immediately," Lydia said. "We'll give her some peace and pamper her. I'm so glad you felt comfortable about asking."

So Em went upstairs and quietly to bed. She would call her driver in the morning. All she really needed this time was transportation to the train station.

CHAPTER TWENTY-FIVE

On impulse, Em left a note for Bob before leaving Hotel Scribe.

Dear Bob,

I'm sorry our paths have not crossed again. I was hoping we could do Christmas together. You still owe me a real night on the town, or maybe I owe you. Thanks so much for sending my Nisei Combat Team story to your paper.

I found Marge in bad shape—combat fatigue, her chief nurse says. I've arranged to take her to visit friends in Geneva. I will stay there with her until after Christmas. The phone number—I don't have it with me at the moment—is listed under Andrew J. H. Blackwell. Merry Christmas and all other good wishes,

Em

With Marge to care for and the time drawing near when Em had promised to meet Frieda Koch, Em didn't feel any jollies over the Christmas season. Having Marge at the Blackwells was going to make it even more difficult to skip out on Christmas Eve day. She and Marge left Paris in mutual silence and found little to talk about on the train journey.

In Geneva, however, Em's spirits rose. In this city, Marge might almost forget the war. Store windows were lighted and decorated tastefully for Christmas, even though the holiday was eleven days away. Em still hadn't come up with a plausible excuse for disappearing on the twenty-fourth, but surely she'd find one. This handsome old city breathed confidence into a person's veins.

Marge showed surprise when Blackwell's chauffeured car met them at the train station. Now, although she didn't say anything, Em could see her sister take notice of everything they passed. When at last they entered the snow-covered grounds of Château Bleu, Marge said in a soft voice, "Remember the Christmas when we had two feet of snow on Christmas Eve? I figured at last Santa could land his sleigh on our roof."

Em laughed in delight. Marge's monotone, don't-care voice was gone. "I remember trying to walk in Dad's footsteps to the barn, and I fell into a drift so deep he had to pull me out."

"It was a long time ago." Marge sounded sad. This, too, was an improvement.

"It seems so now, but sometimes when I think of home, it seems as close as the next town, even here in France."

Marge sighed. "I wish I could be more like you. You always were more adaptable and more adventurous than I."

"Don't ever wish to be like me. I'd hate for you to be like me."

The big car cruised into the circle driveway and stopped beside the wide front steps. Marge looked up at the stately home with Christmas lights glowing warmly through a tall front window. Her tense expression eased. For Em, it was like watching life return to a dead face. *Marge is going to be okay!*

Em let herself out while the chauffeur opened the other door for Marge. Snow had been cleared from the steps and drive, but already a powder of new white covered the swept area of the drive. Em had worn her dress uniform and sensible shoes. As the chill immediately seeped through her shoes, she wished she had worn her boots and battle fatigues. After all, she could have changed when she got here. She rounded the car and took Marge's arm. "Come on. You're going to love the Blackwells."

Before they reached the tall door, Lydia threw it open and came out. "Welcome, welcome! We're so glad you both could come."

Em introduced Marge, and Lydia hurried them inside. "Come to the library. We have a roaring fire in the fireplace. Felix will take your bags upstairs. Em, we put you in the same room you've had before. Marge will have the rose room next to yours. Come along, and we'll have something hot to drink to warm you."

She led them into the gracious old library, Em's favorite room in the whole chateau. Marge moved close to the fire and sat gingerly in a velvet-upholstered chair. "It's lovely here, Mrs. Blackwell," she said. "Thank you so much for inviting me."

"My dear, we are so glad you could come with Em. I hope we can make it a pleasant Christmas for you. And please call me Lydia, as Em does."

A servant brought in a tray and sat it on a trolley near Lydia. "I hope you both like chocolate."

Em exclaimed, "You know I do, and so does Marge. Swiss chocolate, sis—it's the best." Em took the first cup Lydia poured and handed it to Marge. Then she accepted a cup for herself and sat on a chair on the opposite side of the fire.

"Now if you two will excuse me a moment," Lydia said, "I want to run to the kitchen and then change for dinner. We'll dine at seven. Andrew is bringing a guest." She glanced at Em. "Werner Koch will be joining us. He has been asking after you again."

"Oh. I didn't know he was back in Switzerland."

"Apparently he just returned today," she said as she left.

Marge sat her cup of chocolate down and said, "Werner Koch?"

"Yes. A German journalist. Germans, Italians, French—everyone comes into Switzerland to conduct business and meet people. I met Werner last month and then again about a couple of weeks ago."

"He's German—from Germany?"

"Yes."

"Did you interview him?"

"Not exactly. Andrew introduced us, and we sort of became friends."

"Is he married?"

"You mean am I interested in him? Yes, he's married, and no, I am not interested in him."

"Lydia looked at you as if something were going on between you and this Werner Koch."

"Marge, no matter how it may look, please believe me that Werner loves his wife and family. I'm not involved with him in that way. There's . . . something I can't tell you right now, not unless he chooses to tell you. So when he comes, please just let me do the visiting, and don't ask too many questions. Please?" Without question, it was going to be difficult to slip away to meet Werner's wife. What reason could she give when Marge was already anxious?

Marge shrugged. "As you wish," she said in a flat voice, and turned to gaze at the fire.

Em also watched the flames curl up around a fat log, letting the light, warmth, and color mesmerize her. Despite her worries, her eyes felt heavy. She was more tired than she had realized. Marge must be beat. "Would you like to have a hot bath and lie down for a while? There's time."

"Yes." Marge stood up. Although the sad silence had fallen over her again, her cheeks were pink from the fire, and she looked better than she had yesterday.

Em led her upstairs to her room and showed her the robe, slippers, and dresses hanging in the closet. Lydia had asked for Marge's size when Em called. "You can use these. The Blackwells keep gowns of different sizes on hand for their guests, in case anyone wants to change and came unprepared."

Marge shook her head. "Not allowed for me, you know. Not even here in a neutral nation. Do you take off your uniform?"

"I have, but no one who would care ever knows."

"Em, you shouldn't. Your uniform is actually protection . . . in case you became a prisoner of war."

"But we're in Switzerland. No chance of being captured by the Germans here."

"Still, you ought not to be out of uniform." She sounded overly frightened.

"Okay. I won't. Don't worry. But we are safe here. Now you go ahead and take your time soaking in the bath. Just let me know when you get out. I think I'll lie down for a few minutes too."

Marge nodded. She was slipping back into lethargy. Em wanted to hug her and assure her everything was going to be all right, but seeing her in this alien mood frightened her. Marge had always been there for her, an ideal big sister, and now she was gone. Would she ever be herself again?

At dinner Marge responded in monosyllables to the conversation until Werner began to talk about his family, especially his daughter and her heart, apparently damaged from rheumatic fever. Again Em witnessed a transformation on her sister's face. With a burning look in her eyes, Marge asked, "Do you have a good physician for her?"

Werner pursed his lips and shook his head. "I fear she needs more than what our family doctor can do. He is elderly now. If the younger doctors were not in the military, probably he would no longer be practicing, but he does the best he can." He glanced at Em, as if wondering if she had revealed any hint of his plans to get his family out of Germany.

She raised her eyebrows and shook her head slightly.

"What are your daughter's symptoms?" Marge asked.

"Shortness of breath, weakness. She had a heart problem at birth but seemed to grow out of it. She remained strong and healthy until last winter when she had a bad case of flu and sore throat. The illness seemed to awaken the old problem. Now with the privations of war—" He stopped abruptly. "Forgive me, I forgot and am saying too much."

Lydia laid down her fork and said, "Werner, what you say in our home will not be repeated. Please be at ease about that. I didn't know about your little girl's illness. I'm so sorry. Do you have a photo of your family with you?" she asked.

"Yes, I do." He reached into the inside pocket of his coat, removed a photo from his wallet, and handed it to her. "Maria is our oldest, thirteen now, and Anna, seven. We had a son, Frederick, who would be eleven now. He died of a heart condition similar to Anna's."

"What a tragedy," Lydia said. After an appropriate pause, she said, "You must be very proud of your family. Your wife is beautiful. So are your daughters." She glanced toward Em, as if to say, in her polite way, "You've been out of line with this man."

Em's cheeks burned. She glanced at Werner, but he remained stolid, revealing neither discomfort nor concern for whatever Lydia might be thinking or expressing.

Andrew intervened, purposely or not, Em couldn't tell. "Werner, how is your import business doing? Are you able to obtain the fabrics you wish?" As an aside to Marge, he explained, "Werner Koch is a fine journalist, but his family owns a garment factory in Munich, as well as a textile plant here. Some of the dresses, gowns, and sleepwear in our guest rooms are gifts from Werner's factory."

Werner responded with a lift of his chin. "We proceed as usual. As you know, we still have a warehouse full of prewar fabric from Italy and from the east. The Third Reich lacks nothing of necessity. The Fuehrer planned well long ago for conditions such as we face now. Germany is an impregnable fortress."

Andrew nodded. "My friend, business and politics are of no interest to the ladies." He stood up. "Come join me in the library while they have their coffee here."

Werner stood, bowed to each of them. "Excuse me, please." His gaze lingered on Em an instant longer than on the rest. A flicker of anxiety tightened the fine lines around his pale gray eyes. Was he begging again for her cooperation with his desperate plan?

After the men left, Em asked Lydia, "How long have you known Werner?"

"Since before the war. He used to argue vehemently with Andrew about the benefits Hitler was bringing to Germany. He hasn't argued that way for a long time, but he is a loyal Nazi, high up in the party and in the confidence of Hitler. This has been confirmed by the fact he was never a suspect after the attempt on Hitler's life. The Fuehrer ordered many good men executed, including some who were loyal to him."

"Well, what does Werner think about that?" Marge said. "Doesn't it tell him something when some of Germany's best military minds tried to get rid of Hitler?"

"He says such things happen to great leaders."

"He seems too intelligent," Marge said, "to fall for Hitler's so-called charisma."

"My dear, it's not intelligence that's involved. It is something in the German psyche. They crave precision and order, even if it means losing freedom. After the last war they hungered for a way to regain their national pride. But beyond that, Andrew says, they suffered such poverty that they were ready for any way out when Hitler came along."

Lydia turned to Em. "My dear, Werner has, shall we say . . . taken to you. Had he told you about his family?"

"Yes. He talks a lot about his wife and children." She wasn't about to say anything more. "I'm really tired. If you'll excuse me, I'd like to retire early."

"Of course. Rest well," her consistently gracious hostess said.

"Please excuse me too," Marge said, standing as she spoke. "Thanks again for inviting me to spend Christmas here. I really appreciate it."

As Em walked up the wide, carpeted stairs, Marge followed. At Em's bedroom door, Marge said, "Em, there isn't anything between you and Werner Koch . . . is there?"

Em chewed on her lip, thinking fast. She had never lied to Marge. She hoped she could carry it off. For the sake of his family she said, "He's attracted to me, but I haven't done anything wrong."

Marge frowned. "You don't have to accept his attentions."

"Well, maybe I want to."

"Em!"

"Look, nothing has happened between us, and nothing is going to. He just likes my company, and I find him interesting. Ultimately, if I play it right, I may get a tremendous story from him . . . after the war, I mean. Think what it could be. He is close to Hitler."

Marge glared at her. "You should know better than this. You do! You know you're playing with fire!"

"Okay, so I'm playing with fire!" Em yanked open her bedroom door. "Good night. I'll see you in the morning, and I hope you'll be in a better mood."

In her room, she closed her door and leaned against it. She felt as if she had just sprinted a mile uphill. Having Marge suspect the worst of her hurt even more than she'd anticipated.

While getting ready for bed, she calmed down, and then saw a silver lining to the way Marge had reacted. She had reacted normally, as if she'd never been despondent. Just two days ago, nothing would have roused her enough to argue. The old Marge was coming back.

Em walked to the window that looked out across the lake toward the mountains. Tonight low clouds hid the mountains. The snow in the garden below gave off its ghostly light, even without the stars. The whole scene breathed serenity, while indoors, these aged walls sheltered a man whose wife didn't know about his risky espionage ventures, a Nazi who was planning the escape of his family, a nurse suffering from grief and combat fatigue. *And me,* Em thought, *a liar of the first water. Dear God, is it okay to ask you to help me be a good liar . . . for the sake of little children who need help?*

The closest thing to an answer that came to her was the fact she didn't feel guilty. However, she knew very well that her conscience could be a poor guide.

She was in bed and almost asleep when a tap came on her door. Must be Marge. She got up and hurried to the door.

The tall shape of Werner Koch greeted her. "Please," he whispered, "I must talk to you alone. There will be no other time. May I come in?"

She opened the door wider and closed it quickly behind him. "You must be very quiet, or my sister will hear you."

He was fully clothed. In fact he had on his overcoat. "I am leaving, but I can't go without telling you that I've encountered unexpected problems. I cannot take Frieda and the girls to Hamel. I am under constant surveillance. I was able to get her to the ski hut, but I dare not go near there again. Frieda will go to the border on the night of the twenty-fourth. We think, with help, Anna can walk that far. From the border, Frieda needs help. I promised someone would meet her at the border to guide her on to Hamel and help her with Anna. Will you do it?"

"But I don't know the way!"

"I have made very detailed maps. Truly it won't be difficult to see the landmarks. Speed will be important. Frieda will need help, maybe even from the hut, so I included the way to the hut as well as the way to Hamel."

"You mean you want me to go into Germany?"

"The hut is but a few hundred yards beyond the Swiss border. Surely you won't need to go, but if Frieda didn't arrive at the border by 2 A.M. . . . I would hope you could find it in your heart to go help her. Here." He held out to her a sheaf of papers. "These are maps and my drawings of each landmark. I have written specific directions, and the place, the day, the hour. Keep them hidden. It has become more critical than ever that Andrew know nothing about this. I have placed the military documents in a bank deposit box in Geneva. Frieda has the number and the key with her. However, I pray I may come myself, as soon as she is safe, to turn over the information to the Allies.

"Em, I know I ask too much. But I could not leave without asking. It is the lives of my children and my wife I'm pleading for. No matter what I've done, they are innocent."

Her fingers closed of their own accord over the papers, and he reached for the door.

"Thank you," he whispered. "I owe you my life."

"Don't say that. I'm willing to try, but—"

"You said you believe in God. Will not God help you?"

"I don't know!"

"We shall pray, Frieda and I. We believe." When he went out, the latch didn't even click.

God, can a Nazi be a Christian? But he wasn't really a Nazi anymore. She seemed to hear a familiar phrase from the Bible, *O ye of little faith.*

She hurried to her bedside lamp and looked at the papers. There was a standard map of Switzerland and three enlargements of the specific area. Werner had made meticulous pencil drawings of landmarks. He also had included forged identification papers, one for each member of his family and some for her, in case she had to go to the hut. Apparently, if she entered Germany, she was supposed to be a German woman. She'd never carry that off in her uniform—and without her uniform, she'd be treated like a spy.

Dear God, what have I gotten myself into?

In the end, she decided she wouldn't be able to face herself in the mirror if she didn't try to help Frieda and the little girls, but even more urgent—the Allies needed the military information Werner had locked in that safety deposit box. And they wouldn't get it unless Frieda and the children escaped.

Em lay awake for a long time, thinking about her personal D day.

Chapter Twenty-six

The first day at the chateau, Marge slept the morning away. When she awoke, the ceiling of her room glowed bright with the sun's reflection upward from the snow outside. She belted the guest robe around her waist and padded down the hall to the bathroom. Along the way she nearly gasped aloud at the beauty of the chateau—plush rugs, rich oil paintings, and gleaming urns and vases made of porcelain, crystal, and brass. Obviously historical works of art, each container had been filled with winter arrangements of evergreens and dried plants. She had not noticed any of this yesterday.

On the way back to her bedroom she stopped beside a tall window to look out at an idyllic landscape. *Snow gentles the land,* she thought. Even an old shovel left carelessly against the side of the gazebo had become a graceful work of art.

In spite of herself the peace of the view seeped into her soul. But when she relaxed, her grief leaped up. David was dead, his body as cold and hard as the frozen earth in which it had been placed. She shuddered. She didn't even know where they had buried him. She was so angry—it didn't matter that she already knew life wasn't fair. David was different. Of all people, he should have lived. He was good, and she loved him so much.

Choking back sobs, she ran to her room, slammed the door, and cried until she had no more tears. Then she forced herself to gather a change of clothing and headed to the bathroom for a hot soak in the tub.

By the time she was dressed, with her damp hair drying to its own natural curl, she had achieved a certain amount of calm. She went down the wide stairs, wondering if she would be able to find Em in this large home without appearing snoopy.

She tried the library first.

There sat Em, typing. She looked up and then came to give Marge a hug. "Did you rest well?"

Marge hugged her back. "I sure did. I guess you can tell by how long I slept. What will Mrs. Blackwell think?"

"She invited you because she wanted you to have a good rest. So enjoy. Are you hungry? You can have either lunch or breakfast. I'll go along."

Marge's mouth watered at the prospect of good food. Surprised, she said, "I am hungry. I could eat anything. And a lot of it."

"Then let's go find the cook." Em slipped an arm around Marge's shoulders and gave her a sisterly squeeze. "I'm so glad you're here. And to think we'll have Christmas together—I can hardly believe it."

"Me too. This is such a beautiful place. How did you ever meet the Blackwells? You never told me."

"You probably won't like to hear, but it was on one of my impulses that you keep warning me about." As they walked to the dining room, Em told her about bicycling from Dijon to the Swiss border to see what it was like for a French resistant.

A maid interrupted the story to tell them that they'd be served lunch, unless Mademoiselle Marge wished a traditional breakfast.

"Lunch is fine for me," Marge said.

"Then, if you please, be seated, and I will serve you momentarily," the maid said.

"Is Mrs. Blackwell going to join us?" Em asked.

"She said to tell you she has gone to a meeting, but the other auto and Hans, for driving, they are at your disposal. She thought Mademoiselle Marge would like to visit some shops in the city."

"Would you, Marge?"

"Why, yes . . . I think I would."

"Then," Em said to the maid, "you may tell Hans we'll be ready right after lunch."

"Very good, mademoiselle."

Marge, watching Em give directions as if she'd had servants at her beck and call all her life, found herself smiling. Having a sense of humor felt alien. *How long since I've laughed at anything?* After the woman left, she said, "Little sister, I must say you certainly seem at ease with this style of living."

Em grinned. "I do? It's a long way from the ranch, isn't it? When

I'm fortunate enough to be invited here, I try to forget the whole world and just enjoy. It's like reading a good book in order to fall asleep at night—a temporary escape from reality." She pulled out a chair for Marge and one for herself and sat down. "At first I felt a little guilty about having a good time when our men are suffering in the combat zones. But then I decided the only way you can survive war is to snatch whatever beautiful moments you can. Even the troops take leaves when it's possible."

Marge stared at her hands folded in her lap and thought about the field hospital nurses and doctors who worked long hours and seldom got any time off. She looked up. "You're lucky you can do that, but try as I might, I can't seem to forget how it is at the Front. And the minute I remember, I'm back there. I really should return to duty soon. I'm feeling better."

"No!" Em jumped to her feet and loomed over her like a hen defending her chick. "Louise said three weeks, and three weeks it will be—even if I have to tie you to a chair!"

"You? Tie me to a chair? You tried that once, remember? And it didn't work."

Em had lashed her to a chair to keep her from going on a date with a boy they both liked. It was not a happy memory for either of them, being one of the few times they'd had a serious conflict. Now Em sputtered and then began to giggle. "You looked so funny. If only Billy hadn't come along to untie you, it would have worked. Aren't you glad neither one of us married Chester Bolton?"

Marge laughed. "Whatever attracted us to him? His wavy blond hair?"

"No, his skill at marbles. He was the only one who could take my aggies in a fair game."

"Then he was so cute when he was sixteen."

"And such a smug bore when he was eighteen. Amy Patterson deserved him."

They both giggled, remembering the pretty girl who thought she had stolen him from Marge and had clung to him throughout the last two years of high school.

"She couldn't even ride a horse." Em laughed harder.

"And him the heir to the biggest ranch around."

Marge couldn't stop laughing now that she'd started. She laughed until tears rolled. It wasn't really that funny, and yet it was. And laughing felt so good.

When the maid returned with steaming bowls of cheese and leek soup and crusty bread, Marge wiped her eyes and turned her attention to the wonderful cuisine. After roast chicken and glazed carrots, they finished with a fruit compote and chocolate-dipped wafers.

Then following Em's advice to dress warmly, Marge began looking forward to visiting the Swiss shops. She wanted to buy a thank-you gift for the Blackwells. That would be a challenge. Em would have to help her.

In Geneva the shops were filled with wonderful gowns, fur coats, and smaller luxury items they hadn't seen since entering the service. The Swiss clocks entranced her. She selected a special one to send home to her parents, along with some Swiss chocolate, even though they might not arrive until Easter. The shopkeepers promised to pack the clock very carefully, and from the looks of the shop and the price she and Em paid, Marge felt they should.

Em suggested a book for Andrew and a bottle of Lydia's favorite fragrance. Then they also chose scarves and gloves of fine quality for each of them. The shop wrapped the gifts and tied the packages with thick satin ribbons. Before meeting their driver, Hans, they had hot chocolate in a restaurant.

Driving back into the snow-sculpted grounds of the chateau, Marge felt a glimmer of old-fashioned Christmas spirit. She was, however, more tired than she'd expected. All she could think of was how good a nap would feel.

Indoors, when she mentioned her weariness, Em said, "A nap is a wonderful idea. I have a little writing I must finish, or I'd lie down too. Go ahead. I'll call you in time to dress for dinner."

Marge sighed and let go of her habitual sense of duty. To have Em take charge felt incredibly good. "Thanks, sis. See you later."

True to her word, Em woke Marge at six-thirty and sat on the edge of her bed while she dressed. Noticing for the first time that Em was not in formal attire, she asked, "Will there be guests tonight?"

"No. Just family. In fact, I'm not sure Andrew will be home. Lydia sent word that he was delayed at his office."

"And Herr Koch is gone too, I presume."

"I suppose so."

"He didn't tell you?"

"No."

"Is that German arrogance on his part, or doesn't he care about you?"

"Marge, I don't know what he thinks or feels. Really."

"Well, I have a notion, and I don't like it. But then I guess it's your business." Em had tensed up at the very mention of Werner Koch. Now she wore her stubborn look.

"Yes, it is *my* business."

"He has a nice family."

"Yes."

"His poor little girl. I wonder if her heart will hold out through the rigors of war. It's going to get worse for them before it's over."

"Yes. I think the Germans already are suffering serious shortages, despite what Werner says."

Marge thought of little Isabelle and David's love for children everywhere. "I really feel sorry for Werner's children. They both looked undernourished." Isabelle had been robust even during her hospitalization, compared to Anna with dark circles under her eyes.

Marge put on her dress uniform, which someone had brushed and pressed for her while she slept. Someone also had polished her regulation shoes to a gleaming shine.

With her mind still on Anna, Marge said, "I . . . had decided to go with David . . . finish my education and go as a physician to work beside him. I wanted to operate on those who had been wounded, like Isabelle."

Em stared, her eyes wide with questions. "Did you plan to marry David after all?"

Marge felt the tears coming again. She turned away, bit her lip, and pretended to look in the mirror while she combed her hair. She didn't want to cry again and have to go to dinner red-eyed. "We didn't quite get to that."

Em hurried to her side. "I'm sorry. I shouldn't have asked."

Marge held her breath and bit her lip. She did not want to give in to another emotional storm. In order to keep control, she said lightly, "Of course you should have asked. I loved David. If he had lived, I would have married him." There. She had said it out loud. She wanted to talk about him, to tell someone all the things she loved about him. She wanted to remember him. Her memories, so few, were all she had of him. Finding her voice, she continued. "You would have loved him too. He made me really glad I didn't chase after someone like Chester."

Em slipped her arm through Marge's, and as they slowly went downstairs to dinner, Marge told about her first meeting with David. She savored every moment of the telling. When they reached the dining room, she said, "I'll tell you more later."

Neither Lydia nor Andrew came home for dinner, so Marge talked on.

The telling inevitably led to Isabelle. "He bonded with that little girl and may have saved her life, simply by being someone she could trust while her wounds were critical. I guess that's one reason I want to keep in touch with her—because he loved her so much. I hope I can help her after the war. She may never walk normally again, but I think surgeons in the States may put her in better shape than anyone in Europe. We've made tremendous strides in surgical technique, just from operating on our wounded men."

Marge reached for her goblet of water and took a drink. Em waited without comment, so she continued. "Even before I'd considered marrying David, I had this silly dream that if Isabelle's family never turned up, he or I might adopt her."

Em laid down her fork and leaned toward her. "That's not a silly dream. Maybe you still can adopt her."

"You don't think it's foolish, me being single and having to get more education and all? I am serious about wanting to become a surgeon."

"No, it's not foolish. Maybe I can help with expenses. I'm not planning on more education."

"But you may marry. It's a long shot, I guess, for me to even consider it."

"No. Let's make it part of our postwar plans. I want to, Marge. I fell for Isabelle too when I saw her."

"Okay. For sure even the best orphanage can't do as well for her as I could."

"Good! We'll do it."

The maid came to the door of the library. "Mademoiselle Em, you have a long-distance call from a Monsieur Bob Mansfield."

Em jumped to her feet. "Oh! Thank you. I'll take it in here." She went to the phone on the wall.

Em answered and sounded very surprised. As the conversation continued, Marge decided to go her room and get ready for bed. Em would come say good-night as soon as she completed her business.

In her room, Marge changed into pajamas and lounging robe and sat down to write home. After a few minutes, Em came in. One look at her face brought Marge to her feet. "What's wrong?"

"I have to go back to Paris. Marge . . . the fighting in the Ardennes has heated up. Don't worry—it's all well south of your field hospital, but I've received orders to go cover the combat zone."

"But I thought your assignments involved interviewing civilians."

"They did. But I have a new job. I'll be working for the *U.S. National Tribune*, the paper Bob works for."

"Isn't it the biggest national paper, short of the *Wall Street Journal*?"

"Yes. I hadn't even hoped to write for them, but my own magazine refused to print a piece I'd done on the Nisei Combat Team, so Bob submitted it to his paper, and not only are they publishing it, they want me on staff. My first assignment is to report on the Ardennes."

"Em! Congratulations! Why are you looking as if the sky is about to fall on you? This is a great opportunity. You can do it. I've never seen you hesitate before."

Em looked very distracted. "Oh, I can do it all right. And I'm glad they want me. It's just that I must be back here—I want to be with you . . . for Christmas."

"Can't you go and be back by Christmas?"

"Yes."

"So what's the problem? You should be whooping with excitement. Do you feel all right?"

"Yes. No. I hate to tell you, but you will hear anyway. The Germans have taken back St. Vith, surrounded it, in fact. The orphanage is under German control again—"

"Oh no!" The thought of Isabelle in a combat zone again cut deeply. "Has the fighting around St. Vith subsided yet?"

"Yes. The worst should be over for now, that is, until the Allies return to take it back."

Marge began to tremble. She couldn't help it. She wanted to be strong, but her weak knees dumped her onto the edge of her bed.

Em sat down beside her and held her close.

Marge felt as if she were on the edge of a pit darker than the blackness she'd so recently escaped. What scared her most was the fact that she knew her reaction was extreme. "Em," she whispered, "will you sleep with me tonight?"

"Of course I will. You cover up while I run get my pajamas."

Marge obeyed, but she might as well have been curled in an ice cave. She couldn't stop shaking. When Em returned, Marge had to push her words out through chattering teeth. "I'm s-sorry. I don't know . . . what's c-come over me. I can't get a hold on myself. All I can think of is that Isabelle will be killed just like David was . . . after surviving his first wounds."

"No! Your fear is making you superstitious. Listen, what would David do now if he were here?"

"I think he would pray. Funny, how often I never thought to pray until he reminded me."

"Then let's pray. Like we used to at home when Mom would tuck us into bed."

"You pray, please."

"Okay." Em's arms tightened around Marge. "Dear Lord, you know how we feel . . . how we fear for Isabelle and the other children in the orphanage and the nuns. Please send angels to watch over them. Protect them all and don't let Isabelle be hurt again in any way. Don't let her be frightened. And please give Marge peace about this, the peace of our Lord Jesus Christ. Amen."

"Amen," Marge said, and gradually her trembling stopped.

In the night she dreamed that she and Em were back home, sharing the upstairs bedroom of the ranch house. When she awoke from the dream, Em lay sleeping beside her, and the chateau was very quiet.

At dawn Em tiptoed from Marge's room, hoping her sister would sleep in. She bathed, dressed, and packed her bag and typewriter before going down for breakfast.

In the dining room breakfast had been set out on the sideboard. Andrew, having his coffee, looked up from the newspaper in his hand. "I can't believe this. Hitler has launched an offensive. After weeks of retreating and thousands of his troops surrendering, his tanks and infantry are pushing right through the American lines. They've surrounded Bastogne. What has happened? Why don't the Allies stop him?"

She sat down opposite him. "That's where I'm going. I have a new job. I'm on staff now for the *U.S. National Tribune*. They called last night and want me to cover as much as I can of the breakthrough."

With uncharacteristic nervousness, Andrew tapped his fingers on the white damask tablecloth. "One of the advantages of having you as my courier was the fact you worked for a lesser known publication, so you could be almost invisible in many situations. Working for the *Tribune* will draw attention to you."

She stared at him in surprise. Being courier for him had taken such low priority in her mind that she sometimes almost forgot about it. She'd come to think of visiting him as surveillance for Cummins. "I doubt that I shall become famous or more noticeable," she said, wanting to laugh at the thought.

He frowned at his coffee cup for a minute and then said, "How soon do you have to leave?"

"As soon as I can get a train. I'm all packed now."

He glanced at his watch. "I'll drop you at the station when I go to the office. When will you be back?"

She thought fast. Today was December 16th. "I'll be back in five or six days." She had to be, for she must prepare to meet Frieda Koch and the children in eight days. She wished suddenly that she might tell Andrew about Werner's plans. She would feel better if he could know in case anything delayed her return. But of course she must not tell. "If I can, I'll be return sooner. I hate leaving Marge. She's still fragile."

He nodded. "Lydia will watch over her. Look, in a way this is good, your going today. I want you to take a message to Paris for me." He rose. "I'll be leaving in half an hour. I'll have the message and directions ready for you by then."

"Yes, sir."

Em slipped a note under Marge's bedroom door. Then she went down to the entry hall to wait for Andrew. Only time would tell whether she had made a good choice in accepting this opportunity for the job of her dreams. Five days for going and returning was cutting the margin of safety very close. She had to be on the Swiss/German border to meet Werner's family in little more than a week from today.

Chapter Twenty-Seven

Once Em reached Paris, she delivered Andrew's message and telephoned Cummins. He didn't have an assignment for her, but like Andrew, he seemed less than pleased over her new job. "The *U.S. National Tribune* may not give you as much freedom as *USA Living & Review* has. Did you think of that?"

"No. But it will work out."

"I hope so. We need you, Em."

"I'll be as available as ever," she reiterated.

"Oh, by the way, we apprehended Jacques Marchant, but Jeanette managed to slip through our net. She may have left Paris, but you still need to keep an eye out for anyone following you."

"Right." After she hung up, she thought about the father-daughter team, wondering what Jeanette would do now on her own.

Later in the day, with more time to think about the assignment from the *Tribune*, she began to worry about getting back to meet Frieda at the appointed time. She'd managed the so-called impossible before, but if anything happened to delay her, she'd simply have to head for Switzerland and forget the new job. Both Andrew and Cummins would be glad if she gave up working for the *Tribune*.

She was pretty sure her old boss would take her back. For that matter, she had not formally resigned from the *USA Living & Review* staff. So until she notified her editor, she'd be working for both publications. Even though she hadn't signed anything that prohibited freelancing, Albert Greenly might fire her when he saw the Nisei story in the *Tribune*.

Before retiring for the night, she met Bob in the lobby to coordinate their plans. They sat on a sofa in a quiet corner.

"You did say we'll be gone for only three days, right?" she said.

"Yes. Two days for driving and one day at the Front."

"I must be back in Geneva by the twenty-second."

"Well, there's never any guarantee, but that should be no problem. Why the deadline?"

"I promised Marge," she lied.

"Oh." After a moment he said, "Look, this assignment is the chance of a lifetime for your career. The *Tribune* knows you can write. Now they need to know they can count on you."

Her skill at lying must have improved. He seemed to believe that her concern for Marge was her only reason. "I understand, but no matter what happens, I have to get back to Geneva by the twenty-second."

Bob shook his head and gave her one of his hard-nosed newsman looks. "Okay. I just hope you can do that without failing to produce for the *Tribune*."

"I can do this. I would not have accepted otherwise. When do we leave?" she asked.

"First thing in the morning. We're to ride in General Bradley's staff car, so be ready at 0600."

The next morning before six o'clock Em stood with her typewriter case in hand by the front door of Hotel Scribe. Shortly, Bob appeared. "Good morning."

"Good morning."

"Did you wire your resignation to the *Review*?"

"No. I decided to wait. I have to get back to Geneva in five days. If I can't produce a good story for the *Tribune* in that time, I'll still have a job."

He studied her, raised his eyebrows, and shook his head. "I did get a little high-handed about telling you what to do, didn't I?"

"Yes." She smiled.

"Forgive me?"

"You bet."

"I'll get you back here on time, even if I have to conscript an airplane."

She laughed. "Thanks."

The ride north, crammed into a sedan full of army officers, went mercifully fast. No one talked much, so she didn't really learn where they were going until they got there. It was an army headquarters in tents so close to the battle line that once Bob grabbed her and threw her to the floor. An explosion shook the tent floor. When it was over, Bob explained that the whistling sound had been made by an incoming shell.

As the night settled in, the shelling eased, and Em got some sleep in the tent they'd assigned her.

Next morning the heavy gunfire resumed.

"We have to stay here until the Germans stop shooting and start running again," Bob said.

"How do we cover anything just sitting here?"

"We'll get our chance pretty soon."

But the firing did not die down. By noon Em decided to take things into her own hands.

If she could talk to people in a field hospital, she'd get more of what she wanted. A lieutenant at his desk must have felt her eyes on him, for he looked up from the papers in his hand and smiled. She returned his smile and walked over.

"How are you doing, Lieutenant?"

"Fair, ma'am. What can I do for you?"

"I need to get out of here and interview some of the men who've just returned from the battle."

"You wouldn't want to be doing that, ma'am, the battle being what it is. I'm surprised they let you this close to the action."

"It's my job, just like it's your job to be here."

"Well, I wouldn't want my sister out here, so I sort of feel like you shouldn't be."

"Is your sister a war correspondent?"

"No. She's at home, going to school."

"So there you have it. This is my job. That's why I'm here. Is there a field hospital close to here?"

"Why, yes, just yonder over a hill." He waved his hand in a general direction.

"Do you suppose I could go there if I can find transportation?"

"I'm not the one to say, but you could ask Major Russell over there. He'd be the one to decide and maybe give you a jeep and driver."

She had talked last night to Major Russell. He'd been cool toward having her here. His attitude against the press extended to Bob also. He'd said the war had heated up too much for him to have to worry about civilians. Despite their uniforms, they were civilians to him.

Bob was now sitting with his typewriter positioned on the corner of a desk, where he pecked out the first draft of a story. The man at the desk said something to Bob, who then bent his head and typed again.

Em took a deep breath and approached the major's desk. He was on a phone, listening and then giving orders. She fumbled in her jacket pocket and pulled out the ID card Cummins had prepared for her. It was time to see if his magic extended to the battlefront.

When the major hung up the phone, he glanced up at her. "What is it, Miss Emerson?"

"I'd like your permission to visit the closest field hospital, sir. My sister is an army nurse, so I'm used to the way they work. I wouldn't get in the way. I just want an opportunity to talk with a few men who are well enough to talk."

She saw the answer on his face before he spoke. "It's too risky. When you leave this area it will be only to go back to Paris. I realize the war needs to be reported, but I can't take responsibility for your safety."

She held out her ID card. "Will this change your mind, sir?"

He glanced at it and then frowned up at her. "Special permission? How did you get this?"

"It's authentic." She had no intention of telling him anything more.

"I can see it is." He leaned back and lit a cigarette. Through the cloud of his first exhaled smoke, he muttered, "Okay. I'll give you a jeep and a driver, but your friend over there stays here unless he also has a card with that signature and clearance on it."

"He doesn't, and I expect you to keep quiet about mine."

He reached for a piece of paper, wrote an order on it, and called, "Lieutenant Robb. Find Miss Emerson a driver and a jeep."

At the sound of his voice, Bob looked up. He jumped up and came to Em.

"What's going on? Do we get to go observe?"

The major sucked on his cigarette, keeping his eyes on Em. "Not we, Mr. Mansfield. Your friend here is going to visit a nearby field hospital, but two's too many. You stay here. You can go with me out to the next village when I go."

Em breathed easier. He had handled the secrecy astutely. "Thank you, sir."

He nodded curtly and reached for the phone again. Before picking it up, he said, "Be back here before dark. No one is going to go looking for you if you're not."

"I will." She turned, and Bob followed her back to their corner of the tent, out of the way of the soldiers coming and going.

He sat down again at his typewriter. "I'm sorry you can't go out with me—if I go. But how did you work that, getting him to let you visit a field hospital?"

"I just told him my sister is an army nurse and I knew how to stay out of the way. I guess I made a good point about wanting to interview the nurses and medics and the men who were well enough to talk."

"I hate having you take off alone, but that does fit your type of story."

"Sure does," she agreed.

A few minutes later, Lieutenant Robb came for her. "I have your transportation, ma'am."

"Thank you."

She grabbed her coat and snapped her typewriter into its case. Before stepping outside, she fastened the chinstrap of her steel helmet. Small-arms fire crackled off to the right. She couldn't judge how close they were.

The lieutenant pointed out her jeep, and Em ran for it. Before the private at the wheel could hop out and salute, she tossed her typewriter in back and climbed into the front. "What's your name, Private?"

"Private William Polanski, ma'am. I meant to tell you." He blushed.

"No matter. I just wanted to know what to call you. Do you go by Will, William, Bill or Polanski?"

He grinned. "The guys call me Polanski, ma'am."

"I'm Em Emerson."

"How d'ya do, ma'am."

"Where are you from, Polanski?"

This one question led to a long answer. Like most men over here, he loved to talk about his hometown and his family.

The drive to the field hospital took them through farmland, but Em could see forests and smaller stands of trees reaching bare fingers to the sky. Snow alternated with mud ruts on fields and pastures. On the road the jeep churned its way through ice-crusted mud. Polanski seemed to enjoy the challenge.

"I grew up driving tractor, and I have to tell you, this jeep is a gem. She can go through, around, or over anything, so don't worry."

Em smiled back. "Good. How much farther is it to the field hospital?"

"Just over that hill there. I've been there several times. Across country it's probably only a couple of miles back to HQ. It's just, we gotta follow these roads between fields and beside the creeks and all. I bet this sure is pretty country in the spring." He glanced around appreciatively. His face held a refreshingly innocent expression.

"Have you been over here long?" she asked.

"No. I just got here a couple of weeks ago. Got assigned to HQ because I'm a topnotch mechanic. I can make anything work, long as I have enough baling wire."

She laughed, as he seemed to want her to do. By his appearance he should still be in high school, but he was an expert driver. Every spin of the tires elicited instant corrective action from him.

They rounded a corner in the country road and ahead she saw tents clustered at the base of a low hill and marked with huge red crosses on white circles. Leafless trees lined one side of the area, marking the route of a road coming from the battlefront.

Polanski pulled in and parked. Em hoisted her typewriter from behind her and climbed out. The clouds were black, but for the moment neither snow nor rain fell. "Look around for the mess tent. They'll give you some coffee, and I'll meet you there after a while."

When Em stepped into the tent where people seemed to be coming and going, she suspected she should not have come. The tired faces of the orderlies and nurses told her they had not slept in a long time. The room was filled with men waiting for surgical care. Nurses were doing some of the triage that Marge had said the doctors normally did. One nurse looked up and, seeing her uniform, said, "Get over here and help, will you? Hold this man's leg immobile while I cut away his pants."

Em dropped her typewriter against the wall of the tent and obeyed. She kept her eyes on the soldier's face to avoid looking at his wound. The smell of blood was overpowering, and there were other unpleasant odors also that she didn't want to identify. She clamped her teeth together and held his leg firmly.

The nurse slit the man's trousers and carefully washed his leg. A first-aid bandage and tourniquet had been wrapped high on his thigh. Involuntarily Em looked. The nurse removed the bandage and cleansed the skin around a ragged wound that showed the pale line of exposed bone or tendon.

Em gulped and held on.

The nurse loosened the tourniquet, and when blood streamed, she tightened it again. Then she painted the leg with iodine. The soldier, evidently out from morphine, stirred and moaned.

The nurse instantly responded. "You're going to be okay, soldier. You're doing fine." She swiftly painted more iodine around the wound and placed a fresh bandage over it. "There," she said, "you're ready for surgery, and you'll wake up in good shape." With that she stood up and for the first time really looked at Em. "You're not a nurse!"

Em stood up and managed a smile. "No. War correspondent. Em Emerson. I'll be glad to help if there's anything more I can do."

"Well, sure. As you can see, we don't have enough hands. You can go along this line and make sure the aid station's tag is easy for us to see. And bring clean blankets from that stack over there to wrap up any men who are cold. Feel their hands. Talk to the ones who are awake. If you see any faces that look too pale, call me right away."

"Sure. I can do that." She glanced around as stretcher-bearers carried in another man. "Say, I sent my driver to the mess tent to wait for me. If you want, you could use him too."

The nurse straightened and rubbed her back. "We can use any warm body. Go get him, and tell him to help the stretcher-bearers."

Em grabbed her coat. In a couple of minutes she had Polanski back into the receiving tent helping the ward men and ambulance drivers.

She and Polanski worked for several hours without a breather. They both gave blood, as did the nurses and doctors and a few of the men with lesser wounds. Finally there was a lull. The last man in line for surgery was carried into the operating room, and no more ambulances drove up outside.

The nurse who had accepted Em's help came to thank her. "Say, you did all right for a newspaper gal. Have you had experience in a hospital?"

"No. But my sister is an army nurse. Maybe the things she told me helped."

"Well, you didn't faint, and you were right there when I called. And you, too, Private. Ever think of becoming a medic?"

"No, ma'am. And I guess it's too late now."

Em asked what had been burning in her mind the past several hours. "Do you have many rushes like this?"

"It's been this way ever since the German advance began. The quiet times are bad news. We've learned that fewer patients here means more deaths out in the field. For us to run out of plasma and need live donors, that's a first. Glory, I hope it's a last," she murmured, pushing her straggling short hair back from her forehead. "Come on, let's go get a cup of coffee while we can, and you can tell me why you came here. I'm sure it wasn't to assist us."

So Em got her interview, supplied by the nurse, a medic, and one of the doctors. She was about to ask if she might talk to one of the soldiers, but a glance at her wristwatch told her why it was getting dark outside. "Polanski, we've got to go. It's nearly four-thirty."

As they drove out of the field hospital compound, snow began to fall in big wet flakes, and as the wind kicked up, the flakes came fast and powdery. By the time they reached the first sharp curve in the road, the muddy ruts were turning white.

Em was glad she'd included woolen gloves with her gear that morning. The jeep slithered sideways several times, but Polanski straightened it with ease. "Can you see okay?" she asked, when the jeep skidded a third time.

"Well enough. I daren't turn on the headlights. Even though planes can't fly in this weather, a German patrol could take a potshot at us."

Em hunkered lower on the hard seat. With the window flaps down, she couldn't see anything but the white blur ahead.

After a while she said, "Shouldn't we be getting there by now? You said it was only two miles as the crow flies."

"I think it's just ahead." He didn't sound very confident. Then he exclaimed, "Here! This is the final turn. We're almost there."

A couple of minutes later he turned onto a side road that might have looked familiar without so much snow. Suddenly the jeep skidded, slipped sideways, and Em felt it drop into a ditch on her side.

"Don't worry," Polanksi said. "We've got four-wheel drive. This little lady will get us out in a jiffy."

But it didn't. Em sat tight while he tried everything she knew from driving in snow, and a few things she'd never thought of trying. At last he sat there in the growing dark with his chin down. "I guess we're stuck, ma'am. You stay here, and I'll scout up the road a bit. HQ can't be far."

Em roused up. "I'm not staying here. We go together, but I'll have to climb out your side."

He got out and held the door open for her. The snow was only about four inches deep on the road, but the wind was biting cold and starting to pile up in drifts. "Look, we may have to come right back here and stay in the jeep for the night, so let's don't wander off this road," Em warned.

She walked behind him, stepping in his boot prints. When they didn't come to anything soon, she grew uneasy. HQ had not been this far from the main road. Finally she lunged ahead and grabbed the private's coat sleeve. She had to shout for him to hear her above the wind. "We should have reached the tents by now. We're lost."

He stopped, his back to the wind. "You might be right. I was sure this was the entrance to our bivouac area, but . . ." His voice trailed off.

"Maybe we can find a farmhouse for the night—or a barn. Otherwise we'd better go back to the jeep."

"Yeah." He peered all directions.

Em did too. The wind and fine snow had almost obliterated their tracks.

"Come on," she said. "Let's go back to the jeep." She turned and he followed.

Before they reached the jeep, the wind dropped off and the snowfall grew lighter. The surrounding landscape began to take shape. Off to the right, Em saw a stand of snow-covered trees. About fifty yards farther, a dark smudge suggested the shape of buildings. "Look!" She pointed. "There must be a road or path to them."

"There it is. Up ahead I see a break in the hedge," he said. "When it was snowing so hard, I missed it." He quickened his pace and turned into the opening.

Em felt smooth ground beneath her feet. "It's a driveway. Maybe one of the buildings is a house."

No light showed, but blackout precautions would be normal so close to the action.

When they reached the buildings, they saw that one was a house. Em went to the door and knocked. She was about to try to open it when the door opened a crack and a man said something in French.

"We're lost," Em said in English, hoping he'd understand.

"You are American?"

"Yes. Oui. Our jeep is stuck, and we're lost."

He opened the door wider. "Please to come in. Welcome."

The house was cold, dark, and empty, except for the man. "My wife, my children, they flee when the Germans come. I hide in the barn until shooting stop. Now I try by myself to feed and care for the cows, the chickens. Come. I feed you. Then you sleep in warm bed. Tomorrow I help you find way."

"Thank you!" Em said.

"Yes, sir. Thank you," Polanski added.

The man produced potato and cabbage soup, and over the meal they introduced themselves. After they'd had their fill, their host showed them to their rooms by the light of a candle.

Lying snug under homemade quilts, Em said a thank-you prayer, grateful they didn't have to huddle in the jeep all night.

She didn't want to imagine what Bob must be thinking by now. And she didn't want to guess whether Private Polanski could find his way back to HQ.

Chapter Twenty-Eight

When Marge awoke the morning that Em left the chateau, she felt better than she had in days. She was surprised that her first thoughts turned to Werner Koch and his family, especially the little girl with the dark circles under her eyes. While in training, she had nursed a child who had the same sickly look as Anna. The boy had died of heart failure. One could never tell. The physicians said that good care could help, but some conditions were irreversible. Werner Koch's poor wife had lost her son, and now, with two children depending on her, here was her husband making eyes at Em. What a no-good he was.

If David were alive, he probably would find a way to help a mother and her children—even with the war on—if he had a chance. It comforted her to be thinking about what David would do instead of yelling at God the big why.

David never had yelled why. He had analyzed a situation and then figured out some way to help.

She went to her small bag where she'd packed David's Bible. In all the days since he had died, she had not been able to open it and face the pain of possibly finding and reading his personal study notes. Now, in this peaceful setting with no one needing her, she longed for words from him, instead of dreading the sight of his private notes.

The compact Bible fell open at the letter to the Ephesians. David had underlined the last verse of chapter four and the first two verses of chapter five. *And be ye kind one to another, tenderhearted, forgiving one another, even as God for Christ's sake hath forgiven you. Be ye therefore followers of God, as dear children; and walk in love, as Christ also hath loved us, and hath given himself for us an offering and a sacrifice to God for a sweet-smelling savour.*

The old-fashioned words described David. He had lived this way in the midst of the compounded evil of war. Marge perceived for the first time that his goodness had not necessarily been easy for him. It had been a sacrifice.

She wept, as she'd known she would when she read his Bible, but it didn't matter. She didn't have to keep a calm face for anyone this morning. When she finally stopped crying, she thumbed through the worn pages of the Bible. He had marked a number of places and had written dates and comments on the margins. She read a few notes and in the reading grew soul quiet. She felt as though she were talking with David in person. She had God's Word and she had David's words. What a treasure he'd left her. Inside the back cover he'd written his home address in Pennsylvania. She could write to his mother—maybe even meet her after the war.

At the bottom of the page in fresh ink he had written, *My last will and testament: I leave this prayer for the person who reads my Bible. May you love and trust the Lord as I do. He has never failed me. He will never fail you. Joyously, David Whitfield Lewellyn.*

Marge wept again, and when she could cry no more, she felt drained. She bathed, and while she dressed, she realized that the reason David had died didn't seem as important to her as the fact that he had lived and that she'd had the privilege of knowing and loving him.

As she went downstairs, she thought about little Anna again. What could she do for this sick child in Germany? Maybe Em could persuade the father to bring his family to Switzerland, and the Blackwells could find the child a good heart specialist. Or Em could find a doctor. She had such a way with people.

Marge went to breakfast feeling really hungry. The blackness that had dulled her mind and spirit was gone, and she felt sure it would not return.

Lydia came in and joined her at the dining table. "Andrew left and so did Em."

"I didn't mean to oversleep. I had hoped to be up when Em left."

"You needed the rest. I'm sure Em understood."

"Yes. She would. I did rest well. In fact I feel better than I have in days."

Lydia smiled. "I'm so glad. You look better. Now if we can get a little meat on your bones while you are here . . ."

Marge looked at the waffles, the Black Forest ham, and the fluffy fresh eggs scrambled and topped with Swiss cheese. "At this rate, I think you will. Do you have a radio in here? May I hear the news?"

Lydia shook her head. "One rule I insist on is no radios or news reports while we eat. Now, I'd really like to know more about your family. Em told me you have a brother and that you lived on a ranch. I'd love to hear about your home. What is Oklahoma like?"

Marge chuckled. "Well, it's about the opposite of Switzerland. The highest point in Oklahoma is less that five thousand feet, and that's not near Tuttle, where we lived."

Marge told her about her little brother, Billy, and that Em's real name was Lucille. She described her mom and dad and the ranch and a few of Em's crazy adventures. Lastly she told Lydia about her own early interest in nursing, how she'd fallen into helping to care for her best friend's father. She sipped her coffee, then continued. "He was gassed in the Ardennes. Now they're fighting there again. That's why I wanted to hear the news."

Lydia stood up. "Come, I'll show you where the radio is."

In a den she turned on a floor-model radio, and they listened together to the latest report on the battlefronts, but not much was said about the Ardennes. When the news report ended, Lydia said, "I have to go shopping this morning. I know Em showed you around, but would you like to go with me? I plan to meet a few friends for lunch, and I'd like them to meet you, that is, if you feel up to it."

"I do. Thanks."

So Marge saw more of Geneva—and from a quite different perspective. Lydia had been born to wealth, and so had her friends. They were kindly, but certainly looked at the world differently from the way in which Marge did. By the time she returned to Château Bleu, she was exhausted. "Do you mind if I retire early? I'm not really hungry after that wonderful lunch."

"You do just as you wish. I hope today hasn't been too strenuous."

"Not at all. I enjoyed every minute. Thanks for inviting me."

A few minutes later Marge lay soaking in a luxuriously hot bath, thinking about Em and wondering if she was getting the stories she'd hoped for.

Marge nearly fell asleep in the tub. Climbing into bed, she was aware of how pampered the down-filled comforter made her feel.

In the morning the grounds around the chateau looked as if they'd been snowed in. She dressed in her warmest clothing and went downstairs. Lydia again joined her for breakfast and invited her to go to a Red Cross function that afternoon.

"I hope you don't mind, but I'd love a quiet day here, just reading a book by the fire."

"You're most welcome to do that. I'd stay in myself, but these obligations keep coming up. And the Red Cross is one of my volunteer responsibilities. I'm happy to help them."

So they parted for the day, and Marge settled herself in the library beside a toasting fire that the houseman kept going. A maid brought her lunch on a tray and tea and hot cocoa throughout the day. By evening Marge was ready for company, but the Blackwells had each come home alone and had invited no one for dinner.

Shortly after their quiet dinner, Werner Koch showed up. He disappeared with Andrew into the study. Lydia excused herself early for what she called her rejuvenating rest, so Marge decided to go to bed too.

As she passed the study, she heard the men talking despite the closed door. Andrew's voice penetrated clearly. "I wish you had told me sooner. I could have worked out something better."

"I did not dare. I only came now because, with Em gone, I have nowhere else to turn. They will kill me. I have accepted that. But Frieda and the children would still have a chance if Em were here. I had counted on her!"

Marge stood as if nailed to the floor. The door latch clicked. The door swung open, and both men gaped at her in shock.

She was first to find words to bridge the shock. "I couldn't help but hear. What's this about Em?"

Andrew faced Werner Koch. "Tell her what you just told me. It's better than to let her guess. She even may be able to help. After all, she is a nurse."

Marge stared at the German. The horror had not faded from his normally composed face.

He set his mouth in a determined line. "In this I have not much choice. Please, Miss Emerson, there is much that I need to explain. Come in where we cannot be overheard."

She followed him into the study. Andrew entered behind her, closed the door, and locked it. Then he crossed the room and pulled out a chair for Marge beside his desk.

Werner Koch remained standing. He began to pace as he talked. "First, I want to explain that there is nothing romantic between me and your sister. She played her part so well, I could see your concern. She agreed to help me save my family, and this was to be the way." He proceeded to explain that he was high up in the Nazi party and had remained close to Hitler, even until the present.

Gradually he had learned about the evil the Third Reich was committing in the name of progressive thinking. For two years he'd been searching for a way out of Germany that would assure safety for his family. He never found it, but now his time was limited. He had become suspect.

Marge gasped when she heard that Hitler had ordered wives and children to be executed along with any traitor. Betrayal, as the Fuehrer defined it, could be something as small as questioning an order or disagreeing with him. Werner had arranged for Em to help him get his family out of Germany. Incredibly, Em had agreed to meet them and guide them on into Switzerland.

Werner had his own spies who told him that the Gestapo had learned about the plan and the date. They were searching for the hut where Frieda and his children were hiding. They planned to capture them in the act of escaping so they could confront Hitler with incontrovertible evidence that one of his favorites was a traitor. Werner had sent a message to Frieda, through a mountain family who had known him as a boy, that she must leave earlier than planned. Supposing Em would not be able to come sooner, he had made it only two days earlier than originally planned.

"Two days will be enough," he said. "If the Gestapo should locate the hut, still they believe the twenty-fourth will be the night of her escape. They will want to catch her in the act. I was able to come here without observation, but I must be in Munich early tomorrow and accompany the Fuehrer to Berchtesgaden," he said. "I telephoned Em's hotel in Paris. She has gone to the Front, out of touch, and they don't know when she will return. I could think of nothing else but to confide in Andrew, and now in you."

"What was Em going to do when she had your family safe in Switzerland?"

"She planned to accompany them on the train to Geneva. She was to meet Frieda and the children at the border a few kilometers east of Schaffhausen at the small town of Hamel. Right on the border, Hamel looked the safest point of entry. I've known this little town and the surrounding mountains since my early childhood, so I could instruct Em in detail.

"A small rail line will take them from Hamel to Schaffhausen and then to Winterthur. Without changing trains they can connect with the main line into Zurich and then into Geneva. In Geneva I have arranged a safe hiding place with a pastor who has hidden other refugees. After New Year's a doctor friend will have space for Anna in his hidden sanitarium. If my family's departure from Germany remains secret, I may be able to escape.

"My mountain friend told me of one unfortunate complication—my wife is recovering from the flu. She will be all right, but she desperately needs assistance to bring Anna the two kilometers over the snow into Hamel."

Marge, grappling mentally with the risks involved, tried to encompass all these details in order to make an informed decision. Werner obviously had planned with great care.

Andrew interrupted her thoughts. "Marge, Lydia doesn't know about any of this. You must not let her become suspicious."

"I won't. I understand."

"On the strength of that promise," Andrew said, "I will tell you more. Werner doesn't know this. I am with the OSS. Em is an OSS courier, but even she doesn't know that I am an agent. My major task for our government has been to keep ongoing communication with as many German businessmen as possible."

"Em is in the Secret Service?" Marge exclaimed.

Werner Koch said nothing. He rubbed his cleanly shaven chin and rested his fingers across his lips for a second.

Andrew continued. "Yes. It's been important for me to appear ambivalent in my loyalties. Em didn't know whether she could trust me, so she kept her arrangement with Werner a secret. But when I confronted Werner about his infatuation with Em, he finally decided to tell me the truth and ask for my help. But you see what Em has gotten herself into."

"I've always known you were loyal to your country," Werner said, "but could not trust the security of the OSS if you were an agent. Now I have nowhere else to turn."

Marge finally got her voice back. "So how can we help Herr Koch's family?"

"We?" Andrew asked. "You're here to rest and recuperate. All we need from you is your vow of silence and maybe some nursing advice for Em."

"If Em goes, I go."

Werner Koch's expression softened. "You do not mind to help a Nazi?"

"From what you say, you are no longer a Nazi. I'm a nurse, and your daughter needs a nurse. If Em goes, I go with her."

Werner Koch's jaw tightened. His shoulders rose in a shuddering breath. "I did not hope for such kindness after all that my country has done."

"A very dear friend of mine said this war will not be won until enemies forgive each other."

"An unusual friend. May I know who?"

"His name was David Lewellyn."

"Was?"

"He was killed. He was a U.S. Army medic whom I was going to marry." She straightened. "Now I'm going to do what he would do and help your family."

"You give me hope," Werner said. "Andrew, it may work using the two women. To have a nurse would be a wonderful help."

"I hate to see either Em or Marge take such a risk. I can get a couple of professionals."

"No! Our agents will know any agent you choose. Frieda must not be seen with OSS men. I—I would never have a chance if you did that." He straightened and began to pace the floor again. "I do not like to demand, but the information I promised you for the Allies—you will not get it unless you do this my way."

Andrew seemed to turn to stone as he studied Werner Koch. "You play a hard game, don't you?"

"For the lives of my family and myself, I do not want to lose. I know that from inside the OSS, double agents report to the Gestapo. I don't know who they are or where they are, but if you say a word about this to any of your professionals, you will consign me and my family to the death squad. That's why I talked to Em instead of you."

Marge looked from one to the other. She'd offered to help for the sake of the children. To be involved in espionage was another matter entirely. Even as she considered this, however, she still wanted to help the mother and the children.

Andrew heaved a giant sigh and began his own pacing. He stared out the window for minutes. Finally he swung around. "Okay, Werner. You win." He came back to the desk and sat down. "Let's work on the details. I'll telephone Paris again. Possibly Em will be back at her hotel tomorrow."

"Em must be here three days from now and at the border by half past midnight the morning of December twenty-first. She will need to reach the rendezvous location in daylight. I already gave her the maps and the drawings."

"And if I can't reach Em?" Andrew asked.

Werner turned to Marge. "Are you willing to go alone, as Em was?

It is not far, maybe only two kilometers—less than a mile on snowshoes—and my maps are very detailed. I spent many boyhood days there, both summer and winter. The borders are only lightly guarded. The trains in and out of Hamel serve mostly local people and seldom receive attention from either Swiss border guards or the German military. As I said, once Frieda boards she can stay in the same railroad car all the way to Zurich and right on to Geneva."

Having already decided to help Em, Marge said, "I'll go. Em will be here. She will have planned to return here early. I know nothing will stop her from keeping her word."

"Nevertheless, I will draw more maps for you right now," he said.

"You make the maps," Andrew said, "and we'll do the rest. There's no reason why I can't reach Em. I'll keep my mouth shut and my agency out of this. I want you to get out of Germany safely almost as bad as you do."

The men shook hands. Werner Koch said, "Thank you, my friend."

"Will your wife bring Anna's medicines with her?" Marge asked.

"What she has. I have Dr. Schneider's diagnosis and a list of her present medications and dosages written. I was going to give it to Em, but it will be so much better for you, a nurse, to have it."

"Give me Dr. Schneider's full name," Andrew said. "Marge should consult with him. He might suggest something more."

"But—"

Andrew held up his hand. "This I can do without causing any suspicion. I promise."

Werner Koch finally nodded.

They talked for a few minutes more. Then Andrew said, "Marge, maybe you should leave us now. Lydia will begin to wonder why you're in here so long."

"She went to bed early, but I agree. I should go."

Werner reached for her hand when she stood up. "I cannot thank you enough."

"You're very welcome. I think I should thank you. You've helped me too, more than you can know." She opened the door and stepped out before he could ask what she meant. To have a purpose, to feel as if she were doing something for David—she didn't want to talk about this with a stranger.

Now she wanted to be alone. Well, not entirely alone. She desperately wanted Em.

When Em awoke, her face was cold, and she could see her breath. Having slept in her clothes, she made a speedy transition from bed to her overcoat and boots and tiptoed through the small house and outdoors to the outhouse. As she made her way back to the house, a crackle of gunfire exploded like the firecrackers she and her brother used to set off all in a string. Then came a loud burst of artillery, several volleys, so close to the farm the ground trembled and her ears rang. She made a beeline for the house as fast as the six-inch snowfall permitted.

She burst in and found the men in the front room, barefooted but fully clothed.

Their host, Monsieur Ostier, gasped, "They have come back! We must leave the house. If they come through this way, they will use it for their own cover. Quickly!" He pulled on his boots. "Follow me."

Em obeyed. Running for the woods behind the house, she called, "Is it the Germans or the Allies returning?"

"Germans."

"How can you tell?"

"The Panzerfaust, their antitank gun. It makes a sound like no other. Here. Inside! Quickly!" He opened the side door of a shed at the far edge of a cow yard. "The cows, bless them, they will trample our tracks and hide them."

Em doubted that. They'd left a swath of footprints in the snow from the kitchen door across a field to this little shed. Worse yet, the old wooden building didn't look like any sort of protection. Still she obeyed, because she couldn't think of anything better.

Inside the man went to a corner, lifted some boards, and waved them on. "Down here. It was an old cheese curing room, but it has been our bomb shelter and served us well. The building is so small it will not conceal tanks or guns, so they have left it alone. When night comes, if they are not gone, we can sneak out and away."

Em went down narrow stone steps. In the half-light, it looked as if this had been a natural cavern that some housewife had chosen for her cheese-aging room. The cave gave off an earthy, though not unpleasant, odor. The stone floor had been brushed clean. A few wooden boxes stood around the perimeter.

The men came down, and their host closed the trapdoor.

"I made many tracks into the nearby woods," the farmer said. "When I called a cow and her calf, other cows came too and trampled out tracks here in the cow yard. On the floor above, much old straw. The door, it is easy to conceal. With luck, no one will come here. I have candles, but the Boche, they would smell them. So we stay dark."

She heard him rattling around. Something touched her arm.

"Blankets," he said.

"Thank you."

"We have water and a little food. We keep this place supplied, since the Occupation. We hide English flyers in here."

Em stayed on the wooden box she had chosen when she first came down.

From the sound of it, Polanski was across from her. She wondered how long they'd be stuck here.

Artillery boomed again, sporadic rifle fire crackled, then she heard an eerie sound. She'd heard it before down at the house but had been too scared to give it much thought. "The Panzerfaust?" she asked.

"Oui," he said. "A sound your tanks don't want to hear."

The Panzerfaust screamed again, followed by a heavy explosion.

"I'm afraid they got one," Polanski said.

"Oui," their host said.

Guns and artillery fire came from all sides. At times it reminded Em of an Oklahoma prairie thunderstorm. When quiet came, they listened, waiting for the next volley. They waited a long time but heard no guns.

"Have they moved on, you think?" Polanski asked.

"Can't know for a while," Monsieur Ostier said. "Can't go up yet." He sounded stolid and patient.

Em wanted to scream. Not only because she felt trapped in a battlefield, but also because she had to get back to Paris. Bob would be beside himself, and Marge too. *Dear Lord, I have to get to Switzerland!* she silently cried.

Rifle fire erupted, followed by quiet.

Again shots rang out, and bursts from machine guns. "That sounds farther away," she said.

Monsieur Ostier said, "Still close. I go look soon."

The shots continued but didn't come closer.

After an immeasurable time, Em said, "May I have some water and a little food?"

Monsieur Ostier touched her hand with the water bottle. The water had been flavored with wine. She supposed that made it safer. She drank a little and then reached until she bumped Polanski with the bottle. He took it. In the same manner, they all had some cheese and dry bread. Then they settled into listening again.

The gunfire actually sounded fainter. "Can you look out yet?" Em asked.

"Not yet."

She hated just sitting, so she began to ask Monsieur Ostier questions about his family and how it had been during the Occupation.

He answered in monosyllables except where his family was concerned. He obviously loved and missed them. "They are with my wife's mother in Charlaroi. We thought that would be safe. Who would have guessed that, after the Boche fled, they would return? Your armies, surely they will push them back."

"Sure," Polanski said. "It's only a matter of time."

In a bemused voice the farmer continued. "Time—we win in time, but the price, it is always high for a war we did not want."

"That's for sure too, sir."

The two men fell into a conversation about this war and the last, and Em's thoughts strayed to Bob. Would he go back to Paris without her? Or was he trapped in the battlefield too?

Their original plan and permission had been to head back to Paris today. She had to get out of this cellar. Was she behind the German lines? If no soldiers were visible, how would she know?

They would have to rely on Monsieur Ostier's judgment and directions for finding the army headquarters. It took all of her willpower to sit still and wait for this cautious Belgian farmer to decide when it was safe to venture out.

Chapter Twenty-nine

At the chateau Marge slept late again. The excitement of Werner Koch's secret had kept her awake until long past midnight.

Now descending the graceful staircase, she reviewed the details she'd have to remember in order to act as if she knew nothing about Andrew Blackwell's secret life. She wished his wife could be included. She'd always found that playacting of any kind led to problems.

Well, as soon as Em came back, they could plan together. Em would make the task easier. In the meantime, she needed to talk with Dr. Schneider.

In the dining room, the maid said Madame Blackwell had gone out and would return to have lunch with her.

"Fine," Marge said, trying not to look too happy over this brief reprieve from playacting around Lydia.

The phone rang, and when the maid came back, she said, "Monsieur Blackwell for you, mademoiselle."

Marge followed her to the phone in the study. "Hello," she said.

"I hope you slept well."

"Yes, once I finally fell asleep."

"I thought you may have had a hard time after last night. I'm sending my car for you. I've arranged an appointment with Dr. Schneider. He's agreed to give you medicine and instructions. Can you be ready in half an hour?"

"Yes. Lydia is out, you know, but she was going to come home to have lunch with me."

"Don't worry about that. I'll call the Red Cross office and tell her you'll be lunching with me."

"All right. Thank you."

"Good-bye then."

"Good-bye."

She finished the eggs Benedict that Marta had placed on the table for her and then ran upstairs to dress.

In Dr. Schneider's office, winter light from the window cast soft shadows across his face.

Marge, seated beside his desk, supposed he could be anywhere between forty-five and sixty. The certificates on the wall, indicating his several degrees, showed dates beginning in 1925.

He picked up a sheaf of papers. "I have here the records of Anna Koch. I am acquainted with her physician in Munich and am a friend of Herr Koch. I treated his son until it was decided that Frederick should be under the care of his family doctor in Munich." He cleared his throat. "Herr Koch is wise to get Anna out of Germany, especially with the way the war is progressing. I understand you will escort her to Geneva."

"Yes."

"It is my opinion that the influenza and ensuing rheumatic fever she suffered last year has seriously weakened her heart. These cases are tricky. With exceptional care, she may live a reasonably satisfactory life. If she endures the privations and stress of war for any length of time, she may not survive. Although Herr Koch hates to admit it, I have no doubt she has not had the quality of nourishment, and certainly not the quiet, that her body needs to rebuild strength. I sent medicines, vitamins, and instructions to her mother a few weeks ago. For the journey here, I am giving you more medications that will fortify her or treat a crisis. From what Herr Koch described, the journey will not be easy for an invalid. She will need your full attention. Will you have any assistance besides the mother?"

"My sister will go with me."

"Good. Herr Koch said Frau Koch is recuperating herself from flu. She may need a strong expectorant with codeine to suppress her cough, not only for her comfort, but to avoid attracting attention." He set out two bottles containing liquid and three containing pills. "The sulfa tablets are for the mother in case she develops a fever, but I've included a dosage for Anna if she should run a fever."

"I understand, Doctor."

"Excellent. Now, for little Anna. Give her this tonic regularly, as directed. It will fortify her and may prevent need for the other drugs."

He handed her the second bottle of liquid. She nodded and placed it in her purse with Frau Koch's medicine.

He held up the two small bottles of pills. "Although I would prefer not to use these drugs on a child this young, in a crisis the first bottle will strengthen and steady her heart. Check her pulse carefully and administer only if you think necessary. The second will relieve angina. Use only if needed. Here are detailed instructions."

She took the bottles and his typed orders and put them in her purse also.

Dr. Schneider leaned back, resting his elbows on the arms of his chair. "Keep a standard chart, however small, recording what you administer and when and the patient's reaction to the medication. This will help me in treating her when she arrives." He cleared his throat. "And pray you don't have an emergency."

"I shall, Doctor."

He nodded. "How long have you been an army nurse?"

"Three years. Before that I worked in a general hospital for a year."

He pursed his lips, and then said, "Well, you're to be commended for doing this on your leave time. May God go with you."

"Thank you."

He stood up, and she followed suit. Walking her to the door of his plush office, he said, "Give Monsieur Blackwell my regards and Herr Koch, too, if you should see him. Good day."

"I'll do that. Good day, Doctor."

In the reception room the chauffeur stood up. "I will bring the car around, mademoiselle."

"Thank you, Hans."

While waiting for him at the front door of the building, Marge desperately longed for Em. Other than the nursing, this whole enterprise was more in line with Em's skills than her own. The Blackwell car rolled up to the curb, and clutching her handbag full of medicines to her side, she hurried out.

Hans helped her into the car, and when they were underway, he said, "I am to take you to Monsieur Blackwell's office now, mademoiselle."

"Fine." She felt all at odds, unnerved by what lay ahead, yet eager to get started. She hoped to hear that Andrew had talked to Em.

Em waited impatiently when the sounds of battle stopped. It seemed forever before Monsieur Ostier decided he could go out to assess the situation.

Polanski had run out of stories about his hometown, his girl, and his family. So had Em. They waited and waited.

Finally Polanski said, "What if the Germans get him? How long we gonna wait to find out?"

"For now we wait. Maybe he's checking the road or even talking with the folks at the next farm."

Polanski sighed. "I suppose."

"We might as well try to nap. If we have to walk out of here, we may be up all night, trying to find HQ."

"Sure."

Em leaned back against the stone wall. She was going numb from inactivity but was not sleepy.

At last a creak from above alerted her. "What if it's not Monsieur Ostier?" she whispered.

She heard Polanski move. "I'm ready," he whispered.

The trapdoor opened only a crack before Monsieur Ostier called, "It's me—Ostier."

He opened the door wide to let in light and came down cautiously. He nodded at the private's drawn gun. "Good. You are wise. My neighbor says the Americans, they come back. Here, my farm, these hills, we are in American hands. Four kilometers east the Boches make a stand in a small village. If you take road, head south. First highway, turn right. You come where you left yesterday. You see your camp from hill, before you there. Polanski, come help me, my neighbor. We get jeep out."

Em jumped up. "I can help too."

When they reached the jeep, the neighbor was already there with a horse-drawn wagon full of straw and a few heavy planks.

The men set to work shoveling snow. Monsieur Ostier handed Em a small handsaw and told her to bring branches to pack under the wheels.

She brought them by the armful and laid them at the edge of the road. From there the men worked them in front of the wheels. Then they laid a trail of branches and straw all the way onto the road.

Polanski got in the jeep and started the engine. The men levered the low side upward with the planks. With all four wheels spinning, Polanski drove up onto the road.

"Hurray!" Em called.

Polanski got out and shook the men's hands.

Em thanked them, especially their host. "I hope I may come back this way some day and meet your family."

"You come," he said with a big smile. To Polanski he said, "Keep watch."

"I will, sir."

Polanski followed Monsieur Ostier's directions. At last they looked down on the valley they had left yesterday.

"Where's HQ?" Em asked. "I thought sure this was the place."

Polanski slowed and stopped at the bottom of the hill. Muddy tracks of trucks crisscrossed a pasture beside the road, but they'd seen the same evidence of action in other fields. "Maybe we aren't there yet," he said.

Em peered out the windshield and raised the side flaps for a better view. Suddenly she saw what she was looking for. "Look, over there. That tall broken tree stood on one side of the HQ tent."

"Yeah, you're right, and now I can see some of the phone wires still hanging. This is the place." He sat staring at the churned up mud and snow.

"Okay," she said. "So we know they didn't leave in the direction we just came from. If we keep going, maybe we'll catch up to them."

"Or maybe we'll catch up to the Jerries." Polanski looked scared.

Em was scared too. She probably was savvier about how to get along out here than this kid in khaki was, and she definitely wanted someone smarter than herself for the rest of the journey. Taking charge, she said, "Okay. You drive, and I'll stand watch. Just be ready to stop or hit the accelerator or turn if I shout the word."

"Yeah. I can watch too. It's what we don't see that worries me. If the Germans are holed up, we won't see them. Tanks could be aimed right at us. Besides that, it's coming up to sunset pretty soon. We've got to find shelter before dark. Even our own patrols may shoot and ask questions later."

She glanced at him with more respect. He was no dummy. "We'll make it, Polanski. Let's go."

In Geneva Marge entered Andrew's office, hoping to hear he'd reached Em by phone. From the look on his face she knew right away he hadn't.

"I did get through to Paris. I had one of my men go to the hotel and ask for her. She hasn't come back. She went to the combat zone near the German breakthrough with a correspondent named Bob Mansfield. If she doesn't get back soon, we've got a problem. I don't want you to go alone, and Werner is right about not trusting any of my agents or close acquaintances. Even the pastor cannot expose himself to the possibility of scrutiny by German agents."

"Maybe Werner would know someone."

"Werner is back in Germany. He left in the night. No. We've got to have Em. And even then I hate to let you two go. Maybe it was a mistake to commit to this. In my business I can't afford to make mistakes."

Marge bit her lip. "But he said he had valuable military information. How could it be a mistake? Surely Em will check in soon. Is there a way to get in touch with the group she went out with?"

"I'm working on that. I'll give my man one more day. If we don't contact her by then, it will be too late. It will be up to Frieda to save herself and her children as best she can. And we'll have to hope we can get the military information one way or another."

Marge kept her protest to herself. If Em didn't come, she would go alone. It was not impossible. After all, Em had planned to go alone.

With the side flaps of the jeep rolled up for good visibility, Em studied the surrounding landscape. Private Polanski was a good driver, but he was really churning up the slush as they scurried down the muddy road, following tracks left by trucks.

They passed several fields where tank treads had torn up the turf, leaving black muddy trails over the snow. She studied the tracks, searching for any sign of camouflaged tanks or artillery.

Private Polanski slowed and parked.

She glanced at him. "What's wrong? Do you see something?"

He shook his head. "No. I figure we'd better stop and listen. I don't hanker to drive into a live battlefield."

"Good idea." Her respect for him rose another notch. This kid was thinking. They sat very quietly. A heavy gun boomed and then another. "Sounds pretty far away," she guessed.

"At forty miles an hour we could get close in a hurry. I'll take the next road to the left and hope it leads away from the action."

When he made his turn at the next crossroad, Em realized most of the tracks they'd been following went the other way. "How will we find your headquarters? The main traffic went that way." She pointed.

"Ma'am, I want to get us out of here alive. We'll look for HQ later, after we know we're in Allied territory."

"Right." She turned her attention back to watching for evidence of the enemy. The road dropped down between low hills, following the curves of a small river until suddenly they came out into the midst of a village. A woman was walking through the snow beside the road.

Polanski stopped.

Em called to her. "*Bonjour*, madame. Do you speak English?"

The woman shook her head and said something in French.

Trying again, Em asked, "Have the Germans been here?"

"*Les Boches?*" She said something more in a tone of contempt and shook her head. Using both hands she gestured as if shooing chickens and pointed back to where they had come from.

"What do you suppose she means?" Polanski asked.

"I'm not sure." She pointed up ahead. "Boche that way?"

The woman pointed behind them. "Non, non." She pointed over the hills to their left and repeated, "Boche! Boom, boom!"

Em nodded and again this time pointed up ahead. "Boche boom?"

"Non. Okay. Americans." She made a sweep of her arm, encompassing the way forward.

"Oui. Merci, madame," Em said, using up the extent of her French.

To Polanski she said, "I think it's okay up ahead."

He called, "Merci, madame," and stomped on the accelerator.

In about fifteen minutes they reached a well-traveled highway. Private Polanski paused, and then took a right.

"Do you know where we are now?" Em called over the engine noise.

"Not exactly, but I think this goes south, and that should be the direction to our men."

It turned out he was correct. The highway intersected with another highway where convoys were moving both directions.

Reassured that they truly were in Allied territory, Em said, "Now all we need is to find a convoy aimed south and see if they will take me along."

"Okay. If we don't find one, I guess I could drive you and then contact my division."

"Won't they think you deserted if you leave the area?"

"Yeah. I guess they might."

"I'll get a ride, or I'll just stay with you. Let's keep this official. After you check in with your superior officers, they may give you permission to take me to Paris." Having said this, Em chafed over the delay this would entail. Although she still had five days before her expedition for Werner, she felt uneasy being this far from Geneva in such an uncertain situation. The way it looked, she never should have accepted this assignment after promising to help Werner's family.

"Maybe I should head back toward the battle zone," Polanski said. "I think that's where I'll find my corps and HQ." At a lull in the northward movement of trucks, he made a U-turn, putting his decision into action.

Twilight turned the trees black and the fields gray by the time they found the HQ tent in its new location.

Em had no more than climbed out of the jeep when Bob confronted her. "Where have you been?" He grabbed her shoulders and searched her face with frantic eyes. "You okay?"

"Yes. I'm okay." Her heart sang, *He's still here, and he really cares.*

His fierce grip on her shoulders eased, and he stepped back.

She realized they'd acquired an audience. She glanced at Polanski. "We're both okay. We just had to hide to avoid the Germans. Has their advance been stopped?"

"I think so. We'll head for Paris as soon as you're ready." He gestured toward the HQ tent. "Major Russell was about to send me back without you."

"I'll be ready as soon as I find my bag—if anyone brought it here."

"Sure. I grabbed it when we evacuated. How about some coffee?"

"And food?"

"Well, K rations."

"Okay." She turned to Private Polanski. "Thanks for getting me out of there, Polanski."

He flushed and grinned. "My pleasure, ma'am. Any time I can pull driving duty for you, I will."

"Maybe I'll see you again then."

"You bet. Good-bye, sir," he said to Bob. "I've got to report in."

"Good luck, Polanski," Bob said.

They watched him enter the staff tent, and then Em said, "Do you think the major will be mad at him?"

"I doubt it. You came back safely. Who knows, maybe he will get a promotion."

"Would it help if I tell the major he used his head and did a bang-up job of getting us around the German lines?"

"Maybe, but let me get you that coffee and a K ration first. I really need to be in Paris tonight. And on the drive back I want to hear exactly what happened that kept you out all night right in the path of a German counterattack."

"Just get me coffee, and I'll tell all."

"This way." He walked her to the mess tent.

While Em ate and gulped strong coffee, Bob reported to the major. The major delayed them for a few minutes, questioning Em about what she had observed. Then he gave them an army car and driver.

Settled in the backseat where they could talk easier, Em told Bob all that had happened, from helping in the field hospital to hiding in a cellar.

When she finished, he said, "If you were a cat, I'd say you've probably used up eight of your nine lives." He wasn't smiling. He reached for her hand. "I thought I'd lost you, Lucy-Em." His fingers tightened over hers. His warm grip felt like a homecoming. Something inside of her settled into a comfortable balance.

"I wish I had the power to order you not to go into combat zones," he said.

Her answer came out automatically. "It's my work, Bob." Then she wondered if he did have the power. "You won't tell our boss, will you? I'll be more careful, but I don't want to be censored on this new job before I start."

He let go of her hand. "Do you think I'd do that to you, Em?"

Too late she saw how self-centered her remark had been. "No. Of course I don't. You're not like all the others. That was stupid of me. I apologize."

"Thanks." He leaned back and in the process moved away from her. "I'm going to catch forty winks while I can. It'll be a long day of writing tomorrow."

"Sure." *So much for a cozy chat,* she thought. She had offended him by her fear of being put down because she was a woman. But she had apologized, and he'd been wrong too. She was not a child who needed to be protected.

She leaned back and closed her eyes.

CHAPTER THIRTY

Em awoke when the car stopped in front of Hotel Scribe. Her head had fallen against Bob's chest, and his arm around her shoulders supported her there until she stirred. He released her immediately.

She wanted to stay where she'd fallen, but she straightened and smoothed her hair. "We're here," she said, needing to sound casual. It was still nighttime.

"Yes. Can you make it to your room all right?"

"Of course." She got out, took her typewriter and bag, and headed for the front door of Hotel Scribe.

"I'll send your story when I send mine, if it's ready. Probably around noon."

"Okay."

He caught up with her at the door and pulled it open for her. "See you later, then."

Em went straight to her room and didn't bother to undress before covering up for sleep.

In the morning she overslept, so she bathed quickly and put on a clean uniform. Down in the lobby a few press people greeted her on her way to the front desk, but most of the correspondents were already off working.

The concierge looked up from his ledger. "Mademoiselle Emerson, you have several messages. They sounded urgent. Here. Just a moment. I wrote them down and put them in an envelope for you."

He bent over, reached under his desk, and came up with a manila envelope. "I hope it is not bad news."

She nodded and took the envelope. Hurrying to a chair, she pulled out the notes. By the time she sat down, she knew they were all from Andrew. He said nothing about Marge, so she figured Marge must be okay. Every message urged her to call him immediately.

She went to a sheltered phone in the back of the lobby and called his office collect. The secretary answered and immediately put him on the line.

"Em, where have you been?" he shouted in her ear.

"I was out near the Front. What's up?"

"I can't go into detail on the phone. Look, I don't even want you to trust the train. I'm sending my man in Paris to pick you up at the hotel and drive you straight here. Can you be ready in an hour?"

"Yes. How will I know your man?"

"You've met him already. Father Joseph."

"Oh!"

"Are you speaking from a private location?"

"No."

"Then don't say any more. Be ready at the front door of the hotel. He will get you here as the fast as possible. And Em, pack your warmest clothing." Something in Andrew's voice sounded different. He'd always had a take-charge attitude, but now he was snapping out orders like an army officer. What could have happened to change his demeanor?

"I'll be ready and watching for him in an hour."

"Good. On the drive here, try to get some sleep. Good-bye."

Sleep on the way? Surely his urgency was not because of another of his social gatherings. She hung up and went to pack. This time she packed the woolen underwear that came with her fatigues, wool socks, gloves, muffler, and two sweaters. She glanced at the result, all army khaki color. She hated khaki. From the armoire she grabbed the old fleece flight jacket an air force friend had given her and stuffed it in last. She would carry her steel helmet.

She hoped her large bag wouldn't attract too much attention. It might give the impression she was moving out permanently and raise questions she'd rather avoid. With everything packed to go, she suddenly remembered that Bob expected her story at noon. She wouldn't be able to write it.

She scribbled him a note, hoping she wouldn't see him and be forced to lie to him in person.

Dear Bob,

I've been called away. I can't explain, but I have to go to Geneva immediately. I should be back right after Christmas. If my failure to get this story assignment done today loses me the position with the Tribune, I am sorry. But I have no choice. Please tell them I will turn in my story immediately after Christmas if they still want it.

Thanks so much for your help in getting this assignment. I'm really sorry to fail you like this. Someday I will be able to explain. Until then I hope you can trust me and forgive me.

She hesitated over how to sign it. From her viewpoint, *Love, Em*, would say what she felt. But from his viewpoint, she might not even be a friend after he read the message. She settled on, *Good wishes, Em.* She placed the note in an envelope, labeled it with his name and room number, and left it at the front desk. Then she hurried outside.

Father Joseph drove up to the curb in his old Renault promptly at ten.

She shoved her bags behind the front seat and climbed in.

"Hello, it's good to see you," he said.

"I thought you said you didn't work for Andrew Blackwell," she said, preferring to get right to a point that bothered her.

He glanced behind and then pulled away from the curb. Dodging around pedicabs and pedestrians who crossed at will, he said, "I don't really work for him. As I think I already told you, a priest can't do that. Andrew and I are friends from college days. He went into business; I went into the priesthood. When he moved to Switzerland, we met quite by accident. I found out about his industrial undercover work when he tried to enlist me. I declined but decided to do friendly favors for him, like picking up his friends and driving them where they need to go. In return, he has managed to provide me with an auto.

"Now that the Occupation has ended, he obtained this gasoline engine car for me and has helped me locate fuel for it. In his business, he says he has connections for arranging such things. As a matter of fact, I've been searching for you all over Belgium and northern France for the past two days."

"You have? I got caught in an unexpected German counterattack."

"I finally surmised that. At Hotel Scribe I learned that you had left with Monsieur Mansfield for the Front, and then I heard about the breakthrough."

"So you have known Andrew since school days. Did you attend school in the U.S.?"

"Yes, for two years. Then Andrew attended school here in Paris, and so did I for another year. After that, my training for the priesthood took me to Italy. I was there when Mussolini came into power. A sad day for the Italian people."

"I thought they welcomed him with open arms."

"Some did, and some didn't. There are resistants in Italy, just as here. Because I am in the church, I've returned to Italy a few times. My cousins live in northern Italy. I can assure you they did not welcome Mussolini."

She leaned back and stretched to ease her shoulders. "I'm glad to hear that. Tell me, do you know why Andrew is so urgent about getting me to Geneva? I told him I'd be back before the twenty third, but now he's sent you to get me there tonight."

"He didn't tell me anything except to get you there as quickly as possible. It may be early morning before we reach Geneva. Too many destroyed bridges, and the road conditions are not good. Still, driving is faster than the train."

They would drive to Macon, he explained. From there, they would skirt the southern range of the Jura Mountains and enter Switzerland along the narrow valley carved by the Rhône River. "As the proverbial crow flies, Geneva is only about two hundred and fifty of your American miles. But unfortunately we are not crows, and we have winter weather."

"Right." She watched the windshield wipers slap heavy rain to one side and then the other and hoped it would not turn to snow, as it had in Belgium.

As they drove, she told him about her childhood in Oklahoma and how she had gotten into a writing career. He told her about growing up in France, and the gradual growing of the Resistance during the first year of the Occupation. It was a story she never tired of hearing because each person had lived it differently. "Someday," she said, "I'd like to write a book about the Resistance. If I do, will you help me? I mean check things for me to be sure I'm accurate?"

"I'd be pleased to help."

"I hope Andrew will help too."

"He very well may. He seems to think highly of you."

"I'm glad, but I don't know why he should."

"I suspect in his business he has learned to assess people quickly."

"As he did Vivienne?"

"Yes, as he did Vivienne. Of course he had met her in our home before the war."

"I'm still surprised that she was willing to help him with his somewhat unsavory activities."

"You still do not understand. In France we've all been willing to do anything to recover our freedom. The secrets he passed on to the Allies helped us."

The intensity of his voice shook her from her hasty judgment. "I'm sorry. It's true that I don't understand. You've been through more hardship than I can imagine."

"May your country never know war as we have known it."

He grew quiet, and she decided to try to sleep, as Andrew had advised.

They made good time. It was only eight o'clock when Father Joseph parked beside Château Bleu. Visibility had improved after sunset when the clouds disbanded and let the half-moon shine intermittently. Em got out of the car, stretched, and tipped her face to the winter sky. Stars hung low between the clouds.

The front door burst open, and Marge came dashing down the steps to hug her. "Em, I'm so glad you're here. I was so afraid—" Seeing Father Joseph climb out of the car stopped her midsentence.

Em let go of her. "Marge, this is Father Joseph, a friend of Andrew's, and if you remember my mention of Vivienne, he's her brother. Father Joseph, I'd like you to meet my sister, Marge."

While they greeted each other, Andrew appeared. "Come in. Come in. We have a roaring fire to warm you and anything you want to eat. Father Joe, thank you. Hello, Em. I'll answer all your questions later. First, come and please Lydia by eating the food she had our cook prepare just for you."

While the men brought in the luggage, Em went with Marge to greet Lydia. Clearly, their hostess still didn't know exactly what her husband was into or why Em had been rushed here, arriving so late at night. Maybe it was just as well. She didn't like hiding things from this hospitable woman.

For Marge, her sister's arrival relieved a mountain of anxiety. She sat at the long table in the dining room across from Em and Father Joseph, sipping hot cocoa while they ate. The priest glanced at her often, including her in his conversation. She liked him and instinctively felt she could trust him. Was he involved in Andrew's clandestine activities too? She decided no. How could a priest live a lie?

He had an ingenuous manner, but an expression in his eyes reminded her of the look she'd seen on the soldiers' faces when they'd survived deadly wounds—a look that reflected a deep, unquestioning appreciation for life.

When Mrs. Blackwell came and sat with them, Em began to talk about Christmas. "How do you celebrate Christmas here in Switzerland?"

"In the American way. Usually we invite friends in, because we have no family in Switzerland. That's why it's such a treat to have you and Marge with us. Although we aren't Catholic, when Father Joseph comes, we attend midnight mass with him. Tell us about Christmas in Oklahoma."

"We did things in a simple way, but it was always special. Marge, remember the Christmases when we made all our gifts?"

"Yes. We worked in secret. I felt as if it were Christmas for weeks while we prepared surprises for one another. And I loved the day I could finally wrap presents. Mom always saved gift wrap, so part of the fun was ironing the paper and ribbons to make them like new."

"Did you have a religious service too?" Father Joseph asked.

"Oh yes," Em said. "At Sunday school the teachers and children prepared a program for the congregation. We always staged a manger scene with Mary and Joseph and the Babe. I got to be Joseph for several years because I was taller than any of the boys, but my ambition was to be Mary."

He laughed. "Did you realize that ambition?"

"No. Marge became Mary, and they made me one of the three kings."

Everyone laughed.

When they quieted, Marge said, "The truth is that Em was a better actress. She could carry off any part they gave her, and as Mary, all I had to do was sit with a sheet draped over my head and make sure Mrs. Robertson's new baby didn't cry during the speaking parts."

Father Joseph chuckled. "It sounds as if your true talents had begun to show early—you caring for the baby."

In mock offense Em said, "And me trying to be someone I'm not?"

Marge caught a sudden caution in Father Joseph's eyes. *So he is in on Andrew's scheming too.* She came to his rescue. "Em, it's only that you've always been the one who loved a challenge. I don't remember hearing you complain about being a wise man. And I do remember how you practiced walking like a king. You wanted to be the most convincing wise man ever seen in Tuttle, Oklahoma."

Andrew strolled in just then in time to hear Em's rebuttal. "I have to admit I did like the part. I never could act, but it was fun to try."

Marge glanced at him, wondering how he would arrange to get Lydia distracted while he talked with her and Em about the final plan for going after Werner Koch's family.

"Ladies," he said, as if on cue, "I perceive that you are discussing Christmas, and this reminds me that I have a surprise for Lydia, but I need you two young ladies to help me. Would you meet me in the library for a few minutes before you retire?"

"Then I shall keep Father Joseph company while you three plan my surprise," Lydia said, smiling.

"Well, I have finished," Em said and turned to Marge. "Shall we adjourn to said library?"

Marge nodded and stood up.

"This way, Santa's helpers," Andrew said, making an exaggerated flourish toward the door with his hand.

They preceded him out and into the study. He closed the door and moved to the far side of the room. "Please be seated. I do have a gift for Lydia to show you. Then if you don't mind, would one of you wrap it for me? Here." He took two small boxes from his suit coat pocket and opened them. "I have this broach and also a pendant. I'll give her both, but only one for Christmas. Which do you think she'd like first?"

"The pendant would be lovely with several of the gowns I've seen her wear," Em said.

He nodded. "Do you concur, Marge?"

"Yes, although both are gorgeous."

"All right. Please wrap it while I talk." He held out a packet of gift-wrap paper and ribbon.

Marge took it and set to work.

"I need to tell you, Em, that I know about your work for the OSS," Andrew said.

Em's mouth fell open, and her glance darted to Marge. "How did you find that out?"

"I also am in the OSS. Cummins wired me right after signing you on."

Em stared at Andrew, apparently speechless.

"And I found out quite by accident," Marge said.

"First Marge overheard Werner talking to me. I had to tell them that both you and I are in the OSS. Werner's wife must escape from Germany earlier than he'd planned."

"Wait a minute. Slow down. Werner told you his escape plan?"

Marge put the jeweler's box in a larger box and began to fold gold paper around it. "Yes," she said calmly, "and I'm going with you. If you had been late, I'd have gone without you."

Em swung around to Marge. "You've been ill! You can't possibly go trekking on snowshoes."

Marge knew this would be Em's reaction, so she was prepared. "I feel fine. I've felt better every day, and I've been tromping around the gardens here on snowshoes to test my legs."

"This could be dangerous, Marge. You mustn't."

"Do you think I want you to go? But together we can help those poor children and their mother. I feel it in my bones. . . . And this rescue is exactly what David would have done."

Em shook her head. "No! I can manage without you, just as Werner planned."

Marge took a deep breath. "Werner's wife has been ill. She will need me, perhaps as much as little Anna. She's had the flu, and from what Werner told Dr. Schneider, she may be suffering from a secondary infection in her lungs. The doctor gave me medicine for her as well as for Anna. I must go with you."

Em gave a frustrated sigh and clamped her teeth over her lower lip, a sure sign of capitulation. She turned to Andrew. "We need time to get Marge in shape. When are we to go?"

"Werner discovered a plot that makes it necessary for Frieda to leave Germany tomorrow night."

Em's eyes widened. "Tomorrow night!"

Marge watched Em's expression change from confidence to uncertainty at Andrew's words.

Em had always been a loner on her adventures when they were growing up. She could very well feel that Marge was a liability. "I'll be okay, Em. My legs are strong. Together we can do this."

"You don't even have adequate clothing. I brought my winter civilian clothes as well as winter government issue of woolens."

"You both need outfitting. Tomorrow I'll make an excuse for you to go shopping for me," Andrew said. "You will purchase the best winter garb that Switzerland can produce—a well-constructed ski suit and parka. Being in civilian clothing will create no problem as long as you are in Switzerland. The maps Werner gave me show landmarks that you must not cross. The location of the border in that area seems clear."

For Marge, the danger from wearing civilian clothes loomed large. She was regular army, while Em was simply accredited to the WAAC. Until now, without specific details, she'd been mostly concerned about how to care for Anna and Frieda in the cold, primitive conditions. She thought fast. She was still determined to go.

"Because of the risk, Father Joseph will go with you. He's an experienced mountaineer, and I've discovered he's acquainted with the area around Hamel. Best of all, few people would connect him with me or with the OSS, so he fits Werner's requirements."

Having Father Joseph's help made Marge feel much better about the mission.

Andrew stood up. "Let's go out now, or Lydia will begin to wonder why we are taking so long. Tomorrow we will finalize the details, and you'll board the train before noon."

As they left the study, Em whispered, "Even though I hate to have you take the risk, I'm relieved to have your help."

Marge gave her a hug.

They went out into the great hall acting like holiday conspirators. Their efforts were wasted, for the downstairs was quiet. Everyone had gone to bed.

The next day, as Andrew had stated, they boarded the train before noon. Marge wished she were seeing Switzerland under happier conditions. Outside the train window, the mountains and valleys created a Christmas wonderland. As the peaks reared higher and closer around her, however, she began to feel claustrophobic. Having grown up on the Oklahoma prairie, she was unprepared for the overpowering presence of such mighty peaks and deep valleys. The scene that had appeared idyllic from a distance felt menacing up close. She turned away from the window.

Marge and Em shared a seat, while Father Joseph was two seats away on the opposite side of the aisle. They all wore Swiss ski clothes and had stored their skis and poles and arctic parkas in a space at one end of the railroad car. Marge had never skied in her life, but liked the warm sweater, pants, jacket, and boots they'd picked out at a specialty store in Geneva. Father Joseph had advised and approved their choices, and the purchases had been placed on Andrew's account. From the looks of the other passengers, it was not unusual to travel on the train dressed for skiing.

When they reached Hamel, the small town near the border, they would trade their skis for snowshoes. Andrew had it all arranged. If planning made for success, this mission would go well, for in his briefing this morning, he seemed to have thought of everything. By tomorrow they should be back at the chateau, and Werner Koch's family would be safely hidden in Geneva.

Chapter Thirty-One

On the journey across Switzerland, Em's thoughts circled around the way Andrew had concealed his OSS affiliation from her. Now that she knew, a lot of things made more sense. She could see how her courier trips for Cummins had coincided well with alternate assignments for Andrew. However, she never would have guessed that Andrew was with the OSS. She'd only done her work, not realizing that some agents were not allowed to know one another's affiliations. In the process of helping Werner's family, they would have to be extremely careful to protect Andrew's cover.

When the train steamed into Hamel, it stopped only briefly. As they walked away from the station, Em heard it huff on toward the nearby border where it would take on passengers from the German Alps and return to go back to Geneva. She and Marge followed Father Joseph through a maze of small streets and finally into a dark little shop where he exchanged their skis for snowshoes. He made some jovial remarks in German, the language of this border town. Em couldn't understand, but it seemed obvious that she and Marge were the butt of some of them. She smiled, hoping she was projecting the impression of a self-conscious young woman who was embarrassed by such attention.

When they left, outfitted for a trek across snow, Joseph explained the conversation. "I told them Em is my sister and Marge my city-bred girlfriend and that you both intend to beat me in cross-country snowshoeing. That's why he was laughing. Beginners always think there's no skill to snowshoeing."

"Girlfriend? He wasn't very discerning," Em teased, though his priestly collar did not show.

Marge chuckled. "Father Joseph plays a part well."

Em became serious. "We definitely need your mountaineering expertise. How long do you think it will take to get to the rendezvous location on snowshoes? According to the map it is only about two kilometers, but it's certainly not level."

"It's been a long time since I was here," he said, "but the map gives good details of the streams and gullies and where the trail would lie if it were not under deep snow. My guess is we'd better start right away while we have good light. We'll hide and build a snow shelter. Then we wait . . . and pray."

They stopped at another strange little garagelike shop where Andrew had told them they were to pick up backpacks of emergency supplies and snowshoes for Werner's family. The shop owner was expecting them, and the packs were ready to go with snowshoes lashed to each one. Father Joseph took the largest load.

The man who outfitted them let them out the back door, and in five minutes they reached the edge of the village. Following a snow-packed trail created by cross-country skiers, they soon came alongside a broad frozen stream. They lashed on their snowshoes, and leaving the marked trail behind, they crossed over a snow-covered rustic bridge. Dodging under drooping evergreen boughs, they began their trek over virgin snow.

Em kept her copy of the map in a pocket she could reach easily and referred to it often. So did Father Joseph. She wondered how Werner had done so well with the details. But he did say he'd spent many boyhood days in these mountains before the war. No doubt he'd frequently crossed back and forth over the border, especially since Hamel was the nearest town.

Marge stopped ahead of her. "I've got to get out of my coat."

Father Joseph, in the lead, waited. He'd already taken off his outer coat. He spoke very quietly. "Voices carry for long distances in these mountains. We should whisper now."

"Good idea," Em agreed.

"Well, I need to save my breath for walking," Marge said. "How much farther do you think it is?"

"Probably not as far as it will feel," he said. "Are you all right?"

"Yes. I feel the altitude, but I'm okay," Marge replied.

"Me too," Em said. "I forgot about the altitude. Just thought I was out of shape."

Marge tied her jacket to her backpack, and they trudged on in silence. When Em paused to study the hand-drawn map, Marge found a place to lean for resting. They couldn't sit easily while wearing their webbed feet, and the snow was so fresh they'd sink deep without the snowshoes. Em was tired and Marge looked beat. Father Joseph waited silently, not the least bit winded.

At last they came to the outcropping of rock that Werner had marked and named Gargoyle. A barren cliff reared up from the right side of the trail, and sure enough, the odd formation at the top looked like an impressionistic smiling gargoyle. Em pointed to it.

Father Joseph whispered, "The border should be about two-hundred paces down there, inside the trees, and the rendezvous point is at the junction of those two stream beds right over there." He pointed to gaps in the snow-sculpted forest below. "From up here, with this snow field between us and the trees, we have a good view of the area. Let's build a snow cave against the side of the cliff and stow our gear. Then I'll go down to study the lay of the land."

"I think we all should see it in the daylight," Em said.

"Too chancy. We'd leave too much of a trail. I can pick a route along the stream that won't be noticeable."

"He's right, Em," Marge whispered. "Let's stay here and be quiet."

Marge sounded very tired. No way would Em go down and leave her here alone. "Okay."

He pointed to a partially formed cave where snow already had shaped one wall. He set to work scooping and building. Em and Marge copied his actions. In a few minutes they had snug protection against wind and weather. He spread a lightweight ground sheet down beside their backpacks.

Marge sat down, removed her snowshoes, and stretched. "Ah, this feels good."

Em sat on her pack, keeping on her snowshoes until Father Joseph returned from his scouting trip.

They waited for endless minutes. Then, as quiet as a snowflake, he was back and dropped down beside them.

"I looked around as much as I dared," he whispered, removing his snowshoes. "There's an area below the rendezvous point that looks like a trail made by border guards. However, the tracks are not recent. The wind has smoothed them and filled them with snow."

Em thought about what Hubert had said about the patrols on the border of occupied France. They could come unexpectedly, but usually they were regular, like clockwork. Germans lived by their schedules. "If the tracks are not new, a patrol may be due any time," she whispered.

He nodded. "One good thing—I saw no evidence of dogs."

Dogs! Em hadn't thought about dogs.

"Let's pray the guards don't come at the rendezvous time, and let's pray for no dogs," Marge whispered.

"That I have done," he whispered back. "That's why I took so long. I sat there and prayed for a while."

Em was grateful that he'd taken special time to pray. She had no doubt about how close Father Joseph was to the Lord. Looking down the mountainside to where she would face the scariest moment of her life, she offered her own silent prayer. *Lord God, you know me, and how I always want things my own way. Please forgive my foolishness, and please protect us through this night. Help us to get Werner's family to safety. Please. We need you . . . I need you. . . .*

"I'm hungry," Marge whispered. "We should eat something to keep up our energy."

Em grinned. "Yes, Nurse."

"She's right. It will soon be dark. We need to eat and rest and stay warm. I'll keep watch first so you two can rest." He glanced at the radium dial on his wristwatch. "At seven o'clock, I'll wake one of you. You each take a couple of hours and then wake me at eleven. We'll get ready to go and be in place early."

After eating, Em tried to sleep and found it impossible. How could anyone sleep in the snow while lying a few hundred feet from the border of Nazi Germany? She couldn't stop rehearsing every detail of their plan. She, who had never made detailed plans if she could avoid it, found herself trying to think through what they could do if various things went wrong.

She even tried to plot what to do if anything happened to Father Joseph. She'd planned to do this alone, but now she was totally shaken by her naïveté. She'd hate to be without him. He had been an excellent mountaineering companion, affirming her decisions and making wise suggestions.

Em did doze off after a while. When Father Joseph woke her for her turn, she learned that Marge had already taken her two hours on watch and had dropped back to sleep. Em had the third watch.

Father Joseph handed her his wristwatch and whispered, "Marge heard voices. They've been gone for some time now so maybe the way will be clear by midnight. Listen carefully." He handed her his watch and then leaned back to rest.

All was quiet. The snow reflected starlight from breaks in the clouds. When the half-moon came up it would be quite light. That could be good or bad, depending on whether or not German guards discovered them. She listened for voices. The mountainside remained silent. Finally the phosphorescent dial of Father Joseph's watch showed eleven o'clock. She touched Marge and then Father Joseph. "It's time," she whispered. "I haven't heard any voices."

They stood up. Out of the packs they pulled white jumpsuits, booties, caps, and mitts. Their parkas were already white. Then they placed similar white garb for Frieda and the children into two backpacks. In the third they carried water, chocolate bars, and medicines. Marge took that one. They shared carrying the snowshoes.

"If they get across without detection," Father Joseph said, "we can come back here and pick up the rest of the gear."

If not, thought Em, *we'll have to hike out of here with only one flashlight, no ground cover, no extra blanket, and only one ice pick.* Em didn't want to carry extra weight, but she figured the tools and ground sheets were important. They could be lifesavers if needed.

She decided to carry a ground sheet, no matter what. She grabbed it, rolled it tightly, and tied it to her web belt. Then she fastened on her snowshoes and pulled the white cover-ups over her woolen mittens.

Marge finished at that moment too. Father Joseph stepped out ahead and motioned for them to follow single file.

Picking their way down the slope, they stayed in the cleft of a frozen stream bed. Every few steps they paused to listen. Finally Father Joseph crouched behind a snow-mounded rock formation. "We're right near the confluence of the stream beds. In ten minutes they should be here. I'm going a little farther down to assist them. You two stay here."

"I'm coming too," Em whispered back. "With the children you'll need help."

"Me too," Marge said. "No telling how much assistance Frau Koch may need. Cough syrup for instance."

Em couldn't tell for sure in the lack of light, but she sensed that Father Joseph was glaring at them. For a few seconds he stood frozen to his walking sticks, then gave in and led the way down the slope to a stand of trees.

He pointed silently. Just beyond the trees they saw the patrollers' trail he had mentioned.

Em held her breath, listening until she almost could hear her own heartbeat. The family would have to come across that open space—a distance of about seventy-five feet with the trail in the middle. The

Germans or the Swiss must have cleared a swath all along the border for better visibility.

She prayed that the children would keep quiet and that the regular patrol would not come for a long time. Once the Koch family was over the border, they should be safe. The Germans could not legally follow. She didn't dwell on the possibility that out here in the mountains breaking a neutral nation's laws may not count for anything.

They waited and waited. Finally Father Joseph moved. She saw the radium dial of his wristwatch glow for an instant before he covered it. "It's time," he whispered.

They stood up and moved to the edge of the clearing. Em thought she heard the whisper of skis on snow. Then it stopped.

Was it the family? The border guards returning? Why had they not planned a secret signal? Her heart hammered, telling her to flee. She made herself stand still. She was in plain sight if a patrol were to come.

Then she saw the family, nearly invisible, at the other side of the clearing—an adult and two smaller forms. Thank God they'd already thought to dress in white. The little group hesitated. Then they hurried forward. They were all wearing snowshoes. Marge rushed to meet them and took the arm of the woman. Father Joseph picked up Anna and carried her. He whispered in German to the mother.

Em took Maria's hand, and they all hurried to the cover of the trees.

Then Father Joseph whispered, "We've got to get up the mountain as quickly as we can. Frau Koch says we may not be safe until we reach the trail we came on. The border here is tenuous, so we have to move fast until we get over that last ridge we crossed. Come on." With Anna still in his arms he led the way through the trees to the stream bed above.

"Maria, come," Em whispered. She felt the girl trembling through her mittens. She hurried her along behind her mother and Marge.

At the snow shelter they gave the girls chocolate bars and a drink of water. With Father Joseph explaining in German, Marge offered Frau Koch a spoonful of cough syrup. She took it eagerly and whispered, "*Danke*."

Just as they were gathering up the tools they'd left, Em heard voices, distant but clear, speaking German, of course. Em turned to Father Joseph. He stood statue still. Everyone listened.

Frau Koch hissed a command at the children. They grabbed hold of her but didn't make a sound. Father Joseph worked frantically to unlash the snowshoes they'd carried for the family so their packs would be lighter. He tossed them into a drift and whispered, "Come. Hurry. Sounds like that patrol has intercepted someone." Frau Koch's brother had come to the hut against Werner's orders to help her get ready to leave. "Hurry!" Father Joseph placed Frau Koch directly behind him. Em took up the rear, behind Marge and the children.

The children walked well on their snowshoes, hurrying to keep up with their mother. After a short distance, however, Anna stumbled. Marge picked her up. She was small for her age but still too much for Marge to carry any great distance.

Father Joseph grabbed her up in his arms again. Marge removed Anna's snowshoes and handed them to Em to add to her backpack.

Soon Frau Koch began to stagger. Marge plowed ahead and took her arm. Em moved closer to Maria. Walking side by side wearing snowshoes was not the easiest way to go. Maria marched sturdily ahead on her own.

Marge fell back by Em. "Frau Koch seems to want to walk alone," she whispered. In the distance they could still hear men's voices. Someone yelled, "Halt!" A shot split the cold air.

Frau Koch stopped and raised her hands to her face. Then she slogged along faster. At last they topped the ridge and began to descend. Down in the trees again near a stream bed, Father Joseph stopped and whispered with Frau Koch.

Then he came to Em and Marge. "We are well inside the border of Switzerland now. She still fears they will follow. She has no idea who they may have shot, but she thinks they may be Gestapo searching for the hut. If they find it empty, they will come into Switzerland to look for her."

"You mean they would follow us now?" Em gasped.

"Now or later."

Marge went to Frau Koch and put an arm around her shoulders.

Em took Maria's hand. "Let's get them out of here. And we'll have to hide them until they can board the train."

Father Joseph adjusted his hold on Anna and said, "We'll go to the church. I'll put on my robe again, and then we'll think about how to get all of you safely to Geneva."

CHAPTER THIRTY-TWO

Marge preferred bringing up the rear so she could keep an eye on Frau Koch and the children and also on Em. Two kilometers over snow and in rugged terrain was more than Anna and Frau Koch should attempt.

Em and Father Joseph, who was still carrying Anna, led the way now, followed by Maria and her mother. Frau Koch, after pausing to rest, kept on at a good pace. Marge kept an eye on her and let her set the gait. A few times she coughed, but the codeine in the cough syrup kept her from long wracking bouts. Maria was the only one of the Koch family who seemed to be in reasonably good shape for the journey. They walked on and on, following the dim trail through the snow.

At long last they came to the rustic bridge over the river where they had left the main road from the village. Sooner than Marge remembered, they reached the edge of Hamel. Father Joseph led them through the sleeping town to a small stone church. At a cottage behind it, he rapped on the door. After a short time, someone came. Father Joseph spoke a few low words and then beckoned for them all to follow him inside. When the door was closed behind them, he set Anna down on her feet.

The priest of Hamel's Catholic Church greeted them warmly, but as usual Marge couldn't understand a word. Suddenly Anna slumped to the floor.

Frau Koch dropped beside her and lifted her head to her lap. Marge knelt, stripped off her mittens. Anna's hands were so cold she had difficulty finding her faint pulse. It was weak and rapid. She looked up at Father Joseph. "We've got to warm her. Can we have a heated blanket and something hot for her to drink?" She started to reassure Frau Koch and stopped. "Please tell Frau Koch that Anna will be all right. She's just tired and cold."

Father Joseph obeyed and continued to translate while the other priest led them to his sparsely furnished bedroom. With Anna on a bed, Marge removed her coat, boots, and snow pants. "We need that heated blanket," she reminded Father Joseph.

He spoke to the priest, who then hurried out.

Marge pulled off the child's socks and wrapped her feet in her own wool muffler, warmed from being against her neck. Then she covered her with the quilt.

Soon the priest returned with the blanket he had warmed against the stove. Marge lifted the quilt and tucked the heated wool all around Anna.

Her patient stirred and opened dazed eyes. "*Mutter*." She reached up for her mother's hand.

Frau Koch comforted her while Marge poured a spoonful of tonic. She handed the spoon to the mother and pointed at Anna.

Anna swallowed the tonic and closed her eyes. After a few minutes Marge felt Anna's hands again and checked her pulse. She nodded to the mother. "She's okay." Turning to Father Joseph, she said, "Tell her what okay means."

Frau Koch listened then turned to Marge and said, "*Gut*. Anna okay *gut*."

Marge smiled and nodded. "*Ja*. Okay *gut*."

Then Frau Koch glanced at Father Joseph and asked him something.

Father Joseph nodded and left. When he returned, he said, "Frau Koch reminded me to tell Father Desmonde that she and the children need sanctuary, and that no one must know they are here. He's going to wake the station agent, a trustworthy friend of his, and purchase tickets for us. He thinks we can board and be away from here at first light. He will bring a priest's robe for me and nuns' habits for all three of you women. You will be nursing sisters for the remainder of the trip."

"Is this all right with your church?" Marge asked.

"Sometimes the church allows mercies," he said with a smile.

"Have you told Em?"

"It was Em's idea."

"I might have guessed. What about the children?"

"They will be your charges, orphaned by an avalanche. They'll be fine in their snowsuits. The question is whether Anna and her mother will be strong enough. Frau Koch says they will."

"Ask Frau Koch if she has any medicine for Anna with her. I need to know what it is and when she last gave her any. I also need to know how she herself feels. If either of them gets fever or chills, Dr. Schneider gave me medicine for them. I shall have to watch them both carefully."

He talked with Frau Koch, who opened her backpack and handed Marge two bottles. "She says Anna took these according to directions at eleven o'clock. That was"—he looked at his watch—"nearly three hours ago."

Marge held the bottles near the lamp. She recognized the chemical names but couldn't read the instructions. It didn't matter too much. The tonic would not conflict. "Tell her the tonic I gave Anna will strengthen her during the next four hours, but if she feels faint again, I have a pill to give her."

She hoped she would not need the sulfa for either of them, but especially for Anna. An infection could take her quickly if they couldn't keep her warm and quiet. She turned to Father Joseph. "I wonder if your friend could find a wheelchair for Anna."

"I'll see what I can do." He excused himself and left. Marge sat down beside the bed. A bit of color had returned to Anna's lips. Marge decided to try to communicate with Frau Koch. A few basic words in common would help. "Do you speak any English?" she asked.

Frau Koch said. "Little. Few words."

"Good! May I call you Frieda? Easier that way."

"Ja. Easier." She pointed to Marge. "You . . . Marge?"

"Ja!" With appropriate gestures she said, "You tell me German. I tell you English."

Marge worked on words she needed for patient care, like pain, hot, cold, drink, and medicine.

After a while Em brought in extra quilts. "If you can sleep, you'd better. I have Maria curled up by the heating stove." Frieda took a quilt. Marge gestured for her to lie on the bed beside Anna. Marge wrapped up and tried to doze in the chair.

Next thing she knew, Father Joseph knocked on the door. It was light outside, and he was wearing a priest's robe. He laid a bundle on the bed. "Your habits. Em says to put yours on over your ski suit, as she is doing. And the same for Frau Koch—over her regular clothing. I found a wheelchair, but it's not child size."

Marge stood up and stretched to ease her stiffening muscles. "Adult size may be better. We can wrap Anna in more blankets."

Em came in with Maria. "What do you think, Marge? Isn't it better to keep the girls in all of their outdoor clothing?"

"Yes. Trains tend to be chilly."

"The main thing is, if we have to get off, they'll keep warm."

"Will we need to change trains? We didn't on the way here."

"You never know," Em said. "Does Frau Koch understand any English?"

"A few words and phrases. We've been working on that. And she wants us to call her Frieda."

"Good."

"Some English I understand," Frieda said, "but not speak." She groped for more words and then spoke in German to Father Joseph.

He translated. "She says she will be happy to help you with German if the need arises. German is the local language until we travel further south. I told her I'm coming with you, to speak either German or French, so she may not need to translate. Besides, although German is dominant in this part of Switzerland, the railway people all speak French. I've asked her to tell the children not to talk to strangers and to whisper when speaking to her. No point in drawing attention to their accents. When you ladies are dressed, come out to the parlor where I have the wheelchair."

On the walk to the station they attracted a little attention. People glanced sympathetically at the children. Some greeted Father Joseph, but most ignored the three women, hidden by the nursing habits.

They boarded the train with the help of a porter and set the wheelchair at the end of a car where there was space for luggage. Marge helped Anna to a seat near the chair.

At last the train began to move, and Marge leaned back on the seat beside Frieda and Anna. Suddenly Frieda grabbed her hand and whispered, "Gestapo!"

Marge glanced out the window in time to see gray uniforms and the black boots of three men. They were peering into the train windows. For an instant, Marge felt the hard eyes of one on her. She bowed her head, glad for the white nun's wimple that helped to conceal her face. The train moved faster. When she glanced up again, they'd left the station and the Gestapo behind.

She squeezed Frieda's hand and whispered, "Switzerland. Safe."

Frieda shook her head. Her face had grown taut with terror. "*Nein* . . . never safe," she whispered.

Marge patted her arm, wishing she spoke more German or that Frieda spoke more English. Yet she knew that even if she spoke German she couldn't remove her patient's panic. Frieda knew better than Marge what the Gestapo could do. Even so she whispered, "We must not frighten the children."

Frieda nodded as if she understood and glanced at Anna, snuggled on the seat beside her. She bent toward her and whispered something. The child smiled. Marge's respect for the mother grew.

The train steamed through a mountain pass. Marge leaned back to gaze at the serene view of the mountains. *What a contrast to what we are feeling right now*. She tried to rest while she could.

Before long the train slowed and pulled into Schaffhausen, its first stop. The railcar slowly passed a platform full of people waiting to board. Again Frieda grabbed Marge's hand. "I see . . . get Father!" She bent her head down and turned away from the window.

Marge beckoned to Father Joseph a few seats away. He came and knelt beside Frieda. She whispered rapidly. People were standing to leave. New passengers would be boarding soon. Still Father Joseph blocked the aisle. He whispered to Marge and Em. "She saw a man who knows her, the one her husband suspected of reporting him to the Gestapo. Fortunately the man has never seen the children. He was with the people who are about to board the cars behind us. She says Gestapo men were with him. She is now certain they are searching for her. She insists they will find a way to kill her and the children even though they are in Switzerland. I believe her. We've got to get her off this train before they see her."

"But the wheelchair," Marge gasped. "How can we sneak off with a wheelchair?"

"I'll get the porter to help. Can you conceal Frieda's face with something convincing?"

Marge quickly pulled a white handkerchief from her bag and sprinkled some drops of menthol on it. "Tell Frieda to cover her nose and mouth with this. It will look as if she has a cold or consumption. I brought it if she needed it to soothe her cough." She handed the hankie to Frieda.

Frieda needed few instructions. She immediately covered her lower face.

Father Joseph lifted Anna into the wheelchair and a porter helped him get the chair down to the station platform. Marge came close behind. Em held Maria's hands. Frieda, with her face averted, stayed a short distance behind.

As Marge pushed Anna's wheelchair, she saw the same Gestapo men she'd seen at the Hamel station. This time they were boarding with a man in a brown business suit. Marge kept her chin down, watching them out of the corner of her eye. When she got inside the building, she told Father Joseph.

"Good," he said. "If they are going and we are staying, we shall not meet. We'll catch the next train."

He went to the ticket counter to facilitate his plan. Returning, he said, "I told them our little patient had to leave the train for fresh air. They said we could take her on the next train if she has recovered sufficiently. It will be along soon, so we may as well wait here."

Suddenly Em exclaimed, "Look!"

They turned toward the door they'd entered earlier. The Gestapo and the businessman stood there talking and scanning the thinning crowd in the station.

Em said to Father Joseph, "We'll take Frieda and the children to the women's room and meet you out at the street when the way is clear."

She grabbed the handles of the wooden chair and pushed it quickly toward the rest room sign. The women and children followed.

Marge knew that when Em spoke and moved so quickly, she had a plan. She prayed it was a good one.

As other women pushed past them in the rest room, Em whispered, "Get Frieda to take off the nun's habit and we'll wrap my scarf around her face to hide her features. You and I will go as skiers again. If we have to, we'll take turns carrying Anna, but she must walk onto the next train. We will find a better way to transport her if we need to. Tell Frieda we've got to make this change while no one can see."

"I'll try to tell her."

Frieda needed only a few whispered instructions before she nodded as if she understood.

They waited until other women had left. Then they went into the stalls and removed the nun's habits. When Marge came out, Em was already waiting in her ski suit. Her backpack was in her hand.

"Where did you put the habit?" Marge whispered.

"Had to leave it beside the toilet. Come on."

Frieda came out empty-handed too. Em gave her the wide scarf she'd worn for extra warmth and helped her to drape it over her head and arranged it to conceal her hair and lower face.

Each of them took a girl's hand. Em peeked into the waiting room. Seeing no sign of the Gestapo, they hurried out the door leading into the town. Father Joseph was leaning against the building reading a newspaper. Their ploy worked. At first glance he didn't recognize them.

When he did, he led them into a small restaurant near the station.

After they were seated, he said, "I must say, you may fool the pursuers if they suspected you while you were wearing your nun's habits. And the scarf does conceal Frau Koch's face and hair."

Frau Koch responded in rapid German.

He pursed his lips and raised his eyebrows. "She thinks they will still spot her. I'm afraid she may be right. What you've done helps temporarily, but they may see through it sooner or later."

Marge sat thinking. Geneva and Dr. Schneider seemed very far away. Although her patients seemed steady and stable, the sooner they both were under his care, the better.

Em leaned forward. "I know a way we can get them into France instead of going directly to Geneva. For the Gestapo, France is now enemy territory. They couldn't follow us there. We could go into Geneva from France. The Gestapo wouldn't be expecting this."

"How can we spirit them into France any more easily than going on to Geneva?" Father Joseph asked.

"They would never expect us to walk over mountains again, not with Anna. I know a place, and Hubert could help us. I walked it with him already. The little town of Bonnedeux is remote and close to the border. Father Joseph, you could go on to Geneva, telephone Hubert, and tell him to meet us at Bonnedeux. He knows the town well. We'll be at the inn where he has stayed. He can guide us across the border to a farm of his friends, the Charbonneaus. He has walked the way many times during winter. I could almost do it by myself. It's only about two miles. Their farm is right on the border."

Marge couldn't imagine how Em could think this was feasible. "Anna can't do that. She has reached her limit already. It would be a risk for Frieda too."

"We can get a sled," Em said, not deterred at all by Marge's objection. "A sled big enough for Frieda to ride with Anna. Don't you see? Frieda would disappear as far as the Gestapo are concerned. We won't tell anyone her real name. Although the trail goes up and down in places, the inclines are moderate. It will work. I know it will."

The very idea appalled Marge.

Father Joseph sat thinking.

"Won't a sled help enough, Marge?" Em asked.

"How can I know? It sounds terrible. On the other hand we don't know what Frieda will face if we stay on the train." Marge turned to Father Joseph. "What do you think?"

"I think," he said slowly, "that Frieda should decide." He spoke to her at length in German.

She answered in monosyllables and emphatically.

He translated for Marge and Em. "She wants to go directly to Geneva. Werner told her she must let nothing deter her from reaching Dr. Schneider and the hiding place with the pastor that he arranged. She doesn't want to take the children through any more mountains on foot or sled."

Marge nodded. Patients often understood on a deep level what their bodies could and could not endure. "We must abide by her wishes."

"All right," Em said, "then I think it's important that we not board as a group. What if I board a different car—one right next to yours so we can communicate if we need to? I could take the children. Surrounded by all the other passengers we'll be less noticeable."

"No!" Marge exclaimed. "You speak only English and the children only German. How will you get along?"

"She's right," Father Joseph said. "We can get on separately and sit separately, but in the same car."

Outvoted, Em reluctantly agreed.

When they finally boarded the train, Marge sat where she could see Em with the children and was glad Father Joseph had prevailed. A fellow passenger, a woman, was trying to converse with Em. What story would Em come up with to explain that her two little girls spoke German, which she couldn't understand and she spoke only English, which they couldn't understand?

The woman looked like an innocent Swiss woman, but how could a person tell? After seeing the Gestapo actually search a Swiss train, Marge trusted no one.

When the lady greeted Em in Swiss German, Em said that she spoke only English and that she was with the American Red Cross. The woman also spoke English, so Em said, "I'm taking these girls to live with relatives. Poor babies. Their parents were killed when an avalanche destroyed the family home. It took us a while to locate their relatives, but it was worth the effort. So much better than keeping them in an orphanage."

The woman smiled benignly. "So much better. I've always appreciated the work of your agency. How encouraging to see a young woman like yourself, far from home, helping unfortunate people."

Em nodded. "Thank you." She did not want to converse. She leaned back and looked out the window of the train, hoping the woman would take the hint. In a way she did. She pulled a notepad from her purse and produced a pencil stub for each girl. The children began to draw.

Em closed her eyes. Keeping her ears open, she stole a peek from under her lashes from time to time.

Finally Maria touched her hand and whispered, "Anna, go." She gestured toward the end of the car.

Em had taught them these and a few other basic requests. They were quick learners. She smiled, stood up, and excused herself to the woman. Taking Anna by the hand, she made her way down the aisle. The girls studiously ignored their mother. She had coached them well. At the end of the car, they passed Father Joseph seated beside the aisle. He was reading a small black book and didn't look up.

Leading the children into the next car where the rest rooms were located, she nearly gasped aloud when the first thing she saw was the shiny black jackboots of a German military man. She didn't raise her eyes to his face. Seated beside him was another German in uniform. A man in a brown business suit sat across from them, and him, she recognized. Unable to avoid facing him, she glanced away and led the girls onward. She was positive this was the man who knew Frieda, the one she'd seen in the previous station. The misfortune of having them on this train and in the next car overwhelmed her. Then she steadied herself by the fact that Frieda said he'd never met the girls. She hoped he'd never seen their photographs either.

Chapter Thirty-three

Em hurried through the next car to the lavatory. It was occupied. "Only one minute." She held up one finger, hoping they would understand. Maria smiled and whispered to Anna.

When the door opened, Em stared in shock at the woman facing her.

"Mademoiselle Emerson! You here?" Jeanette Marchant looked startled. She glanced at the girls.

"My friend's children," Em explained quickly. "How are you, Jeanette, and how is your father?" She was amazed at how quickly she fell into the part she must play.

"Ah, my father, he has been detained, accused of betraying France. I am sick for him."

"Oh no." Em groaned and felt she was convincing.

"But I must tell you how happy you made him to send the published story. I can never thank you enough."

"I'm glad if it made him happy. His story certainly inspired our magazine readers." Suddenly aware of the girls staring at her, she said, "Excuse me, please. I must tend to the children." She sent the two into the small rest room and waited outside. Jeanette did not seem eager to leave.

Em didn't know what more to say that would stay in keeping with her façade as the correspondent. "Are you on your way back to France?" she asked and then regretted the question.

Jeanette fielded it well. "I am staying with relatives in Switzerland awhile. It is what my father wished." At last she started to move away. "Maybe some day my father and I can return the pleasure you gave to us."

"But you already saved my life!"

"Ah, that was nothing. A fortunate moment in the midst of misfortune. They were street tramps. Poof, and they were gone." She moved away with a tiny wave of one hand. "Au revoir, Mademoiselle Emerson."

"Au revoir." As she watched the young woman proceed toward the car Em had just walked through, she marveled at the other woman's skill in deceiving. She seemed to be so much on the up and up. And she'd probably still stalk Em if she thought she'd learn anything about Vivienne.

While the girls tended to their needs Em thought fast. With the Gestapo in an adjacent car, surely now Frieda would be willing to leave this train and accept the idea of crossing over to France. The man in the business suit had the eyes of an executioner. Despite being in a neutral country, Frieda was not safe with this man in pursuit. According to Andrew and Cummins, when it came to duty, Nazis were not only heartless, they also were thorough. Jeanette was an unknown quantity.

When she took the girls back down the aisle, she positioned herself between them and the three German men.

Entering the railcar where the Gestapo were sitting, she nearly turned and fled. Jeanette was sharing a seat with the one who sat facing Em's direction. They seemed to be in earnest conversation. *Oh, Lord, help us! Could Jeanette possibly know he's looking for these children and their mother?* Em braced herself and hurried the girls toward the door just beyond the Gestapo. *Please don't let them recognize the girls,* she prayed. *Please!*

Just before she reached them, Jeanette glanced up, still talking. Her eyes met Em's. Em caught her breath.

A tiny smile curved Jeanette's pretty lips. Then she exclaimed something in German and pointed out the car window. The man who had been so attentively listening to her, turned and leaned to look out, as did the other two. Em hurried the children toward the door. As they passed the men, Jeanette glanced up at her, smiled, raised one eyebrow, and quickly turned back to the window. Was she intentionally distracting the men?

Once outside of the car, Em signaled the girls to be quiet while she beckoned through the small window of the next door to Father Joseph. He stood up casually and came to the rattling little porch between the railcars.

"The man Frieda knows and two Gestapo men are in this next

car! Not only that, a Frenchwoman seated with them knows me. Her father was arrested as a Nazi agent after I had interviewed him as a French patriot. She and the Gestapo are all seated, so you can't see them until you enter the car. The men didn't seem to notice the children, but all they have to do is walk through our car to the rear for a smoke, and they will see Frieda. And Jeanette, the Frenchwoman, got a good look at them while she talked to me beside the rest room."

Father Joseph stood frowning but not coming up with anything to counteract her fears.

"Look, as I said before, we can change trains and take Frieda to Bonnedeux. We can hide there, and you can send Hubert. If we do it right, Werner's family will drop out of sight as far as the Gestapo is concerned."

"But Anna needs a doctor."

"If we take her to a doctor in Paris, Dr. Schneider could collaborate with a French doctor until we bring her back to Geneva."

He sighed heavily. "You don't know Paris. They've lost so many men, including young doctors, she wouldn't get the best treatment. But maybe you and Marge could bring her from Dijon straight back into Geneva. I think your plan does offer more hope than staying on the train with those executioners."

"Would they kill them in a public place?"

"They have their ways. They'd snatch them and make their deaths look like an accident."

"Then we must get them off," Em said. "Can we change trains and get to Neuchâtel? I remember we passed through there shortly after leaving Bonnedeux."

"A connection to Neuchâtel will be coming up soon. All right. You go sit down with the children. When the train stops, get off and go immediately to the rest room with the girls. I'll tell Frieda and Marge to meet you there. Then one of you buy your tickets. I'll go on to Geneva and have Andrew call Hubert. If I can, without slowing Hubert, I'll come with him to Bonnedeux."

"Tell Hubert I'll be at Duvall Inn, where he told me he had stayed."

"Duvall Inn. All right. Your success will depend on not being seen. A small town can be more risky than being on the train. There would be fewer places to hide if the Gestapo were to follow you."

Em nodded. "It all depends on getting off this train unnoticed. So far they don't know Frieda is aboard."

"Don't count on that. It may not be an accident that they are seated in the car next to us."

The girls watched them with worried expressions.

He said something in German, and they smiled, but not with much enthusiasm.

"I explained they will be getting off with you soon and will meet their mother in the train station. You'd better go take your seats. I'll stay here for another minute or two. When the train stops, do not try to leave until I stand up. Timing may be important. When you go, get out fast."

Em took the girls' hands and made her way back to their seats. The woman across from Em was reading a newspaper now. She made a few friendly remarks and returned to her reading.

Soon Em saw Father Joseph return to the car, walk past Marge, and as if by accident, drop the book from under his arm into Marge's lap. As she handed it back to him, Em saw him slip her a note. Marge kept her hand closed around it, concealing it. Em looked away, lest anyone follow her gaze to Marge.

The curving route and Em's tension made the journey seem endless. The children curled up against each other and closed their eyes. She hoped they could nap. They must be very tired.

At last the train hit a straightaway and put on speed, then it entered the outskirts of a city and slowed. This was it. Em touched the girls, waking them. They sat up slowly. She pointed out the window to show them the town they were entering.

As the train pulled into the station, she kept her eyes on Father Joseph. He just sat staring out the window. Maybe this was not the place to get off. Others were leaving the train. Then a few people boarded, hoisting their luggage in front of them. They settled in seats. Suddenly Father Joseph stood up, flashed her a signaling nod, and stepped across the aisle to help a woman hoist her basket into an overhead rack.

"Come, girls," Em said, and grabbed their hands. She hustled them down the aisle. When she reached the steps down, the train shuddered and started to move. With a firm grip on each girl's arm, she jumped off and hurried into the station. Without a backward glance she made a beeline to the rest room. Inside, she leaned on the wall for minute. Anna whimpered, "Mutter!"

"She's coming, sweetheart. She's coming." Em knelt and wrapped her arms around both girls, pulling them close.

The door swung open, and Frieda burst in, followed by Marge.

Frieda cried, "He saw. He knows!" She grabbed the girls and hugged them to her.

"What happened?" Em gasped.

"Father Joseph had to run interference for us," Marge cried. She was almost as pale as Frieda. "The man in the brown suit saw us trying to get off and actually grabbed hold of Frieda's shoulder. Father Joseph fell against him as the train took on speed. Pinned him against the wall and knocked him down. When we jumped, the train was going so fast, I was afraid we'd fall under it. Oh, Em, I don't know what happened to Father Joseph, but we've got to get away from here fast. What if those men manage to jump off? They really mean to get Frieda!"

"You all stay here," Em said. "I'll purchase tickets and find out how soon we may board the train to Neuchâtel. Pray it is soon."

The station agent sold Em the tickets and said the next train would not be due for more than an hour. Em thought fast. The man had a friendly smile, a kindly attitude, and spoke good English. She decided to be honest with the ticket agent. "Please, sir, is there a place where my friend's child, who is ill, could rest away from other people? She is very weak."

The man hesitated, then said, "I'm sorry, we have no invalid room . . . but if it would help, you could bring her into my office here behind the desk. I have a sofa there, and I can shut the door for her privacy."

"That would be wonderful. My friend has a nurse with her and her older child. Would you mind . . . all of us in your office?"

"Not at all, mademoiselle. Bring the little family."

"Thank you. Thank you so much."

"It is nothing. Bring them."

She hurried back to Marge. "Our train will be here in an hour, but the ticket agent will let us wait in his private office, out of sight. I told him the truth, that Anna is ill and needs to be quiet and that you are her nurse. He was really nice about it. Come on."

She opened the rest room door and peeked out to make certain the way was safe. Then she led them quickly to the private haven she'd acquired.

Frieda sank down on the couch and leaned back, panting. "Is gut," she said. "Much gut."

Looking at her, pale and frightened, with her children crowding against her on either side, Em thought of Werner. If he was dead, he had laid down his life for these three. She prayed he was still alive . . . and Father Joseph too.

Safely hidden in the ticket agent's office, they waited. Marge checked Anna and medicated her. Then Frieda held her. Maria leaned on her mother and soon both girls dozed.

When the ticket agent tapped on the door, they all jumped. He came in smiling. "Your train is in, ladies. You may board now."

They filed out, Em going first to scout the area. Marge thanked the man for the resting place. He nodded and wished them a good trip.

People were boarding. They followed. Em chose seats near the door. Almost as soon as they sat down the conductor came through for their tickets and the train began to move. As they picked up speed, Em saw the man in the brown suit hurrying into the rail station waiting room from another train that had just arrived. She nudged Marge and whispered, "Look!"

Frieda spied him too and gave a gasp of alarm.

"It is him, isn't it?" Em said.

Both Frieda and Marge nodded. Since he apparently had recognized Frieda, it would be easy for him to put two and two together if he learned about the women and children the ticket agent had sheltered in his office. And the agent could tell him where they were going. The man's persistence was terrifying. If they already had killed Werner, why wouldn't they just give up on Frieda and let her go? Maybe they thought she also had information that would help the Allies. Actually, she did. Only she could open that safety deposit box in Geneva.

Em pressed her hand to her forehead and rubbed her temples. *Think. Think what to do!*

"Now what?" Marge whispered.

Em tried to stay calm. "I don't know. If Herr Brown Suit has a car, he may drive and beat the train to Neuchâtel. But I don't know any other place where we can get off and still find a train to Bonnedeux."

"Then we must stay on as planned."

"But if he comes—"

"I guess we'll have to pray to be invisible," Marge said. "Look, David said something about praying without ceasing. He said he talked to God in his mind all the time, just as he would to anyone else he knew and loved, and when he did this, he often felt the presence of God. If we can pray like that, I think we'll be able to do whatever we must. I'm going to try."

Em wanted to remind her sister that David had been killed despite his conversations with God, that God was not a magician in the sky who made a business of granting favors. But she couldn't be that cruel. Marge was still grieving over David. Instead, she said, "Okay, you pray, and I will too. I don't know how to tell Frieda to pray, but I hope she is."

Marge nodded and began to whisper to Frieda. The children, sitting beside Em, watched and then returned to playing a finger game that Em had taught them.

Em was becoming fond of these little girls. They deserved a chance for a new life. *Our Father, please,* she added silently, putting her whole heart in the plea. *Let them live to see a world at peace, free of fear.* Every few minutes she thought of something to silently mention to God. She'd never done this before in her life, but then she'd never been in such danger before, not even when she was caught in that battle in Belgium. She'd been under the gun then, but not in its sights.

For all her words of assurance, Marge desperately wished Father Joseph was still with them. If she couldn't have David for spiritual strength, Father Joseph was her second choice. She hadn't realized until now how much she'd relied on Father Joseph, not just for the obvious—his knowledge of German and his physical strength—but also for the way his presence had made her feel stronger in her own faith. Because he was confident of God's care, she'd felt more confident.

Yet she was scared to death. She'd come off sounding full of faith with Em, but now in the privacy of her own thoughts, terror crept in. *Oh, God, help us. Help my unbelief. Give us, with this family, safe passage to freedom.*

Frieda sighed and leaned back. Marge clasped her hand and rubbed it. She let her fingers rest lightly where she could feel her pulse. It was steady but rapid. Marge whispered, "Try to rest. We'll watch over the girls." She wasn't sure how well Frieda understood the words.

Frieda squeezed her hand and whispered, "Danke."

Still holding her patient's hand Marge prayed again. *You know, our Father, how much we need your help. For the sake of these children protect us all. And please, will you tell David that I'm carrying on for him?*

Several hours later when they reached the station at Neuchâtel, Marge gave Anna another dose of her tonic. They didn't have to change trains, so she hoped the stop would be brief. Already the shadows in the snow were taking on the blue tint of evening.

More passengers boarded. Marge watched the platform and saw no hint of their pursuers. Soon the train rolled on toward their destination near the border of France.

The children fell asleep, but Frieda, now wide-awake, stared out the window at the fading light.

"Em, how long until we get there?" Marge asked.

"Maybe an hour. It's not so far, but each time the train stops, we lose ten or fifteen minutes. Don't worry if it gets dark. That might be better, and I know the way to the inn."

If they have room, Marge thought. *If they are still in business, if—no, I won't think that way. God has brought us safely this far. Surely He won't let anything happen now.*

Night fell fast after the sun went down. Clouds lowered over the mountains. A stormy night in December was no time to be in the Alps wondering whether they'd find lodging. *Dear God, let there be a room for us. Frieda is so tired, and the children too.*

When the train finally pulled into the station, they hurried out onto the open platform. Snow was falling thickly without a whisper of wind. If she were not so scared, it would be a winter wonderland.

"Down this way," Em said, holding the girls' hands. "It's not far."

"Stop to rest whenever you feel like it," she said to Frieda. "We'll wait."

"I go . . . okay," she said.

Marge never could tell how much English the German woman understood, but she usually responded with the correct behavior.

Em stopped several paces ahead, waiting for them to catch up. She pointed. "It's that two-story building ahead on the right."

Snow was falling faster, frosting their shoulders and knit caps. Arriving at the inn Em went inside first. There was no sign outside, so Marge, if she had been alone, would not have recognized it as an inn. She followed Em, who stood inside a tiny lobby brushing snow off the children. The concierge greeted them in French.

"I'm sorry," Em said, "I speak only English. Do you speak English?"

"A little," the man answered.

"We need a room and also supper. Can you accommodate us?"

"Room—*une* . . . one. Bed—*deux*." He held up fingers for them to count.

"Oui. Merci!" She took out Swiss money Andrew had given her and held it out. "How much?"

He looked at what she offered and selected a bill. Marge, watching, felt he was honest about what he took.

Then Em asked, "Supper . . . for five?"

"Oui. You come. I show." He led them to a doorway that opened into a small dining room, and he beckoned them on. "Room. Come."

At last after a few hand signs and simple words, they were settled in a clean room with the promise of a fire in the enameled stove. Outside the window Marge saw the snow climbing the windowpane. She turned to Frieda. "Shall we go eat now?"

"Ja," she said with her eyes on her children. "Eat now. Danke."

The supper was served family style at long tables. The rustic room with a large fireplace at one end made Marge feel as if she were back in a Welsh pub. There were other guests, but no one was speaking English.

Marge ate quickly. She noticed Em did too. Frieda helped the children and took a little longer. By the time they finished, all three of them looked more alive than they had since Marge first saw them. Andrew probably was right about food shortages in Germany. Of course Frieda had been ill as well as Anna, but Maria also needed meat on her bones.

When they returned to their room, Frieda tucked the children into the bed she would share with them. They fell asleep quickly.

Marge went to the window. Snow was swirling in a breeze now.

Frieda came and stood beside her. "Snow good. No trains . . . tonight."

"Yes. No trains, no cars. Sleep and rest well, Frieda." She gestured toward the bed.

"Medicine? Anna?" she asked.

"In the morning."

"Ja. I sleep now."

"Good night," Em said.

"Good night," Frieda repeated.

"Me too, Em," Marge said. "Let's go to bed. They need the light off, and I'm beat."

After they were snugly wrapped in the plump quilts, Marge whispered, "You're sure this is the place Hubert will come to find us?"

"Yes. This is the inn. Hubert will know. It would make sense for him to come by train to Bonnedeux, but he might choose to walk on the route we will take out. That way he could scout out the way. Either way, he should get here tomorrow. All we have to do is stay out of sight until he comes."

It all sounded good to Marge, but one thing had troubled her ever since she'd left Father Joseph on the train. "Em, if those Germans on the train suspected Father Joseph of anything more than stupid clumsiness, they might have hurt him or worse. What will we do if Father Joseph never got to Geneva?"

She felt Em stiffen. "Don't even think that!" she hissed.

Em listened to Marge's breathing slow as she fell asleep. Sleepless herself, she stared wide-eyed at the pale light that marked the window. She thought of how narrowly they'd escaped from the Gestapo to catch the train to Neuchâtel. She wondered how much Jeanette Marchant had to do with them getting away. She'd probably never know for certain, but from the beginning she'd found it difficult to think of Jeanette as an enemy. Impulsively she asked God to bless the young Frenchwoman.

The wind rattled the glass. She slipped from bed and tiptoed to look. The air outside had turned to swirling snow. She couldn't tell how much was falling and how much the wind lifted from the ground and hurled back into the air. If the storm closed the roads, they'd have more time to cross the border without detection. Of course the storm also might delay Hubert's arrival. She shivered and hurried back to bed.

Whatever happened, she must be prepared in case Hubert did not come. The next choice she dreaded; she'd have to walk into France without him. She would wait a long time before trying such a feat, even though she remembered clearly certain landmarks along the way. One way or the other they'd need the same equipment and supplies. First thing in the morning she'd buy snowshoes and a sled.

In the morning the snow stopped falling after breakfast. Em took advantage of the clear sky and went out to purchase their snowshoes and a sled. She found a small shop where the owner made many kinds of outdoor gear. A sled drew her attention. Shaped like a small dog sled, this one was designed to be pushed by hand. She tested the feel of the handles. The shop owner came over. "Good morning," Em said. "Do you speak English?"

"Yes. You come from the spa, yes? The sled, good for children and for shopping."

"Good for a grown-up too?"

"Oh yes. Strong. The runners, they are like my skis. Built to glide. The brake, it stops. Locks in place. You like to try?"

"I'm not sure. I need to think about it. Thank you for showing me. I do need snowshoes." She selected three adult sizes and two children's.

He tied them into two bundles and opened the door for her. "Nice day for children to walk or ride a sled right here in town," he said. He waved his hand at the mountain slope above the town. "Not good to go up mountain. Too much new snow. Avalanche danger."

"Oh. Thanks for the warning. We won't go there."

The five pair of snowshoes made a heavy, awkward load. She stopped twice to rest her arms before she reached the train station. The inn was in view. One more rest, and she would make it.

Storekeepers were out shoveling the snow from doorways, and a horse pulled a sleigh down the street. When it passed her, the driver smiled and nodded. She nodded back and hoisted her load again.

A few feet farther on she saw him—without a doubt it was the man who had been following Frieda. Now he was entering a bakery. She'd never forget that profile, for she'd marveled that even his profile looked cruel.

And yet she might be mistaken. No trains had come in this morning. Not wanting to pass the baker's shop, she turned aside into another street. There stood the answer, a black car, the kind that can be hired in cities for driving in the country. It had no accumulated snow on or around it. Obviously it had been parked recently.

She piled the snowshoes next to a building and hurried back to the bakery. She didn't dare go in, but she must be certain this was the man who knew Frieda. She stopped at the window with her cap down and her collar up. She pretended she was studying the breads on display while she peeked from under her lashes. The man's back was to her as he paid for his order.

When he turned she glimpsed his full face before she moved away. It was the man. He had followed. Her knees began to tremble. *I've got to get Frieda and the children out of here as quickly as possible.*

She didn't dare retrieve the snowshoes. She strolled on, looking in the shop windows as she went, until she saw the man leave the bakery and disappear in the direction of the car. A couple of minutes later the car prowled up the hill toward the part of the town where businesses and an alpine spa and resort hotel stood. Once his car was out of sight, Em hurried back, gathered up the snowshoes, and rushed on to Duvall Inn.

Chapter Thirty-Four

By the time Em reached their room in the inn, she'd made up her mind. Keeping her voice steady, she told Marge about seeing Herr Brown Suit. "We're going to cross the border at first light in the morning, even if Hubert doesn't come."

Frieda must have followed her meaning pretty well because she grew pale and said, "Ja. We go. We go."

Marge, on the other hand, argued. "How can you be so positive it was the man? I don't think we should go without Hubert. We can stay out of sight right here."

"You said yourself Hubert might not come. If he isn't here by morning, we must leave. I know this is the man we saw with the Gestapo. He will be searching the town, asking questions. How many English-speaking women do you think there are in this small town, and with two children?"

"How would he know we speak English?"

"People have already noticed that we are strangers. We can't blend in with the locals, and if he checked at the shop where I got the snowshoes, he would start searching. We can't just hope that he won't find us. Look, even though I walked that trail before it snowed and walked it only once, I know the way. It's not that far. I know we can make it."

"Maybe you can, but Anna is exhausted. Walking across the room left her panting this morning."

"We'll push her the whole way on a sled. Frieda too, if she tires."

"What?" Marge turned wordless at the suggestion.

Em told her about the sled. "It's about five feet long, with room enough for an adult to sit holding a child and have extra foot space for bundles. It's lightweight, like wicker furniture, but made of tough bent wood and is strong enough to hold an adult. You push it like a baby carriage. I'll go buy it right away. Even if Hubert comes, we will need it."

Still Marge looked doubtful.

Em turned to Frieda. "Do you understand? The man who was following you is here. He may find you."

Frieda nodded. Her faced twisted as she tried to find words to say what she wanted. "He must not. We go . . . now."

Marge went to her side. "Are you sure? Can you go again on snowshoes?"

Frieda nodded. "I can do." She encompassed them all in a sweeping gesture. "We go. Anna on sled."

Em went to her, knelt beside her, and took her hands. "You will ride too, if you tire. To France. Not far."

Marge stood with her hand on Frieda's shoulder. "If the wind comes up again or more snow, we must not try."

"I agree we can't go out in a storm. I'll go buy the sled and ask the concierge where we may put it."

In the little shop the shopkeeper greeted her with a wide smile. "Have you decided, madame?"

"Yes. I think the sled will do nicely." She paid the asking price on the sled, not knowing if haggling was part of the custom here.

The man gave her a canteen for water and wax for the runners, so she evidently had paid top price. Well, it was almost Christmas, and no doubt he could put a profit to good use.

When she reached the inn, she left the sled at the back door by the kitchen and went to discuss its storage with the concierge.

His eyebrows went up at the mention of a sled, and he scratched his head. "The carriage house," he finally said. "Come, I will show."

He led her out the back of the old inn and across a snowy yard to a small building with a high-pitched roof and wide doors across the end toward the street. He opened a side door. "Here." He helped her lift the sled inside. "Ah, I see that Krueger gave you his good wax. Let the runners dry. Then once wax, and it will last. He does good work. He put one coat of wax. You will be glad you bought from him."

"That's good to know. I think the sled will bring much pleasure to my family. My mother has been ill. We came here for the air."

"I did notice the fragile madame. How young she looks despite illness."

"Yes. Losing weight as she has, she's looking like a bride again.

She was married very young. Until this illness, people thought she was my sister."

As they went out, he said, "The door, I leave unlocked. You can get in any time, madame. Tell your mother I wish her well." He paused. "Will you be wanting to stay on at the inn awhile?"

"Yes. I'd like to pay for a week in advance. Let me do it now, please."

"Certainly."

He headed for the front desk, and she pulled out the money Andrew had provided. It would be nearly gone after this and another meal, but they shouldn't need Swiss money again until she saw Andrew in Geneva.

The man wrote her a receipt. "Lunch will be served soon. Shall I save a table for your family?"

"Would it be possible to eat in our room? My mother and children are still tired from traveling."

"Certainly. I will send up. Nice hot soup and fresh bread with our best cheese. Hot chocolate for the children?"

"Very good. Thank you."

She went on upstairs, where she intended to stay until she felt the sled had dried off enough for waxing.

"We can have lunch in our room," she announced. "I'll ask for supper to be brought to us too. I said Frieda is my mother and that she has been ill. Of course she looks too young, but when we go out we can keep her face mostly concealed with her scarf again and let her lean on you, Marge. The girls can hold on to me as if I am their mother. This is just in case anyone sees us. If Hubert doesn't come, we should try to leave before most people are up tomorrow." *Oh, please, God, help Hubert to get here.* She explained about the sled in the carriage house. "I'll wax the runners this afternoon, and I think I'll buy some sausage and cheese to carry for a snack."

"How will we keep Anna warm in the sled?"

"I'm afraid we'll have to borrow a couple of these down-filled quilts. I'll return them when I come to back to Switzerland. Besides, I paid for a whole week's lodging."

"We go at night . . . in the dark?" Frieda asked.

"In the morning, but still dark. You and Anna will be covered, hidden by quilts. If anyone asks, you will be my mutter. Only don't speak."

"Is gut. The girls?"

"Mine," Em said, pointing from them to herself. "I shall be their mutter."

Frieda addressed the girls in German. They listened, keeping their wide eyes on Em. Then Frieda said to Em and Marge, "They know . . . to do it."

A maid brought their food on two large trays, and after lunch they set the trays outside the door. A short time later, Em took the snowshoes to the carriage house in two trips and then stayed to wax the sled runners.

She applied wax with her fingers, then looked for a rag. Fortunately she found a scrap for an applicator and an old hemp bag to use for buffing. When she was finished, she ran her hand over the smooth surface. The craftsman had done excellent work. If it weren't for the frightening circumstances, the sled ride would be fun. Hopefully she could make the children feel as if it were an adventure.

When she returned to the inn, she studied the windows on the back of the building, hoping they could drop the quilts out rather than carry them. Seeing no sure way to do that, she decided she could just tell anyone who might ask that her mother longed to ride in the snow and the quilts would keep her warm.

The concierge greeted her when she came in through the back hall. She returned his greeting and hurried upstairs.

As usual she knocked on their door before entering. Inside, she met a palpable climate of fear. "What's wrong?" she asked Marge.

"Frieda saw the man. He walked by on the other side of the street. At least now we know for sure that you saw him."

Em felt like a deflated balloon. She had counted on Hubert getting here; she had counted on waiting until morning. She hurried to the window and peered up and down the street. "Did he show interest in the inn, or was he just walking by?"

"He looked at the inn, if that's what you mean."

Em retreated and locked their door. During her forays out, she'd been leaving it unlatched. "Get everyone ready to go. We'd better leave as soon as possible. If we're careful keeping to back streets and alleys, we can make our way to the road that leads to Hubert's trail across the mountains." She glanced at her watch. "It's two o'clock. We've got more than two hours of daylight."

"Em, what if it starts snowing?" Marge looked about to wring her hands.

"We'll make a shelter if we can't see well. Fresh snow could be our friend. It would cover our tracks." Underneath her rational words, Em was terrified. But she was more frightened of the man who was searching for Frieda than she was of spending a night in a homemade igloo.

Still, it was only fair to include Frieda in the decision. She tried, with hand gestures and the few English words that Frieda had used correctly, to explain the choices—to go on an outing now and end up sneaking away without Hubert as their guide, or to wait for him, not knowing how long they'd have to wait . . . or whether he would come at all.

Frieda's anguished eyes went to her children. Then she said, "Go now."

Marge double-checked every item placed in their bags, and then she reviewed with Em. *As if we are pilot and co-pilot about to take off in a bomber,* she thought. "Matches—do we have matches?"

"I bought some at the outdoor store and also a small tin filled with candle wax and paper, as well as an emergency burner for melting and heating snow to drink."

"Good." Marge ticked off her next concern. "It's too bad we left our white coveralls back in Father Desmonde's house. Our every move will be visible against the snow."

"I know, but it's too late to worry about that. We'll have to try to stay in the shelter of trees."

"Uh-huh. Let me see . . . I have all the medications and the water in the canteen."

"And I have the food, which we shouldn't even need."

"Unless a storm hits, and we get snowed in," Marge commented, almost to herself.

"Right," Em responded quietly.

For the first time Marge saw Em's fear. "You sure you can find the way?"

"I wouldn't be doing this if I weren't sure," Em shot back. "And do we have a better choice?"

They both glanced at Frieda, who was ready to go and listening intently.

"We're going to get you to safety," Marge said to her. "Try not to worry." She patted the woman's shoulder, knowing her words must sound foolish. Frieda knew the risk and had voted to go.

"Okay," Em said, "Let's go. I'll carry the quilts." She pulled Frieda's cap low to her eyes and her scarf up over her nose and mouth. "Frieda, hold my arm." She rolled the quilts into a manageable size and held her elbow out to her.

Frieda spoke to the children, and they silently crowded close to

Em's other side. Marge shouldered two packs. Maria carried a small one.

They slowly descended the stairs and crossed the back of the lobby to go out the back door.

The concierge called after them, "Enjoy your outing, mesdames." If he noticed the quilts in Marge's arms, he said nothing.

"We shall. Thank you," Em responded.

At the carriage house they brought out the sled and had Frieda hold Anna and sit on the padded seat with quilts under and around them. The snowshoes and other packs fit at their feet. "We're off!" Em exclaimed, pushing the sled into the snowy street. Traffic, mostly pedestrian, had tromped down a packed path over the new snow.

Marge watched Em push awhile, then she volunteered. "You can keep an eye out for where you want to go."

"Good idea," Em said.

Maria scooped up snow and threw it into the air. Marge figured that to anyone watching, they must look like a family out for pleasure.

Em led them in a circuitous route on small streets, past shops and homes. A few townsfolk smiled and greeted them, but most paid no attention to them. Gradually they ascended gentle grades until they crossed the railroad tracks. From the last snow-covered alley that ran beside the railroad tracks, Em turned onto a little road that led directly away from the town. Now there were no footprints, nothing but smooth new snow from last night, but Marge could tell it was a road. Whoever lived up this way had not ventured to town today.

Em stopped. "We've got to put on the snowshoes now." As she spoke she lifted them off the front of the sled.

Marge set the brake and stooped to fasten hers. Frieda got off the sled to walk too, now that she didn't have to pretend she was the grandmother.

"Let me take a turn pushing," Em said.

"Okay."

They tromped up the mountain road while the shadows deepened from blue to indigo. In the shade of the mountain Marge studied Anna's face, felt her cheek, and tucked the quilts around her face so that not much showed but her nose. "Ask her if she's cold," she said to Frieda.

Frieda did. "She says she is warm."

"Good. How are you, Frieda?

"I gut. Walking is gut."

To Em Marge said, "It's best to keep Anna riding unless she begins to chill from inactivity. I hope the quilts insulate enough. Once she walks, she'll get her outer clothes wet. Then she might chill when she has to rest again."

"I agree. Up ahead by that jutting rock is where the trail meets the road. The route should be well defined even in the snow. There are several landmarks I can follow to get to the farm. Once we cross the border, it's all downhill."

Marge and Em took turns pushing the sled, refusing to let Frieda use her energy for that. Em was right about the trail being visible. Although the trees stood close together in their snow mantles, a narrow corridor led them onward. The way would be clear if the whole route was like this.

Frieda was lagging, and Marge's legs were getting tired so she called a halt. "Let's stop and rest a few minutes, Em."

"Sure. Should the children have a drink?"

"Yes. And we all should eat some of the chocolate."

The canteen, wrapped under the quilts to keep from freezing, held a couple of quarts of water. Two folding metal cups had come with it. Marge used one cup for Frieda, and the children and she and Em shared the other one.

They all stretched and then sat on the edge of the sled. After a few minutes Em said, "Time to go. Rest stops have to be brief, or we'll chill."

They slogged on. The trail dropped into small vales and then ascended. Their whole progress moved them higher and higher but still within the timberline. It was growing darker among the trees. A slight breeze swayed the smaller snow-laden branches of the trees. Marge pulled her scarf up over her nose and wrapped Anna better. "You said it was less than two miles. How far do you think we've come?" she asked.

"That's hard to say. We may be halfway, but you know how mountain miles go."

"Frieda is wearing down. Maybe we should have her ride again."

"Let's wait as long as she can. Will she tell us?"

"Probably not. I'll keep an eye on her."

On the next slope Maria stumbled and began to cry softly.

Marge helped her up, unfastened her snowshoes, and set her beside Anna. Taking care not to get the girl's snowy feet near her sister, Marge pulled one quilt around her.

They glided down a slope with the brake on and shoved the sled up the next. Em looked carefully around. "Here, I remember we went straight across this open area just above the timberline, and then there was a deep creek bed to follow almost to the border. I'm sure we're more than halfway now."

They crossed the open snow at a snail's pace. Marge was bone weary, and she could tell that Em was too. "When we get to the trees again we've got to rest," she said. Her chest burned from the icy air. Away from the shelter of the trees a breeze gusted. If she weren't working so hard, she'd be chilled. Frieda was almost staggering. "We've got to rest," Marge repeated.

Em grunted, and they both pushed on the sled. "When we stop, I'll make a tow rope out of something so we can pull as well as push. I wish I'd thought to buy rope."

Marge wished they could have stayed within the protection of the timber, but she kept that to herself. When they finally crossed the snowfield, the trees deflected the wind again.

They stopped, and Marge removed her scarf. "Here. Let's use this for a rope."

Em took hers off too. She knotted them together and then tied one end to the front of the sled.

Frieda struggled to Marge's side. "I help."

"No. You must not," Marge ordered.

Em took the lead, pulling, and Marge pushed. The sled glided, lighter and faster. Frieda brought up the rear.

Suddenly Frieda cried, "Look!" She pointed behind them to the snowfield.

At first Marge saw nothing, then she spotted a dark smudge, moving, following their trail. "Em, do you see? What is that? A dog? A wolf?"

Em came and stood close, studying the distant movement. Finally she said, "It's a man. We are being followed."

Chapter Thirty-Five

At the sight of the faraway figure moving steadily along the trail they'd left, Em had to fight against panic.

Marge's whisper seemed to come from far away. "Could it be Hubert, trying to catch up with us when he found we'd left the inn?"

Em sucked in a deep breath. Her head cleared. "I wish. We can't take a chance. We've got to stay ahead and get to the Charbonneau farm. Frieda, can you walk faster?"

"Ja. Fast." She went to the front of the sled, unwound her scarf, and set about tying it to the sled.

"No!" Marge cried in a stage whisper. "Just walk."

"I pull. We go fast." She tugged without waiting for them to help.

"Let her try," Em said. "It may lengthen our lead. Under cover of the trees, we may escape." She knew they couldn't hide. There was no way to conceal their tracks across virgin snow.

They took off as fast as snowshoes would permit. Fortunately they'd all become adept by now, and they more than doubled their speed. The sheltered route among the trees followed a frozen, snow-covered stream bed with curves and rises that slowed their progress again. Soon they were gasping and had to stop. During the pause, snow began to fall, at first scattered flakes and then thick and stinging against their cheeks as wind swept through the treetops.

"Come on," Em urged. "If enough snow falls, the wind will erase our trail."

They raced again until, gasping, Frieda slumped onto the front end of the sled to rest. Marge went to her and took her pulse. It was hammering like an engine out of synch. "Em, she's got to ride. We'll have Maria walk again."

Frieda stood up. "No. I walk."

"I think you should let her," Em said. "Anyway we don't have time to argue about it."

Frieda grabbed her tow scarf, and Em joined her. They took off again. Fortunately they hit a downgrade. Then another shallow gully, formed by summer melt, intersected the one they had been following. Em saw a way to confuse their trail. "Look, we can turn here and follow this gully. Then after the storm we can find our way back here easily." She led them downhill, and turned them around. "Now let's go up the mountainside as far as we can from the trail. Anyone tracking us may not be able to tell whether we went up or down. If we have to cross open snow higher up, the wind will wipe away our trail. Have Maria get out and walk. The lighter sled will make less trail. Hurry!"

Frieda caught on right away. She even had Maria help her pull as they tugged the lightened sled up the creek bed, crossed over their own trail, and climbed higher.

Em lunged ahead, and Frieda kept pace with her.

Marge was ready to drop. She couldn't imagine how Frieda kept going, but still they climbed.

The higher they went, the harder the wind lashed at them. The trees braving this height showed only their tips above the snow. Em pulled them to a halt behind the protection of the tallest tree where the wind had piled a snow wall into a ridge on either side.

"Look at our tracks," Em said. "They're nearly gone already! And the snow is coming down thicker than ever. We've got to wait here until this lets up. Let's dig in and make a shelter like the one Father Joseph made. Frieda can wrap up with the children on the sled for warmth."

"You think that man will go back if he can't find us?"

"I don't know. But I'm sure he can't find us here as long as this storm continues."

Marge looked at the snow whipping by and had to agree. The tree turned out to be a cluster of three trees. They definitely cut the wind. "Okay. Let's make a nest."

Having no shovel, they used the children's snowshoes to scoop and toss the snow. Frieda silently helped. When they had a depression deep enough, they pushed the sled close against the trees and made Frieda wrap up with the children on the sled. Then Em and Marge huddled together against it. The wind rushed above them, scarcely dipping into their shelter. However, fine snow drifted in, and Marge felt as if the mountain were sucking out her body heat. Shivering violently, she fought sleep but finally lost the battle.

When she awoke, the wind had subsided. Overhead, vivid stars marked breaks in the clouds. The half-moon lighted the snow. She moved, wriggling her hands and feet. They were almost numb. Shaking Em, she whispered, "Wake up, Em, wake up!"

"Hmm. Oh! I'm freezing."

"That's probably true. We've got to move, or we will freeze for sure." She struggled to her feet and went to Frieda. Not a finger or nose was exposed to the night air. She touched the lump where Frieda's head should be. "Frieda, are you okay?"

The quilt moved, and Frieda peeked out. "Girls sleeping. Gut, okay."

"Are you warm enough?"

"No, but . . . okay."

Marge carefully tucked the quilts back in place.

"We'd better jump up and down or do something," she said to Em.

Em staggered to her feet and stamped up and down. "Let's dig out the snow that blew into our cove," she suggested.

So they deepened their shelter and built the sides higher. Then Em climbed out carefully and went to the other side to look down the mountain. When she returned to Marge, she whispered, "Far as I can tell, our trail up to here doesn't show, and there's not a sign of movement in any direction. If we can stay warm, we're safe here."

"We have to get Anna down and into a warm place as soon as possible. And Frieda too. I'm not sure how much either of them can tolerate. Let's try to move before daylight."

Em didn't answer.

Marge turned to her. "Em?"

Em stood hunched, chin down.

"What's wrong?" Marge whispered.

"I'm not sure I can find my way in the dark. I'm not even sure I can find Charbonneaus in the daylight. It all looks so strange now."

Marge put an arm around her. "We have to go. We'll need to get down to the cover of the trees before full light."

Em covered her face with her mittened hands. Silent sobs shook her. Marge had not seen Em cry like this since childhood. She wrapped both arms around her and held her tight.

Finally, Em whispered brokenly, "I was so sure of myself, and now

I've led us all out here to freeze to death. I couldn't see a single recognizable landmark down there. Even the way we came up is a like a blank piece of paper. I am so sorry!"

At Em's heart-stopping admission, Marge could only cling to her all the harder. *This cannot be the end. We must save the children.* For a moment she felt as if David were standing there beside her speaking to her.

Then she heard herself say, "You can do it. I know you. Once it's light, you'll see the way. Come rest a few minutes. Then things will look better."

Em let Marge pull her down beside the sled again. She huddled against Marge, shaking with fear as well as cold. The sky was growing lighter. There was nothing to do but get up and try to make it. After a brief rest, she straightened and staggered to her feet.

Marge stood up beside her. "Ready to go?"

"Yes. Wake Frieda and the girls while I look around." She climbed out of the shelter and strapped on her snowshoes. Searching the pale slope in all directions, she cautiously moved out from the screen provided by the trees.

After detecting no sound or movement, she returned to the shelter and helped to hoist the sled out and put Anna back into it.

Marge examined Anna carefully and gave her some medicine. She took almost as much time checking Maria and Frieda. She said, "Frieda and Maria need to walk to get their circulation going. I wish Anna could, too, but she's not strong enough."

"For going down," Em said, "I'll handle the brake, but you and Frieda tie your tow mufflers where you can and help pull back too. I wish we could go down at an angle, but that would leave a much more noticeable trail. Also, we have to go down the way we came up, steep or not, or I won't find the trail."

In the half-light they inched down the steep slope to the timberline. Inside the trees Em called a halt. "Wait here. I'll scout ahead. Keep your feet moving and, Marge, give everyone some of the cheese and sausage now."

"Okay, but don't you get out of sight."

"I won't." Em moved around the sled and tromped ahead. Em didn't want to say so, but they should have come to the other stream bed by now. Since they hadn't, she didn't know which way to go.

Suddenly a voice called out in German. It sounded like a command to halt. Panic tore through Em. Even though she was several yards away from the sled, she heard Frieda gasp. Em froze. The voice had come from somewhere below them.

An explosion of shots rang out, then more men's voices came through the trees. Em couldn't tell whether they were speaking German or French. Remembering the man who had shot at her and Hubert and Estelle, she feared it was German. What a fool she'd been to leave the train and think she could get into France safely this way. She edged back to Frieda and whispered, "Can you hear what they are saying?"

Frieda hesitated and then said, "Nein."

"Now what?" Marge whispered.

They waited, listening. The voices became more distant. They were moving away, but which direction?

Slowly the sound of voices dwindled to nothing.

Em began to breathe again. "If we keep going downhill," she whispered, "we may come upon their tracks. They must have been on a trail. If it is our trail, all we need to do is turn left to reach the border. I'll be able to tell shortly whether it goes to Charbonneau farm. Shall we try?"

"Yes," Marge and Frieda whispered almost in unison.

"Should Maria be in the sled again?" Em asked.

Marge felt Anna's neck. "I think so. Anna needs her warmth."

Marge and Frieda took off Maria's snowshoes and wrapped her up with Anna.

Em nodded. "Okay. Tell the girls they must not make a sound."

Frieda whispered to them and tucked the quilts snugly around them.

Em walked in front of the sled. Every few paces she stopped to listen, then moved on. Abruptly she came to the trail she'd hoped to find. Ski tracks sliced over the snow. After a few minutes of study, she found some marks that clearly indicated the skiers were headed to the right. By her calculations that direction led away from France.

When she returned to the sled, Marge was checking Anna again. The expression on her face indicated the child was not doing well.

"She cold," Frieda whispered.

Marge had each of the younger girls unfasten the front of their coats and hug each other close so they could share body warmth. Then she wrapped them again in the down quilts.

"Okay, Em. Let's go!" she whispered. "We'd better be close to the border."

Em helped Frieda pull the sled while Marge pushed. They moved faster but had to rest more often, and Em knew they were leaving a trail a blind man could follow.

She could only hope she'd read the ski tracks correctly and that the skiers really were traveling away from them. The shooting was a frightening puzzle. All she could think of was to reach the Charbonneau farm as soon as possible.

The route now was consistently downhill, so she felt sure they were on the right path. Maybe they already were over the border. If so, the farm should show soon with its open field where the Germans had patrolled during the Occupation.

They came to a clearing in the forest. In the gray morning light, nothing looked familiar. Dreading to leave the concealment of the trees, she signaled a halt. "A good place to rest," she murmured.

Marge set the brake on the sled. Em went to the back of the sled for a drink. The canteen, in its hiding place under the quilts, held only a little water. She passed it around before drinking herself.

Marge pushed her knit cap back and wiped her forehead. Then she pointed. "Is that a building over there to the far right? See? Just peaking above the rise in the center of the meadow!"

Em followed her gesture and squinted. The snowfield, with no real shadows defining anything, looked flat and featureless.

Suddenly everything snapped into focus, like one of those trick drawings that can look like two opposite things depending upon how you're thinking. "It's the Charbonneau barn! We're here! The trail—it actually led to here." She gulped. She didn't want to cry again.

"Thank God!" Marge exclaimed. "Thank God!"

Em went to the front of the sled and pulled with all her might, cutting sideways across the pasture that she'd last seen carpeted with green grass.

Frieda spoke to the children in German. They answered and began to talk to each other. Em instinctively wanted to hush them.

Marge did. She asked them all to stay quiet so as not to startle the French farm family.

Em led them straight past the barn to the stone house that stood at the bottom of the long hill. The lights were on despite the early hour. A dog barked.

"Napoleon!" Em called.

The dog bounded to meet them and sniffed everyone thoroughly. Then it escorted them to the house, still barking. Em pulled the sled right to the door. Before she could unfasten her snowshoes, Madame

Charbonneau opened and gasped at the sight of her. "Where is Hubert? He went to Bonnedeux to walk with you. Georges and Father Joseph, they have gone to meet you. Did you miss them all and come alone? Oh, come in and warm yourselves! I fix hot food. The children, and so cold! Do come in!"

She herded them all into the kitchen, where her adolescent daughter and three young sons stepped forward to help. "My daughter, Claire," her mother said, "Emile, Pierre, and Robert. Boys, help Claire bring more wood for the fire. We must warm our guests."

The small young boys looked to be between the ages of five and seven. The older boy was on the edge of puberty. They had greeted the women and girls with silent stares. Now they jumped into action, all talking at once while Claire made sure the little ones pulled on boots and caps with their coats before they went outside.

Em helped Marge place Anna in a chair close to the iron stove. Frieda began to remove Anna's coat and sweaters to let the warmth reach her skin.

Marge helped. "Please, Madame Charbonneau, can you heat a blanket to wrap her in?"

"Oui. Quickly I shall."

Em helped Maria out of her heavy clothes and sat her close to the iron heating stove. Then she took off her own coat and ski jacket. The radiant heat was heavenly.

Claire and the boys came in with armfuls of wood for the woodbox. Claire added a few chunks to the firebox of the stove and poked them into place for quick flames.

In short order the women had Anna wrapped in heated blankets. Madame Charbonneau gave them mugs of hot milk laced with her ersatz coffee. For the children she added a spoonful of honey.

Em decided ersatz coffee never had tasted so good as she obediently sipped the cup Madame Charbonneau had handed to her.

Frieda's pale cheeks began to take on some color, but Anna, shivering uncontrollably, looked like a wax doll.

Marge hovered over her patient. "Madame, do you have any bottles we can fill with hot water to help get this little one warmed up? Frieda, if you hold her on your lap, I'll wrap you together."

Frieda sat in a big rocking chair holding Anna while Marge, Em, and Madame Charbonneau tucked bottles of hot water into the folds of the warm blanket around them. Finally Anna stopped shivering.

Em and Marge, feet to the stove, sat limp and drained. Em gave a long sigh. "I have never been so thankful in my whole life."

"Me either." Marge reached over and squeezed Em's hand. "You made it, little sister. You saved us."

Em shook her head. "Not me. You know it wasn't me. We are here by God's mercy."

Frieda, who had been silent, exclaimed, "Amen! Gott's mercy!"

They sat staring at the stove and the flicker of flames that glowed in the door windows until Madame Charbonneau said, "The men, they should come soon. How is it they did not see you?"

"We were higher up the mountain," Em said. "We heard voices down below and a couple of shots. We couldn't tell if they were speaking German so we stayed out of sight."

Madame stiffened. A look of horror crossed her face. "Shots? The Boche! They could kill Georges and Father Joseph!" She began to pace the floor, ringing her hands. "Mademoiselle Emerson, after that man shot at you and Hubert, Georges saw other signs of the enemy up there."

"Oh no!" Em exclaimed.

Marge rose to her feet and rested her hand on Frieda's shoulder as if to steady both Frieda and herself. "Em! You never told me someone had shot at you!"

"It didn't matter once it was over. Hubert came back later and said they had killed a man who was a collaborator. I thought that was the end of it."

Madame Charbonneau stumbled to the rustic kitchen chair and collapsed onto it, her strong face pinched with anxiety. Claire hurried to her mother and put her arm around her shoulders. "Maman, Père will be all right. You know how he is careful. No one will catch him."

Madame Charbonneau patted the girl's hand, but bit her lips as if to steady them. "Yes, child, certainly you are right." She didn't look up. Em saw fear still sharpening the lines in her face.

Claire straightened. "I will go to feed the cows and look to see if Père may be coming even now."

Madame Charbonneau straightened. "Don't go up the hill. Stay at the barn." She made no effort to hide her fear this time.

"Yes, Maman." With chin down, she went quietly to get her coat.

Once she was out the door, Madame Charbonneau said, "I have had to watch her so closely. She thinks it's safe now that France is free."

"Have you actually seen Germans hiding up there?" Marge asked.

"Georges has. That's why he and Father Joseph went to meet you. Georges thinks they are spies, rather than soldiers, but to me it's all of the same cloth. I despise them all. I made Georges teach me how to shoot his gun."

Em glanced at Maria and Frieda. Anna had dozed off. Clearly Maria understood what had been said. She had her chin down, as if to hide. Frieda sat stiffly, watching Maria.

Poor kid, Em thought. *She definitely understands that she is in enemy territory.* "Are you getting warm, Maria?"

The girl looked up, and with a flicker of a smile, she nodded.

"Would you girls like to lie down and rest for a while?" Marge said. "You must be very tired."

Maria nodded.

Marge stood up. "Frieda, let me carry Anna. You must rest too, now that you are warmed up."

"Ja." Frieda stood up, swayed, and caught hold of the chair back to right herself. "Madame Charbonneau, I pray your husband be safe and come back soon."

Madame Charbonneau's expression softened. "Oui. Merci." Em thought she was going to say more, but she turned and led them to a bedroom. "This way, please."

Em lingered by the stove, wondering what to do next. Despite her exhaustion, she couldn't sleep when there was still so much to be done. As soon as possible, they had to take Frieda and the children to Geneva. If Father Joseph didn't return soon, what were they to do? What if something had happened to him and to Georges Charbonneau? Who could go and look for them? She could barely think in a straight line. She got up and went to the window.

Snow lay deep in sheltered areas and against the animal sheds and barn, but out on the hillside wind-scoured patches of frozen grass marred the clean white blanket.

Out of the corner of her eye she saw something move. Expecting a cow or goat, she caught her breath at the sight of three erect figures. They stood at the edge of the woods as if conferring, then they separated into a stealthy line.

Madame Charbonneau returned to the kitchen.

Keeping her voice low, Em said, "Madame Charbonneau, three men are coming down the hill from the border."

CHAPTER THIRTY-SIX

"Three men?" Madame Charbonneau put her hand to her throat and then hurried to the window to stand beside Em. "I can't see. It's too far! Is one of them Georges?"

"I don't know."

Madame Charbonneau called to Claire, who had just returned from the barn. "Take your little brothers upstairs to the loft, and stay there until I call."

Claire picked up the smallest boy and led the others away without asking any questions.

"You think it's Germans?" Em asked.

"I do not know." The older woman went to spy from behind the curtain. "I can't see them at all now. Friends would approach openly." Even as she spoke, shots rang out. "Oh, dear God!" she cried.

Em gave one hasty glance outside and pulled her away from the window. "Is the door locked?"

Madame Charbonneau ran and bolted the front door and then the back. Another volley of shots erupted.

Marge burst from the bedroom. "What's happening?"

"We don't know," Em said. "I saw three men coming down the hill. Then they disappeared, and the shooting began." She turned to Madame Charbonneau. "Do you have a gun for me?"

In the bedroom Marge found Frieda and the girls clinging to one another. "What is it?" Frieda asked.

"We don't know. Keep the girls calm. The doors are locked. If anyone threatens, we can defend ourselves."

Frieda murmured something to the girls in German, and they all sat wide-eyed, listening.

After a few minutes they heard men's voices.

"French! They speak French!" Frieda said.

Marge listened intently. "Yes! Stay here and be quiet. I'll go see who it is. The fewer people who see you the better."

In the kitchen she immediately recognized tall blond Father Joseph. The other two she'd never seen before.

"Come," Madame Charbonneau motioned to her. "You are safe. It is Georges and Father Joseph and Hubert."

Marge turned to Father Joseph. "The shots . . . we were afraid you were Germans."

His mouth tightened. "When we met Hubert, we were ambushed by the man who had been after Frieda. Georges shot him, but he escaped. Then the man followed us, quite invisibly. We never guessed. He apparently had decided to kill us after we led him to the farm. Georges got a good view the second time he shot at us and killed him. His body is up there at the edge of the forest. We will carry it down later. We didn't want to upset you or the children by traipsing in without warning, packing a dead man."

"You're sure he's dead?"

He nodded. "We checked."

"Then Frieda and the children are safe." The fear that had put iron in her backbone dissipated, leaving her limp.

The man named Hubert spoke. "We hope so. We can't be sure. We've got to get her out of here right away. Father Joseph left his car in the village below."

"What about Werner?" Em asked. "Has anyone heard from him?"

Father Joseph shook his head. "Let's keep Frau Koch's hope alive. How is little Anna after the trek through the mountains?"

"She's all right," Marge said, "but both she and Frieda need to be under a doctor's care."

Hubert said, "Andrew has arranged for Dr. Schneider to check them as soon as we reach Geneva. Then he will get them to a safe place until Dr. Schneider can hide them. Get them ready to go as quickly as possible."

Marge felt as if everything were passing by her in a blur. "Right now?" she blurted, and then caught herself. "Sorry. I'm so tired, I'm not thinking clearly. Of course I'll get them ready."

"I'll help Georges hitch the horses to the sleigh," Father Joseph said.

"A sleigh," Marge repeated.

"Snow has closed the road to the nearest village," Em said. "So Father Joseph had to leave his car down there. Come on. I'll help you get the children dressed."

An hour later everyone, except Hubert, squeezed into the large black sedan Father Joseph had brought from Geneva. Marge recognized it as one belonging to Andrew. While Father Joseph drove them expertly to a major highway, Marge leaned back on the plush seat and closed her eyes. Her patients were safe. At last she could sleep.

In Geneva Father Joseph drove them to an old building that looked like some kind of a museum. To Em's surprise, Andrew met them at the front door and whisked them inside and into a private room where Dr. Schneider greeted them.

The doctor quickly and gently examined Anna, and then he and Marge left the room for a private consultation. Em supposed this was the medical version of debriefing.

Em had slept during the drive, but still she had to stay standing just to keep awake.

Frieda huddled with the girls. Em went over and whispered, "Do you have the key to the safety deposit box?"

Frieda nodded. "I will not give until Werner is safe."

Em smiled and stepped back. It would be Andrew's job to handle that.

Marge and Dr. Schneider returned. The doctor nodded to Andrew. "I will go with the family to the room you secured here for them and examine them more thoroughly." To Frieda, he spoke in German, and from Frieda's expression, his words must have been encouraging.

Then Frieda stood and came to Em and Marge. "We go now." She took their hands in her own. "I cannot say . . . with English . . . such gut prayer I give to Gott for you. Danke."

Marge squeezed her hand. "We shall pray for your husband and for Anna."

Frieda grabbed them each in a fierce hug. "Gut-bye, *mein freunds.*"

"In America," Em said, "we say, 'I'll be seeing you.' "

Frieda smiled. "Ja. Is gut to see you again."

The family left, and Em and Marge went to the car with Father Joseph and Andrew. As they drove to Château Bleu, Em said, "I'm growing to hate good-byes more and more. I've begun to think of Frieda as a friend."

Father Joseph, who was still driving, said, "That's what she called you. Freund is friend. I have this private theory that when you face death together you come away with part of each other in your heart."

"Thanks for putting it in such fitting words for me. May I quote you?"

He threw back his head and laughed. "Ever the journalist! Yes, you certainly may quote me."

His teasing remark about her journalistic sense made Em suddenly homesick for Bob. He should be here. He would laugh at her too, but he would understand as no one else could. She turned to Andrew. "I have a friend in Paris who had hoped to spend Christmas with me. Would it be too much of an imposition to ask—"

He raised his hand. "Say no more. We would love to have another guest. Telephone when we get to Château Bleu. This will be a most happy holiday for me and for Lydia to have all of you here. You will stay, of course, Father Joe?"

"My people in St. Hilary need me more than ever this holy season—our first Christmas of freedom in five years. Thank you for asking, but I want go home."

"Home," Marge said. "May we all be able to go home for Christmas by this time next year."

"May the Lord grant it," Father Joseph responded.

At the chateau Em went to call Bob as soon as she could politely pull away from greeting Lydia.

When the buzz of the phone in his hotel room repeated the fourth time, her spirits sank. She might reach him indirectly in time for him to come for Christmas, but she had so wanted to hear his voice right now. A click in her ear ended her disappointment. "Mansfield here," he said in a clipped tone.

"Hi, Bob, it's Em."

"Em! Are you back in Paris?"

"No. I'm calling from Geneva."

"Em, I have amazing good news. Susie knows I'm her father, and she's taking it okay!"

"That's wonderful! How did she find out?"

"My sister told her. I started writing more often to Ruthie after you suggested keeping a journal to show Susie some day. Then just yesterday I got this letter from Ruthie saying she and her husband, Clarence, decided to tell Susie about me. Susie has always known she was adopted. Seems that she had begun to ask about her real father and mother. I have Clarence to thank for insisting that Ruthie know about me. It was big of him to do that." Bob was as close to babbling as Em would have been under the circumstances.

Before she could respond, he exclaimed, "I even have a letter from Susie with a recent snapshot! She explained how she loves Clarence but is so happy to know I am her dad too. She says she understands how I must have felt, and she even thanked me for placing her with Ruthie and Clarence. Can you beat that? Isn't she a great kid?"

"Yes. What a wonderful Christmas present. I'm so happy for you!"

"Are you on your way to Paris? I've been hoping you'd make it back for Christmas."

"Oh, I almost forgot why I called! Can you come here for Christmas, Bob? I need to stay a few days longer with Marge, and my friends really want you to come. They asked me to invite you."

"How about you, Lucy-Em? Do you really want me?"

"I really, really want you."

He laughed, and she could tell that all of his reservations about her were gone. Maybe someday she'd find out what they had been, but it didn't matter now.

"I'm on my way." he said. "Tell me where I'm going."

She gave directions. Then she said, "I love you, Bob."

"I love you too, Lucy-Em. Do you think we may be able to keep track of each other long enough to get married?"

"Yes! Absolutely yes!"

He groaned, managing to sound both happy and unhappy. "I never planned it this way. I wanted you in my arms. I wanted candlelight and violins in the background."

"I think I hear the violins," she said.

When she hung up, Marge had already gone to her room. Em dressed for bed and tapped lightly on her door.

"Come in." Marge was sitting up in bed.

Em dropped down on the edge of her bed. "I was afraid you'd be asleep already. I wanted to tell you that Bob and I are going to be married."

"Oh, Em. I'm so happy for you!"

"You do like Bob?"

"Very much. Have you decided when?"

"Not yet. We'll talk about it when he gets here."

"What a holiday this will be for you."

"Marge ... I'm sorry ... about you and David. Me becoming

engaged must make it all the harder for you. I can't imagine how you must feel." As she said this, the thought of Bob even being wounded horrified her. She fought down an irrational dread that something might happen to him on the way to Geneva.

"Don't be too sorry," Marge said.

"What?"

"About David. He's more alive now than we are. I know it in my bones. I'd love to have him here, but I will see him again, and I'll tell him all that I failed to say when he was here."

Em weighed her sister's words. Despite how tired they both were, Marge's face held a quiet radiance. "I have a feeling he knows right now, sis."

Marge smiled tenderly, like the times long ago when she played the part of Mary beside the manger in the Christmas pageant.

Em didn't want to share her worry that something could happen to Bob nor did she want to be alone with her happiness. "May I sleep with you tonight, sis, like old times?"

"Sure," Marge said and threw back the covers. "Just don't get your cold feet on me like you used to."

Em lay down and turned off the bedside lamp. "I'm so happy, Marge. But I'm scared too. Can this kind of happiness last?"

"Don't even question it. Bob's a good man. You'll both make it last." Marge was quiet for minute, and then said, "Marry him soon, Em. You can't count on tomorrow. Before you came in, I was thinking about how I was ordered to France, scared to death that someone wanted me dead, and yet here I am. Then I thought about how Rufe Johnson died, and yet Werner Koch's family has been spared, and him a Nazi. There's just no way to understand God's purposes. But if I survive this war, I will try to make a difference in the world . . . as David intended to do."

"Me too, Marge." *Funny,* she thought, *to think that God could have special plans for us, two ranch girls from Tuttle, Oklahoma, but I believe it.* Aloud she said, "Marge, you're going to make a good difference. And so am I."

Marge didn't answer. She was asleep already.

In the morning when Em awoke, she slipped out of bed without disturbing Marge. Bob would be coming today, and she wanted to look her best. She'd soak in a perfumed bath and do her hair and then put on one of the lovely dresses Lydia had placed in her bedroom closet. A glance in the mirror she passed told her she looked as tousled and unkempt as she had expected after the ordeal she'd been through.

Wrapping up in her borrowed robe, she tiptoed out into the upstairs hallway. There on the top step of the broad staircase sat Bob, reading a newspaper. He heard her and stood up. "I couldn't wait downstairs to see you." He came toward her, arms outstretched.

She stepped into his embrace and hugged him close. "Now this is really coming home for Christmas," she murmured against his shoulder.

He kissed her, and she forgot all about how messy she must look.

EPILOGUE

Neither Lydia nor Bob learned the full truth about what Marge and Em had done during the three days they'd been gone from the chateau. Lydia had long since learned not to ask Andrew too many questions. Bob, having sat in on high-level briefings from General Eisenhower and General Bradley, was accustomed to not learning all the details he might wish. He had Em's promise that someday she would tell him everything. Until then he was happy just to have Em, secrets and all.

On Christmas morning Andrew announced that Werner had reached Basel and was in safe hiding. Andrew left for several days to secretly deliver Werner's maps and blueprints to Allied headquarters.

In January Em and Bob were married in Paris, first by civil authorities to make it legal in France and then by Bob's army chaplain friend to make it legal in the United States. For Bob's sake, Em asked for and received a discharge from the OSS. Her by-line in the *U.S. National Tribune* remained Em Emerson. Despite the fact she couldn't write Werner Koch's story yet, she'd already acquired a name for producing unique human interest articles. More important to her were the letters she wrote to her new stepdaughter, Susie. She looked forward with Bob to visiting Susie in person.

When Marge returned to duty, the Allies were battling their way back to the Siegfried Line after the German breakthrough, which became known as the Battle of the Bulge. As soon as St. Vith came under Allied control again, Marge went in search of Isabelle. She found the Babe well and in good spirits, hopping energetically on crutches. Marge told the nuns that she wanted to adopt Isabelle and began the necessary paper work, even though nothing could be finalized until after the war.

The war was far from over. Hitler had conscripted boys and men from fifteen to sixty-five to fight to the death for the Fatherland. They were obeying. As the Allies struggled into Germany, Marge continued to nurse the wounded and the sick in the field hospital. And Em continued to write about ordinary people who, in fighting for freedom, became extraordinary.